seven
shades
of you

A.M. JOHNSON

Editing and Formatting by Elaine York,
5Allusion Graphics, LLC/Publishing & Book Formatting
www.allusiongraphics.com
Proofreading by Kathleen Payne Proofing
Cover Design is Amanda Bockman

seven shades of you

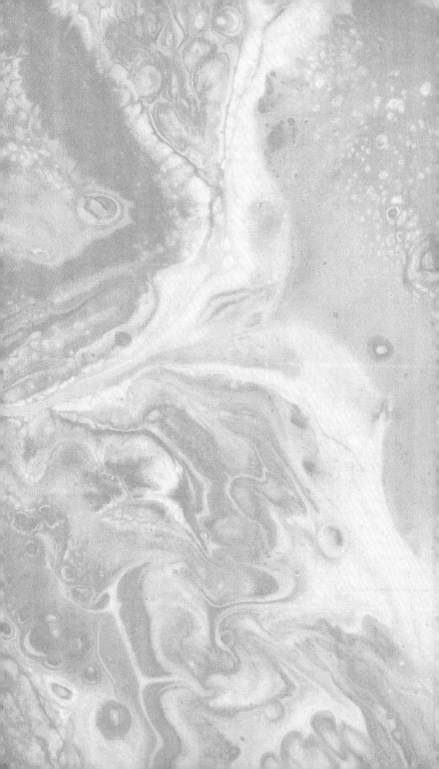

To You...
Yes, You,
You behind that mask.
Slip it off.
Breathe.
Find your gravity,
And believe,
That you deserve the love you give.

For Cornelia
For always calling me by my name,
for showing me I am worthy of love, and for every mile
that keeps us apart, is a beat of my heart
that knows how dear a friend you truly are.
You, my love, belong to ALL the colors.

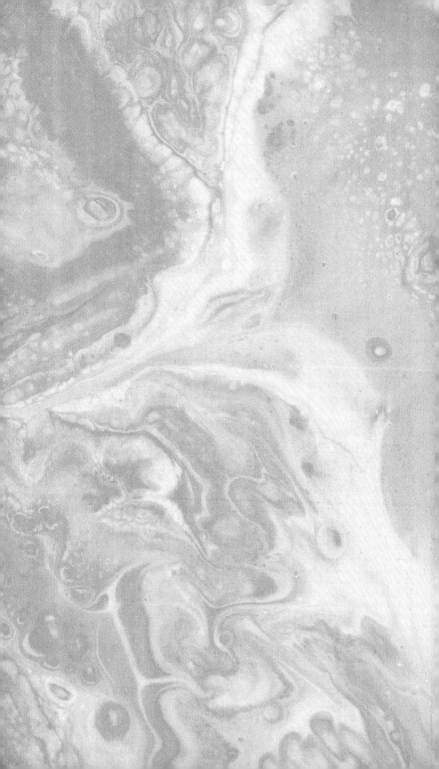

"We're all pretty bizarre.
Some of us are just better at hiding it,
that's all."

John Hughes
The Breakfast Club

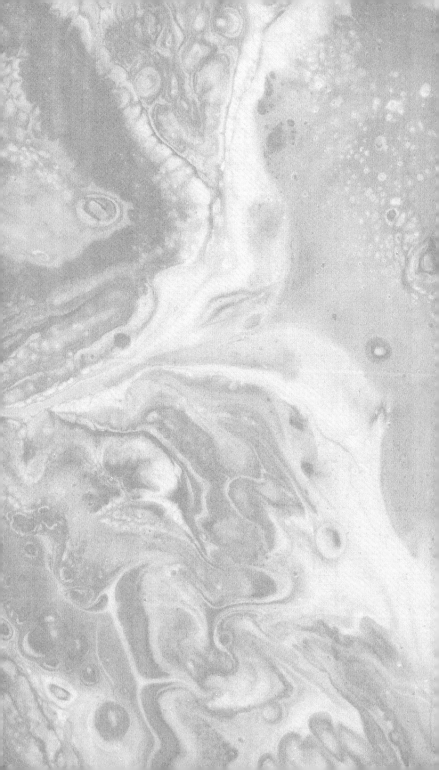

Kai

It was hazy, the stale scent of gasoline mingled in the frigid air, evaporating from the frozen concrete floor of the garage. The moonlight stuttered across the car door handle as he attempted to open it. Once, twice, and then again. His brows dipping into a furious line as he swore under his breath. Vodka-tainted puffs of fog spilled from his lips as he sighed. The door opened, and the dome light illuminated the front seat. Warm and welcomed, he fell into the leather.

"Let's go," he growled to himself, shoving the car key into the ignition with haphazard fingers.

The engine revved as he slammed the door shut. Kai closed his eyes with a wry smile. The world spun, his heavy body sinking into the driver-side seat, relief flooded his veins.

Silence.

"Do you like it here?" she asked.

"Not really, no." Kai wouldn't smile, he wouldn't give in.

"I like it here. It's quiet. I think better when it's quiet." She pushed the long strands of her hair behind her ear with shaking fingers.

He couldn't remember her ever being this beautiful. She was always twisted limbs and sad eyes.

"You always say that." His lips lifted into the smile he'd tried so hard to hide. "I like the quiet, too."

"Some days I wish I didn't have to speak at all. I wish I could sit on the back porch and let the sun speak for me."

"What would it say?" he asked, inching closer, letting his pinky dust hers.

"It's a secret." She turned her head, and the thin hospital pillow crinkled as she faced him.

"You told me there were no such things as secrets."

"I did, didn't I?" She laughed and placed her hand over his. The heat of it made his smile grow wide.

"You did."

"The sun would tell the world I missed it, it would remind the grass how much I miss its itchy blades, it would tell the wind to break up the quiet so I could remember the day was not over yet."

"It's not over, Mom." Kai's eyes burned and his nostrils flared. "When you get home, I'll have Dad set up your rocker on the back porch, okay?"

She exhaled a long breath, and his shoulders relaxed as she beamed at him.

"You make me so proud... every day... so proud."

The grating hum of his old, beat-up Impala nagged, keeping him rooted into the present. Rooted in the day that seemed to never end. All he wanted was a minute to think. Quiet. Sleep. Glorious and uninterrupted. No one to remind him—every second of every day—that he'd failed, or how much they'd needed him. No one to remind him how selfish he truly was, or how, no matter what, he'd always be the poor kid from Rockport with a mom who was dying and a father who never gave a fuck.

Quiet. Sleep.

No one to tell him the garage was a dangerous place to leave a car idling. No one to remind him to breathe, to wake up, to...

Indigo

The Beckett House cafeteria buzzed with students trying to balance trays stacked with food and books, and cups of coffee, smudges of color whipping across the room, around the tables. The smell of bacon and eggs and maple syrup lingered in the wide-open room. Winter break was over, the second week of spring semester had commenced, but a light shower of snow sprinkled white flakes just outside the large floor-to-ceiling windows, dusting the fir trees outside in a glow, almost light blue in the gray dawn light, reminding us January wasn't quite done yet.

The table I'd sat at last semester with my brother and his friends had a few open seats this morning, but I knew the one across from Royal was reserved for me. I set my tray with cereal and milk onto the table, but before I could sit down, my brother flashed me his winning smile. "Hey, Pink, can you grab me a side of salsa?"

He still needed me. Even if it was for small things like sides of salsa, or what songs he should add to his study playlist. Royal needed me and that was all that mattered. I nodded and gave him a mirrored smile, one he'd recognize as well as his own. We were twins, in heart, body, and mind. Well, except I was a girl and he was a guy... who liked guys... or maybe just one guy, but I digress. We were born on the same day, and even though I'd been born first, he was my big brother in all the ways a girl could need. A protector. And I protected him.

"The green kind, not the red," Camden, my brother's boyfriend, suggested before I got too far away.

"I'm well aware of what type of salsa my brother requires, thank you very much." I raised my eyebrow, trying to keep the grin off my face but failing, and Camden chuckled.

"Would you mind grabbing me some, too, Pink?" Corbin, one of my brother's teammates, spoke around a large bite of his breakfast burrito.

I tried not to be too pleased he'd started using my nickname, Pink, regularly after spring semester had started. I can't say that Royal loved it, though, when Corbin called him Blue. It was our thing. A way to annoy our parents and their obsession with all things blue. Indigo and Royal had become Pink and Blue and the rest was history. Corbin feeling friendly enough to call me Pink felt better than it should have.

There wasn't much to say about a girl like me. A girl with light blonde hair and pale, sea blue eyes. I was just another girl who'd been discarded in the halls of her high school, the halls of her mind. A girl with thoughts no one would ever understand. A girl who tasted the sunset and listened to the voices living inside her paint brush, inside her ears. I wasn't afraid of the murmurings. They spilled across the canvas in loud shouts and muted whispers. They made up my soul in coppers and caramels and matched my deep blue heart. Each beat another picture. Each swath of color another facet of who I'd become.

My adolescent years hadn't been easy, and I had the social bruises to prove it. Not once had I gone on a date. No prom for me, no smiles from that hot guy in my algebra class. My father had once said that loneliness was just another chapter, another cog in the wheel of life's failures and successes. I'd listened and owned his words. There wasn't much to do about who I was anyway. I was the shy bit of yellow in a duet of gold. My brother Royal flourished inside the heat of others. Where I'd won a scholarship to St. Peter's College for art, he'd won a scholarship for swimming. He was a go-getter. He'd fought for what he wanted in everything even if it meant he'd lose it all. This past fall, our first semester, he'd met Camden and had fallen in love, quickly and wholeheartedly. What the world thought had never been important to him, or to me, but I hadn't the inclination to chase after things like he always did. I'd rather sit inside my family's art studio, or the one here on campus, and create a better life. A life that made me smile regardless of all the immature chatter that floated around me.

There is nothing special out there for you.

I exhaled, shaking off the intrusive thought. I knew better than to listen. Those spiteful voices inside my head, I'd inherited them from my father. We suffered together. But, because of him, my family, I never had to suffer alone in the dark words, the evil fingers that tried to pull me into the depths, the dank realization of my own mind. My father had taught me to ignore them, taught me how to paint through the depression. Because of him, my family... I lived and breathed and felt normal on most days.

He gave birth to us.

I shut my eyes, willing the voices into silence, and tuned in to the chaotic hum of the dining hall as it rose to the top of the wood-and-metal-beamed ceiling. When I opened my eyes again, the words in my head had evaporated. I moved quickly to the breakfast bar and grabbed a few cups of green salsa before I made my way back to the table. The familiar faces of St. Peter's ignored me as I walked by. I was a ghost in overalls, with paint-stained Converse and a smile, wasted, for the *no one* who would notice.

"Here you go," I said as I placed the cups onto the table and pulled out my chair.

Corbin was deep in conversation with Dev, another one of my brother's teammates, and hadn't noticed I'd returned. This table was a reflection of my brother's gifts. Gifts I wished I could harness.

You'll always be alone.

"What are they saying?" Royal's asked, his voice rough with concern. I kept my eyes on the table, hyperaware of everyone around us. My brother, his boyfriend Camden, and my suitemate Daphne were the only ones at St. Peter's who knew about my illness, and I wanted to keep it that way for as long as possible. "Pink?" he whispered, leaning closer.

"Same as usual, I'm feeling off today, Blue, no big deal."

"Have you seen Dr. Sand?" he asked, and I finally met his worried, azure eyes. My eyes.

"I have an appointment today."

"Try not to miss it, okay," he said, his tone soft and careful.

"I won't."

I'd become well acquainted with the Behavioral Health Center on campus. Dr. Sand managed my illness, schizoaffective disorder, or depression with psychotic features. I never liked the latter, psychotic features, it always sounded defeatist and scary. My father and I heard things, saw things that the world couldn't, and yes, at first, I'd hated it. Originally, I'd been terrified. I'd wake up in cold sweats, having nightmares that I'd never truly wake up from. Dad had explained to me what they were, the voices, and once I was old enough, I understood. Those persuasive ramblings in my head, they were all just mind games. Dad told me I had to fight them, told me I couldn't let them win. So I fought. Therapy, meds, and the love of my family. Art and color. It was a prescription. A reality. My life.

It was difficult, being away from home, from my dad, from my mom. Royal hovered, making sure to sit with me for every meal when he could, nag me about my appointments, and he always asked about the voices, knowing there was nothing he could do to stop them. But he had a boyfriend now, friends, his swim team—a life. A life I would never really fit into, and I wondered sometimes if he viewed me as one of his failures. What would it have been like to have a sister to double date with, to socialize with? What would it have been like for him to not have to always be the big brother? When we both decided to move to Oregon to go to college, I'd promised myself I'd give him the space he needed to flourish, and he had. Royal had bloomed, the brightest gold, and it was a color I'd struggled to create on my own canvas since our arrival.

Our family suffered as one, loved as one, and celebrated as one. Royal was my second half, Mom and Dad were my center, and as I watched my brother take his boyfriend's hand in his, I whispered to myself.

I'm not alone.

I wasn't sure if Blue heard me, or if his smile was just his usual brotherly affection, but I smiled back before bringing a spoonful of cereal to my lips. In class, if I whispered to myself, or if I got caught gazing into the great wide nothing, I wouldn't care. I'd always been taught that I was special... that I saw the world... that I belonged to color, and that was pretty freaking awesome as far as I was concerned. Raised by artist parents and a brother who treated me like I was his queen. I was one of the lucky ones.

"How's he doing?" I asked as I flopped down on my brother's bed, the cheap dorm room mattress groaned under my weight.

Camden didn't protest as I laid my head on his chest. "Good." He cleared his throat. A tell I noticed he had whenever he was nervous or uncomfortable about something. It made me smile.

"Good," I repeated and Camden relaxed, his breathing less rigid.

The color of his tone, orange and warm, as he said, "We're... happy. Being out, being able to love him in front of everyone, I was nervous, especially after what happened last semester, but I think it's going to be okay."

He rested his hand on my back, and I snuggled in a little closer, the familiar scent of his soap somehow made me think of home. Some people might find it odd I was this open, this close with my brother's boyfriend, but it had become our way. Camden had spent the entirety of Christmas break with our family, his own family shunning him after he openly started dating my brother. Camden was one of us, ours in the way the color blue belonged to the sky. Not truly blue, but a reflection of color through a spectrum of light. His spectrum illuminated under Royal's light and we all basked in it. He was ours. He was family.

"I think so. I've always thought so."

He chuckled and it rumbled around in his chest. "I wish I had your optimism."

"There's still time. I will teach you my ways." I smiled as I rolled over onto the pillow. "When is practice over again? I'm starving."

Camden lifted his arm and glanced at his watch, worry creasing his brow. "He should be here by now."

"He said he would be late, that's why he had us meet him here instead of Beckett. Don't worry, I'm sure it's fine."

Camden turned and stared at me. His gray eyes shadowed by the mop of dark chocolate hair hovering over his brows. "Will I always be nervous when he's late coming home from practice now?"

I wanted to lie, to tell him the vision of my brother—his boyfriend—black and blue, would fade over time. That the fight last semester would be the last obstacle they would ever face, but the truth wasn't something I could ever hide, from myself or from the ones I loved. "Probably for a while. I mean, it's all still fresh, Camden. What happened last semester was scary. And I wish it wasn't true, but there are people in this world filled with hate. But Royal's team seems to accept him?" He nodded, and I asked the question I'd been too afraid to ask my brother for the past month. "How's Kai?"

Kai Carter was the hero, the mystery, the only boy to ever make me look twice. He was a brazen brush of violet against the muted gray canvas of St. Peter's.

Camden shrugged, his gaze fixing on the wall. "He's quiet. We haven't spoken much since the semester started. I feel like I don't have a roommate anymore. He's never around."

"Royal told me Kai finally texted him."

"Yeah." Camden's smile was lined with sadness. "No explanation for the freeze-out over winter break, though. Just a quick, *no worries, see you in the pool,* very vague."

"He's good at vague," I mumbled to myself.

"How do you mean?" Camden stared at me, straightforward, with stark-white honesty.

"Have you ever noticed he ignores me?"

"He does?"

"I think so." I picked at the dried spot of yellow paint on my hoodie, avoiding Camden's gaze. "You know, come to think of it, not since last semester, when we first met in the cafeteria, has he ever directly spoken a word to me. What he did for you and Royal, defending you guys like he did, you'd think he'd want to know me. I'm his best friend's sister." I bumped my shoulder into his and forced a smile. "I mean, you let me snuggle with you, and you hate people."

"I don't hate people."

I raised my eyebrows and won a rare smirk.

"I don't. They just make me uncomfortable."

"I don't make you uncomfortable."

"Yes, you do."

"I do?"

He nodded and my smile dimmed. "But I like you. I like the awkward way you push into my space. It's nice to know someone cares enough to break my boundaries."

I rested my head on his shoulder. "Royal's not the only one who loves you... I hope you know that."

He picked up my hand in his. Staring at the way his large fingers swallowed mine, he said, "I know." He cleared his throat again. "There's more to Kai than I think anyone cares to notice. Maybe he ignores you because he's afraid you'll notice."

Royal hadn't told me much about his best friend. But I wasn't blind. Kai was the guy who walked into the room and every girl noticed. Tall and broad, that violet aura, dangerous with dark eyes that promised things they shouldn't. He was hard to miss. Even when he swam, he commanded the water to his will, more so than even my brother could. He was the kind of guy who stood up and fought for his friend; he harnessed strength, bled it dry, and gifted it to others. Without his help last semester, I wondered if Camden and Royal would have ever had a chance. Maybe Camden was right, and his indifference was purposeful, but it was too late, I'd already noticed the way he wore bravado like I held a paint brush. It was a safety net and there was a weakness in me, the same low voice that told me I was alone, I was invisible. And I craved the strength he so readily gave to others.

"Maybe," I agreed, ignoring the blanket of silence that had covered us.

Camden's phone chirped and his lips spread in a slow smile, his cheeks turning a shade of pink only my brother was capable of creating.

"Practice was good?" I asked, and Camden nodded, reading the screen of his phone.

"Yeah, he apologized for being late, said to meet him at Beckett in five minutes." Camden sat up and tapped out a message.

I shouldn't have, but I looked at the screen.

I miss you, too. Stay with me tonight.

Quickly, I averted my eyes, both embarrassed that I'd eavesdropped on such an intimate sentence, and wistful, wondering if one day I'd be lucky enough to have such an invitation.

Kai

The elevator smelled like piss, thick and overpowering, and I wondered what the hell I was doing here. My shoulder ached, and my ears hadn't stopped ringing with my mom's worried voice.

"It's for the best. You... You have to stop, stop trying so hard to be perfect, baby. You can't hold on to every thread when you're stretched so thin. You'll break... you're breaking..." Her voice had cracked, and I'd done all I could to prove her wrong. I'd kept silent. Holding in my anger, like always. She deserved none of it. *"You're not the same."*

The same. Same as what? I'd wanted to ask. I couldn't reconcile her definition. Captain. Son. Best friend. Smart. Loved. Same didn't fucking apply to me anymore. The only idea I tried to hold on to as the pinch in my rotator cuff screamed, *you are definitely not the same,* was the word sober. I wouldn't graduate like I'd wanted, like I should have been able to next summer. I wouldn't lead my swim team to any more victories, and I sure as hell wouldn't support my mother's decision to let *him* back into her life. Sober had become my *same*, or the closest thing to it. A clear head was the only way I'd be able to find my way out of the mess I'd made of my life. At least, that's what I kept reminding myself every time my mouth felt dry, and the weight I struggled to hold threatened to sink me. I exhaled an irritated breath, already annoyed with myself and it wasn't even ten yet. I stepped from the elevator and scanned the placard above the doorway.

Behavioral Health Center.

What the hell, Mom? This was too much, I screwed up, but I didn't need some stranger telling me how to feel about it. I'd drank too much, as usual, fallen asleep in a running car... in the garage. It hadn't been some grand gesture, I hadn't wanted to die. I'd wanted to fucking sleep. I'd wanted the pain to stop. I'd wanted my parents to listen. I'd wanted winter break to be over, tired of living in the shadow of my mother's worried gaze and my father's disappointed glares. Everything had become too—heavy. How could I help my mom when she didn't think I was capable? How could I make *him* understand that you don't walk out on your family and then expect them to take you back with open arms when your new life falls through? I'd never planned on drinking the whole bottle of Absolut. I'd meant to escape for a while, drive down to the beach, but I'd passed out in the front seat of my car with the engine running. An accident. Plain and simple.

A long, knowing sigh spilled from my lips. It wasn't simple. I was man enough to acknowledge the truth. The very "sameness" that had escaped me—everything I thought I could handle—had me pushing through these damn clinic doors. The waiting room appeared blessedly empty, but as I rounded the corner, my heart stopped.

Shit.

I took two, maybe three, quick steps backward.

Why was she here?

My tongue suddenly fat in my mouth as I peeked around the corner. A familiar dry feeling coated my throat, the feeling that made my fingers tremble, made me want to find the closest bar and grab a beer, a feeling that balked at the words, sane and sober, and wished for drunk and quenched. I couldn't deal with much more today. Being here was enough, but... I craned my neck to get a better look.

"Damn it," I whispered.

It was her.

I closed my eyes, clenched my jaw, as I recited the words I'd told myself before every race, before my hands cut through the water like blades, before my body brought home the win every time. I found a piece of myself behind the solitude.

I can do this. There is nothing that will ever stop me. I am fire.

Shallow breaths pulled through my lungs as I finally took a step forward. I focused on the corn silk color of her hair, the soft white of her skin, the way she sat with one leg curled under her body, the other dangling, her paint-covered shoe threatening to make me smile. The thing was, even though I'd like to pretend she was invisible, she'd been impossible to ignore. It had been impossible not to steal glances when I could, to wonder what she'd been thinking, and hating every single guy who had looked at her freely and with interest. From the first time I'd laid eyes on her, the first day of fall semester, in that darkly lit hallway between art studios, she'd haunted me. After that brief moment, I'd thought I'd never see her again, but she'd woven herself into my life, and part of me hated her for it.

Hated her paint-crusted fingernails, her shoes, her glowing cheeks, her funny little smiles. Hated her delicate lips, her laughs—never for me—the soft bend of her elbow, the light dusting of fine hair on the slope of her neck, and how, if I stared at her long enough, those very same hairs would stand and prickle with goosebumps.

She was too good for me.

She was his sister.

And I'd only ruin her.

"You should reconsider." Professor Hintz frowned, his coal eyes scanning the drawing I'd handed him. "You have an artistic hand."

"I won't have the time this fall. I made captain." My smile was smug and he shook his head.

"All this talent, Mr. Carter..." His fingertips brushed the page. Wistful and wanting. "I wish I would have had half of your talent when I was younger. You should be taking my class, not floating in some pool."

My jaw flexed. "It pays my way, I don't have the luxury of wasting away inside a studio like you."

17

He chuckled and met my glower. "I suppose all that anger makes for a better artist in the end. I'm sure I can sell this piece tonight at the show. I'll get you the funds by the end of the week." He scanned the page again with a nostalgic exhale. "She looks sad, like she'll never get to embark beyond the window she stares through. You captured her sorrow perfectly. Who is the subject?"

"My mother."

He'd sold my drawing for two-hundred dollars that night, and when I'd gone to pick up the cash, I'd seen her there, staring at some painting on the wall next to the professor's office. Her hair had been pinned to the side, her overalls too baggy on her fragile frame. Like a ghost, she'd whispered to herself, laughed quietly to no one at all, at least no one I'd seen. She'd passed by me, her eyes forward, like she hadn't noticed I was there. Her scent had hovered around me, soaking me in sweet lavender, and when Professor Hintz had called my name, I'd wanted to leave the money behind, follow her, ask her name, find out if I'd imagined her, if maybe I'd overworked myself into a delusional state.

I hadn't imagined her, though, or her scent, or her paint-stained fingers, that quiet smile. She turned out to be my teammate's sister, a fucking cliché. Indigo O'Connell, the most beautiful girl I'd ever seen in my entire, pathetic life, was Royal's twin sister. I had no other choice but to look the other way, to run. She was everything I could never have, everything I didn't deserve.

I stared at her longer than I normally allowed myself, standing in the doorway of the therapy office waiting room. She lifted her eyes, and I swallowed as her ice blue irises caught me, assessed, a small smile working at the corner of her lips. I ignored her as I sat on the opposite wall. I kept my head down and pulled my phone from my pocket, avoiding her gaze. Acting like I didn't know her, knowing I knew her better than she thought. The hair on the back of my neck stood, goosebumps raining down my arms as she watched me. Royal was more than my teammate. He was my best friend, and I'd purposely kept my distance from his sister. Never speaking to her directly, never allowing her into my world, assured I'd never be tempted. But sitting here, without any buffers, especially after what had happened last semester, I felt like an asshole. Staring at the blank screen of my phone, I thought, maybe if I stayed silent now, I could at least keep some things as they were. I didn't need any more distractions, anymore reasons to fail, and she was definitely not good for my sanity. Besides practices, I wasn't really speaking to her brother at the moment, either. At least, not yet, I wasn't ready...

I clicked open the notifications on my phone and scrolled through the fifty or so messages from Royal. I was angry at myself for not texting him back over winter break, but after everything that had gone down, the fight, my academic probation, having to repeat the entire fucking semester, I'd made friends with the black and empty spaces inside my head. I wasn't the leader he looked up to anymore. Shit, I needed this appointment more than I was ready to admit. I had nothing to offer him or his sister.

"Hi." Her shy voice broke through the silence, and my mouth fell into a scowl.

Indie waited. Her wide, big blue eyes met mine, and my stomach sank. They were too clear. Too light, like she could see deeper than she had any right to.

"Hey." I lifted my chin.

Christ, what did she see when she looked at me? The asshole who couldn't text her brother back? A coward who couldn't even look her in the eye for more than a couple of seconds?

Her smile confused me.

"Something funny?" I asked, sounding more irritated than I intended.

She mashed her lips together, fighting her smile. "Nope." Her smile grew, and my grip on my cell tightened. "It just looks like you want to throw your phone." Her eyes lowered to my hands, and I followed her gaze.

I shoved the damned thing into my pocket. Not offering conversation, I closed my eyes, like the asshole I'd gotten so good at portraying, and leaned back into the soft, vinyl cushion of the waiting room sofa.

"Did you check in?" she asked, and I opened one eye, the muscle in my jaw pulsing.

"No."

"You have to check in. They won't know you're here, otherwise."

"Thanks." I stood from the couch and made my way to the front desk.

I filled out the necessary paperwork.

Name: Kai Carter

Age: Twenty-One

Reason for your visit: ~~Depression.~~ My mother made the appointment.

I filled out the form, dreading the next few minutes of scrutiny I'd have to endure inside the waiting room. Why was Indie-freaking-O'Connell sitting in that damn chair? I didn't want anyone to know I was here. Shit, I'd been forced. I was under serious duress when my mom and dad had suggested it. High on carbon monoxide and my father's vodka, I'd made a shitty decision, but I wasn't depressed or suicidal. I'd admitted to my drinking problem and had sober handled. So I hadn't expected my dad to be waiting for me when I'd arrived in Rockport for break. And maybe I didn't give a shit that my father had come crawling back. What did it matter that I was pissed at my mom for forgiving him? Not a damn thing. Except... it meant everything. My entire life I'd always been compared to him.

You look so much like your dad. You have your father's eyes. You have so much of your father's determination.

Just like him.

I shook my head as I plopped down onto the sofa again, grimacing at the pain in my left shoulder. My heart rate increased as the pain shot down my arm. This pain. This goddamn pain hadn't eased up since the fight. I didn't want to think about how this shit would affect my race times. How this pain could affect my scholarship.

"You okay?" she asked, her concern only fortifying the wall I'd spent months building to avoid her.

No.

No, I wasn't.

I wasn't okay at all.

I hate Ellis and how he ruined everything with his ignorant mouth.

I hate what he said about Royal.

But mostly, I hate what he said about you.

These were the words that stewed inside my head, and I'd never speak them.

Ever.

I allowed myself to meet her gaze, avoiding the question. "Nice shoes."

I was a sarcastic prick.

She laughed, dropping her leg and wiggling her feet. The white Chuck Taylors were covered in splashes of paint. Yellow and blue, red and pink. "I think so."

"That's right... your parents are hippies."

"Painters," she corrected, her pink lips curled into quiet dimples as she laughed.

The sound of it lifted some of the pain from my shoulder, and I chuckled, feeling lighter than I had all day.

"Thank you," she whispered. Her ghostly pale eyes appraised me, and I feared she'd see it, see the empty, shallow nothing inside.

I licked my lips, swallowing past all the doubt choking me as I asked, "For what?"

"I wish..." She bit her lip and shook her head. "It's unfair, what happened, you should have—"

"What's done is done." I gave her a halfhearted smile and winced, the ache in my left arm throbbed as I shifted, uncomfortable under her gaze.

"You were there for him, when he needed it most, for both of them, Royal and Camden. You didn't deserve to be punished. You were protecting your friends. My brother…"

I hadn't missed the way her eyes had begun to swell with unshed tears. *Shit*. She shouldn't be crying, not for me.

"It was reckless," I admitted. "I could have grabbed Coach, I could have done a number of things that didn't require my fist down Ellis's throat."

I shouldn't have liked the way she smiled at my statement, or the way she hiccupped a little when she laughed.

"We never talk… but I wanted to say thank you. Thank you for protecting my family."

I sat up straighter, wanting to be the hero she saw sitting on this couch. I wanted to be more than the guy who drank too much, the guy who could barely afford the textbooks in his backpack.

"I told Camden to tell Royal I'd do it again in a heartbeat."

She nodded, a quiet grin in her eyes. "Maybe you should tell him yourself."

Indie lowered her eyes to the drawing she'd been working on in her notebook. I watched as her pencil moved fluidly over the paper, only pausing to lift the book from her lap as she readjusted, pulling her foot under her body again. My stare lingered for a few seconds as I tried to figure out why she was here, sitting in the on-campus therapy office. Was Royal here? Was she waiting for him? Had what happened last semester messed him up, too? I suddenly wished I would have answered every text he'd sent. I should've called him, told him I didn't regret what I had done, let him know that I envied him, that I would protect him and Camden every day if I needed to, that my silence was selfish, and he deserved so much more than a friend who couldn't gather the courage to face his own shadow.

"I'll call him today."

Indie lifted her eyes. "He'd like that."

Her attention fell to the page, and I dared a glance at the picture she'd been working on. It looked like a self-portrait, but half of it was faded and seemed to drift off the edge of the paper. Perhaps it was the fact her eyes were no longer focused on me, or maybe I'd found a voice inside her drawing, a kinship, that had me fumbling my words before I could stop them, creating some tie to her that I could hold onto, at least for the next five minutes.

"I'm thinking of taking an art class this semester."

A warm blush tinged the arch of Indie's cheek bones, her pencil hovering mid-stroke; she glanced at me from under long, straw-colored lashes. "Yeah?"

I nodded, my confidence hidden somewhere underneath the mass of unease growing inside my stomach. "Yeah... I'm thinking of dropping my upper-division writing class. The professor is a dick."

She laughed and fiddled with the end of her side braid. She always had her hair pulled back, and I pushed down the wonder growing inside my fingertips. They itched to pull apart the black tie at the end of her braid. I could only imagine how pretty she'd look with her hair down, falling over her elegant neck.

Around my knee, there was a large tear in my jeans. I picked at the frayed edges as a distraction, turning to look at the reception desk, and hoping for an escape from my thoughts.

"Do you like art?" she asked, her curiosity a warning I should heed.

Too close.

"Sure." I exhaled as I turned to face her, attempting to lace the word with boredom, calling on my inner asshole to shut down this conversation before I said something stupid. Her smile dimmed and regret tightened my chest. "Royal says your whole family is really talented." I nodded my chin at her art pad. "Is that you?"

The color of her cheeks deepened, and I couldn't help my smile. I liked that she reacted to me. "I'm not sure."

"Looks like you."

She bit her lip and stared down at the shadowed face on the page.

"Maybe it is," she said more to herself than to me.

"Kai Carter," a man in beige slacks and a bland sweater called my name from the door by the desk.

"That's me," I said as I stood, plastering on my all-American, of course it wasn't a suicide attempt, no, I don't want to drink myself into an oblivion, smile. I tapped my finger on the edge of Indie's drawing, flippant, and as "sane" as I could muster. "We should do this again sometime."

She giggled and hell if I didn't feel it in my spine. "I'm here almost every Tuesday."

She was here for herself. I filed that piece of information away to dissect later. "Every Tuesday..." I repeated, and she nodded, her smile not at all tempting, or beautiful, or sweet. I was such a liar. "It's a date, then."

It was just another lie I could add to my list of lies, but it'd made her entire face light up, the blush of her cheeks leaking all the way to her ears, and just like that, my day wasn't as shitty as when I'd stepped into that fucking cat piss elevator.

Kai

"You seem uncomfortable?"

"And?" I asked, pushing forward and resting my elbows on my knees. The fake leather upholstery had only added to my body heat, leaving a streak of sweat down my back. The chair squeaked under my weight. "If I said this entire fucking office makes me uncomfortable, what would you do? Write it down? Make a note on that pad of yours about how angry a young man I am? How I'm unwilling to open up?"

His top lip quirked into a burgeoning smile. "Are you?"

"Am I what?"

"Unwilling?"

Unwilling to talk to a stranger? Absolutely. Some asshole who thought he could fix all my problems because he had a title after his last name. LPC. Licensed Professional Counselor, aka therapist, or as I liked to call him, emotional rapist. The past twenty minutes, my silence an obvious no, but he kept pushing, pushing until I gave him what he wanted. Answers I didn't have.

Brian, according to the name badge hanging from his lanyard, sighed and shifted in his seat. The beige monochrome of his office matched his pants and sweater, the small green succulent sitting in his windowsill the only splash of color in this eight-by-ten cell. He shut his notebook, focused his eyes on mine, and my pulse quickened.

"Let's start with the basics, then?" He shrugged, and the gesture made him seem younger somehow. Made his receding, blond hairline and pot belly seem less aggressive as he assumed the same position as me. No doubt some sort of therapy technique. Was mirroring a thing? He rested his elbows on his knees, clasped his hands, and placed them under his chin. "You're here on an athletic scholarship?"

"Yes."

"Swim team."

I nodded.

"And you like swimming?"

"Wow, you figured that out?"

He chuckled. "I did. It's why they pay me the big bucks."

Without thinking, I laughed at his response. So, he was a smart ass. I could handle the sarcasm. His nosy questions, not so much.

"I played college football."

"Yeah?"

He hummed his agreement. "Yup, I was an Oregon Duck."

"No way?" My excitement was obvious, and he smiled. "That's my favorite team."

"You're from Rockport, I'm surprised you're not a Huskies fan."

"Why the hell would anyone be a Huskies fan?"

"Amen."

"Amen." The tension in my shoulders relaxed. "What position did you play?"

"Tight end." His grin seemed forced. "I hear your specialty is the four-hundred-medley relay. Freestyle, right?"

Irritation stretched itself back into my muscles. His segue graceless. "You seem to know everything about me... makes me wonder why I'm even here."

"You're here because you mixed a bottle of vodka with a sidecar of carbon monoxide." A serious line spread across his forehead, marring his laid-back approach.

"It was an accident."

"Tell me about it, then... Tell me how you accidently almost killed yourself."

"Everything you need to know is in that notebook. Am I right?"

"Is that how you see yourself?" he asked, and I realized his eyes were more gray then blue. Hard and intimidating, his gaze turned almost paternal. "Are you a few lines on a sheet of paper? No will? No personality? No heart... soul? Just a story to be told by others? A perception... an assumption?"

"I have no story." I turned my eyes to the small green plant, staring at the minuscule specks of brown decay. The tiny dots covered the tips of the leaves, ruining the illusion, disfiguring the vibrancy the plant had offered the bland room, peeling back its disguise.

"What happened in that locker room, Kai?"

"Didn't I tell you to get ready for practice?" I barked, but Ellis paid me little mind, his douchebag, smug smile, all for Royal.

"Tell me something, O'Connell. Is it biological?" Ellis smirked, his target set, his claws out, his posture ready for the fight, unwilling to let it go, to be a better person. It was like the entire room was holding its breath... waiting, hoping—wishing for blood. Royal's entire presence shook with repressed fury, his hands balled into fists at his sides. Ellis leaned in enough for me to notice and whispered, "I mean, it'd be a pity if your sister was a dyke, she's got a fuckable ass."

The memory made my knuckles ache. Half hoping I could punch the fucker in the face again, half wishing I'd have minded my own damn business. That was the thing that gutted me the most. My regret. I'd told Royal I'd do it again, and maybe it was the truth, but there was this hateful, spiteful part of me that was furious. That scolded. If I hadn't stepped in, if I would have just let Royal fight his own battle, maybe I would still be captain and not repeating my entire fall semester. That part of my heart, the small yet powerful fragment never seemed to stop hurting. It made me wish for something to drink, someone to bury myself in, something to help me forget I wasn't truly the man my friends, my family, believed me to be. I'd become a coward.

"I got into a fight," I finally answered, but Brian wasn't buying it.

"You were defending your gay friend."

"I'm no hero." I'd defended Royal, but I hadn't thrown the first punch until Ellis said what he'd said about *her*. About Indie.

"Your teammate, Ellis, he said some pretty awful things, got expelled for it, and you did what you thought was right and just, but you're conflicted... why?"

"I'm not conflicted."

"But you are, Kai, and that's the problem you're not willing to face."

I faced it every day when I looked in the mirror.

"You lost your captain title, you didn't get to take your exams, effectively holding you back an entire semester. That has to sting, does it not?"

I stood abruptly, the chair sliding backward a few inches. "What do you want me to say? That I wish I hadn't fucking punched him? That I should've let Royal deal with it? I almost lost my goddamn scholarship, and you know what, I wouldn't change a thing. I'd do it again." My voice shook. "I'd do it again, okay?"

Brian's eyes were filled with pity, too much damn pity. "Okay."

Pacing, I ran my fingers through my hair. "Ellis is an asshole who got everything he deserved."

"I agree." Brian held out his hand indicating I should sit down again. I hesitated. "Have a seat. Pacing makes me nervous. This office isn't big enough." He gave me an understanding smile. "Please."

I fell into the chair, wishing it would break apart and lay my ass out on the floor, giving me an excuse to leave.

"You were punished for doing something you felt, within your moral compass, was right. It's normal to be angry, even with your friend, Royal. Kai, the feelings you're having are normal, but the way you're dealing with them is not. Your mother said—"

"When did you speak to my mom?" The muscle in my jaw threatened to pop.

"Yesterday."

Heat flushed my cheeks as I tightened my hands into fists. "What did she say?"

"She said she thinks there's more going on in your head than the fight. She thinks you're mad at her and that's causing you guilt. She recently let your father move back in?"

"I'm done." I tried to stand, but Brian placed a soft palm on my knee.

"Stay, we only have a few minutes left."

I sucked in a long breath and leaned back into the chair. Brian set his hands in his lap, his astute gray eyes assessing me and said, "She's sick."

My throat thickened, my tongue dry and swollen with all the things I couldn't say, wouldn't say, ignoring the burn in my eyes, the pinch in my chest, I nodded.

"She has multiple sclerosis. That has to be hard for you, to see your mother so weak?"

"She's not weak." I managed the words, my mouth sticky, my palms sweaty. The walls of the office narrowed, stealing the space, my breaths accelerated as if I was fighting to win a race.

"You're right, my apologies. She's ill, not weak. In fact, for her to be doing as well as she is, she must be very strong."

I gave him another clipped nod.

"But you're angry with her?"

My nostrils flared, the burn in my eyes turning to liquid at the lashes.

"Time's up, Brian." I scrubbed my face with my palm and stood.

He didn't have the right to know. He didn't have the right to know any of this shit. He was a scavenger, feeding off my problems to make himself feel better. He had no idea what it was like to watch your mother's seams unravel, to watch her fall and then never get back up again, to feel the world breaking your fucking back, your heart, disappointing you and giving everything away to the people who didn't deserve it. He had no idea what it was like to have a mother who would die before she was even fifty years old.

Brian stood and held out his hand. I was respectful enough to shake it, to wonder what suffering he had stowed away in his own pockets. His suffering was his alone, and I'd never walk in his shoes, and he'd never walk in mine. The only difference between us was I didn't practice under the delusion I could help myself by collecting people's most miserable secrets.

"I hope to see you next Tuesday." He let go of my hand, and I didn't look him in the eye.

"Sure."

I shoved my hand in my pocket, his heat still soaked into my skin, making my lie feel heavier than it should. Or perhaps it was the lie I'd told earlier, to Indie, when I'd said every Tuesday would be ours. It wouldn't be. It couldn't be.

She was a silver lining, and I had no business wishing for such extravagant things.

Indigo

I couldn't deny the pleasure it gave me, the light hum of the projector, the quiet cast of blue darkness that descended on the lecture hall before the first slide illuminated the large, white screen. Professor Blackwood stood in front of the auditorium, remote in hand, staring up at his exhibition. These were the moments time afforded me an indulgence. Time, even the briefest of seconds, to catalog my world in color, to push away that voice in my head, and see everything as it should be. The blue haze... before the room was flooded with the brilliant gold, red, and green of Picasso.

"Can anyone tell me the title of this piece?" Professor Blackwood scanned the large room, squinting through his bifocals to find a victim.

Reading at a Table, oil on canvas, painted in 1934. I keep these words in my chest as the girl with long, dark hair in the front row raised her hand.

"Miss Marigold?" Blackwood's excitement was evident in his wide eyes as he stepped in closer toward the girl.

His uncanny ability to remember every student's name, well, at least their last names, baffled me.

"The Reading Girl." She sounded confident.

"Are you quite sure?"

"Um…" she stuttered, flipping through the pages of her textbook.

Anxiety stewed in my chest, not for the girl, but for the correct answer on my tongue. The internal battle to speak my mind, but the fear of this large room, and its fifty or so inhabitants…

Know it all.

Freak.

I cleared my throat, a poor attempt to drown out the voice in my head, and the professor turned his attention to me.

"Do you disagree, Miss O'Connell?"

The entire first three rows of students turned their heads, the tandem motion creating a wave-like sound of fabric rustling this way and that throughout the classroom.

"No, sir," I whispered past the raspy feel of my throat.

"No?" He raised his brow.

"Well…" I floundered, my palms sweating as *Miss Marigold* squinted her eyes, shrewd and annoyed. She'd found me wanting and turned back toward the slide display. I wasn't someone worth worrying about. I channeled the strength my father had always taught me to have, breathed through the voices strangling me silent and spoke with a clear and sharp tongue, "*Reading at a Table,* oil on canvas, painted in 1934 for his lover, Marie-Thérèse Walter."

Professor Blackwood's lips slowly spread into a grin, making him seem younger than his salt-and-pepper hair had colored him. "Very good, Miss O'Connell."

The room steeped itself in green as the girl quickly glanced over her shoulder, piercing me with blue eyes that might've been beautiful if they weren't so mean. In high school, that look would have wilted me on the spot, but this was my world. It didn't matter if my voices were still haunting me, I wanted this, wanted to feel at peace in my own skin, pave my own way here at St. Peter's, prove to myself I was more than just a sister, a daughter, a painter. I was a fresh start, a wheel of brand-new color, the first stroke of a brush on plain white canvas. I stared at the slide, at the women depicted by Picasso. Gold hair. Pale skin. It was like looking at a self-portrait. She was alone. For all the bold colors he'd chosen, she appeared sad and empty, sitting at the table, falling, drip by drip, into herself. Last semester I'd learn to be on my own, to not rely on Royal, and as much as I liked it, I understood the woman, Picasso's lover. I understood how at times, even under the eyes of those who love you, you could still feel empty.

Blackwood pressed his thumb to the remote in his hand, switching the visual.

"And this?" He gazed at the new painting. "*Woman in White.*"

"Neoclassical," a boy three rows down spoke without raising his hand.

"Yes... and..." Professor Blackwood prompted, a bored expression dipping his brows into a straight line.

The boy sat up taller, his shoulders filling the space of his chair. He tilted his head, allowing several long seconds to pass before he finally said, "Oil... water-based, on canvas."

"And crayon," someone answered behind me.

Professor Blackwood exhaled. "Yes... yes, but how does it make you feel. It's such a contrast to the previous painting."

"It's boring," an anonymous voice in the crowd teased.

"Boring." The professor balked. "Do explain."

The room filled with laughter when no one claimed the task.

"It's not boring, it's depressing." I recognized the gruff voice as it floated through the room, my heart beating a little faster, my breath caught in my lungs as I turned to find him sitting two rows behind me. He was all the way against the back wall, baseball cap pulled low over his dark eyes, but the familiar, tight line of his jaw was all the confirmation I needed. Broad shoulders, stiff and strong, how had I missed him sitting there this past week? Had he decided to transfer his class like he'd talked about at the clinic the other day? The hair on the back of my neck stood as he stared at me for a few quick, fumbled beats of my heart. Kai slid his gaze to Blackwood as he continued, "It's exactly the same as *Reading at a*

Table, but with less color. Both women seem sad." The room stilled, leaned in, like it was waiting for more, and I leaned with it.

"Sad," Blackwood mused.

"Yeah. Sad." Kai tapped his pencil against his left forearm. "I think she seems the saddest." He nodded at the screen, the bright white of the painting casting a dusky glow over the class, but he stood out, violet and controlled. "The other woman, Picasso's lover..." His throat bobbed as he swallowed, his lips caressing the word lover. Heat flashed and melted into my stomach. I didn't hide from my reaction to his voice, to the word, to the way he licked his lips before he said, "She owns the color despite Picasso's attempt to disfigure her, she wears it, like her loneliness, she belongs to it. This chick, she's all beige and pale, and yeah... a little boring."

The class laughed again, and to my surprise, so did the professor. "Very astute, Mr.—"

"Carter, Kai Carter." His eyes met mine briefly before I turned. Embarrassed by the way my cheeks had flushed.

She belongs to it. To Color. To Loneliness. Like me.

He doesn't see you.

He doesn't see you.

He doesn't see you.

The witch chanted inside my head as the lump formed inside my throat. I whispered softly to myself, "You're wrong."

But when the lights came on, and class was over, I'd looked over my shoulder, hoping to catch his attention, but he was gone. Disappeared, like always. I hadn't told Royal, or anyone that I'd seen him at the clinic. I understood the need for privacy, the hope that maybe one day I wouldn't need the privacy anymore anyway. That the noise would fade, and happiness would become a primary color I found in every piece of my day, mixing itself into the foundation of who I was. I was a lifer, though, and I couldn't stop myself from wondering if he could be, too. If his visit to the clinic would really become a weekly "date" or if the conversation we had was simply a forced nicety, a politeness gifted to his best friend's sister.

I slipped my bag over my shoulder and pulled my phone from my pocket as I walked to the auditorium door.

Me: I'm tired of the cafeteria. Let's go to Annie's?

His response was almost instant.

Blue: Hell yes. I need pancakes if I'm going to make it through another practice tonight.

Me: You always need carbs.

Blue: Meet us at my car.

Me: I have to drop off a few things at the studio.

Blue: Camden says hurry up, he's S-T-A-R-V-I-N-G.

Me: Camden never whines.

I giggled as I read his next response.

Blue: Fine it was me, but hurry up, okay. Powdered Sugar Utopia awaits you, Pink.

I placed my phone in the back pocket of my overalls and made my way down the long hall of the art building. The walls were covered in hand-sketched drawings, part of the junior class exhibit from last semester. I marveled over the charcoal pieces, the talent, only stopping when I noticed a small area of the wall was blank except for a sheet of paper that had been taped to its surface. It read, NEW EXHIBIT COMING SOON. Excitement bubbled up inside my veins, wondering what new talents would be placed on these walls. Maybe one day my work would be, too, left up for pondering and speculation. The corner of my lip pulled between my teeth as I tried to suppress my smile.

One day at a time, Indie. My dad's voice echoed inside my head, drowning out the earlier witch. I could see his weathered smile, feel the touch of his hand on my shoulder.

"Always in such a hurry," I whispered with a smile as I opened the studio door.

The lights were on, but the place was empty. The large, open space was cooler than the rest of the building, all metal beams and concrete floors. If it wasn't for the kiln and pottery majors, we'd all freeze to death this winter. I rummaged through my bag, grabbing the new brushes my mom had gotten me for Christmas, and placed them in my bin in the right corner of the room. Every art student had his or her own Tupperware tub filled with their supplies. There weren't very many of us, maybe thirty-five, including all mediums. Sculpture, pottery, painting, drawing, restoration, and history. Vigrus Hall, one of the girls' dormitories, named somewhat for the patron saint of artists, was where the entirety of female art students resided, including myself. We were a small, quirky bunch, sometimes intermingled with those taking their humanities requirements, but preferring the solitude of our studio space. I'd really only made one friend, an art major, as well, named Daphne, and that was mostly because she was one of the four girls living in my suite.

Daphne's bin was next to mine on the studio floor, and I laughed at the disheveled mess. Her lid was tossed on the ground, her supplies half open, half spilled, her paint brushes crusted. I leaned down, grabbed her lid, and gently snapped it in place.

"Indigo O'Connell, you keep your hands off my shit." Daphne's shrill voice echoed off the deserted walls. She shot me a smile, her lip ring sparkling under the bright lights. She opened her bin, scanned its contents, and with a dramatic sigh said, "Thank God, I finally got it organized."

"That's organized?"

She ran her long fingers through her black hair. The pixie cut she'd gotten last semester had grown out, and flopped over her forehead.

"I have a system." She picked out the crusted brushes. "Well, fuck, these are ruined." She tried to throw them in the trash, but I plucked them from her grasp.

"A little turpentine and they'll be as good as new."

"Really? Because I already spent most of my student loan on housing." Her lips curled up into her famous, *I am up to something*, smile. "And maybe a bottle of whiskey." Her eyes floated to the ceiling. "Or two."

"You can't get caught with that again, Ari will lose her mind."

"Ari is a stuck-up bitch."

"She's really sweet once you get to know her."

Daphne narrowed her eyes. "You're too soft, Indie."

Ari was another one of the four girls living in our suite, and honestly super nice. "You're mad because she's dating Gus."

"I have a thing for jocks, so sue me." She blew out a long breath and sat on one of the stools by her easel.

I giggled. "Just be careful."

"All great artists have vices." She waved her hand dramatically, speaking in a deep and terrible British accent.

"You should've majored in Theater."

"You know, I still might."

My phone vibrated in my pocket, and I didn't have to look to know it was my "starving" brother wondering where I was.

"I'm heading to Annie's with Blue and Camden if you want to join us."

"Speaking of fine jocks." She smirked, and I shook my head.

"One, that's gross, he's my brother, Daph, and two, he's gay."

"Bi."

"Whatever, Daphne."

"He had a girlfriend once."

"He's in love with Camden."

"I could turn him."

I huffed out a laugh. "You could try."

"Is that a challenge?" She stood, her full lips stretching across her face.

"God, no."

Her laugh was infectious. "Fine… at least tell him I said hi."

"You can't come?"

"I have art history in thirty minutes."

"Brush up on your Picasso."

"Ugh, Blackwood loves him. Pablo was such a chauvinist."

"I think the whiskey has officially pickled your brain." I paused, staring at the black and white stripes on Daphne's shirt, debating if I should tell her about Kai.

"What?" she asked, pulling at the seam of her shirt. "Did I get paint on it again?"

"Kai Carter was in my art history class today." I hadn't meant to blurt it like I had, but the words rushed out on one big breath.

She looked up from her shirt. Daphne had gone to high school with Kai but had run in different circles. I always wondered if they ever had a thing, if he was her reason for *bedding* jocks as she liked to call it.

"Weird."

"Maybe that was one of the classes he had to retake? It's a humanities requirement."

"Art History One is required, not Two, and besides, he would have finished that his freshman year. Maybe he's hiding out, he's good at that."

My stomach did a full somersault. "What do you mean?"

She shrugged, pulling her paint brushes from my hand. "He runs hot and cold. Always has."

44

"Did you guys date in high school?"

Please say no.

She grinned and tugged on my side braid. "Why so interested?"

"I'm not." I took a step toward the door.

She hummed, a doubtful glint in her brown eyes. "I didn't really know him in high school. He was a junior and I was a freshman. We grew up together, but then one day he pulled away, went his own way, I guess. Shit happens when you have an almost three-year age difference. He was the one who got away." She said the last sentence with a wistful lilt and then laughed. "You should see your face. All doe eyes and shit. Kai is *not* your type."

"I never said I was interested."

"You didn't have to."

"You're crazy."

"And I drink too much, tell me something I don't know." Her face took on a serious expression. "Indie, listen..."

"Gotta go." I turned toward the door, pulling my phone from my pocket and waving it over my shoulder. "Blue gets hangry when he has to wait too long."

She didn't try to stop me. "Don't forget to tell him I said hi."

"I will."

Once the studio door closed behind me, I leaned against it, closed my eyes, and exhaled. I should've let her finish that sentence, but there was this feeling growing, maybe more powerful than it should be, that yearned for more. That elusive *more* I'd craved. More feeling. More light. More color. Red. Like the love my parents had for each other, like Royal had with Camden, and maybe Kai wasn't it, maybe he wasn't my type, but when he looked at me, I could admit to myself. In this hallway filled with feeling, filled with thoughts bled across the walls in black and gray smudges, in this place, like my church, I could confess it. When Kai actually looked at me, when he took those stark, infinitesimal minutes inside that clinic waiting room and truly looked at me for the first time, I'd never felt so seen. So known. Maybe I'd created something out of nothing. It's what I did, what I was good at, but he wasn't one of my paintings.

He doesn't see you.

"But he did. He did see me." I spoke, a small smile on my face, and hoped he'd see me again on Tuesday, like he'd promised.

Kai

Everything drowns under the water, sound muffled and muted. Like these insecurities I held in my hands every day, they floated away in the current created by the very same hands. Each breath I took propelled me forward, toward something tangible, toward the hard surface of the wall, to the win. My ears broke the surface first as my lungs burned with fatigue. The whistle blew, and the smile on Coach's face lit the fire inside me. The fire I'd thought I'd smothered with beer and whiskey.

"Carter, welcome back," he shouted loud enough it echoed off the tile floors as he leaned down and tapped the top of my head with his clipboard.

My swim cap pulled at the hair on my nape, but I ignored the pinch and watched as Royal's long body sliced through the water. My eyes flicked to the clock, and just like last semester, he was fast as hell. His broad arms and shoulders moved with effortless grace, and he touched the wall before anyone else.

Coach's whistle was between his teeth, the shrill sound taking on a more aggravated tone as he stalked toward Sherman. "Do I need to cut you?"

"No, sir." Sherman ran his hands over his cap, pulling it from his head, his eyes darting across the lanes, his lips curling into a scowl as he stared at Royal.

Coach lowered his body into a squat, his voice a rough whisper as he ripped Sherman a new one. "I don't give a crap where you come from, who your parents are, or what problem you have with your teammates. You don't get your times up—you're done. Don't make me do this. You're better than this, kid."

"Wow," Royal whispered. "Do you think Coach would actually cut him?"

I watched as Sherman dragged himself from the pool without another glance in our direction, stomping off, his head down, and his swim cap and goggles balled into his fist.

"I think Coach will do whatever it takes to get this team back to where we were before the break."

"I feel like this is my fault."

"Bullshit." I shook my head, not in the mood to rehash everything all over again. "Sherman is a fucking bigot and should've followed Ellis out the door."

"He was our friend."

"Was, Royal. Was being the operative word."

Royal cast his gaze to the surface of the water. "Everyone's been cool, even some of the guys I didn't talk to last semester, but it hurts a little more, knowing Sherman thinks there's something wrong with me. He ate lunch with us almost every damn day. Now he looks at me like I shit in his cereal."

"There's nothing wrong with you, Royal. You're gay. You love who you love, we don't need assholes like Sherman Hollister on this team fucking up the chemistry."

"We need our captain back."

The weight of Royal's statement hit me in the gut as I turned to face him. "Not happening, O'Connell. It can't. What's done is done, and I'd do it all over again. You know this."

I was a broken record, repeating the same lines over and over since practices had begun. I believed them, so why couldn't he? Planting my palms on the slick surface of the deck, I unsuccessfully tried not to strain my left shoulder as I lifted myself out of the water. I grit my teeth, concealing my quiet wince of pain.

"Listen, I know I messed up by not answering your texts over break, but... everything at home... let's just leave it. It wasn't the best Christmas I've ever had, and it probably won't be the worst."

"Did you get in trouble?"

"Not exactly. My mom's got more important shit to worry about than me losing my captain title."

"Is she doing okay?"

I didn't want to talk about my mom. My dad. Or how everything I'd struggled with, worked so hard for, had basically exploded.

"Yeah, man, but like I said at practice the other day, it's all good, O'Connell. It's better this way. Everything happens for a reason, right? You and your boyfriend get to be out." The smile I gave him was genuine, but the concern in his eyes made it falter.

He eased himself from the pool, wiping the water off his arms, he held my gaze. "It feels different. You... and me. It's weird. I feel like we broke up or something."

A smirk formed on my lips, and I gave him a teasing punch to the shoulder. "Awe, do you miss me? Does Camden know you're in love with me, too?"

"You're a jackass." Royal's anxiety melted.

Feeling lighter than I had in over a month, I said, "I miss you, too."

He rolled his eyes. "Sure."

He grabbed a towel from the bench and threw it at me. As I stretched to grab it, the muscle in my left shoulder pinched and I almost dropped it.

Laughing, I tried to hide my discomfort. "I'm serious. It's strange never having Camden around anymore. I actually want to listen to his crappy music."

His eyes on my left shoulder, perceptive, Royal asked, "What's up with that?"

I gave in and rubbed my fingers into the muscle. "What? I'm not allowed to miss my roommate and his depressing music either?"

"Your shoulder? You're favoring it when you swim. Tonight's the first night you've come anywhere close to your usual times. Is it bothering you?"

"It's fine, a little tight is all." I averted my eyes and headed toward the locker room.

Royal's cool fingers rested on my shoulder, stopping me in place. "What do you mean it's a little tight?"

"Jesus, can you two talk about your sex lives later? I'm wilting away from hunger. Pizza at Stacks, remember?" Corbin breezed by, his big, goofy smile reaching his eyes.

"You're disgusting." Royal dropped his hand from my shoulder and playfully shoved the back of Corbin's head.

"You love it." Corbin flashed us another grin before escaping behind the locker room door.

"You going with us to get pizza?" Royal asked, distracted from his previous interest in my shoulder.

Hating that I had to be thankful to Corbin for anything, I nodded.

Unconvinced, he asked, "Why don't I believe you?"

Guilt burrowed inside my stomach. I'd let the distance between us linger, made him doubt our friendship, made him think he wasn't worth my time anymore. I was such an asshole.

I lifted my chin, and my lips formed into a wolfish grin. With the mask in place, I found the pieces of myself Royal needed, the captain he couldn't let go of. "I wouldn't miss it, not even for that redhead in my Calculus class."

Royal's smile stretched across his face as he cupped the back of my neck with his palm, pulling his forehead to mine with a chuckle, he said, "I really have missed you."

The soles of my shoes were sticky with spilled beer and liquor as I walked toward the group of booths near the back. Most of the team had packed themselves like sardines around the pool table, drinking beer, scarfing pizza, and flirting with the usual sorority girls. The scene at Stacks hadn't changed since I'd started at St. Peter's my freshman year. The only difference tonight was that I'd chosen to be good. Scratch that, I had to be good. I could drink from the pitchers of beer offered, chat up some chick, and maybe even get a blow job before the night was over, but I had to try. I owed it to myself, to the team, to try. My race times were inconsistent, sucking air and water into my lungs like a rookie. It didn't help that my shoulder felt like shit for the most part, but I hadn't had a sip of alcohol since the beginning of the semester, and already the pain had begun to improve. I hadn't wanted to die after weight training with Royal this morning, and tonight, despite the ache, I'd made my best time at practice since our last meet back in December.

Instead of pushing my way through the pack of wolves around the pool table, I decided to slide into the booth with Camden and Royal, not giving a damn about the few outliers glaring at me. The ones who'd blamed Royal for "ruining the team." Sure, most of the guys were chill with the gay kid in the locker room, but there was a small minority that hated. I could see it in the way they watched him in the showers, see it in the way they clenched their teeth when he walked out onto the mark, felt it in the way they watched me and wondered if I was secretly into guys, too. I only hoped Royal hadn't caught on yet, he deserved his happiness.

"It's packed tonight." Royal shot Camden an apologetic smile.

"I'm surprised you're here." I chuckled and elbowed Camden.

"I don't mind it as much anymore." Camden's silver-green gaze was only for Royal.

"We don't have to stay long." Royal reached across the table and covered Camden's hand. His thumb tracing long lines against his skin.

The gesture would have never happened last semester. All the things I thought I'd lost, in this moment, seemed selfish. I stood up for this, for these two people. Their intimacy, out for the world to see, it cracked me open in a way that hurt. The pain of it spread down my chest and ribs, reminding me how alone I'd allowed myself to become. No alcohol-induced numbness to hide behind, and as much as I didn't want to admit it to myself, I loved it. This feeling... as I took a deep breath, this feeling that hurt, I welcomed it. Welcomed the warning that I was alive somewhere inside this shell.

"Thank God." Corbin flopped down across from me, and I held back my smile as Camden cringed. "Can I use your discount, man? I'm low on cash, and I don't want to use my credit card."

"I don't work here anymore." I cut my fingers through my hair as the entire table stared at me. "What?" I shrugged. "I quit last week."

"Why?" Corbin asked, as if my quitting had been a personal affront.

Royal's worried frown was hard to ignore. I let it anchor me as I spoke. More than anyone, he deserved the truth. "I was drinking too much. I need to be healthy, get my shit together if I want to prove to Coach I can be captain again next year."

"For real?"

"Yeah, Corbin. For real." I laughed, hoping no one heard the way it trembled, or noticed the few beads of sweat that had begun to form on my hairline.

"Good." Royal held up his fist and I bumped it, ignoring the way my heart raced at my admission.

I had a problem.

A problem.

I wanted to drink.

Sweating because I wanted to drink.

Sweating because I wanted to pick a random girl from the growing swarm to make me forget for five minutes, maybe ten, about the life back in Rockport I carried on my shoulders. All because I'd felt that intimate pain crack down my chest, because I wanted that pain, because I liked the way Royal treated me with respect, because I wanted to deserve it.

"Kai?" Corbin's brows furrowed. "Dude, did you hear me?"

I shook my head, the sound of the room rushing in around me.

"Don't you need the money, though?"

"I picked up another part-time gig... on campus, actually..." I wiggled my eyebrows, trying to make light of the shitty job I'd accepted a few days ago. "Building maintenance."

"What the hell do you know about maintaining buildings? You're a business major." Royal's skeptical blue eyes danced with humor.

"My dad was a mechanic," I argued.

"Not the same thing." Camden's cool tone made me laugh.

"Alright, it's a fancy title for the guy who mops the floors and takes out the trash. Give me a break, it pays, and that's all that matters."

Corbin almost spit out his beer. "A janitor?"

"Yeah, shithead, a janitor, someone has to pick up after all you spoiled-rich idiots."

I bit back my smirk as he back-peddled.

"I mean, yeah, cool, a janitor, that's... you know... admirable."

Royal tapped his fingers on the tabletop. "You should've applied for a library spot. I could ask..."

"There weren't any. Trust me, this isn't ideal, and it's only temporary. Just until something better opens up, but working in a bar wasn't a good option anymore. Sorry, Corbin, you'll have to find some naïve girl to buy your drinks from now on."

"For the record, *I* don't need a girl to buy me drinks. *And* I don't think you drink too much. I say this without any ulterior motives. You should get your job back." Corbin stood, a slight scowl on his face as he assessed the crowd for an unwitting female to pick up his tab.

"For the record, I think—"

"Yeah, I know, Kai, I'm an idiot." Corbin's lips split into a smile, all teeth and sarcasm as he walked away.

Royal leaned in, asking in a voice I could barely decipher, "Are you doing okay, then? I mean, you've given up drinking altogether?"

I collapsed backward into the booth, scrubbing my clammy palms over my face with a long exhale. "For now."

Camden spoke as he laced his fingers through Royal's. "It's probably weird being the third wheel, but if you need people to keep you on track, we're here for you."

I huffed out a laugh and bit the corner of my mouth. "Thanks, Dad."

"You're welcome."

I was busy thinking up some witty comeback when my phone chimed in my pocket. Last semester I wouldn't have hesitated to check the message, but I'd been avoiding so many people lately, the notification sound, that quiet chirp and vibration in my pocket had started to give me anxiety.

Daphne: So this is how it's going to be?

This was exactly why I hated checking my messages. *Shit.* Another bad decision come round to collect. My thumb hovered over the screen, debating whether or not I should answer. Ghosting her wasn't an option. This fucking campus was too small, and Rockport was even smaller.

Me: Hey, Daph.

Daphne: Hey, Daph? Really?

Me: I'd say I'm sorry but you wouldn't believe me.

Daphne: No, I wouldn't.

I waited a full minute before I let out a sigh and typed the one thing I should have had the balls to say to her in person.

Me: I fucked up.

56

"Well, look who it is." The sound of her voice should've startled me, but I had a feeling she'd be here tonight. Daphne was always here, just like me, hiding her shit life inside a bottle. "Hey, Pink, grab us a few menus."

Pink.

Indie was here, smiling and shiny, covered in more paint than usual. Pale blue and purple streaks covered her overalls, and the tips of her blonde braid were speckled with white. That damn braid. I couldn't fathom how gorgeous she'd be, pink cheeked with a halo of gold on my pillow. My jaw strained enough, I felt it down to my molars. I wasn't supposed to fucking think about her like this, I shouldn't think of her at all. Her iced blue eyes found mine, sought me out as Daphne shoved in next to me, trapping me, pinning Camden up against the wall, and making it impossible for me to perform my disappearing act. I dropped her gaze, following the script in my head. She was invisible.

"Do you guys need a menu?" Indie asked, sweet and soft.

Last Tuesday we'd had an actual conversation, and ignoring her would make me seem like the biggest prick in the world. Camden and Royal both answered no, in unison, while I lifted my gaze and gave her a half-hearted smile and shook my head.

It would be a good thing if she hated me, if she only thought of me as her brother's douchebag friend. But as she slid into the booth, menus in hand, and took a seat next to her brother, I didn't want her to hate me. I liked the way she watched me, thinking I hadn't noticed her noticing me as she handed Daphne the menus.

"Haven't seen you around, Carter." Daphne batted her lashes, flicking her tongue over the ring in her lip. "I've missed my barmaid."

I wanted to slink away, panic wedged itself inside my throat as she leaned in, flirty as ever. I never hid the fact I was a whore, but I didn't want it paraded in front of Indie. What happened between me and Daphne over winter break was a mistake, and maybe I was a dick for messing around with her in the first place, but she knew damn well what she'd wanted that night. Fueled by Jameson and anger, we'd both needed to feel something beside the disappointments of our day to day. We used each other to get off, and as callous as that sounded, she had been the one who'd set the rules.

One night, Kai. Can I just feel good for one night?
One night. No call backs.

She hadn't texted me for the rest of the break, not even when classes had resumed. I hadn't heard from Daphne until yesterday. She sent me a text asking if I wanted to meet her at the lake for drinks. I hadn't responded. And never planned to.

"So, you get a new job or something?" Daphne pulled a flask from her pocket, bringing it to her lips, she took a long sip.

I watched as she screwed on the cap, thirsty for more than the water inside my glass. Jameson, Heineken, hell, even Budweiser would've made this awkward situation much more bearable.

"I did. I start next week." She dangled the flask in front of my face from her fingers, offering me sin and absolution. I shook my head. "Can't, we've got a meet in a few days." With a fake smile, I gave her a gentle shove. "Move your ass, Daphne, I need to use the bathroom."

She squeaked, always the drama queen, and stood, her smile just as fake as mine as she murdered a southern accent. "So polite."

"You know me, always the gentleman." Her Cheshire grin fell, and I hid my shaking hands in my pockets. "Actually, I'm probably gonna take off." I skated around the uncomfortable silence that had descended, capturing Royal's attention, I asked, "Weights in the morning?"

"Bright and early."

I steadied my hand enough to hold out my fist. Royal bumped his knuckles against mine. "You coming home tonight, Camden?"

I chuckled as he blushed all the way to the tips of his ears. "Probably, I need to practice."

"Good, you know I can't sleep without your moody bullshit in the background." He rolled his eyes, my derisive choice of words making Royal snicker.

"You still have ear plugs from last semester, I imagine?" Camden asked, and I nodded, holding back my grin at the annoyed crease between his brows. "Then use them."

Chuckling, I avoided Daphne's pointed stare and shifted my gaze to the bit of sunlight sitting next to Royal. Indie's head was tipped down, her purple fingernails picking the splatters of paint from her braid, and allowed myself to look at her, a small indulgence, before I left.

59

"I'll see you in the morning, O'Connell." The sentence was meant for Royal, but as Indie lifted her chin, her lips tilted into a shy smile, and fuck it all, I smiled back.

I couldn't lie to myself and say I hadn't hoped my transfer would land me in the same art history class as her. I also couldn't deny I almost transferred out when I'd realized she was actually in the damn class. In the end, my masochistic tendencies won, and I kept the new schedule.

"Don't be a stranger, Carter." Daphne eyed me as I turned to leave.

She barely waited until I stepped outside to send me another text.

Daphne: Want to fuck up again? Meet me tonight.

The cotton mouth feel of my tongue, its sour taste, made me nauseous. I could say yes. Meet her somewhere, share a bottle, use each other until we were sloppy, and hated ourselves all over again.

Me: I can't.

Daphne: You mean you won't.

Me: You're right. I don't want to do that to you.

Daphne: Such a hero.

A hysterical, sad, humorless laugh forced itself from my lungs as my head fell back. Thick clouds parted, exposing tiny pin pricks of light that glittered against the purple and black sky. I sucked in the frigid air, the tip of my nose numb as a damp fog parted from my lips.

Hero.

Captain.

Not anymore.

It would be easy to type those three letters, but the last time I said yes to her, I'd wound up passed out in a garage and almost died.

Me: 'Night, Daph.

I slipped my phone in my pocket, not expecting a reply, and started toward campus. When I was finally in my bed, sober as a rock, I checked my notifications.

Nothing.

I smiled.

I smiled because I'd done the right thing, and hopefully, this time, it wouldn't cost me everything.

Kai

"I'm fine."

Her soft laugh made the corners of my mouth ache for a smile. "Fine..." She hummed and the static sound crackled through the receiver and down my spine. It made me nostalgic for home. I pictured my mom sitting on the couch, her blanket over her feet like always, a book in her lap, and a cup of coffee at her side. Our house always smelled like coffee, it didn't matter if it was ten in the morning or at night, the woman had a cup of coffee by her side. "Wasn't it you who said women only say they're fine when they're ready for a fight?"

I could hear the humor in her voice, and I sank down onto the dorm room sofa feeling relieved she sounded healthy. "You seem... happy."

She breathed out a sigh, probably at my blatant avoidance. "Today was one of the rare good ones. Sunshine kind of day."

I wish you could still sit on the porch, I wanted to say, but instead asked, "Did home health come?"

"Don't they always? I hate to say it... but I don't think I like this new nurse. She threw away my coffee without asking if I was finished. She said it was bad for me. I mean..." *What does it matter?* I wanted to finish her sentence. *I'm dying so what does it matter?* But she said things in her own way, her own *lay it down nice and gentle for the sake of our son* sort of way. "If I want to drink coffee, I'll drink coffee, life's too short for this is bad and this is good."

The angry, still volatile, part of me, the ever-present being that lived inside me, stretching itself out, long and permanent under my skin, begged me to tell her there were worse things than coffee. Dad, for starters. But I'd get the same answer as the nurse.

"I'm glad it's a good day, Mom. Can you at least feel the sun, did the nurse leave the blinds open?"

"She did." The silence thickened, and I could hardly breathe or swallow. "You're allowed to have good days, too."

I hung my head, my fingers pinching the bridge of my nose, desperate to push away the burn building beneath the lids of my eyes. "I'm getting there." The gruff quality of my voice gave me away, and I heard her slight intake of breath.

"Kai," she whispered.

"The therapist helped." A lie.

"Kai." She'd seen right through me all the way from Rockport.

63

"I'll go. I promise."

"Taking care of yourself is your only job. Repeat the words."

"Mom, I'm not nine."

"Repeat them."

I chuckled at her watery laugh, wishing I could sit next to her on our porch again, peeling away the aged gray paint, turning over the splinters of wood in my hand, days with sunshine that would yawn for miles, when all I had to worry about was my father, making sure he'd set up her rocking chair, when everything felt impossibly optimistic and light. "Taking care of myself is my only job."

"That's my Kai bear."

I shook my head, but couldn't stop my smile from spreading, from cracking me open a little bit wider. "You, too, Mom, you need to take care of you, lay off the coffee."

"Anything for you."

Camden's bedroom door opened and he emerged sleep tousled. His hair stuck up and out in every way but down as he yawned, lifting his arms over his head like a cat, his signature, disgruntled expression on his brow.

"Gotta go, Mom. Be nice to the new nurse, you can't keep running the young ones off, Rockport is small, you'll end up nurse-less."

"Now that would be a good day."

"Love you.

"Love you, too. Therapy... Kai, don't—"

"Harpy."

"Bull."

I laughed out loud. "Tuesday."

"Thank you."

I hung up the phone as Camden plopped down on the other side of the couch.

"You and your mom have the weirdest conversations." His silver green eyes were at half mast, sleepy, he leaned back and yawned again. "Why does your mom need a nurse?"

He stared at me, waiting for an answer, but I was struck by the fact Royal had never told him. He'd kept my secret, even to his boyfriend.

"Hey, I'm sorry, it's your business, I shouldn't—"

"She's not well."

Cold crept its way up my neck, making every part of my body feel stiff and used. Telling Royal about my mom, then Daphne, now Camden, every person who knew the truth made my mom's death sentence that more real. "She has MS. Multiple sclerosis. One of the worst kinds. She has good days, and bad days, but the bad days are fucking winning, and I—"

The air in my lungs disappeared, making it difficult to form a sentence. My ribs squeezed as I fought myself, fought the emotion that would lead me down a dangerous path, the path I couldn't travel anymore, not if I wanted to be here for her. Not if I wanted to have some semblance of a life when she was gone.

A shuddered, weak breath passed my lips. "And I'm falling apart."

Camden's posture was as frozen as I felt. "I don't know what to say."

"I don't need you to *say* anything. It's nothing new, she's been fighting this for years."

"I had no idea." He shook his head. "I mean, I had a feeling there was more going on with you, the drinking was..."

The muscle in my jaw contracted. "Save it. I have a problem. I know."

"I'm your friend, Kai. What you did for me, I'm here if you need help, if you need—"

I stood. "You don't owe me anything."

He exhaled a defeated sigh. "I know that." Camden unfolded his long limbs and stood, resting a warm palm on my shoulder, he caught me off guard. He wasn't the touchy-feely type, at least not with anyone besides Royal. "I have a mother who threw me away like I was a useless piece of garbage, and if my dad called me tomorrow to tell me she was sick, I'd still mourn her. Being alone sucks, I did it for years..." I opened my mouth to speak and he held up his other hand to shut me up. "I know you have friends, girls, but you're alone, Kai, and you don't have to be." He released his grip on my shoulder.

"Noted." I gave him the best smile I could muster. "You know, if the whole music gig doesn't work, you could probably take Brian's job."

"Who's Brian?"

"My new therapist."

"You have a therapist?"

"Yeah, I guess I do."

Camden's phone rang, and his eyes darted to his bedroom door. I laughed. "Tell Royal I said I'll see him in the gym."

He hesitated, but gave in with a nod. I planned to razz him later about how fast he practically ran to grab his phone. A lot of shit in my life had taken a nosedive, a full-on spiral down, but I kept reminding myself some things had turned out okay. I pushed open my bedroom door to grab my stuff for the gym, and as I lifted my backpack, the sketch book I always carried fell from a large, unzipped pocket. It flipped open as it hit the carpet and a pair of blue eyes stared back at me. This was the first drawing I'd rendered in a long time, Indie sitting on the couch at the therapist's office. I'd gotten the length of her chin all wrong, and her cheek bones were too thin, but as I knelt down, I let my fingers run over the dark gray lines of the pencil, smudging heavy shadows along the page.

My eyes drifted from the drawing to the ridiculous swimsuit model posters hanging over my bed. Everywhere you looked in my room, the posters, the football in the corner, the empty stack of beer cans I'd erected last semester into a pyramid sitting on my windowsill. My persona. My perfectly placed stereotypes displayed for the world to see.

"Taking care of myself is my only job," I whispered as I put away the sketch pad and shouldered my bag.

I grabbed my phone out of my pocket, flipped through my contacts, and hit the call button. As the phone rang, my heart galloped, speeding through the oxygen in my blood.

Lightheaded and unsteady on my feet, his voice was almost unfamiliar.

"Haven't heard from you in a while."

"I've been busy." I cleared away the anxiety in my throat and pulled at the confidence I'd wielded every day of my life. "Listen, Professor Hintz—"

"My buyer relocated to Seattle, Mr. Carter. Though, I'm sure I could—"

"I don't have a piece to sell, well... not this very moment. Actually..." I summoned that courage, that feeling I got on the mark as the water settled into a placid calm before the storm, before I dove in and made it mine. "I'm calling about the TA position you have posted on the work-study website."

"You have someone in mind?" His voice seemed bored, distant, as papers rustled in the background.

"Yes, sir. Me... I mean, I'd like to apply for the position."

"You're not an art major."

"I'm not."

"The position is for art majors, Mr. Carter."

My left hand curled into a fist as I raised it and closed my eyes.

"Yet."

"Yet? What do you mean, yet? Are you thinking of coming over to the dark side?"

"I am. I mean, I want to, but I have some questions, do you have time this morning to meet with me? I have a class at ten-thirty but—"

"Meet me at ten." His tone was electric. "I have to say, you abandoning your pursuits of pie graphs and expense reports should be shocking, but I knew you'd come around. You're too talented."

I opened my eyes, my lungs filling slowly, my muscles rolling out along my limbs. "I sure hope so."

"I'll see you at ten."

I didn't move for what felt like a full minute. My phone in my hand, the conversation I'd just had repeating itself like a needle jumping on those old vinyl records my mom listened to when I was a kid. Camden laughed and the muffled sound of it, coming through the wall we shared, shook me awake.

Art major.

Taking care of myself is my only job.

Life's too short for this is bad and this is good.

I took a few steps and leaned over my bed, my fingers gripping the bottom of the Miss July centerfold, and as I tore the picture from the wall, something long forgotten tore loose inside of me, as well.

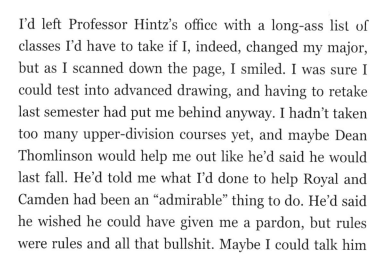

I'd left Professor Hintz's office with a long-ass list of classes I'd have to take if I, indeed, changed my major, but as I scanned down the page, I smiled. I was sure I could test into advanced drawing, and having to retake last semester had put me behind anyway. I hadn't taken too many upper-division courses yet, and maybe Dean Thomlinson would help me out like he'd said he would last fall. He'd told me what I'd done to help Royal and Camden had been an "admirable" thing to do. He'd said he wished he could have given me a pardon, but rules were rules and all that bullshit. Maybe I could talk him into switching a few of my classes despite the cutoff date passing last week. I was busy, making plans inside my head, or I'd have seen her coming a mile away.

"Hey, you."

She wore a dark green sweater that hung off her shoulder, her skin exposed like porcelain. Her braid was loose today, stray pieces of gold tickled the line of her jaw as she stood in front of me, cute with nerves as she bit her lip.

"Kai, I almost forgot..." Professor Hintz stumbled out of his office, another sheet of paper in his hand. "You'll need a portfolio, nothing crazy, just a few pieces, all Teaching Assistants have to submit one. Don't look so grim." He shot Indie a smile. "Good morning, Miss O'Connell."

"Professor." Her pink lips matched the color of her cheeks as she smiled.

"Portfolio, by Monday."

I avoided Indie's curious stare as I nodded. "Monday."

The door to his office shut, stealing the air from the hallway. "You're going to TA for Professor Hintz?"

"I'm going to try." I started to walk toward our shared art history class, wishing I wasn't such a rude asshole, wishing she didn't make me so fucking nervous.

She kept up, sliding easily alongside me. "Do you even paint?"

I stopped at the annoyed snap of her words. Incredulous and out of breath she gazed at me.

"No."

"You don't paint, but you're going to TA for Professor Hintz?" Confusion dripped from her lips, and I couldn't help the smile that quirked at the corners of my own. She was agitated, pulling at the strap of her bag, maybe even a little angry, and I had no doubt I was headed straight to hell. I liked it. I liked that I made her feel something.

I shrugged, loving how her cheeks had turned red. "Never painted, no desire to, but it's better than being a janitor."

"Do you always get everything you want?"

"Usually."

But not you. I'll never have you.

She narrowed her eyes. "How do you plan on assisting a painting class if you've never painted?"

I raised my hands. "I don't know, maybe I'll change my major."

"To art?"

"You ask a lot of questions." I started to walk again. "More than your brother. Which is kind of amazing if you think about it, because, well... Royal is Royal."

She ignored me. "It's your junior year."

"And it's your freshman year."

She huffed a small, aggravated breath, and I paused outside the auditorium door.

"Why are you so bothered by a guy changing his major?"

"Because. Art is real, and serious, and... for some people, the only way to belong to something." I wanted to reach out and feel the heat of her cheeks, feel that passion, steal some of it for myself, enough to get me through this day.

"Art is real for me." I'd spoken softer than I'd intended, and her eyes found mine, eager, that curiosity

71

bleeding away the ire. "No, Indie, I don't paint, but I can draw, I've been drawing my entire life."

"I didn't know."

"Not many people in my life do."

"Oh." The word floated sweet and perfect in the air between us.

The long, elegant line of her neck, the same line I'd botched in my hurried sketch the other day, moved as she swallowed.

Feeling bolder than I had any right to be with her, teasing, I thumbed a stray piece of her hair, loosened from her braid by the wind. "And now my secret belongs to you... just like art."

Indigo

The heavy, coal-colored lashes that framed his dark brown eyes were the focus of my drawing. The tip of my pencil moved in a slow circle around the pupil, dilated and open, remembering how he'd looked at me, with intent, with purpose, a black hole sucking me in. Goosebumps marched down my arms as I imagined those very same eyes watching me from the back of the classroom. We weren't even friends. Not in the traditional sense. Friends by association. Acquaintances linked by the branches of the swim team family tree. This boy who'd done nothing but ignore me, who'd worked his way under my skin regardless, had given me a piece of himself today, and I couldn't for the life of me figure out why.

Kai had shared this big, colossal thing with me, the moment red and bright. I'd wanted to steal some of that color for myself. After he'd turned away, leaving me behind, more gray than blue, outside the auditorium door, pretending his words were real, that I belonged to his secret in some weird friend, but not really friends, and hey here's this piece of my puzzle do what you will with it sort of way.

Professor Blackwood, on his soapbox regarding the Surrealist and Modernist movements, asked the class for their opinions, successfully dragging me from my looping thoughts. The usual suspects all raised their hands, and I used the moment to steal a glance over my shoulder, instantly wishing I hadn't. With a flexed jaw and deep, brooding brows, Kai stared back at me. I quickly brought my attention forward, to the slides on the screen, embarrassment flooding my cheeks and neck with heat. Dropping my shoulders, I attempted the smallest possible posture and stayed that way until the end of class. I didn't look at him when I packed my bag, and I definitely didn't look for him as I made my way up the stairs to the door. It was this precise reason I wasn't prepared, and why I sucked in a surprised, not at all a relieved or hopeful breath, when I found him leaning against the wall just outside the classroom.

The navy St. Peter's swim team hoodie he wore stretched across his chest and shoulders, fitting itself against his muscles in a way it would never fit my brother. Kai's tall frame was broad and built, leaning out around his waist like all swimmers, but he seemed stronger, harder. Growing up with a brother on the swim team, I guess I'd become desensitized to the male body in some ways, going to meets all the time, it had become my status quo. But Kai was a piece of art. A sculpture, a presence on the mark, in the water, and now, his long body standing out amongst all the paintings, the color and line surrounding him.

"Hey." The gruff sound of his voice was at odds with his lopsided grin.

He'd waited for me?

He doesn't care.

I blinked, letting the voices clear before I answered him with a quiet, "Hi."

A few seconds of silence ticked by, uncomfortable and sticky, until we tried to speak at the same time.

My laugh tickled with nerves, I said, "Sorry, you go first."

Kai cut his long fingers into his thick, chocolate hair, and I stared at his knuckles for something to look at. Anything but those eyes, those eyes that hadn't ever given me the time of day, but here, in this moment, saw right through me.

"Ladies first." He shoved his hands in his pockets, stealing away my distraction and forcing me to meet his gaze.

His smile real and warm, seeped into his irises, and I struggled to find my vocabulary, anything at all to say. This wasn't like me, and I swear to God, his smile got wider the longer I gawked at him. I blurted the only thing I could think, the one thing that had been bothering me since we'd walked into the classroom ninety minutes ago.

"I'm sorry if I was rude... earlier... Your major, it's not my business. I mean... we're hardly even friends."

The light in his eyes faded, his grin forced. "I didn't mean it that way."

"You're right."

"I'm right?" The grip I had on my bag tightened as I hugged the strap to my chest.

"The friend thing... I feel like that's kind of my fault."

"Kind of?"

His shoulders relaxed as he laughed. "You're Royal's sister."

"And?"

"And he's my teammate."

I shrugged my shoulders, confusion settling between my brows. "You've lost me."

"It's a respect thing."

"For me or for Royal?"

He slipped his thumbs under the straps of his backpack, his fingers curling around the black fabric until his knuckles were white. "Don't worry about it." He chuckled. "Just some self-imposed bro code."

"That says we can't be friends?"

"Come on." He tipped his head to the right. "I'll walk you to Beckett to meet your brother."

"That seems like something a friend would do..."

He rolled his eyes. "I'll make an exception."

"I feel so special."

He coughed out another laugh. "You're a smart ass... I would've never thought."

"Because I'm quiet?" I guessed as we headed toward the east side of campus.

"Yeah..." He slowed his pace, the tight edge of his smile softening. "You're different than your brother."

I lowered my chin, watching the concrete like my life depended on it.

You're strange.

A loner.

Different didn't have to mean odd, or weird. My dad used to tell me, unique was a quality painted in stars and silver. As much as I'd appreciated his advice, I'd wanted to argue that sometimes different was the color silver turned as it tarnished. Murky and dull, and unwanted. Something to scrub away in hopes of revealing a treasure underneath. I didn't want to be different. I wanted to be a girl, walking across campus with this cute guy, having a real conversation that didn't involve her brother.

"Hey." He tugged on the strap of my bag. "That's not a bad thing."

I swallowed and managed a smile. "He's a force, hard to miss."

"He's a pain in the ass."

I laughed and it loosened the doubt twisting around my ribs. "He can be."

"It would be weird to have a twin."

I didn't think the world could handle two Kai Carters. "He's my left lung."

"Like that black and white fish thing."

I crinkled my nose. "What?"

"That thing, it looks like two fish hugging."

My head tipped to the side as I laughed. "You mean the Yin and the Yang?"

"Sure." His laugh was quiet as he watched me. "Is that what it's called?"

"Yes."

"I'll have to look it up."

"You don't believe me?"

"I do... but it doesn't sound right."

"I'm right." My cheeks ached from smiling so much.

He stopped short, his eyes falling to my mouth. "You're probably right."

"I'm right." I pressed my lips together to stop myself from grinning like an idiot, and he started to walk backward.

He pointed toward Beckett. "Enjoy your lunch, O'Connell."

"You're not coming?" I asked, even though I was used to this disappearing act.

"I've got a major to change, remember." He shot me another heartbreaking smile, two girls who happened to be walking by stared at him with abandon, as he waved at me. "See you around, Friend."

Friend.

Liar.

There was this hidden, brash, burning orange inside me that ignored the false whispers inside my brain. This tiny seed, telling me to hold my head up high, begged me to throw him a flirty comeback. Like Daphne, I could've called him out for his cute, smart remark, but instead I kept my feet firmly planted in reality, and offered him a shy wave of my hand, not making more of his sudden chivalry than I should. Corbin and Dev would have walked with me, and actually had on many occasions. It didn't have to mean anything.

But it did.

To me, it did, and I couldn't stop myself from thinking about that big, colossal red moment when he'd touched my hair, and his pupils had become that black hole, open, wide, drawing me closer. I wanted more. His secret felt like more, and he'd given it to me, given me more without even knowing it. More than normal, than sitting alone in my silence, than everyday heartbeats. I'd been waiting for *more*, a definition I'd given to something I'd started to believe never existed in the first place. A fairytale I'd conjured based on the love my parents shared. A hope that, like my father, I was worthy of a happily ever after, too. And perhaps this was a simple crush, a product of naivety, my heart painting its own creation, tired of the blank canvas I'd left behind inside its walls. I wanted it to unravel something, even if in the end, the ghosts in my head won, and all that was left of my more was a friend who filled out his sweaters, leaned against walls like a sculpture, and left me wanting.

"Has she emerged yet?" Ari asked as she plopped down next to me onto the sofa.

I kicked my feet onto the couch and stretched them over her lap. "Is she home?"

There wasn't any light peeking out from under the door of the room Daphne and I shared. The four-bedroom suite quiet except for the soft music playing from my iPad. We all shared the small place, but were lucky enough to have a nice, open living room and, if we had the time, could actually cook something if we wanted in the tiny, galley kitchen. I didn't think any of us had actually used the stove, though. We'd all agreed at the beginning of last semester on a communal pantry, stocked to the gills with all kinds of snacks for late-night study binges, and tended to use the dining hall for big meals. The pantry had been Imogen's idea, my other suitemate, which ended up being kind of comical since she was never here. She was a senior and the chief editor of *The Silver Wolf Gazette,* St. Peter's student-run newspaper, spending the majority of her time in the journalism offices.

"Daphne came home this afternoon and hasn't left her room that I know of." Ari raised a flawless, arched brow. "Pretty sure she was toasted, too."

"She's been drinking a lot more this semester."

Ari's laugh held no humor. "She just hid it better last semester. Indie, you're too sweet. She's a bit Jekyll and Hyde, if you ask me, but you spend more time with her than I do." She pulled her thick curls into a messy knot, using the elastic on her wrist to hold it in place. "If she's not careful, she'll end up just like my cousin who lives in Malibu. Expelled and living in rehab."

"Your cousin was expelled?"

"Yup, last year. We shared a dorm on the third floor. Drunk every damn day. Alcoholism runs in my family, but I don't touch the stuff."

"Me, too. My grandfather was an alcoholic, died of cirrhosis." I'd never met him, but the stories I'd heard my dad and his brothers tell never sounded like he was a man I would have wanted to meet. "Does Gus drink?"

"Hell no. He kills his body enough playing football, and besides, if he wants to continue to be my boyfriend, he knows better than to bring that shit around me."

Ari wasn't more than five-feet-two inches, but her big green eyes and attitude made her seem six-feet tall. Which was probably a good thing since her boyfriend was at least six-foot-four. She reminded me so much of my uncle's wife, Melissa, it made me homesick sometimes. Maybe it was the Hispanic accent, or the big heart, either way, Ari made me want to call home more often than I should.

"I used to think people could drink and be okay, but I don't know. Indie, I've seen it ruin so many lives, and Daphne... she's in a bad way."

I stared down the hallway leading to our rooms, worry itching its way under my skin. Daphne drank a lot. It didn't matter if we were out or in the studio, she always had a flask. At first, I'd thought it was normal college kid stuff, but realized quickly there was a difference between partying every now and then, and needing it to function. I didn't drink, with the medications I took for my depression it had always been something I was cautioned against. Daphne never seemed to mind that I didn't partake in her late-night, one-woman parties when we painted together, but lately, she'd become more vocal about how boring it was to be in the studio all the time and had been spending her nights at Stacks, or at least I thought that's where she'd go at night. I shuddered to think what else she was into.

"I'll talk to her," I whispered more to myself than for Ari's benefit.

"Girl, you are not her mother." Ari pinched the underside of my calf, and I squeaked.

"Ow. What was that for?" I swatted at her hand, and she giggled.

Even through her laughter, she sounded stern. "I'm serious, Indie, if you're worried, talk to the campus counseling office, we have an awesome Behavioral Health Center."

I bit my lip, casting my eyes to the coffee table. I never lied to Ari about my mental illness, but I hadn't gathered the courage to tell her, either.

"That's a good idea."

Ari stood, not so gently shoving my legs off her lap. "I'm headed over to Warren House to see Gus, want to come?"

"Royal has practice."

"Hang out with me and Gus till he gets home?"

Ari's boyfriend lived across the hall from my brother. And as much as I appreciated her invite, I didn't want to feel like a third wheel.

"That's okay, I think I'll harass Camden, see if he'll eat dinner with me before I head into the studio."

She shook her head. "I still wish your brother wasn't gay." Ari's grin colored her cheeks as she said, "He's too cute, damn it."

I almost snorted. "What about Gus?"

"I like Gus."

"Gus is cute."

"Gus is hot," she corrected with another giggle.

I exhaled and rested my head on the soft arm of the sofa. "The entire athletic department is hot."

She smacked my foot. "See. I knew you were holding out on me."

Heat bloomed in my stomach and cheeks. "I don't know what you're talking about."

"Mm-hm." She pulled her purse over her shoulder. "You're a terrible liar." She stared at me for a few agonizing seconds, and I almost, almost opened my mouth to tell her, the urge to actually share these confusing feelings, my thoughts, to see if I was out of my mind to even think about him. "I'll get you to tell me. Or should I ask Royal?"

"You wouldn't?" I sat up a little breathless.

"Of course not, but you just proved I was right. You like a guy." Her smile was smug.

"Maybe. I'm not sure. It's too new."

"I can work with new." She slipped her phone in her back pocket. "Tell me when you're ready, but just so you know, I'm dying a little inside the longer you hold out."

She laughed as I reached over to the coffee table, grabbed a balled-up piece of paper, and threw it at her, missing by a mile. "Go see Gus."

"Alright, alright." Her laughter died down as she stared at Daphne's door. "Make sure she's okay before you go?"

"I will."

"Bye, chick."

After she left, I stood and walked to Daphne's door. I listened for any sign of life coming from her room and heard nothing. Feeling like a thief, I opened her door, slow and soft, until I could see the small twin bed and her half-naked body bathed in the white light of the moon, streaming in through her open blinds. Her arm dangled off the mattress, pale and still, the measured rise and fall of her back as she breathed was my only reassurance.

I quietly said her name, and I took a few steps. "You okay?"

She didn't answer.

Her paintings and band posters were hung on the walls, the dirty laundry still strewn across the carpet. All normal college girl stuff, but as I scanned the floor by her bed, I noticed a pack of cigarettes and a bottle of what looked like whiskey, half empty, laying by her hand. It all seemed staged and unreal. My friend, lying in a tank top, covered in gray and secrets, and I had no idea what to do. It was six-o'clock on a weeknight and she was already passed out. Had she been drinking all day? Did she even go to her classes?

And like the universe had decided to reach out and flick me on the nose, my phone buzzed. I stepped out of her room, pulling it from my pocket, and dragged my thumb over the touch screen. My therapy appointment reminder flashed in bold yellow. Ari was right, if I tried to say anything to her, she could take it the wrong way, blow me off. Dr. Sand would know what she needed more than I would, wouldn't he?

You're useless, sick girl.

I closed my eyes and took a few breaths, the words in my head sharp and black. Stress always made them worse, stronger. They'd find the holes in my self-made walls, but I knew I wasn't useless, years of therapy, meds, and love had taught me that. If I could be happy, live a

84

good life, Daphne could, too, my only hope was that she still wanted a life at all.

Kai

"And you don't find that impulsive?" Brian tapped the chewed cap of his pen against his chin as he leaned back in his chair.

"More like inevitable." He hadn't bought my smirk, and I sighed. "It was impulsive, but art is something that's... I don't know, it's mine. It has nothing to do with them..."

"With them?"

"My parents. When I put my pencil to paper I'm able to create something that is unique to me."

"There are lots of artists in the world. What about swimming, that's something you're good at, that you like?"

I lowered my eyes to the thread dangling from the hem of his left pant leg. "Not anymore."

"Because you lost captain?" I didn't like the way he'd asked, with such reproach. "Kai..."

"No one will ever be able to recreate the stroke of my pencil. There are talented swimmers who can recreate form and function. I'm an extension of a learned and practiced skill." I lifted my eyes and stared straight into his dull irises. "My art is mine."

"You can still have art and be a business major. Swimming is still yours even if you're not captain."

"Business was never my thing, though. It may seem impulsive to you, but for me, it's a regret I'm finally able to rectify."

He leaned back in his chair, crossing his legs at the ankles, the perfect picture of open and understanding. "Explain."

"My father was a mechanic, struggled to support us, and when he got a job selling parts, our lives changed. We weren't rich or anything close, but my mom got health insurance, and we had food on the table."

I didn't like the way Brian picked me apart, deciding, weighing my motives. It was invasive. But I promised myself, my mother, that I could do this, would do this. It didn't matter what he thought as long as he listened. I did my part, vomiting up all my imperfections and leaving them at his feet. What he did with it after I was gone? I didn't care. As long as I was lighter, more like me in the end, he could sit in that chair and pick at my scabs all day long.

"I figured business was the financially smart thing to do."

"Then why change halfway through?"

"Because..." I fought with myself. Half-truths left me heavy, but the full truth would cut me open. Brian waited. He wanted blood. "Because my father is a piece of shit who drinks too much, cheats on his sick wife, and there isn't enough money in the world worth becoming like him." My hands shook and I pushed them into the pocket of my hooded sweatshirt.

"That's fair."

I chuckled but it fell flat. "That's fair... but..."

"But creating financial freedom for yourself by choosing a career path that may seem similar doesn't make you like him, Kai. You're not him. Even if you sold parts for a living, you're not him. It's how you live your life... your choices are yours. Swimming is yours, art is yours, and business can be, too."

This man with all the credentials, all the big letters sitting in a bold font after his last name, his badge hanging proudly from his neck on a relatable superhero lanyard, had no idea what he was talking about. He didn't get it.

"I chose business because I wanted to make sure I could get a job that would help support my mom when my father finally left for good, a job that would give me the means to hire home health nurses, and not worry about the cost of her prescriptions. But I don't want it, Brian. That's the point. I never wanted it. And I feel fucking selfish for hating it, for hating her sickness, for hating my life. Every day all I want to do is drown, forget about all the shit. And that makes me just like him. I'm changing my major because it's the only way I can save myself, save myself for her."

Heat flooded my face and neck, my eyes spilling over with angry tears as I wrapped my hands into tight fists. The pain in my shoulder throbbed as I sat stiff and unmoving, waiting for judgment.

Brian swallowed as he moved to the edge of his chair. "Does he know?"

"Know what?" I asked, more like snapped, and he shook his head.

"I want you to tell him. That's your assignment for next time. Tell your father everything you just told me."

"Fuck that. He doesn't need—"

"He does, and you might be surprised at what he has to say." Brian rested both his elbows on his knees, lowering his voice, he said, "It's not your job to save her."

I couldn't stop the heavy rise and fall of my chest, my nostrils flared as I breathed, attempting to calm myself, to dislodge the boulder inside my throat. I didn't need his verbal pat on the shoulder, his *there-there*, but he'd hit way too close to home.

Taking care of yourself is your only job…

"The last time I talked to my mom she said something along those lines. She told me to take care of myself and that's what I'm going to do."

"Okay."

His answer was too easy. "That's it? Okay?"

"I wanted to make sure, Kai. Make sure this wasn't another impulsive risk you were taking."

"It's not."

"Okay." He smiled, and I exhaled.

"Do I still have to talk to my dad?"

"Yes. It's part of the process. Part of taking care of you. He needs to know how you feel."

"He doesn't give a shit how I feel."

"Tell him anyway." He stood, and I stared at him.

"Why?"

"Sometimes it feels good to hold people accountable. Sometimes you have to get rid of all the shit in your head. Get it out, or the wound you have will get infected."

"Infected. I like that." He held out his hand. I took it as I stood.

"I'll see you next week."

"Yeah. Yeah." I shook his hand and grinned.

I reined myself in as I opened the door to the hallway, my head running a mile a minute. The idea of talking to my dad made me feel sick to my stomach. Made me want to drive straight to Stacks, miss my afternoon classes, and call out to work tonight. But I'd told Dean Thomlinson when I'd spoken to him yesterday, if he'd let me switch my classes around, I'd be on my best behavior. I'd even put in my two weeks' notice with the maintenance department before I switched to the teaching assistant position. Getting drunk and avoiding my responsibilities was the last choice I should make, not to mention, it's exactly what my father would do.

I let out a long, aggravated puff of air. "Shit."

"Talking to yourself in the Behavioral Health Center is dangerous business."

Indie stood with her hand on the door to the waiting room, her hair in a messy knot on the top of her head, the change from her braid exposed more of her long neck.

"Thanks for the tip." A smile formed on my lips of its own volition.

"Anytime." She bit the corner of her mouth and let the silence warm between us.

"Coming or going?"

"Going, my appointment was earlier than usual." She opened the door, and I followed her to the elevators.

"You really come here every Tuesday?" I asked, trying not to notice the way her lashes touched her cheeks as she blinked, or how I could see the pulse in her neck, and how I must have seriously needed a drink because all I wanted to do was lean in and smell her heartbeat.

She pressed the button to call the elevator, avoiding eye contact. "Most of the time. Not always, though." Her blue eyes found mine, and the elevator doors opened with a loud ding, the smell of cat piss leaked into the hall. I hated that the stench would bleed into her skin, her hair, she shouldn't have to smell like that all day long.

"These elevators are disgusting."

She laughed. "It's like St. Peter's dirty little secret."

"Right? They spend so much money on everything else, but they can't get new carpet for these damn elevators."

"There's no money in behavioral health."

"I guess."

Once the doors shut, the energy changed. Everything about the small space tingled and burned, the smell faded into the quiet singe. The rush of my pulse was loud enough I was sure she'd be able to hear it, too, and when I turned to look at her, I found her staring back. Indie wore a simple gray sweater and jeans. The absence of color made her eyes this crazy fucking shade of blue, almost like a picture of the Caribbean, but without any green. Pure and bottomless.

"Did you do it?" she asked.

"Do what?"

"Change your major?"

"I did."

She smiled, and I smiled, and I realized we'd both unconsciously leaned in toward the other, some force pulling us in against our will.

"I'm excited to see your work. Hintz is a curator of talent. If you're assisting him, you must be good."

Pride filled my chest despite my nonchalant shrug. "I've sold a few pieces, but nothing big."

"You've sold a few pieces?" she asked, shock written in her whisper.

"What?"

"Kai, I've been painting my entire life. Seriously, I have my hand prints on canvas from when I was eighteen months old. I haven't sold one piece."

"Have you tried?" I asked as the elevator doors opened to the first floor.

"No. I'm not ready to let go," she whispered as we made our way to the front entrance.

The cold, fresh air was a relief, the strange heat of the elevator, the small space, drifted on the wind as we stepped outside of the building.

"What does that mean?"

Indie was distracted by the students on the lawn. Several girls giggled as they passed us, the guys they were with spoke loud enough I could have heard their cheesy pickup lines from across campus. I recognized one of the girls, some chick I'd met last semester. By met, I meant slept with once and never heard from her again, not that I'd wanted to. She waved, and I nodded my chin with my signature smile, hating myself a little in the moment. Hating that I was "that guy" to most of the people here and would always be.

"It doesn't matter," Indie muttered, fidgeting with the strap of her bag, she started in the opposite direction of where I was headed. I followed her anyway.

"I want to know."

"Why?"

Because I'm selfish and want things I shouldn't. I want to know why she couldn't let go of her paintings, why she was in the Behavioral Health Center in the first place, why those girls had made her nervous. I wanted to know her, even if the details weren't mine to have.

I gave her a crooked smile. "It's kind of cool you can't let them go."

"Cool?" She raised a brow, the smile on her face skeptical.

"They're like your little art babies."

She rolled her eyes. "I knew you were making fun of me."

I raised both of my hands. "I swear I'm not. I'm being serious."

"Your laugh suggests otherwise."

"I'm serious, Indie." I toned down my smile when she finally looked at me.

She wet her lips and stopped walking, the breeze sent goosebumps along her neck and collar bone. My fingers ached to reach out and smooth them away.

"I'm not ready to give away something so personal. I don't want to sell my secrets, the parts of me I'm still learning to love."

Her nose was pink from the wind, her skin stretched soft over the arch of her cheekbones, she was absolutely stunning, and I'd give her my last twenty if she'd tell me one of those secrets, one of those things she was still learning to love.

"I'm crazy?" she asked, and I nodded.

"Certifiable."

She laughed, pressed her lips together, and then laughed again.

"I guess I am." She tipped her head back, looking at the sky, and I kept my eyes on her face as she tried to compose her smile, waiting her out.

I gave in and spoke first. "I have to go. I have my first class with Hintz in five minutes."

"That's on the other side of campus."

"I know."

She stared in the direction of the art building. "You better hurry, he hates it if you're late."

I pulled my hood up and over my head, protecting my face from the weather. "Full of advice today."

She let go of the strap of her bag and pushed a piece of loose hair from her eyes. "Like I said before, anytime. I'm in the studio almost every night... if you need help with any of his assignments."

I knew she meant it literally, but in my head, where I kept the thoughts about her full lips and breathable pulse to myself, I wanted to pretend her invitation was more than it was, that if I showed up at the studio, she'd show me the parts of herself she couldn't let go of, the secrets she'd never sell, and I'd let her see mine too.

Indigo

Thick rivers of yellow paint dripped down the canvas, mixing in with the gray and red, creating a marching army of brown that swirled around the previous layer I'd thrown last night. My arms ached, the chill of the studio sticking to the fine layer of sweat on my skin, I stepped back to survey the damage. Alone, I stood in front of the six-by-eight-foot painting, the music blared, my usual tactic. Smother the whispers, the doubt, until all I had left was a peaceful, white noise. A beat, beyond the pulse in my wrists, a guiding rhythm I could use to create. If Daphne was here, she'd tell me to turn it down, tell me she couldn't think, but she hadn't shown up again, texting to say she had a date and to not wait up. She'd been avoiding me after I talked to her, on Dr. Sand's suggestion, about coming with me to sign up for therapy, brushing me off with a quick *I'm fine*.

You let her go.

You'll let her drown.

Help was something you could only offer the willing. I pressed my lips together as the song switched to Prince's, *I Would Die 4 U*, one of my favorites, and the words scratching around in my head were honed and bleached to that perfect white. I leaned down to grab the other bucket of green paint, some of the lime color spilling, splashing onto the floor and decorating the bottom of my jeans. I hummed to the tune, trying to clear my head, leaving the world behind, making sure the voices stayed far away. My love for the eighties was cultivated by the pop beats. Artists sang about dying for love, the heavy lyrics dressed up in purple sound. Drum machines and guitars and synthesizers, all buttoned up by the poets who made them fly beyond the paper they'd been written on. Music filled the room, taking up all the space, and half-way through, I found myself smiling, bobbing my head, singing, and fading into the white noise.

I dipped my brush into the paint and waved my arm with as much anger and feeling as I could muster, stretching the muscle and the paint across the canvas. It was messy and fun, and any darkness hidden inside my corners dispersed. I found being alone like this, without my dad, or my mom, or even Daphne, I was able to do something different, something I'd never done before, something beyond the form I'd been taught all my life. It was a war of color, the East versus the West, and I was so immersed in it, I didn't hear the door open or close. I was alone, until he chuckled.

"What the hell are you listening to?" Kai's laugh warmed my entire body, like a sweater, it wrapped around my cold, damp skin.

I lowered my brush and rested it on the side of the bucket, hyperaware of how naked I felt. He'd caught me mid-ballad and embarrassed. He was here, looking at me with a crooked smile, oblivious, not knowing he'd stepped into my sanctuary, a realm where my insides were out, my thoughts a disarray of spectrum, a place where I couldn't hide behind forced confidence. He stared at me for a few breaths before his gaze fixed on the large painting behind me.

"Prince." I answered too late. His eyes had gone wide, his lips parting as he took a step forward. "It's Prince," I continued to ramble. "I have a thing for eighties music, more for eighties covers, but sometimes the original is better."

Shut. Up.

You invited him.

He'll see it. He'll know.

You can't hide us.

I closed my eyes, willing myself to take a breath, to find the center, the big empty. My father, my meds, all the years I worked on feeling normal and quiet, Kai split me open with one look. Nerves fed the demons on my back, but like I'd always been taught to do, I opened my eyes anyway.

Kai swallowed, his arms—corded with muscle—lay at his side. His dark brown eyes devoured the piece, my painting. My blood sang at what I thought might be awe inside his expression. When he finally spoke, my heart fell one-thousand stories, like a leaf falling from a tree, in the wind, twisting and turning, until it met the ground with a delicate end.

"Wow," he whispered, long and exaggerated, coming to stand next to me. We both stared at what I'd been working on for the past few days. "It's like I'm standing in front of a Jackson Pollock."

My fingers trembled as I pulled on a smile. "I wish."

"Indie." My name an admonishment, but hearing it in his rich, rough, tone, burnt orange, it conjured glints of fall fireside flames, and made my heart heat inside my chest. In my periphery, I saw movement as he turned to face me. "This is fucking amazing... how many layers have you created?" he asked, and when I didn't turn to look at him, he stepped closer to the painting, holding his hand up as if to touch it, but leaving a good three inches of space between his skin and the wet paint.

"Five, so far."

He looked over his shoulder with a smile. "It's chaos."

I smiled, my neck, cheeks, and ears burning. "I don't usually paint like this, but—"

"You should always paint like this." He stepped even closer, tilting his head as if to listen to the color, hear the war in action as I'd laid it out to be heard.

"Abstract is my father's thing, my mother is... more literal, I've always been a blend of both." He absently nodded as he moved back a few steps, tipping his head back to take it all in. His broad shoulders spread in the center of the rectangle, his t-shirt stretched as he breathed, the ball cap he wore backward made his hair curl around the edges by his ears. He was too perfect standing in front of my destruction.

"Is this for a class?" he asked, facing me again.

The tan of his cheeks had been touched with pink. It was the first time I could read him, that blush of color, there was no arrogance in it, just real, honest, and raw interest. It made the truth slip past my lips before I could decide if it sounded too weird.

"It's the dissection of my inheritance, my attempt at finding something that hasn't come from my DNA." I could hear him breathing as I found the brave bits of red in the room and collected them, drawing me closer to where he stood. He smelled like boy. Spiced and soapy and warm. I smiled, wanting his eyes on my mouth, and when he found it, I watched him watch me speak as I said, "Something only I am capable of. Something they can't take away from me."

"Your parents?"

I shook my head, knowing I couldn't tell him the truth, knowing the minute I mentioned the voices in my head, any progress we'd made as friends would be tainted, and I'd never see this honest set of his eyes ever again.

"Everyone, in general, I guess. Royal has his own thing, I have painting, and it may sound childish, but I'd like to set myself apart from my parents as an artist. Make my art mine in its conceptions."

His Adam's apple moved under the smooth skin of his neck as the song on my playlist switched to some dark, ambient instrumental Camden had recommended. The shift drew his attention to the speakers. He didn't say anything for a while, the seconds ticking by, and as if he had to shake himself awake, he sucked in a long breath, the honesty graying around the edges of his mouth, he said, "You have the weirdest taste in music."

"I'd like to think it's eclectic."

"You keep telling yourself that, O'Connell."

"I like to paint, music is a mood, and I like to have them all."

"Can the mood be from this decade?"

"You don't have to stay."

He held his hand to his heart in mock offense, I almost snorted. His jaw pulsed, and he looked over my shoulder at the painting, his confidence flickering like a dying bulb. "Just finished up with work, figured I'd stop by since I was in the building."

"You're working with Professor Hintz already?"

"No, I had garbage duty tonight. Building two and the art campus. Very important stuff." He shoved his hands in his pockets, and I liked the way it made the veins stick out on his arms. I wanted to draw them on paper, use them as the standard. Every male arm should look like his.

"Do you miss Stacks?"

"Honestly, not really. I miss shooting the shit with my teammates, but it's better that I left. I don't have to do this cleaning gig for much longer, two weeks, and I'm the property of Professor Hintz."

I laughed at his wolfish grin. "God help you. Do you know how picky he is?"

"I guess I'll find out. He extended my deadline. I have to have my portfolio ready in two weeks. He wants a painting and..."

"And that's why you're here?" I'd hoped my disappointment wasn't as obvious as it sounded to me. I'd invited him, offered to help him, but that naïve hope, the girl who'd never been kissed, whose fingerprints remained on her own flesh, with hands aching to be held, wanted him to be here for her.

"If you're willing, I could use the help." His eyes flicked to my canvas. "Because if he expects this, I'm screwed."

I grabbed my brush from the side of the bucket and placed it into another tub filled with turpentine. "He expects you to try. He sees something in you if he's allowing you to assist him. You've sold drawings... you can do this." I covered the buckets of paint I'd been using with their respective lids and walked over to the supply closet. Kneeling down, I rummaged through all of the blank canvases until I found a small six-by-six-inch square. "Start here."

Kai took the canvas from my hand. "What am I supposed to do with this?"

I shrugged and tried not to laugh at the irritation gathering along the creases of his forehead.

"You get to listen to my shitty music and paint a mood."

He raised his brows. "Hope you have black paint."

"See, already equating mood to color, you're ahead of the game."

"Are you making fun of me?"

"Maybe."

His chuckle was dark as he reached for the end of my braid. My skin came alive at the playful tug, the relaxed intimacy of the gesture. "Watch yourself, O'Connell, don't dish it if you can't take it."

I stood taller than I have in my entire life, conjuring my brother's laid-back ease, and said, "I can take it."

He rubbed the back of his neck, and I admired the way his muscles moved under his skin. The air in the room a golden static as he cleared his throat.

"I surrender, okay, this is your pool, teach me how to swim."

I took the canvas from his hand and nodded my chin toward the back wall with all the brushes and bottles of paint. He followed me in silence, not speaking or interrupting, as I explained to him the different types of brushes, where he could find the water color, oil, pastels, and acrylics, everything he might need for a basic painting.

"What if I wanted to add my own mediums?" he asked.

"How so?"

Without answering me, he picked up the newspaper we used sometimes as a drop cloth, a bottle of white and red paint and set it all down on a table. He motioned for the canvas in my hand and I gave it to him. Kai studied the room, and I didn't say a word as he moved around like he owned it, grabbing a plastic bowl, glue, and not one paint brush.

When he returned to the workstation, his lopsided grin made me laugh. "Are you gonna watch me?"

I held up my hands. "Not if you'd rather me not."

"I'd rather you not." I wasn't sure if he'd meant to be harsh, but my smile faltered, and he exhaled a long breath. "I mean, how would you feel if Picasso was here, watching you?"

"I'm no Picasso." The compliment broke my face open, and the smile I'd tried to hide had no chance.

He rubbed the back of his neck again. "You're my Picasso alright. And I feel like a dumbass."

I bit back my smile, pinching my lip between my teeth. I nodded. "I've got a drawing I need to work on for class in the morning. I'll just sit at the other end of the table. You won't even know I'm here."

"This music of yours will remind me."

"You can change it."

Just Like Heaven by the Cure started to play.

"This is fine."

We worked without words for almost an hour, the music getting sleepier as the playlist went on. I'd lied about having a drawing due in the morning, wanting to sketch his arms as he worked. I'd begun shading the curve of his biceps when he swore under his breath.

"This is shit."

I didn't look up from the table, afraid he wouldn't want me to.

"Is this total shit?"

I glanced up and loved that his hat was off, his hair messy and tipped with white and red paint as if he'd dragged his angry fingers through it.

"Do you really want my opinion?"

"Yes." The one syllable more like a growl.

I hopped off the stool and circled the table. At first glance, what he'd accomplished was pretty spectacular for a first attempt. He'd used the newspaper for a decoupage canvas, the white and red paint strewn across the words in abstract lines and shapes by his fingertips.

"I like it and I don't."

"Okay. What the hell does that mean?"

"It means you're trying too hard." His body tensed. "What are you trying to convey here? What does it mean to you?"

"Nothing."

"Nothing?"

He let out a stuttered breath. "It means I'm not a fucking painter."

I lowered my voice, feeling his frustration in bursts of shadow and black. I'd been here several times, wanting the piece to be exactly what it was like in my head, and failing.

"How did you learn to draw?"

"I didn't... I just... knew." He raked his paint-covered hands through his hair and sank down into his chair.

"I'm the same way with a brush... it comes naturally to me, but it took me forever to learn how to draw, to get things to look real. Everything I drew looked like a cartoon version of whatever the subject was, but over time, and I'm still learning, I got better. You will, too. Hintz liked your drawings?"

"Yeah, he's the one who sold them for me."

"He'll push you, Kai. Like he pushes all of his students. You don't need to know how to paint to be a TA. You'll learn."

"I will." His shoulders set in a stern line.

"You don't have to be a painter. Hintz wants your eye, your hands—your pencil. He sees something in you and that's huge."

He looked at me, his jaw a sculpture of its own. "You're good at this pep talk stuff, you should come rile us up before meets."

I huffed out a laugh. "Royal would hate that. Swimming is his canvas."

"Dissection of inheritance." His gaze drifted to my painting. "Royal said he's not artistic at all, was he lying?"

I leaned against the table. "No. He can't paint, and I can't swim, it's like somewhere our coding got mixed up and we both lost a gene."

"Wait." He picked up his hat and pulled it on backward, his smile conspiratorial. "I think I'm high on fumes... did you say you can't swim?"

"I almost drowned when I was five and never went back."

"So you haven't actually tried."

"Like I said, I'd rather—"

"Paint, yeah, I got it." He stared at me in disbelief for a minute and then rapped his knuckles on the tabletop before he stood. He picked up his painting and tossed it in the trash.

"I'm going to let you in on a little secret about me. I never do anything half-ass. When I chose swimming, I gave it everything I had. I want to do the same with this. I can draw, but if I'm turning my life upside down, I want to do it all. I want to paint how I feel, Indie. Like you do. I want to translate what I see in every medium if I can. If I'm doing this then I'm all in."

"Good."

"And I want to learn from the best."

"Hintz is a genius."

"I'm not talking about Hintz." He smiled when I shook my head. "Help me and I'll teach you how to swim."

"I don't care about swimming."

"Yeah, you do."

The water was as frightening as the mess inside my head. I had a hold on my voices for the most part. I could medicate myself, shut them out, paint them away, but inside the water, I had no control. My body had never been mine, shared by the monsters inside, never stepping foot inside another pool was something I'd done on my terms.

"I really don't, it's Royal's—"

"I'll feel better knowing I'm helping you in some way, too."

"So, really, you're just selfish?"

"What? No?"

"Is that a question?"

"Let me teach you how to swim. It's... a safety thing."

I narrowed my eyes. "A safety thing?"

"Yeah. What if you fell in the lake or a pool?"

"Random. But I don't own a suit."

"Then buy one." He looked at my painting one last time. His eyes lingered over the layered splatters of paint and then dusted over my color-crusted arms and clothes.

"I'll help you, and you won't owe me anything. Except... I might like to see some of your drawings."

"I'll show you whatever you want," he said in a half whisper, his attention wandering back to my canvas. "And I'll teach you how to swim."

"Water scares me."

Such a child.

"And that's exactly why you need to learn. This entire room scares the shit out of me, but I want to make it mine."

He was dusk and dawn. Chasing the rays of the sun as they moved beyond the horizon every day. I preferred the night and its never-ending expanse, a place I could settle inside, a void to find my own palette. But he stared at me, waiting, his pupils lined with a light ring of amber. The same look Royal had before a meet, the look I had when I finished a painting, the adrenaline of want. Wanting to succeed, wanting more, and he wanted me to say yes.

"Fine..." His smile was triumphant, slow moving and cat-like. "But if I drown, you'll have to deal with my brother."

He held out his hand, sliding his skin against mine, kick-starting my heart as the heat of his palm relaxed my limbs.

"It's a deal, then," he said, letting the seconds unfurl between us as he shook my hand.

"It's a deal."

Kai

She'd attempted to hide it, but I'd felt the way her fingers, fragile and hot, trembled as I'd taken her hand in mine. She was the first to let go, her big blue eyes digesting our deal, like a deer in headlights. She took a step back with a cute-as-hell, nervous giggle. A tightrope formed under my feet, that line, dangerous and selfish, not thick enough to hold us both if she chose to tread across it with me. I shouldn't have come here, shouldn't have pushed my way into her world, but the smile on my face, the battering ram in my chest, the way I could still feel her touch in my palm, said *walk the fucking line, let it snap*.

"I'll text you a time we can meet up for lessons. This week's kind of—"

"Whenever." She waved me off, taking another step backward.

I held out my hand and chuckled when she exhaled. "Give me your phone, I'll program my number."

She reached into her pocket and handed me her cell. I added my name and number to her contacts and sent myself a text so I'd have her number, too. This was happening. I was letting it, but this could be one of those "just friends" type situations. I was "just friends" with a lot of girls. It didn't matter that Indie was stunning and talented and...

I suppressed a sigh as I handed her back the phone. I was supposed to be taking care of me, not torturing myself.

She stared at the screen of her phone as I said, "The pool is a ghost town after eleven on most nights. I still have the key code to the locker rooms."

"Still?" She smiled and it was the same smile she reserved for her brother or Camden. Part of me was grateful for it, that friend zone, brotherly type smile. It put me in my place. It stole away the shiver, the feel her hand had left behind. The other part of me, the guy who always got what he wanted when it came to girls, the eager asshole who wanted more than he should ever ask for, saw a challenge in her lips.

"It was a captain perk." I wouldn't drop my mask; I wouldn't let her see how much I hated having to say it in the past tense. It didn't really matter anyway; the title was just that, a badge I wore to complete a façade. I loved swimming, leading, but it wasn't everything that I could be, or I hoped it wasn't. I wanted to believe there was more to me than race times, and badges, and beer.

"You're still captain to Royal, to your team, you know that, right? They still look at you as their leader."

I debated on giving her a stock answer or the truth. The giant painting, Indie's heart, hovered behind her, reminding me how remarkable she was, and I decided she deserved nothing but real. This cute girl, with paint everywhere, who had created an entire galaxy, layered on top of another, until it was infinite, until it was its own universe of color on one canvas.

I met her eyes, and she held on to my gaze. "I wish they wouldn't."

"They look up to you."

Gritting my jaw, I shook my head. "They shouldn't." The silence that descended made it hard to breathe. "I guess what I'm trying to say, is maybe it's a good thing. A chance to do something else, something more."

She bit back a smile. "More is good."

"I think so... My therapist thinks he knows better. "

"Occupational hazard," she suggested, scrunching her nose.

I had the urge to reach out and smooth out the skin with my thumb.

"Change is good. The dude can think whatever the fuck he wants."

"My dad told me that I should go after my dreams, but to be smart enough to realize the difference between chasing and running."

"I'm not running," I said, and Indie's cheeks flooded with chagrin.

"I'm sorry, I didn't mean—"

"I got your meaning." I'd done a complete one-eighty these past few weeks, and each day was harder than the next. Balancing who I was with who I could be. What I wanted and what I didn't. My old life was a place to drown. This new life a patchwork path, to fuck if I knew where, but it was worth a try. It had to be. I pushed down my irritation and smiled. "I'm not running."

She dropped her chin, her smile gone. She tapped the toe of her Converse on the concrete floor a few times before she looked at me. Her eyes seemed off, more vacant, and she swallowed. "I say things and I don't think. The words just fall out of my mouth. Call it a coping mechanism."

"A coping mechanism?"

She laughed, and her eyes filled with humor and color again. "A conversation for another night, I think."

"You're kicking me out?" My smirk made her lips spread farther up her cheeks and it was like I'd won an award.

Making a girl smile wasn't that hard, I did it on a daily basis, but I wanted to earn Indie's smiles, every last one.

"No, please... stay as long as you want. I might be poor company, though. I need to work on this piece a while longer before I call it a night. Want me to grab you another canvas?"

Yes.

"Nah, I should go, I've got dryland training at five in the morning."

"I don't think I'd get up at five for anything."

"Not even to paint the sunrise?"

"Not even then." She brought her finger to her temple. "I'd rather imagine what it looks like. Choose my

112

own colors, make it my own personal fete of nature, with coffee, at a more reasonable hour."

"So what you're saying is only late night swimming lessons?" I asked and took too much pleasure in the blush on her neck.

"If you want me to show up." She reached down, popped the lid off one of the buckets on the floor, and I took that as my cue.

"Thanks for helping me out tonight, I promise not to crash your art party too much."

"Crash all you want. If you're serious about painting, I'm here."

I was serious about drawing. I was serious about learning how to teach. I was serious about making a life out of art. And as much as I should deny it, I was serious about getting to know her. In any capacity.

"Thanks."

"Of course."

She smiled, and I turned toward the studio door.

"Hey, Kai?"

"Yeah?"

"I believe you." Her eyes found the laces of her shoes. "You're not running. I just wanted to make sure you believed it, too."

She didn't know me. She didn't know the first thing about my life. Yet her assumptions were spot on. Some days I couldn't be sure I wouldn't wind up at Stacks drunk on cheap beer, and other days, I was sure I had the right motivations, I knew the way. Today was one of those days.

"I'm trying."

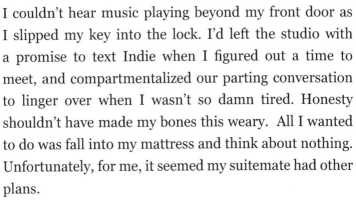

I couldn't hear music playing beyond my front door as I slipped my key into the lock. I'd left the studio with a promise to text Indie when I figured out a time to meet, and compartmentalized our parting conversation to linger over when I wasn't so damn tired. Honesty shouldn't have made my bones this weary. All I wanted to do was fall into my mattress and think about nothing. Unfortunately, for me, it seemed my suitemate had other plans.

I groaned as I shut the door, announcing my presence. "You have a private dorm, last time I checked?"

Royal moved quickly to the other side of the couch, leaving Camden, and his disheveled hair and shirt, to fend for themselves. I tried not to laugh, but the shock on Royal's face was too much to handle.

"Dude, your face..." I held my fist to my lips, but my laughter broke free. "You guys were totally about to bang."

Camden rolled his eyes, stood up, and left the room.

Royal's face was officially as white as a ghost. "Don't be a dick."

"You'd like me better if I was."

"That joke is getting old." He flipped me off as he lifted himself from the couch. He pulled the front hem of his shirt over his loose belt buckle and asked, "How was work?"

"It was a blast." I eyed the sofa. "Is it safe for me to sit here or do I need to buy a new one?"

"Don't be gross."

I chuckled as I sank down into the soft cushions and propped my feet onto the coffee table. "I wasn't the one about to get down in the middle of the living room."

Camden reemerged with his backpack over his shoulders, his dark brown hair, not as messy, flopped over his forehead. "There's lo mein in the mini fridge," he said as he purposely walked into my legs, effectively knocking them off the coffee table.

"Passive-aggressive much?" I whispered, then realized. "Wait, you guys got Chinese without me?" I had an addiction to Chinese food, one Royal and Camden did not share.

"No, Royal got it for you on his way here," he said, matter of fact, threading his fingers with his boyfriend's. They both looked at each other, having some silent conversation, making my third wheel status loud and clear.

"You don't have to leave. Sorry, I was trying to be funny." I ran my hand through my hair and leaned forward. "Seriously, I'm gonna shower and crash. Stay. It's late. We have weights in the morning, remember?"

Royal nodded. "Let's stay?" he whispered, and Camden stared at me.

"You're covered in paint." Camden's assessment drew Royal's attention to my hands and I pushed them into my pockets.

"Shit, it's in your hair." Royal chuckled. "I thought you said you were on garbage duty tonight?"

"I was... I..." Camden's shrewd, silver eyes watched me, and once again, I had to choose the truth over a lie. And if I wanted to prove to myself running wasn't an option, then the people I cared about had to know me. The real me. Unsaturated. Zero proof. Kai Carter. No warranty. Available as-is. "I worked on a project for class after work at the studio."

Royal's brows dipped. "The... art studio?"

"Yeah, I'm hoping to get a TA job with one of the professors I've sold some of my drawings to. This janitor job sucks." It didn't matter how nonchalant I was, or how I had infused every ounce of no-big-deal into my body language, Royal gawked at me. "What?"

"I didn't know you drew."

"I did." Camden slipped his bag off his shoulders and set it on the floor against the couch. "You're always doodling on the takeout menus. He's pretty good."

"Thanks." I laughed at his dismissive tone.

"Can you TA if you're not majoring in art?" Royal asked.

"I changed my major."

"When?" The accusation in his voice jarred me.

"This week, it's not a big deal."

"It's a huge deal, Kai. What the hell? Why didn't you tell me?"

"I just did."

"Okay." He wouldn't look at me, his cheeks splotched with red.

"Hey," Camden whispered as he slipped his fingers gently around Royal's wrist. "It's late, let's go to bed."

Royal leaned in and kissed him on the mouth. "I'll be right there."

It wasn't weird because it was two men, it was weird because I hadn't really been around to watch how open they'd become. It made me smile. Camden noticed my regard and blushed.

"Don't be too long." He disappeared behind his bedroom door, leaving his boyfriend scowling at me.

"Christ, Royal. It's *not* a big deal."

He sat down, and I allowed him his silence. A minute, maybe two, passed before he said, "I thought we were cool. That everything between us was straight."

I turned my head to face him and he stared at me, his blue eyes so much like Indie's it unnerved me. "We are. I literally just decided all of this a couple of days ago. My mom—"

"Is she okay?"

"Yeah... for now, but she said something to me, and it sort of woke me up. I've been living my life for her for so long, I forgot how to live it for me. And I know she won't be here forever, and she told me I needed to start planning for that. I don't want to... deal with it, Royal, but I have to. Live for her, live for me, it's the same thing. She'll get to see me happy for once, I hope."

"You want to be an artist?" he asked, skeptical.

"I'd like to teach, and I'm good at drawing, and I love it, it makes me feel something. Pie graphs and spreadsheets are draining."

Royal let out a breathless laugh. "You're a junior."

"I'm already behind."

"Because of me."

"Because of what happened." I shoved his shoulder. "Not you, dude."

"Promise me you won't leave me for my sister." He smirked, and my palms began to sweat.

"Promise. She's only in my art history class, you're still my favorite O'Connell."

"Good. Sometimes I think Camden likes her better than me."

"I doubt that." I leaned back and changed the direction of the conversation. "You think we're ready for the meet this weekend?"

"I think so. Dev's been busting ass at practice. What do you think?"

"We'll have it handled. Bonus... my shoulder hasn't been giving me such a hard time since I cut back on the booze."

"I knew it was bothering you. That because of me, too?"

"Were you always this whiny?"

He pinched the back of my arm, and I punched him in his side. We were both laughing and out of breath when I said, "As much as I appreciate the foreplay, I'm pretty sure your boyfriend is waiting for you."

He shoved himself to his feet. "You're hilarious."

I blew him a kiss, and he swatted my hand as someone knocked at the front door, ruining the brilliant comeback sitting on the tip of my tongue.

"Probably one of the guys," he guessed. "Corbin stopped by earlier wanting to discuss his times from last practice."

Royal headed to the door as I said, "He should be talking to coach, not me."

Royal unlatched the lock, looking over his shoulder at me as he opened the door. His mouth moved, but I didn't hear a word he'd said.

"Daphne? It's late." I stood too fast, feeling lightheaded; I took a deep breath to catch my bearings.

Her eyes were glassy, ringed with smudged black coal, she wet her lips as she slurred, "I missed you."

Royal gave me a questioning look and I lifted my shoulders. A silent *I have no fucking idea why she's here* that he didn't seem to believe by the slight smirk he gave me.

"Hey, Daph, come on in." Royal held the door open and locked it behind her, assuming she might stay for a while.

I wanted her gone five seconds ago.

"See you in the morning, dude." Royal clapped my shoulder and whispered, "Try to keep it down."

"It's not like that."

"Not my business." He gave me another smile and left me standing in the middle of the living room.

Daphne waved at him as Camden's door shut with a final click. She approached me on drunk legs and rubbed at her nose, her smile fading. Her blood-shot eyes filled with tears as she set her hands on my chest.

I lifted her chin, trying to figure out if she was drunk or high or both. My thumb caught one of her mascara-stained tears as I wiped it from her cheek. "I'm not doing this with you."

seven shades of you

She sniffled and pulled away from my touch. "I know."

"Why are you here?"

She rubbed at her nose with one hand, and tugged the sleeve of her hoodie with the other. "I don't know what I'm doing anymore."

"What's going on?"

Her tears started to fall in earnest and she shook her head. "I don't know."

"Daphne," I cautioned as she turned to face me.

"I need help."

Kai

Dry skin, red with irritation, framed Daphne's nose. Her fingernails were bitten into flat stubs, a few of them scabbed where the cuticle met her skin. Her overgrown pixie cut looked like it hadn't been washed in a few days. She smelled like she'd been sweating whiskey, her skin's pale complexion hung over her hollow cheekbones like a wet dish rag.

I swore as her tears turned to sobs, taking her clammy hand in mine. "Come on."

The light in my room added a new dimension to her pallor, casting her cheeks in more of a light green than white as I shut the door. Soft music leaked through the thin wall separating Camden's room from mine, creating a timely buffer of sound.

"Are you hurt?" I asked, lowering my eyes to hers, willing her to look at me.

She didn't answer at first. Choosing to stare off into the distance, she brought her nails to her mouth as she scanned my room.

"Do you know anyone who could sell me a few pills tonight?"

"You're fucking kidding me?"

Daphne's fingers started to shake. "Imogen's out..." She grabbed her flask from her back pocket and shoved it into my chest. I grabbed it, keeping it from falling to the floor. "Have a sip." Stepping into my space, she offered, "I've got more in my car."

My temper flared. "You drove over here?" She could hardly walk.

"I need something, Kai, and if you're not willing to take the edge off... One of your teammates... I guarantee you they use, there's no way all of you could deal with the schedules you keep without a little help."

"I don't use pills, and anyone on my team caught using would be out on their asses." I grabbed her hand and pushed the flask into her palm, holding it there until she curled her fingers around it.

She laughed, her head rolling back. "Piety doesn't look good on you."

"Daphne," I said her name in a calm whisper and pressed my thumb and finger to the bridge of my nose.

"If you hadn't found me in the bar that night over break... you would've what? Gone home with a stranger? I helped you that night. Help me now." She tried to place her hands on my chest again, and I gently took her wrists and lowered them to her sides.

"Yes." I backed off, creating distance between us. "I would've gone home with anyone that night if they were willing."

"Whatever." She waved her hand and swayed where she stood. "I don't want a do over, I—"

"Good, because it's never happening again."

She narrowed her eyes. "I want a number, you have to know someone."

"No."

"No, you won't give me a number, or no, you don't know anyone?"

"I don't know anyone, and if I did I wouldn't tell you. This shit could kill you, Daph."

She ran her hands through her greasy hair. "I have it under control."

"Obviously." I reached for the door.

"Kai, please. I'm hurting." She started to cry, and I couldn't tell if she was for real or trying to reel me into the rabbit hole. "Fucking Imogen."

"You've been taking her meds?" I asked.

"So, what? She doesn't use them anymore. She got a prescription for Adderall to help her study, but didn't like how it made her feel. It was wasteful. I helped myself."

"Adderall is dangerous if you don't need it for an actual diagnosed reason, Daphne."

"You know my diagnosis."

"Shitty parenting is not a diagnosis."

"Shitty parenting was enough for you to get wasted and fuck me."

"Get out." The muscles in my arms and shoulders contracted, my control the only thing stopping me from picking her up and physically removing her from my room.

"I'm sorry." She raised her hand to touch my face and I opened the bedroom door a crack.

"Don't."

"I didn't mean your mom, I didn't mean it... I..." The mascara streaking down her cheeks was the only human thing about her in that moment. "I didn't mean your mom."

She stared at the floor as I measured my anger.

"Let me help you, I can take you to the Emergency Room."

"No way." She shook her head hard and fast.

Anger had always led me down the wrong road, and if I let her walk out of here tonight, the prospects were horrifying. Someone could take advantage of her. What would she be willing to do to get what she needed? What if she couldn't find any pills and ended up taking something worse.

"Stay here, sleep it off. I'll take the couch. In the morning we could go to the campus clinic together." Her face was blank of emotion. "I was in a bad way that night over break, and I didn't realize you were, too. I used you to escape, and that makes me the biggest fucking asshole on the planet, but if I let you walk out of this dorm tonight, it would be unforgivable."

"I used you, too," she whispered and wiped under her eyes. "I can't stay here."

"You have no choice." I shut the door and locked it. "It's here or the E.R., Daphne, and I'll sleep on the floor in front of the damn door if I have to."

She sat down on my bed and let her head fall into her palms. Her shoulders shook as her chest opened up with wet sobs. I didn't sit next to her, affording her a somewhat private breakdown. I didn't have anyone with me when I was sitting at rock bottom, and I was lucky to still be breathing.

She sniffled and patted the mattress. "You don't have to sleep on the floor."

"Actually I do. I wasn't lying, we were a one-time thing, and you're in no place—"

She shrugged. "Suit yourself."

I ignored her, grabbing a hoodie from my desk chair to use as a pillow. Sleeping on a hard floor wasn't ideal for my shoulder, but I didn't trust that she wouldn't bolt the minute I fell asleep on the couch. At least this way, I'd have a better chance of hearing her if she tried to leave.

Daphne kicked off her shoes and lay flat on my bed. Her eyes on the ceiling, she said, "Thank you."

Royal's laugh filtered through the wall as I turned off my light, reminding me I'd have to skip the gym in the morning to get Daphne to the clinic. I couldn't tell him Daphne's business, especially since she was Indie's roommate, but I didn't want him thinking this sleepover was anything but platonic. Stretching out on my floor, the strain of this day pressed my lids closed, and I told myself I'd worry about everything in the morning.

A light thump on the wall, a low voice, maybe Camden or Royal, I couldn't tell, made my eyes pop open.

"Are they always this loud?" Daphne asked.

"They usually stay at Royal's place." I shoved the hoodie into a tighter ball and rolled onto my side.

"One nice thing about having a virginal roommate... quiet nights."

The word virginal spun in my head over and over. I'd watched as Indie used all the strength in her arms, throwing paint onto the canvas. Intent and passionate... I internally cringed as heat gathered at the base of my spine. I shouldn't be thinking about heat or that fucking word... virgin.

"Maybe if I'd been raised by artists and not addicts, I wouldn't be in this mess."

I suppressed my groan and rolled onto my back. "What are you talking about?"

"Nothing... Everything..." Daphne exhaled in the dark, the tension pouring from her lungs. She was wired. "Indie... Royal... they're so perfect."

"No one is perfect."

"I don't really know Royal, but Indie is perfect. Well, not perfect-perfect... there's always the *voices thing*, which is crazy, but still, I'd swap places with her in a heartbeat. In a freaking heartbeat. Perfect family, hot brother, and Christ, she can paint."

The voices...

It was an invasion of Indie's privacy, Daphne rambling on and on, and I hadn't had a chance to process everything she'd already blurted out before she dropped another bombshell of information.

"She crushes on you."

"Stop talking."

The gruff command didn't faze her. "You invited me to stay, and I can't sleep." I heard her shift to the edge of the bed. "Why do you ignore her?"

"I don't know what the hell you're saying."

"You do. It's like Indie doesn't exist to you. At least, that's what she thinks."

I swallowed, an ache forming under my ribs. "She said that?"

Daphne rolled away from me, the springs of my mattress singing, and disregarded my question. "Kai?"

"Still here."

"What do you think will happen tomorrow?"

"That's up to you."

"That's not an answer."

"It's all I've got."

I waited for a response, but Daphne had gone quiet. She'd either fallen asleep or was too lost in her own thoughts to pester me with any more of her verbal digressions. As for me, I was wide awake, thinking about Indie. Virginal. Voices. Crush. These words, her secrets, private pieces Daphne had inadvertently given me, and it didn't matter how long or how many times I tried to fit them all together, turning them in every direction, the puzzle pieces wouldn't fit. I'm not sure when I finally dozed off, but I dreamt about a girl named Pink, and no matter how hard I looked, I couldn't find her.

The next morning I was startled awake by a loud knock, forgetting how the hell I'd ended up on my floor.

"Kai?" Royal whisper-shouted and it all came back to me like an ice cold bucket of water on my head.

"Shit." I scrambled to my feet and stared at my empty mattress.

She was gone.

"It's four-forty-five." I opened the door and he cringed. "Sorry, I didn't want to wake—"

"There's no one here. I'll be out in a second." I hadn't meant to shut the door in his face, but I needed a second to regroup.

Daphne shouldn't be my problem, but she'd forced my hand last night. I grabbed my phone from the desk, the notification light flashing.

I opened the lock screen and read the awaiting text.

Daphne: Didn't want to wake you. Thank you for last night. I wouldn't have made it without you.

Me: Please tell me you'll go to the clinic today.

I tossed my phone into my gym bag, changed out of last night's jeans and threw on a hoodie and sweats. Royal had waited for me, sitting on the couch, playing some game on his phone.

"I'm going to brush my teeth. Grab us a couple protein bars from the pantry?" It wasn't really a pantry, but a coat closet where I stored all my dry goods.

"Sure." He pocketed his phone, and I closed the bathroom door.

I splashed cold water on my face, shocking myself into submission. I had too many questions running through my head. Daphne was like a wrecking ball, creating havoc everywhere she landed. I worried how long it would take her to find someone willing to share their pills. And everything she'd said last night had been on a constant loop. Invisible. Crush. Voices. I'd deleted the virginal thing as inconsequential. Indie and I—there was no Indie and I. We were barely becoming friends and that's all we would ever be.

I used the towel hanging on the back of the door to dry away the heavy beads of water clinging to my face and lashes. I glanced at myself in the mirror before I left. Dark circles shadowed my eyes. I'd shown up at the gym half-drunk more times than I cared to remember, this was nothing. I pushed down my exhaustion and taped on a smile as I met Royal in the living room.

"Long night?" he asked, the innuendo blatant.

"She's just a friend."

"Okay."

"I'm not kidding."

"I said okay."

Comfortable with the silence, we'd made our way to the main doors of Garrison Hall before he asked, "If you were more than friends... you'd tell me?"

It was damp, the rain more like sleet, cut like a knife to the bone. "Probably." I grinned and pulled my hood over my head.

"I tell you everything."

"That's not my fault."

He bumped his shoulder into mine. "It could get complicated... if it ends badly, she's my sister's roommate."

"I'm not into Daphne." I stopped, not giving a shit about the weather, or that I couldn't feel my toes or my fingertips. "She's pretty low right now, and I know what that feels like. I want to help her if I can."

"You're supposed to be working on you."

The fog left behind by our breath dispersed in the sudden wind. "I am."

We continued toward the gym, our pace faster than before, the elements winning. "Good."

I didn't roll my eyes, or give him a smart-ass comment. For starters, I was too tired to be witty, and he was right. I couldn't be Daphne's savior when I was still trying to save myself.

"She said she'd get help... said she'd make an appointment at the clinic."

"If you want I could ask Indie to—"

"Don't involve your sister. If Daphne wanted her help she would have asked."

He nodded, and by the time we got to the gym, we were both frozen through. Royal shed his damp hoodie, revealing a shirt underneath, and I regretted not grabbing a dry shirt for myself. He guessed as much, and once we were in the locker room, he unzipped his bag and threw a shirt at me.

"Give it to Camden after you wash it."

I stripped out of my soaked sweatshirt. "You expect me to wash it?"

He pushed his finger into my cheek. "So funny."

"Do I want to know where that finger's been?" I asked, pulling the dry shirt over my head.

The material stretched as I tugged it down over my chest. It was a size too small, but it was warm.

"It's too early for this shit." Corbin practically fell onto the bench behind us, drenched from head to toe. "I swear to God it never used to rain this much."

"Didn't you say that last week?" Dev asked, slinging his bag onto the floor at Corbin's feet. "Watch it, don't get my bag wet."

"Fuck you."

"You wish."

Dev's chuckle was cut short as Coach yelled from his office door. "Enough dicking around, I want you all ready and in the weight room in five minutes."

"Great, he's in a mood." Corbin replaced his wet shoes with the pair he kept in his locker.

"I think the Canucks lost last night," Royal said as he shut his locker.

"We're screwed." I smirked.

Dev's grimace was comical. "You're a masochist."

"You know it."

We managed to finish getting dressed without any further bickering. Royal and I always teamed up for weight training, and Dev and Corbin wandered off to find their usual partners. Luckily, Sherman stuck to himself, and the rest of the guys trickled in a few minutes later. The first few sets weren't that bad, but the sleepless night reared its ugly head as I tried to bench press an extra five pounds, per Coach's order. The addition was minimal, something I should have been able to do without issue, but I could feel the pain of it deep inside the curve of my shoulder.

"Stop." Royal took the bar from my hands and I slid out from underneath it. "You'll pull something."

I stretched my arm across my chest and winced. "Shit, I overdid it."

"You think?" Royal removed the weights from the bar. "Have you had anyone look at it yet?"

"No."

"No?" he gave me a look that would make my mother cower.

"Chill. It's feeling better, but if it's still bugging me next week, I'll make an appointment after my therapy session."

"I accept that plan."

"Thanks, your Highness."

"You're welcome."

He loaded his weights on the bar, and I debated whether or not I should ask him about his sister. What Daphne had unearthed last night hadn't faded with my morning routine, or the pain in my shoulder.

I pressed my lips together until my curiosity got the best of me. "By the way... I ran into Indie at the Behavioral Health Center."

His hands hesitated over the weights. "Oh?"

"She didn't mention it?"

"No." He finished loading his bar and I moved, letting him take his place on the bench. He waited, his jaw working in the process. "She's extremely private about ... everything." Royal met my curious gaze. "Don't say anything to anyone about—"

"I wouldn't."

"I know. But I wanted to make it clear. That's not up for discussion, unless she says it is."

"Noted."

Lying down, he wrapped his fingers around the bar. "Thanks."

The tension in his shoulders relaxed, but mine remained. Royal didn't say much after I'd opened my big mouth, not until we were back in the locker room, he asked, "You going to answer that?"

My phone vibrated on the top of my bag and I saw my dad's name flash on the screen.

"Not right now."

Royal headed to the shower, and I picked up my phone once the screen went dead. I had a message from Daphne. A missed call from my mom and the one from my dad. I bypassed all of them and pulled up my contacts.

Me: Can I stop by tonight?

I didn't think she'd respond right away, but my phone buzzed in my hand before I could put it back in my bag.

Indie: The studio?

Me: I feel like crashing your art party.

She sent a single red balloon emoji.

Me: Is that a yes?

Indie: You don't need an invitation. It's open to all the students.

Me: Will bring food for help.

Indie: Just bring you.

Just bring me...

I could do that.

And maybe a question or two.

Indigo

Wednesday night was my least favorite in the studio, usually I didn't show up until after eleven. The evening sculpture class ended at nine, but the students always loitered, finishing up their projects for the night. Most of them were nice, sending meaningful smiles from their secret corner of the studio. Some of them never bothered to lift their heads at all. I felt a kinship to those particular students. Art wasn't a spectator sport.

Normally, I would've been with Camden right now, biding my time with my head on his lap, listening to whatever new music he'd found that week, and making a playlist to bring to the studio with me later. But tonight, I found myself with headphones covering my ears, absorbed in the instrumentals from last week's playlist, surrounded by familiar strangers, working on my present for Camden, and worried when Kai would show. I knew he had swim practice only because Royal had swim practice, but I wasn't sure if he would come straight from the Aquatic Center or not. I ignored the negative thoughts in my head, promising me he wouldn't show, that his sudden interest in me was most likely an attempt to boost his grade, and chose to focus on the tiny, black musical notes I was meticulously painting onto the canvas. My fingers trembled slightly from the painstaking effort. They needed to look like notes, not black splotches.

A light touch made me jump, and I was grateful I didn't have my brush to the canvas. I steeled my irritation, expecting to see Kai standing behind me. Instead, I was met with a giant, off-kilter smile I didn't recognize. I pulled my headphones around my neck only to catch half of what he was saying. "...so dope. I've never seen you here, are you new?"

I stared at the dark mop of hair that hid his eyebrows and shadowed a pair of almond-shaped gray eyes. When I didn't answer immediately, he held out his hand. "Hunter. Sculpture major." His thin lips pulled back almost to his ears, his teeth overly white.

I waited a few seconds longer than socially acceptable before I took his hand. His palm was dry and calloused, rough against my skin. "Indie. Art major."

"Painter?" he asked. Withdrawing his hand, he ran fingers through the thick strands of his hair, exposing raised brows that were too neat and reached into the deep lines of his forehead.

"Painting is my emphasis."

His shrewd eyes flicked to my painting, and he bit back another growing smile. "I can see why. This is sick."

135

Sick.

Sick.

Sick.

He continued to talk, but I couldn't hear past the rush of blood pounding in my head.

"I like the lack of color," he said.

"I'm adding the color later."

"I think it looks perfect as it is." His eyes were as colorless as my painting. "But I'm excited to see the final result."

You won't. I wanted to say, but my anxiety wasn't his fault. The panic building in my chest wasn't because I was talking to a stranger, well, not all of it, at least. I glanced at the door prepared for it to open, willing Kai Carter to walk in and scatter the vultures.

"It's a present for a friend."

He assessed me. "Like a boyfriend?"

"My brother's boyfriend."

"Cool." He zipped up his black hoodie and stuffed his hands into the pockets. "I don't usually... I mean, I'm thinking this is..." He sighed, took a deep breath, and laughed. "Would you want to maybe go—"

"I brought dinner," Kai interrupted, ignoring the fact I was in the middle of a conversation. His voice was deep and gravel, and all the apprehension I'd been harboring, chewing on since he'd texted to tell me he wanted to come to the studio tonight, evaporated into thin air.

"I told you, you didn't—"

He leaned in and I held my breath.

"I should feed you," he teased, setting the bag in his hand onto the work table. Kai tugged on the end of my braid, a new habit that felt oddly intimate, like it was our thing now, even though I could count our real encounters on one hand. "It's the least I could do." Hunter shifted on his feet, drawing Kai's attention. "Who are you?"

"Hunter." He stood as tall as he could manage, his small, skinny build seeming boyish compared to Kai's six-foot-plus broad frame.

"Sculpture major," I said.

Kai nodded, but didn't offer anything to the conversation. Hunter looked at me, then back at Kai, and asked, "The brother?"

My laugh was a mixture of incredulity and nerves. "No, he's..." Was he my friend? Royal's? Both? "A friend of mine." Warm and honey-colored light filled my stomach. Of *mine*. Mine.

Hunter's expression deflated, and he scanned the back of the room where a few of the students from the sculpture class remained.

"Are you and Gunther—"

"Hunter," he corrected Kai, his lips flat.

"Are you and *Hunter* in a class together?"

"We just met." I smiled and wondered at the stiffness in Kai's shoulders and jaw. Guilt prickled in my fingertips, maybe he thought we'd be alone, maybe he didn't want spectators either.

"I didn't catch your name," Hunter said.

"Kai."

The moment stretched and stifled until I finally chose to be the one to speak. "You were asking me something?" I reminded him.

Hunter shook his head. "I can't remember. Anyway..." His smile reappeared, but it wasn't as bright, and his black hoodie, black shoes, black mop of hair, seemed just as staged. "Cool painting, maybe I'll see you around?"

"Sure." I felt my cheeks flush at the hopeful tone of his voice.

Hunter caught up with the sculpture students as they were leaving, not looking back as he headed through the studio doors.

"What a tool." Kai chuckled under his breath.

"Why is he a tool?" I asked, unable to hide my annoyance.

How many people had been just as quick to judge me, cast me aside without a second notice? Too many.

"The kid's got no follow-through." His smirk, a touch too arrogant, aggravated me.

"I don't know what that means." I turned my back to him, rummaging through the bag of take-out, keeping my hands busy and my eyes off his.

I could feel the heat radiating off his body as he approached me, standing close enough it startled me when he spoke. "He was about to ask you out."

"He was not."

Kai left little space between us, his arm brushing mine as he reached into the bag and pulled out a white and red container. The small touch made me shiver.

"That dude was about to ask you out. I'd bet my season on it. What did you think he was about to ask you? Hey, uh...would you maybe want to go... play board games in my dorm room...naked?"

I shoved his shoulder, and despite my earlier annoyance, I giggled. "That would be a terrible date."

Terrible and terrifying. I'd never even kissed a guy, but there was no way I would admit that to Kai.

"Only terrible because you'd be with *Hunter*." He grinned, smug, like he'd won some nonexistent argument, and grabbed two sets of chopsticks from the bag.

"It's terrible on many levels..." I took a set of chopsticks from his hand and tore open the paper wrapper. "You really think he was going to ask me out?"

He hummed as he dug into a container of lo mein, and I popped open the other box, frowning at the sweet and sour chicken. My least favorite.

He swallowed his mouthful of noodles and licked his lips. I tried not to stare. "Definitely." He pointed his chopstick at the take-out box on the table. "Royal always gets sweet and sour chicken, so I assumed..."

"Royal hates Chinese."

"I know, but he says he'll tolerate the chicken."

I laughed and shut the lid. "My Uncle Kieran is addicted to this one Chinese food place in Salt Lake. It's been open forever, and I'm pretty sure he's the only person keeping them in business."

"So you're a hater, too?"

I shook my head. "No, not really, I'm more of a lo mein girl."

He grinned, lowering his chopsticks back into his container. "Soul mates." He held out the container, offering it to me. "Here."

"I'm not even that hungry," I lied, and he rolled his eyes.

"Take it, unlike you and your picky-ass brother, I'll eat whatever is put in front of me."

I took the container and stared at his chopsticks sinking into the noodles. They'd touched his mouth, his tongue. I shared food with Royal, with Camden, even Corbin in the cafeteria all the time, but this, I couldn't explain it. I wanted my lips where his lips had been, his tongue... the thought poured an unusual heat through my body, dripping red all the way from my cheeks to my stomach.

Kai grabbed my untouched container and plopped down onto one of the stools. I sat next to him, aiming for casual, and for a few minutes, everything was quiet as we ate, as my lips touched his lips, through some weird conduit.

Pathetic.

"I'm not," I whispered and he noticed.

Oh God, he noticed.

I could feel my embarrassment crawling up my throat and refused to look at him as he searched the side of my face.

"Can I ask you something?"

I pushed the container of food away, no longer hungry.

Can I ask you something?

Why did that sound ominous? Gloomed with gray and touched with edges of blue.

"Of course."

"You don't have to answer me... tell me to fuck off if you want..." He pushed his dinner away, too.

Kai's eyes were more than brown, coffee with a touch of milk. Warm and deep. Serious and sweet. His emotions were written in the way his pupils dilated; no way he could hide what he was feeling, if only someone was brave enough to look.

He rubbed the back of his neck, his lips parting with a slow breath, he asked, "I was forced to see a therapist, and I kind of hate it, but I kind of don't either."

"Are you asking me if I hate my therapist?"

"No... well, maybe." He laughed, releasing my growing anticipation.

"I want to say I do. I want to wish I didn't have to be there. But it's been a part of my life for so long, I can't even try to wish it away anymore. It's part of me."

"Why..." He'd tipped his chin, shrinking the space between us, his tone soft, his violent purple giving over to an electric yellow. "Is it a part of you?"

My head was static. I waited for the mean words to form in my brain, push me to feel guilt for my sickness, and it could've been the way he watched me, his curiosity more a veil for something else. I didn't know what he thought of me, what Royal had told him, probably nothing, and I wanted to be scared, but he smiled and shook his head.

"You don't have to tell me."

"I want to."

It was the truth and it hurt a little to admit it, but it was a good pain, like finally tearing off a hangnail. I'd always be alone if I didn't let others in.

"I'll make you a deal."

"I like deals."

"I know, I'm appealing to your competitive nature." I dropped my gaze to the table. "I'll tell you why I'm in therapy if you tell me why you are."

The strain in his smile was evident. "Okay."

I tore the chopstick wrapper into tiny pieces as I spoke. "I had really bad mood swings as a kid, still do. There were times when it was hard to get out of bed, and there were times when I couldn't sleep for days. I hid it for a while, but my dad was the first to figure it out. He and I share the same illness. Mine started a little later than his, but I don't fluctuate as much as he does..."

"Bipolar?" he asked.

I stuttered through a breath. "With psychotic features."

He didn't even pause to take in what I'd said.

Psychotic.

Freak.

Useless.

There was no shock, or horror, when he asked, "What does that mean?" And all I could hear in his voice was genuine curiosity.

"It depends on the person. Voices, hallucinations, paranoia." I stole a glance, his forehead and lips too smooth to read. "I mostly deal with depression. And sometimes... I... I have negative, intrusive thoughts, but my dad, he had all of them, has, all of that. We both work really hard in therapy, and with meds, he's stable most of the time."

"What about you?"

"Nine times out of ten? I'm good. I'm lucky to have my dad, he taught me how to handle it, to paint through the darker days. I'm lucky..." My breath caught in my throat and a familiar burn filled my eyes. I exhaled, centering myself, closing it all down and smiled. "Freaky?"

That soft smile returned and I found myself lost in it as he said, "Not at all."

"You can be honest." I rolled a piece of the torn wrapper between my fingers, too anxious for his truth.

"You hear voices?"

"Yeah."

"And they're always mean?"

"No, not always."

He turned to look at the painting I'd been working on. "And they help you paint?"

"I paint to keep them away. I paint to see color when there's none. I paint to remember who I am, when all I remember, all I hear, is the dark."

He raised his hand, and for a second I wanted him to touch my cheek. I held still, waiting for it, the warmth of him, but he lowered his palm to the table and said, "You're brave."

My mouth was dry, my throat sore from the sentiment. "My dad calls me his 'brave girl', and some days I feel brave, and others..." I laughed, trying to lighten the mood.

"I get it. Most days I feel like I have shit handled and others... I can't seem to find solid ground." Kai gave me a shy smile, his hand at the back of his neck again. "I guess it's my turn now?"

"You don't have to tell me."

He pressed his lips together, his jaw working, he held me captive and said, "But I do... I want you to know me."

Kai

She was completely intimidating.

Indie had a fragility about her. Her pale skin, bright eyes, soft blonde hair. Quiet and introverted. Even now, sitting here in jeans and an oversized sweater that devoured her frame, I might've missed the strength inside of her.

Voices.

She heard voices in her head, telling her dark shit. She'd given me this secret and I felt absolutely useless. I had no right to be depressed or anxious about anything. Here she sat, smiling—shy and beautiful—at *me* like I was about to give her the whole world, a piece of me, and I was, but it weighed nothing. It was insignificant. I made my problems—hers were born.

"Are you seeing a therapist because of what happened last semester?" she asked.

"Sort of." I was nervous, my hands clammy as I fisted them in my lap.

Indie watched me, waiting, and I was terrified she'd realize that I was a giant asshole with nothing to be sorry for. That my mother's illness was a crutch for me to blame my father, the world, for everything that had gone wrong in my life. I was scared she'd see me as I saw myself every day in the fucking mirror.

"I'm angry all the time, I guess…" I swallowed, trying not to focus on the gnawing sensation in my gut, or the hammer inside my head, my pulse making my face and chest flame. I uncurled my fist and tapped the tabletop, keeping my eyes on the gray metal surface. "I started drinking too much and I messed up over break. My mom wanted me to get some help."

"Only your mom?" she asked, and I couldn't look at her.

I mashed my teeth together, took a second to answer, keeping my gaze fixed down, I said, "My mom has multiple sclerosis. Her illness has progressed to a point where she can't walk, can't get out of bed. She has a nurse who comes to the house daily. She gets these painful fucking wounds on her back and hips, but she's always smiling. My mom is the most positive person you'll ever meet. She doesn't ever say *I'm done* or *I can't take it anymore*. She won't give up on anyone, not even a cheating husband."

"Kai," Indie whispered despite the fact we were alone in the room, the pity in her voice hard to take, and I realized my hands were shaking.

I stood, almost knocking the stool over in the process. "I'm sorry. I'm… Shit. I don't know what I am."

"You're still angry."

The statement grabbed me and pulled me in, and when I faced her, there was nothing but understanding, and it cooled the burn of my building rage.

I nodded. "Yes."

Every muscle in my body was tight. Tight with anger, fear, and something I had no name for, something darker, something that had led me to the garage that night.

I walked toward her painting. It was a plain white canvas with a black wave of detailed musical notes. It was incredible. If I stared long enough, the notes appeared to move, the light catching the metallic black paint as I walked toward it. More of her chaos displayed for the world to see. I'd never be that fearless. I'd only ever drawn the world as it was, as everyone else saw it, not how it had locked itself up in my brain. Distorted, turning the air in my lungs into resentment.

I could smell the light lavender of her skin, the powder of her soap as she approached me, and I was calm again. Pushing my hands into my pockets, I continued, "I'm angry that she took him back. That she never stands up for herself... that I always have to." I braved a glance in her direction. "I'm selfish."

She shook her head, leaning in, not quite touching me, but the charge of it, the imminence, I was being stripped of my skin. I was raw with it.

"I don't think you're selfish."

"You don't know everything."

"Then tell me."

We stared at each other, a quiet standoff. *I showed you mine, now show me yours.* I should have been thinking

147

of what I would say next, tell Indie I wasn't as brave as her. Tell her I was a coward who struck first because I was terrified of becoming like him, like my dad. But all I could think about was how tempting her lips were. How her top lip had a slight bow in the middle, and when she pressed it to her bottom lip, it formed a heart. How it was the most inopportune moment, and all I wanted was to kiss her, distract her from the conversation, and prove to her just how selfish I was.

Thank God, she didn't give me the chance.

"You said you wanted me to know you, so tell me." She smiled. "I, of all people, know what it's like to have secrets."

I brought my attention back to the painting. "That's kind of why I don't want to tell you. My shit doesn't even compare."

"Pain is not a contest," she said. "Scars are scars. The blade may be different, but it still cuts us all the same."

I smirked despite the mood. "You just went all Yoda on me."

"Maybe you need a little Yoda in your life." Her bottom lip was trapped between her teeth, a poor attempt at hiding her smile.

"You should teach my therapist."

"I probably could, when you spend at least eighty percent of your life in a behavioral health center, you learn a thing or two."

"Shit. I wasn't meaning it to sound—"

"I know."

She closed the space and bumped her shoulder into my side. I wanted to wrap my arm around her waist and keep her there. Like a lifeline, I needed the light weight of Indie's touch in order to tell her the worst parts of what I'd done. But I shouldn't attach myself to her like that, shouldn't allow her the possibility to sink with me. Royal would never forgive me. I would never forgive myself.

"I mean it, though... I have a mental illness, it doesn't mean the things you've gone through are any less important."

"It's the way you handle it. Your pain." I raised my hand and waved it at her painting. "I chose to get drunk and kill myself." The last part slipped out and I winced. "I mean... I didn't try to kill myself."

"You didn't?" she asked in a thin-trembled whisper.

I allowed myself to look into her eyes again, find that strength, and maybe use it to get through these next few sentences. "I don't think so. I got really wasted one night over break. I'd gotten into a huge fight with my dad, and I was still messed up over everything that had happened with Royal. Mad at myself for not calling him, mad at *him* for not standing up for himself. Kind of like my mom hadn't stood up to my dad and let him come home after he'd been shacked up with his girlfriend.

"I expected a chill Christmas with my mom, time to process everything with school. My dad being home was like the whipped topping on the mountain of shit that was my life. I finished off a long night of drinking with another bottle of vodka, passed out in a running car inside the garage."

"Oh my God."

"I don't think I meant to do it, but maybe I did. I can't remember much, but I know I wanted to go somewhere. I couldn't be in that house anymore. And once I got in the car, I was too tired to move. Bone tired, Indie, and I fell asleep."

"You could've—"

"Died."

We didn't speak for what felt like an eternity. Her eyes glued to the painting, I started to sweat. I hadn't ever felt this weak in my entire life.

"Kai... " Indie looked up finally. She was so small compared to me. The top of her head barely level with the center of my chest, but I knew she was the bigger person. "It was an accident?" she said, but it sounded more like a question.

"I told you I was a self-centered asshole. I put my mom through the scariest night of her life all because I have daddy issues."

"You didn't get into a fight with Ellis because you're self-centered, Kai. You did it to protect Royal. It's the same with your dad, you're not standing up to him because you think you'll gain anything from it. You do it because your mom can't. You're *selfless*. That's the problem. You think nothing of what you do for others, for yourself, and you almost threw it all away because, yes, you had a self-indulgent moment, but you're getting help."

"I was forced to get help."

"Semantics... you're going, right?"

"Right."

She exhaled a rough breath. "Then that's all that matters."

She was over-simplifying, something Royal usually did, and I couldn't help it, I smiled.

"It's cute how much you're like your brother sometimes."

She lifted a doubtful brow. "Cute?"

"Or weird, but I was trying to be nice."

She shoved me, her small hand barely registering on my bicep and I chuckled. The moment came and went, and the silence that fell wasn't uncomfortable. We were two kids, with scars made by two different blades, hoping that maybe one of those scars matched. At least, I hoped. Even if hoping for her was the dumbest thing I could ever do.

"I would have preferred weird," she said, her smile pulling wide.

Knowing her was worse than watching her; at least from afar I could create reasons to stay away. Up close, like this, with her scent in my lungs, and her heat in the air, not even Royal was justification enough to stay away. As if the universe agreed to disagree, my phone chirped in my pocket.

Indie gave me a polite smile as I checked the message.

Royal: Where are you? We're grabbing dinner at Annie's. Want us to bring anything back to the dorm?

I typed out a quick text, not wanting to face the fact I should probably tell him I was with Indie. I was a self-proclaimed man-whore with a drinking problem. Not exactly the type of guy you'd want hanging around your sister. I was anxious that Royal wouldn't approve. He was the one who'd made the passive-aggressive joke about not choosing his sister over him. I'd gotten his meaning.

Stay away.

Me: Already ate. Thanks.

Royal: Will you be headed home soon?

Me: If you're asking if you and Camden have time to bone, then yes, bang your little hearts out.

Royal: I think you need to talk to your therapist about your unhealthy obsession with my sex life.

Me: Or maybe we could talk to the dean and you could give me your single dorm and I wouldn't have to listen to your sex life.

Royal: We listened to yours all last semester.

Me: Touché.

Laughing, I could feel Indie's curious gaze.

Royal: We're staying at my place tonight, asshole. But figured if you were home, we could've all hung out instead.

Me: Aww... sorry my plans ruined your threesome fantasies.

Royal: See you in the morning.

Me: Use a condom.

Grinning and proud of myself, I slipped my phone back in my pocket. Indie had cleaned up our take-out, placing the half-empty boxes back into the bag.

"Thanks," I said and pulled the bag toward me, tying the handles into a knot.

"No problem." She picked at the hem of her sweater, not giving me eye contact.

Everything I'd admitted suddenly seemed like a giant black cloud in the room.

"Did you still want to paint?" I asked.

She glanced at the pocket where my phone chirped again. "I'd like to... you're sure you don't have somewhere else to be?"

"Nah, that was Royal asking me if I wanted anything from Annie's."

"Oh." Indie bit the corner of her mouth. Looking at me from under the veil of gold lashes, she asked, "Does he know you're here?"

A pit formed in the center of my stomach. Unsure if she would want him to know, if she'd think I was hiding it, which I kind of was. I didn't want to hurt her feelings.

"No." I took a step toward her. "Should I have told him?"

"What do you mean?"

"I mean, I don't usually check in with Royal and tell him my whereabouts."

"Okay." She tugged the sleeve of her sweater. "Do you want him to know?"

"Know what?" I played dumb, hating myself for it when she blushed.

"That you were here. With me."

"Do you?" I turned the question around, making it her choice.

Damn it, I didn't want her to think she was a secret. I wanted to be friends with her. Just *friends*. It didn't matter how easy those bottomless blue eyes twisted me up.

"I don't want him to know you're going to teach me how to swim."

Not the answer I had expected. I wanted to ask why, but I let it slide. "Done."

She exhaled. "Thanks."

I debated if I should ask, but the selfish parts of me, the parts she refused to notice asked anyway. I liked having this, possibly having her to myself for a few hours a week. Something no one knew about. Something that was mine. "Would you mind keeping this between us, too? You teaching me how to paint?"

Indie paused, and maybe she was going to ask why, but let it slide, too. Giving me a small smile, she said, "Of course." She tipped her chin toward the supply closet. "Grab a canvas. I want to work on landscapes."

"Landscapes?"

"Anything you want... forests, oceans, mountains..."

"How about the sky?"

"Like a sunset?"

"No, open, clear and blue." *Like your eyes.* "Stretched low to the horizon, I think."

Her lips spread gradually, her smile revealing itself in stages of excitement. "Simple, but more."

"Definitely more."

Kai

Sleep was one of the things I missed about drinking every night. The black, empty, and bottomless dreams were long gone, opening up sharp points of light, restless, and illuminating. Dreams that were impossible to sleep through, waking me sometimes three or four times a night. My five o'clock alarm was rendered useless, already my eyes fixed on the bright blue sky I'd painted the night before. I'd painted a wish. A wish for my mother, for myself, even for my fucking father. I wished everything could be as simple as that open sky. That my dreams weren't as violent, that I was capable of forgiveness.

Sweat lingered on my forehead as I pushed back the covers and got dressed in a pair of sweats and a long-sleeve t-shirt. I didn't even bother to look in the mirror, knowing already the dark circles under my eyes would only piss me off. The pain in my shoulder grated as I reached down and grabbed my gym bag. I opened my bedroom door, and made my way to the bathroom to brush my teeth before leaving for the gym. It was early but I wanted to get there before Royal.

I'd stayed at the studio until midnight working on my painting with his sister, and thanks to my screwed-up brain, the little sleep I'd counted on was wasted. I needed some time to clear my head, figure out how I planned to avoid telling him I'd started a relationship with his sister. Even if we were only friends. Friends who had a secret trapped inside an art studio, and maybe one of those friends wanted to be more than just friends. Maybe he wished he could stop thinking about other said friend's fucking pink lips for five seconds. Lying to Royal about my friendship with Indie was my only option. She'd asked me not to tell him, and I'd asked the same of her. If dishonesty was the only way I'd get to spend time with her, for now, I'd rather lie by omission than point blank. I was good at rationalization when I needed to be, and for argument's sake, Royal didn't need to know. Not yet.

Coach was already in the locker room when I arrived, listening to the morning sports news radio. I didn't offer him a hello, just my usual smile and wave as I headed to my locker. Like always, he nodded his chin, his lips parted with a stilted hello, and I felt his gaze on my back as I made my way to my locker. He'd never outright ask, but his heavy-handed assessment every morning, judging if I was hungover, was easy enough to read. I didn't blame him. My sobriety was a day-to-day challenge and everybody on the team knew it. It was why I got here early on the days I didn't walk with Royal. It was why I busted my ass at every practice.

Show.

Prove.

Some of the guys had begun to stumble into the locker room as I left. The smell of the gym, sweat and hard work, was a weak comfort as I sat on the bench press waiting for Royal. I stared at the phone in my hand. Last night's dream still a thick fog surrounding me; I clicked on my father's name in my contacts, and opened up a message.

I want you to tell him. That's your assignment for next time.

In my dream, more like a nightmare, I'd gone home to talk to my father. He'd told me my mother had died, and I'd tried to speak, but my words had only choked me, suffocated me, until I was on my knees, sobbing, with blood on my hands. When I'd raised my head again, his face had been mangled, and the joy I'd felt at seeing his tortured expression—it made me sick. The nausea real. It happened like this, often, I'd wake up to the sound of my mother gasping, and it didn't matter how many times I tried to think of something else, the dream always happened. Nothing changed. All the elements the same, and, as I typed out the words on the screen, my fingers shook with the fear I'd set this recurring dream into motion.

Me: Will you be around this Sunday?

I pressed send and the burn returned to my throat. The gym door slammed open, a boom of laughter and deep voices spread through the empty room. Royal trailed behind, the smile on his face made me smile, a temporary fix. A twinge of guilt damped my grin as he approached, his eyes reminded me of Indie.

"You didn't wait for me?" he asked.

Standing, I motioned for him to sit. "I didn't lift one pound, I promise." I held my hands up in surrender. "Do you nag your boyfriend as much as you nag me?" I asked, looking for a couple of twenty-pound weights to add to the bar.

"No. I don't need to nag him." He smirked.

"'Cause you're so good at giving head, right?" Sherman's scowl killed Royal's smirk on the spot.

I was about to intervene, stand up for him, when Royal stood from the bench and shrugged. His nonchalance a front I hoped only I could see through. "Why? Are you asking for a demonstration?"

"Fuck you, fa—"

"I swear to God, Sherman," I said, balling my hands into fists.

Royal stepped in front of me, his eyes on mine. "Leave it, I don't care. If he has such a problem with my sexuality, it only calls into question his own."

"Sherman, stop acting like a third grader with a crush and pick on someone you actually have a chance with." Corbin sat on the bench next to the leg press and patted the cushion.

The invitation was met with a glare and a middle finger.

"Oh, he's full of it today, isn't he?" Corbin's smile bordered on giddy, and I chuckled as Sherman stalked off to the other side of the room.

Most of the guys gave him a wide berth with chuckles of their own.

Annoyed and itching to punch something, I said, "That guy's a prick."

"Wants Royal's prick."

"Shut up, Corbin." Royal attempted not to smile and failed.

"It's the truth." Corbin grinned. "Twenty bucks says he comes out by the end of the semester."

"Don't you have weights to lift?" I asked Corbin.

"You'll see. Maybe he'll bring Ellis to the Spring Fling."

"That's not funny," I barked, any humor I had left dissipated with the mention of that asshole's name.

"Spring Fling?" Royal asked.

"Come on, you haven't heard?" he asked and Royal shook his head. "Every spring, Greek Row puts together a themed dance to raise money for the athletic department. It's epic. The senior class tries to best the previous class's attempt."

Royal laughed. "And here I thought I was done with stupid high school dances."

Corbin's forehead creased into a serious line. "Dude. You have no idea. Spring Fling isn't a dance. It's tradition."

"It's just a dance... and a reason for people to get shitfaced and laid," I added.

"You haven't gone to one so you're not part of this convo."

"Corbin." I placed my hand on his shoulder. "I beg you. Go away. It's too early for any of this shit."

"Whatever. I'm going again, and you should bring Camden, leave this boring asshole home."

Royal smiled as Corbin walked away. "Didn't take him for a formal dance kind of guy."

"Don't let him fool you, he just goes for the alcohol and sorority girls."

"Figures."

After weights, we showered and walked to Beckett to meet Camden and Indie. Usually this would be my cue to leave, I'd go grab something fast and eat it on my way to the library. But I didn't want to avoid her anymore.

"You taking off?" Royal asked as we entered the loud, overheated cafeteria.

"Nah, since I changed my schedule I have an extra hour before my next class."

"Sweet."

We decided on breakfast burritos, which Camden said had become a Thursday morning ritual. I watched as they stacked several containers of green salsa on their tray, and followed behind them to the table. I kept my eyes on her the entire way across the room, she kept her head down, busy reading a book as she stirred her coffee with a spoon. Indie's hair was, surprise, surprise, braided, long and gold, over her right shoulder. She had on a turquoise, hooded sweatshirt, and I couldn't wait to see how the color would reflect inside her eyes. She didn't look up from her book once, not even for her brother when he offered her a good morning.

We all took a seat and Camden asked her, "Has he made it to the castle yet?"

Even then, her eyes never left the page, and I watched as she lifted her finger, a small smile blooming on her lips.

Too curious, I asked, "What are you reading?"

Instantly, she raised her head, her cheeks turning the brightest shade of red I'd ever seen. And like I'd hoped, her eyes had absorbed the color of her sweatshirt, and I couldn't look away.

"*The Empire of Solistar*," Camden answered for her.

"It's a book my Uncle Liam told them about over the holidays. It's based off of some children's book he loved as a kid. I don't understand the appeal." Royal gave his sister a teasing smile.

"It's romantic," she said quietly.

"It's a series," Royal said, taking a bite out of his burrito, completely oblivious to the shade of his sister's cheeks.

"What's a series?" Dev asked as he sat next to Indie, and Corbin took the other seat on her left.

Camden explained for the next five minutes the ins and outs of some dude named *The Painted Prince*, and the entire time, my breakfast sat on my tray, untouched as I tried not to look at her, frustrated with myself as I lingered over her smile, or stared at the paint under her fingernails. The same paint I'd watched drip down her fingers as she'd poured her version of the sun onto a canvas last night. Silence was what I had always given her, but here, now, watching Dev and Corbin tease her, playfully bump their shoulders into hers, Dev's hand only inches from her hand, it was torture. Jealousy and irritation sank into the pit of my stomach.

I stood abruptly and Indie was the only one who noticed. Her full, soft bottom lip pulled through her teeth, her gaze curious and unsure. I was sure everyone had gone quiet, there was no way the people at this table couldn't feel the tension. It coiled in every one of my muscles as I bent down to grab my gym bag.

When her eyes met mine again, I'd found my breath, and I gave her a secret smile before I spoke to no one in particular. "I forgot, I've got to meet one of my professors before class."

"The teaching assistant job?" Royal asked, and I nodded as I threw my wrapped burrito onto his tray.

"Teaching assistant?" Dev asked.

"I'll let Royal fill you guys in." I raised my chin, and Indie's lips spread into a quiet smile of her own. "See you later."

I'd addressed her and her alone, but I didn't think anyone noticed.

Before I could leave, Royal asked, "Dinner after practice tonight?"

"I might have to work."

"Let me know."

"Will do."

I didn't chance another look in her direction, and waited until I was outside to pull my phone from my pocket.

Me: Swim lesson tonight.

162

I was almost down the stairs before my phone chirped.

Indie: I told you I didn't have a suit.

Me: That clothing store, north of Stacks on Beech Street sells suits. This is a lake town, you know.

Indie: What time?

Me: Eleven. I'll meet you at the studio so you don't have to walk alone.

Indie: I'm feeling nauseous.

Me: Don't punk out on me, O'Connell.

Indie: I'll see you at eleven.

I didn't get a chance to smile at my win because my father's name flashed across the screen with an incoming message.

Dad: No plans for this Sunday, why?

The team had a meet this Saturday, which meant no Sunday practice. My mouth was dry as I typed, the pain in my shoulder flaring more in this instant than it had in days.

Me: We need to talk.

Indigo

Daphne rummaged through her backpack, her music manic as I walked into our room. She had clothes piled and spilling off her small, twin mattress. She'd warned me on the first day I met her she lacked the "organizational code" in her DNA, but this was bad, even for her. I scanned the chaos and noticed two more suitcases sprawled on her bed, and her side of the closet was empty.

"Going somewhere?" I asked as she stuffed a few articles of clothing into her bag.

She glanced at me, peering over her shoulder, a deep frown on her face. She looked more awake than I had seen her in days. Actually, I hadn't seen her for a couple of days.

"Yeah, I was invited to Greek Row for the weekend." I would've known she wasn't serious even without the snarky attitude.

I sat on my bed, staring at her back as she picked through a pile of tank tops. Setting my bag at my feet, I sighed and her posture stiffened.

"Spit it out, Indie. Subtlety isn't your thing." Daphne turned, giving me the full force of her appearance.

She was gaunt with dark circles under her eyes. Her hair was wet from what I assumed was the shower, the lack of makeup on her face made her seem even more pale than normal. She looked thin and weeded through. Gray draped over her silhouette, not an ounce of color left in her.

"Did I... do something to make you angry?" I asked.

Her shoulders sagged, tears pooled on her bottom lashes. She shook her head and swallowed. "No, Pink. I'm not mad at you."

"Talk to me. What's going on?"

Like I hoped she wouldn't, she turned and grabbed a handful of clothes, shoved them in her bag, and zipped it.

"Where are you going?" I asked again.

She sucked in a breath, or maybe a sob, she wouldn't look at me. My eyes filled with tears as I stood.

"Don't touch me. If you touch me, I won't leave this room, and I have to leave, Pink. I have to go."

"Go where?" I asked, feeling the hand of panic on my throat.

She swung her bag over her shoulder and looked at the bed. "You can keep whatever I left behind."

"Daphne, you're freaking me out."

She took a step toward me, her hand out as if to touch me, stopping when the front door slammed shut.

"What the hell is she still doing here? Get out!" Imogen's cheeks were red, her face contorted into a sneer. I'd never seen her so upset.

"Don't worry, I'm gone." Daphne shut her two suitcases, pulled her phone from her pocket, and whispered, "Fuck my life."

"Will someone please tell me what's happening?" I asked and earned the wrath of Imogen's glare.

"Ask your junkie roommate."

"For the record, I never liked you, Imogen." Daphne's smile sat wrong on her face. It was twisted in a way that made me think of pain.

Imogen brushed her long, silver blonde hair over her shoulder. "Trust me, the feeling is mutual."

The comment landed without damage, and Daphne laughed as she pushed her cell into her back pocket. "My ride's here."

"You mean your parents, or your dealer."

This time Imogen struck the right chord. "My parents. Asshole. Now get out of my way and stop being a bitch. You ruined my entire life." Daphne's voice shook as she tried to grab both of her suitcases at the same time.

"Your parents?"

"She's been expelled." Imogen's tone bordered on gleeful. "Hopefully, they're taking her skanky ass to rehab."

"Expelled? Daphne, what the—"

Daphne's phone rang and she didn't let me finish. "I have to go. I'll call you, Pink. I promise." She grabbed her other suitcase and I watched as a tear trickled down her face. She was almost to the door when she stopped, her head falling in defeat, she said, "I'm sorry, Indie, I'm sorry for everything."

I didn't get a chance to ask her what the apology was for. She practically shoved Imogen into the wall as she stormed past. The front door opened and never shut.

"She can't even close the front door."

Her hands were full. I wanted to say, but I was still piecing through this train wreck of an afternoon. Imogen exhaled and left my room, I assumed, to close the door. I stared at Daphne's bed.

Expelled.

She was gone.

A few t-shirts and tank tops were scattered on her black comforter. All of her Andy Warhol posters were left behind, too. Maybe she'd left them like bread crumbs. Maybe she'd come back.

Expelled.

"Imogen." I called her name louder than I had intended and she jumped. "What the hell just happened?"

"She got caught buying coke from some guy in Kappa Sig."

"Cocaine?" My bones felt too heavy as I sat on my bed.

"She's been stealing my ADHD meds. I had a whole bottle and didn't realize they were missing. I cleaned out my bathroom bag the other day and they were gone. I'd let her have a couple last semester, so I know she was the only one who knew where to find them. When I asked her about it the other night, she denied it. I told the dean."

My stomach was sick. "Why didn't you tell me? I could have—"

She narrowed her eyes. "Could have what? Helped her? You are so naïve. She needs rehab and I hope to God her parents are taking her there as we speak."

"I didn't see it." That wasn't entirely true. Since the semester started, she'd changed. Drinking more and more, it was why I'd asked Dr. Sand how to help. When I suggested therapy, she'd taken it as a joke, and put even more distance between us. But cocaine? "I guessed something wasn't right... I had no idea it was that bad."

"If I wasn't so angry that she stole from me, I'd feel sorry for her, but she knew what she was doing. After what I told the dean, the campus police were going to pull her in for questioning, but they caught her red handed... it's not my fault."

Addiction was a sickness. Instead of fighting voices, Daphne fed hers.

"I feel terrible for her. Addiction isn't that black and white. Yes, she knew better, but maybe there's more there that we don't know about."

"Her parents were addicts. My boyfriend's roommate told me that last year. The two of them went to high school together."

High school.

I thought about Kai.

"My brother's best friend, Kai, went to high school with her, too."

"Isn't he the one who got Ellis expelled?"

"Ellis got himself expelled."

Her face softened. "I know, I'm sorry, I didn't mean... I'm pissed off. I shouldn't take it out on you."

She was pissed off? My best friend was gone. Using drugs. And I had no idea.

"I've got to go into town," I lied. "Need anything?"

"No, thanks." Her attitude had almost completely cooled. "Want me to walk with you?"

"I'll be okay." I gave her a small smile, and she nodded.

"Ari will be home soon, she's gonna flip when I tell her. She suspected Daph of stealing her necklace last week."

I walked toward the front door, not wanting to listen to any more of Imogen's insights, debating on if I should call Daphne the minute I left the dorm, or Blue to ask him what he thought. Still shocked, I figured calling Daphne would only serve to make me more confused and angry. Not ready for excuses, I decided to call my brother.

The weather was chilly as I stepped outside. It didn't matter that the sun was out, painting the firs in several shades of green, it was February and winter's cold touch still drove the wind. I pulled out my phone and dialed my brother's number. The phone rang as I made my way toward Warren House.

"Hey, Pink." He was out of breath.

"Can you talk?" As soon as I spoke, tears fell down my cheeks.

"What's wrong?"

"Are you home?"

"I'm at the gym."

I heard a few beeps and a soft whirring sound—I hadn't noticed at first—as it fell silent in the background. I sat down on the bench near his dormitory, quickly wiping the tears from under my eyes with my free hand.

"Daphne got expelled for drugs."

"Holy shit, really?"

"I had no idea."

He was silent.

"Did you know?" I asked.

"Kind of, but… She stayed at our place the other night and—"

"She stayed at your place and you didn't tell me?" I was incredulous.

"She was with Kai."

"W-what?"

My pulse tripled, hollowing out my chest, leaving my heart in a free fall.

"I don't know, Pink. She slept in Kai's room, and the next morning she was gone. Kai shut me down when I asked him about it, said she was struggling and to leave it alone."

He's with her.

He doesn't want you.

My throat was thick and dry. "He knew."

"I'm not sure. He did tell me she promised him she'd get help. What happened?"

"She got caught buying cocaine from a frat guy." I fell back onto the bench and shut my eyes.

"Cocaine?"

"That was my reaction."

"I wish we could have helped her."

"Imogen thinks her parents will put her in rehab."

"It helped Aunt Mel."

"Mel wanted the help."

My Uncle Kiernan's wife, Melissa, struggled with drugs when she was younger. Mel had told Royal over break, when he'd asked her about Kai's drinking, "You can't help those who don't want the help in the first place."

"Maybe this will be the catalyst. Kai said they're just friends, but maybe there's a deeper connection, maybe he can reach out to her. I'll talk to him."

"Okay," I said and opened my eyes.

A deeper connection.

The hollow spread to my ribs.

Just friends.

The voices in my head laughed at me.

"I've got practice tonight, but you should come over after."

I was supposed to meet Kai for my swim lesson, but after everything today, watching someone I *thought* was my best friend, walk away, I wanted to be alone. I was unsettled. My head ached and so did my heart.

"Thanks, but I think I'm going to the studio."

"I'm here if you need me. Camden's got a song to write, so I'll be flying solo if you want some company."

"Love you, Blue."

"You know I love you, Pink."

I slipped my phone in my jeans pocket and walked back to Vigrus, my mind spinning through the last thirty minutes. It was selfish for me to think about Kai, with Daphne possibly en route to rehab, but I couldn't help it. I'd come to St. Peter's with the hope I'd find my own way. I was good at being Royal's twin. Good at sharing his smile and eyes. His friends were my friends. Kai belonged to Royal, too, but I'd let myself believe he'd become mine. I couldn't let myself get attached to the idea of Kai more than I already had. Kai Carter had more life experience in his pinky than I had in my entire existence. He had a reputation. He was a man, and I was girl. It didn't matter if he was the only guy I'd ever thought about kissing, or how his smile made the voices disappear, how his attention had set me on fire. But that was him. Who *he* was. I wasn't special. How many girls had he struck like a match?

Naïve little girl.

He never saw you.

Ari and Imogen were in their room when I got back, I could hear Ari's voice over the music playing in my own. I shut my door and turned off the clock radio Daphne had left on. I let a few minutes pass, waiting for Imogen and Ari to crash through my bedroom door, ready for gossip. But the apartment was quiet. I started to fold the left-over things Daph had left behind, creating a neat stack on the center of her bed. I checked her two drawers in the dresser we shared and found more abandoned clothes. She probably wanted a new start, new things for a new life. Hopefully, a clean one. I pulled what looked like a sports bra and underwear from the back of the top drawer. The dark red material like a sign from the universe dangled from my hand. I puffed out a laugh and stared at the bikini. It still had the tags on it.

Slipping off my shoes, I threw the suit onto the bed. Daphne had once said Kai wasn't my type. She wasn't entirely wrong. I'd never had a chance to develop a type. I didn't know what I liked. I could see a guy and find him attractive, but no interest was sparked. Kai was my type. Him. His loyalty to my brother. His mystery. I smiled. And maybe his body was perfect, too, but in the studio, he'd showed himself to me, cracked open his façade and showed me he understood the dark as well as I did. My physical attraction to him shouldn't stop me from being his friend. He trusted me, and I needed to trust myself. Trust what I wanted. And I wanted him in my life. I wouldn't let this thing with Daphne, my self-doubt, those voices, undermine what Kai and I had started to build so easily.

Before I could talk myself out of it, I tried on the bikini.

It was five after eleven when Kai showed up at the studio, wearing his faded SPC swim team hoodie and a smile that made my knees feel gooey.

"You're looking a little sick, O'Connell. Don't worry, I won't let you drown."

"That's good." I picked up my bag, the red bikini burning a hole through it, or more like my nerves.

"Got everything you need?"

"Yup."

Kai's grin lightened his eyes and I smiled in response. Leaning down, he touched my shoulder; the small sensation sent a thrill down my arm and erased my doubt about deciding to go through with this. "I promise. You've got this."

The sky drizzled down around us as we walked to the Aquatic Center in a comfortable silence. I wondered if Royal had mentioned Daphne to him? It felt intrusive to ask, but she was my friend, and anything he might know that could help her was worth it.

"Did you hear about Daphne?"

"Yeah." His jaw flexed as he looked at me. "Royal said you were pretty upset. I should have texted, we don't have to do this tonight."

"It will be a good distraction."

His chuckle surprised me. "You'd rather be painting."

"You sound like a bumper sticker."

My favorite lopsided smile appeared. "I'll make you a shirt."

The Aquatic Center loomed ahead of us and I lost my humor. He must have noticed.

"I'm sorry about Daphne," he said.

"Royal said you were trying to help her?" I asked, keeping my eyes on the front doors of the building.

He punched a code into a small metal box right off the entrance. A soft click sounded, and he pushed through the door, holding it open for me.

He paused inside the large, empty lobby, his dark eyes finding mine. "I should have said something to you the other night. She stopped by, she was strung out. I was afraid to let her leave. I told her if she stayed I'd take her to the clinic in the morning, help her make an appointment, but she snuck out sometime in the night."

"I didn't realize you guys were... close." I wanted to cringe at my reluctance. I couldn't care who he was *close* to.

His jaw pulsed again and he turned toward the hallway by the front desk. "I've known her since we were kids."

"I know."

"I should have told you."

"She should have come to me, I'm her best friend."

He looked at me, his eyes darker than they were just seconds ago. "A girl like Daphne has only one friend. Herself."

"I'm angry, too." I wanted to reach for his hand, but I was afraid he wouldn't want me to.

"Good thing you have a distraction." He smirked, lightening the mood as he twisted my earlier words. "The women's locker room is to the right, down the hall. You can enter the atrium from there." He pulled my braid. "Don't try to sneak off, O' Connell."

My laugh was uneasy as I watched him walk toward the men's locker room. I wanted to run, but not because I was afraid to swim, but because of the suit in my bag. When I tried it on, it fit better than I had expected. The top was tighter than I would prefer, my curves bigger than Daphne's but smaller than the world's standards. I worried about what he would think of my body as I walked into the locker room. The lights flashed on automatically, illuminating a wall of mirrors and rows of lockers. I set my bag down and stared at myself. I saw the women he used to flirt with at Stacks when he'd worked there. Tall with slim waists, curvy hips, and more in their bras than Daphne and me combined. Compared to them, I looked like a boy.

It was too late to back out now.

I changed into the dark red suit, clipping the strap behind my neck. It really did look more like a sports bra than a bikini top. My skin was translucent under the fluorescent lights, and my eyes trailed along the line of my reflection in the mirror. My hips hardly flared. An hourglass I was not. My thighs were lean, not necessarily sticks, since they touched toward the middle. I had no abs, and I hated that the suit was cut so low. My hip bones jutted—too prominent—reminding me I probably needed to add more protein to my diet. I stared at my boyish figure and wrapped my arms around my chest.

He'll break you.

So delicate.

My thoughts hissed and hummed until my eyes started to burn.

I should leave.

"You get lost?" Kai's voice echoed through the locker room.

The pool door was hidden behind a row of lockers; he couldn't see me as I called back, "Almost ready." His laugh lingered after the door shut. I threaded through my braid with fast fingers and pulled my hair into a tight bun. I avoided the mirror as I folded my overalls and set them on the bench. Without another glance, I exhaled.

"Here we go."

I watched him as he finished his lap. The open atrium was warm and humid against my bare skin. The water splashed onto the tiled and concrete surface surrounding the regulation-size pool. I'd always observed from the safety of the bleachers. The pool seemed endless from ground level. It disappeared into the horizon of the huge, three-story floor-to-ceiling windows on the opposite side of the room. He moved through the water with grace. Elegant and violent, sharp and fast, I lost my breath watching him. My suit pushed against my breasts as I tried to breathe, the rise and fall of my chest more dramatic with each inhale and exhale. Stepping close to the edge, I waited.

He stopped mid stroke, his body breaking free from the water. His tan, wet, skin more real this close. The size of the pool wasn't the only thing distorted from the height of the bleachers. His shoulders seemed massive. The cut of muscle in his arms, his chest, dripping under the surface of the water. I lifted my eyes to his, heat flaming in my cheeks and neck as he stared right back.

Kai

W*ow.*
The word repeated in my head.

Don't say wow.

I had to remind myself how to breathe.

Christ.

Take a breath.

Skin. Too much pale, flawless, endless, smooth skin.

Don't say it.

"Wow." It whispered through my lips anyway.

"What?"

"Hi." I forced a smile.

Draping her arm around her waist, Indie's smile had a nervous edge to it. "Hey."

This was the worst fucking idea I have ever had. That suit. That goddamn red suit hid nothing as she leaned to sit on the pool's edge, exposing a modest amount of cleavage. Unsure of the water, she kept her eyes down as her feet slid into the pool, and my swallowed words stayed stuck in my throat. I watched as goosebumps trailed up her limbs, her nipples hardening under the fabric of her top, I tore my eyes away.

Tension weighted me in the water. Let me drown and never again think about her in red. Never again think about how soft the flat plane of her stomach would feel under my palms. How delicate her hips would be in my grip. How much I wanted her elegant legs wrapped around my waist, hidden under the surface of the water, chest to chest, close enough to feel the gentle push of her body, of those nipples, her breasts, understated and perfect. Made with elusive lines, her shadow small, she'd fit—snap into place—against my stubborn stone.

"I'm kind of terrified." She laughed, gripping the pool wall.

I had to say something, had to pull my shit together. This was Royal's sister, not some girl I should've been perving out about. The thought killed any burgeoning heat, and like I'd dipped my balls in a bucket of ice, I found the words I needed to say.

"Do you think I'd let you sink?"

Indie glanced at me, her golden lashes hiding the full color of her eyes as she chewed the side of her cheek. "No."

"Then jump in." Finding my breath, I smirked as her eyes widened.

"No way."

"It's the shallow end, O'Connell."

She pressed her lips together, her smile fighting to escape.

I wanted to close the distance, take her hands in mine, and pull her in, but I didn't trust myself. To see her like this, practically naked, in her simplicity, no makeup, no artifice, most likely with paint still under her nails, stunning. I had to picture something, anything, glue Royal's face to hers to stop myself from getting hard. My suit was less than forgiving to the casual observer on my best days. An erection would be like a neon-freaking-sign tonight.

"Come here."

She shook her head.

"Indie."

Her cheeks went from porcelain to pink, and fuck it, I loved the reaction.

"Are you going to make me drag you in here?" I asked and took a tentative step toward her through the water.

She laughed again, curling in on herself, she held out her hand to caution me. "You wouldn't."

"Obviously you don't know me very well."

"Kai," she warned, but I didn't listen.

I lowered my body the rest of the way into the water and slowly swam toward her.

"Don't you trust me?" I asked, trying to sound as serious as possible.

"Not at all."

This was the worst idea I'd ever had, and maybe it was some basic need inside me that had to touch her, that drove me to the wall of the pool, that watched the pupils in her eyes dilate as I stood in front of her and said, "If you didn't trust me, you wouldn't be here."

Indie's lips parted, and I tried not to watch the rise and fall of her chest as I reached for her waist. I swear she stopped breathing altogether as my fingers found purchase on her skin. She was soft and warm, and as I lifted her from the edge, she grasped my shoulders, holding on to me for dear life.

I let my hands linger, even as her feet touched down on the floor of the pool, keeping a few inches between us, I promised, "I won't let go until you're ready." I heard her suck in a breath, her fingers flexing against the muscle in my shoulder, she shivered. "Are you cold?"

"A little." She looked up at me with a fragile smile.

"We should keep moving, let your body adjust to the temperature."

"Okay."

Releasing her, I said, "You can't learn to swim until you learn to float."

"Float," she repeated, her hands still holding me like I was a raft.

Gently, I took each of her wrists and lowered her arms. Her spine stiffened, and I smoothed the pad of my thumb over the back of her hand. "Trust me."

"I do."

I'd never been this close to a girl without it leading down an explicit road. Every part of me wanted her, wanted to pull her body against me, but Indie wasn't what I was used to. She was the promise of something better, something more, even if I had to force myself to keep it platonic, she was worth the acute pain.

Don't cross the line.

181

I slid my hands up the length of her arm, turning her to face the side of the pool. Letting go, I brought my palm to the small of her back and said, "Lean against my hand."

Every touch was like dragging my skin through the hot flame of a lighter, a battle for control. My fingers trailed along her spine a few inches higher, resting on the clasp of her suit.

"What now?" she asked, a shudder in her voice.

"You make it sound like I'm getting ready to murder you."

She grinned. "Maybe you are?"

"Murder by drowning. Harsh."

She splashed me with a wave of water and I coughed as I inhaled it on a laugh.

"Not funny."

"I was running interference," I offered once I caught my breath.

"Interference from what?"

I didn't give her time to think and scooped her into my arms. Her scream echoed through the giant room. She struggled as I tried to cradle her legs.

"Indie, I've got you."

She went still as I pulled her closer to my chest, her legs relaxing over my left arm. She brought her hands to her chest, trembling, she rested her chin on her knuckles.

"I feel stupid."

"Don't."

"I'm like a little kid."

"Trust me, you are not." I wished the words away as soon as I said them.

She stared at me. "I'm trying to figure out if you just called me fat."

I chuckled, and the fear evaporated from her eyes.

"Definitely not fat."

She didn't say anything, and the silence pulsed around us, heating my skin and hers. I realized I was tracing idle circles with my thumb between her shoulders blades and stopped when her face flushed.

"Still nervous?" I asked, trying to quietly step back over that imaginary line without being noticed.

"Not as much."

"Good. Because in order to float, you have to be calm."

"Floating in a pool is the least relaxing thing I can think of."

"Lean all the way back." Her eyes widened. "I'll hold you up until you're ready."

"You swear."

"I swear."

Indie hesitated, and I was the total asshole taking advantage, stealing as many touches as I could, placing my hand on her lower back, and drawing calm fingertips across her skin. She relaxed under the touch and let herself fall backward as I guided her in the water. My right arm was under her shoulders as my left skirted dangerously close to the swell of her ass. She'd closed her eyes, and I was free to stare at her, admire the way the water absorbed into her silhouette, the way the stray wet strands of her straw-colored hair framed her heart-shaped face. Beads of water trickled down the front of her neck, on the tops of her thighs, her stomach, and my mouth went dry as I thought about tasting her, tasting each one of the drops warmed by her skin.

I was dying. Indie had come here thinking she would drown, but I was the one fighting to keep my head above water.

I moved my hand to the center of her back, letting the space between our bodies widen, and her eyes flew open. "Don't let go."

"I won't. I'm giving you some room."

"I don't need room."

I couldn't help it, I laughed. "Just listen. Hold your arms out. Let them float, too."

Reluctantly, she did as I'd asked. I shifted my hold, taking the weight of her torso with my left hand, and letting her neck rest in the palm of my right. Her legs began to sink.

"You need to relax."

"I can't."

"You can." I kept my voice low and steady, and her skin prickled as I pressed the tips of my fingers softly along her neck, her pulse. "Close your eyes." She watched me for one, two seconds, before her lashes fluttered closed and gave in. "Think about something, think about art…"

More time passed in silence, the quiet rhythm of her breathing the perfect soundtrack. I could tell the moment she'd stopped overthinking, her body weightless and buoyant with ease. I kept my hands as motionless as possible, barely touching her, letting the water take over.

184

"Am I floating?" she asked, breaking the spell as her body dipped back into my hands.

My laugh was quiet. "You were. Stop thinking about it."

"Kai?"

When I looked down again, her eyes were open. "Yeah?"

"It's not very relaxing... being inside my head."

"Are they worse... when you're stressed out?"

She closed her eyes, and I wondered if I'd embarrassed her.

"The voices? Yes."

"I'm sorry, I didn't—"

Blue eyes found mine. "Don't be sorry. It's not your fault."

"It's kind of my fault. I'm making you do something you hate."

"I can't live in a bubble." Her lips spread, her smile reaching her eyes right before she closed them.

"Does it help to talk?" I asked.

"Sometimes."

"Then tell me something."

Her fingers dusted against my bottom rib, but I was sure she hadn't noticed. I noticed though, and my heart thrummed inside my chest.

"Like what?"

"I don't know, a memory? Something you don't usually tell people."

"I already told you about my voices."

"You're more than your voices, Indie."

She kept her eyes shut, and I watched as she swallowed.

"Before Royal and I were born, my dad and his two brothers renovated the apartment we live in. It's really nice, kind of like a loft. Industrial. We have our own studio and everything."

"Sounds cool."

Indie let her arms sway in the water as she continued, her body like a feather in my hands. "I think I was nine or ten, Royal and I had wanted to have a sleepover, and I remember I woke up because I was cold. It had snowed all day, white, white, white, and Royal had stolen all the blankets." Her laugh felt almost private. "There was music playing, and I followed it down the hall to the studio. I heard my dad laughing, and it was so rare. He smiled all the time, but he was laughing, full and open, and it pulled me to the door. I didn't want to get in trouble for being up late so I cracked it open as quietly as I could."

"What happened?" I whispered not wanting her to realize she was floating all on her own. I wasn't even touching her anymore.

"Nothing. I mean, nothing anyone else besides me would notice, but it had been the biggest moment of my life. I opened the door and my mom was wrapped up in my dad's arms with her head leaning back, smiling as he buried his face in her neck. He had red paint all over his chest and arms. It was on her pants and in her hair. The painting behind them was covered in what seemed like a thousand different shades of red. It was the safest I'd ever felt. It wasn't anything more than an embrace between two people, but I felt it, I felt the color red as it filled my heart, and maybe it was the beginning of my illness, but ever since then everything has a color."

Red.

Like her suit.

"Everything?"

"Everything."

"What color am I?

"Violet."

Violet.

Bruised.

She opened her eyes.

"You're floating."

"Oh my God."

I took a few steps back and let her drift in the water on her own.

"Kai, don't let me sink," she said, the panic in her voice palpable.

"Stop thinking."

"Kai?"

"I'm right here." I reached for her, touching her back with my palm. "See, I told you. I've got you."

She moved before I could stop her. It all happened too quickly, and in hindsight, I probably should have warned her that we'd drifted toward the center of the pool. It was deeper here, and with how short she was, there was no touching bottom when she tried to stand. Her head went under only for a second before I grabbed her waist and pulled her toward me. Indie's legs enveloped me, her arms clasped around my neck as her breasts crushed against my chest with each frightened breath. If she wasn't so freaked out, I might've enjoyed this for a second, but she'd buried her face in my neck, and I hoped to God she wasn't crying.

I rubbed soothing lines across her back with the heel of my palm as I walked us toward shallow water. "Shh. You're okay."

Trembling hands fell to my shoulders as she pulled away enough to look at me. Her irises were blue flames against her pale skin. "I'm not crying." Indie shoved my arm, her legs winding around my body even tighter, drawing us closer together. "You said you wouldn't let me sink."

"I told you to float."

Her mouth was maybe three inches from my mouth. Each breath we took shortened the distance for two agonizing seconds, and I watched with envy as a rivulet of water dripped over the curve of her lips. I clenched my jaw, imagining what it would be like to lick them, to bite with soft intentions. Her fingers were a hot brand, and I was driven by reckless need as my hand slipped lower than it should have, the tip of my thumb teasing the waistline of her bikini. The humidity of the room was electric, heavy, and as I leaned in, her eyes fell to my mouth. She exhaled and it tickled my lips. Every hair on my body stood with the static of her. Her scent surrounded me, mixed in the air with the smell of chlorine. I could kiss her, and by the way her heart thudded inside the crook of her neck, I could convince myself she wanted me to, tell myself lines were meant to be crossed, but I'd already messed up enough for one year.

"You can put your feet down now."

Indie met my stare, her eyes glassy as she found her footing. The pull between us snapped like a rubber band stretched to its limit.

Letting go of her waist, I pushed a wet piece of hair from her forehead. "I'm sorry. I didn't mean to scare you."

She exhaled and it stuttered past her shy smile. "I really floated?"

I nodded. "All by yourself."

"Can I try again?"

"Yeah?"

"You can't let go, Kai, ever."

"I won't."

"Swear on something."

"I swear on Chinese food."

"Now that's a promise."

Her laughter washed over me as she raised her hands to my shoulders, and I thought, with the brush of her fingertips on my skin, I understood what it meant to feel red.

Indigo

My palms rested on the surface of the water, my arms extended, I floated. Left alone inside my head, all I could hear was the thundering beat of my heart. I was grateful Kai had only switched on a few of the lights; the dim fluorescence seemed to illuminate the water from underneath, affording me a thin veil to hide behind. I'd like to pretend he hadn't noticed the effect he had on my body. Melting every nerve, sending a flash of heat down every limb. Silent in the water, his touch hot against my thighs, my arms, my back, every part of my body wanted to know his fingerprints. I only hoped the blush blooming in my stomach hadn't made its way to my face. He was too close to miss it. Even with my eyes shut, it was next to impossible to try and picture anyone else in this pool with me. The scent of his damp skin heightened the smell of his soap, and the warmth of his breath dusted over my cheeks as he exhaled.

"I want to ask you a question, but don't answer it if it's too personal." The butterflies in my stomach took flight at the sound of his voice.

"Okay."

I kept my eyes closed as his hand trailed up my thigh, holding my breath as he skirted around my backside, following the line of my hip to the small of my back. My pulse was alive in places I didn't even think I had a pulse. I inhaled, hoping he didn't notice the army of goosebumps scattering across my belly.

"Does it bother you... that Royal doesn't hear voices, too?"

"No, I wouldn't want that for him."

"I think you're the stronger one."

I opened my eyes and found him staring down at me. Kai's wet hair was slicked back, all the angles of his face, his sharp nose, solid chin, his jaw cut by the stormy gray shadows from the low overhead lighting.

"Strength is defined in many ways, our experiences are different."

"Not by much, you were raised equally?"

"Yes."

"Then your experiences are the same. But you have this constant internal thing... He got off easy."

I smiled as his brows dipped into a serious V.

"You know that's not true."

I brought my feet to the pool floor and immediately wished I hadn't. Kai dropped his hands into the water, and I shivered at the loss of his heat.

"Because he's gay?" he asked.

I shook my head. "Because... his love isn't accepted everywhere he goes. My voices are mine, private, no one sees them like they see Royal and Camden. When they hold hands, or kiss, they're judged. If I ever date anyone, I won't have to worry about who's watching."

"If?"

I turned my eyes toward the clock on the wall, dipping deeper under the water until my shoulders were covered. Making myself as small as possible, hiding behind that imaginary veil, I said, "I... I've never dated anyone."

"Never?" he asked, his tone scratchy and disbelieving.

"Never, ever." I gave him a small smile, but wouldn't look away from the clock.

"Never." He whispered more to himself than to me.

I told myself it didn't matter what he thought, but I looked at him anyway. He ran his hands through his hair, and I watched as the muscles in his arms, his biceps, tightened and relaxed with the motion. He was sculpted and perfect and had probably dated a million girls. I wished for my overalls and paint brushes, my studio, my armor. What was happening between us? Was I like a sister? A friend? More? He'd said I was strong, but he didn't understand that the demons in my head fed on the emptiness in my life. My foundation was weak, but I'd been taught to never give up, never stop building.

He flicked the water with his fingers, his lips curling up on one side, he asked, "So... does that mean..." Kai's throat bobbed. "I mean, if you've never been on a date, then..."

He let the question fall into the abyss where all stupid boy questions go to die, my stomach fell with it. "No."

"No?"

I tried to float on my own but couldn't, taking a giant breath, I sank under the water. My head filled with muted sound, like cotton stuffed inside my ears. The water blue and clear, sucking me in. I didn't necessarily want to drown, but it was better than answering that damn question.

Kai's powerful hands grabbed my waist and pulled me above water. I inhaled too soon, coughing. "Shit, Indie, are you okay?"

"Yes, I—" I couldn't think, let alone speak. For the second time tonight, his mouth was inches from mine. His coffee-colored eyes searched my face, looking for any sign of distress. "I'm fine," I promised.

I blinked heavy wet lashes, and the droplets of water landed on my lips. Kai's pupils dilated as I licked them away, his jaw tight as his fingers dug into the skin of my hips.

"I thought you were trying to drown again." His low, gruff tone resonated in my bones, down to my knees. "You're okay?"

"I'm okay."

He let the grip of his fingers relax.

Don't let go.

The voices scratched little laughs inside my temples, but I ignored them, too preoccupied with the way his hands lingered.

Every breath he took dusted his bare chest against my body. Violet and blue, watercolors brushed on a moment. Honest. Skin and hands and mouths, this was how it was done. Knowing a person, reaching inside to figure them out. Uncomfortable questions, embarrassing answers. He wanted to know me. I wanted him to touch my face, kiss me, see for himself what I hadn't done.

"I was…" I lowered my chin. "It's embarrassing."

He released my hips, but didn't step away.

"I didn't mean to—"

"It's all right. I shouldn't be embarrassed."

He lifted my chin with the tip of his two fingers. "No, you shouldn't." In my head, this was when he'd lower his chin, press soft lips to mine, and I'd die in that watercolor sea. In reality, he lowered his hand, his eyes worried over mine. "I shouldn't have asked you such personal questions."

"Friendship is personal, Kai."

"I guess it is." His grin made it easier for me to tell him the truth.

"No, I haven't. Kissed a guy. Or anything else that goes along with dating…"

"Huh."

"Shocking." I smiled and shoved his chest.

"More like unbelievable."

I pushed the fallen pieces of my hair into my bun as I said, "I was the weird, artsy girl with a cool brother. I was too quiet to be noticed."

"I guarantee you were noticed. I bet the cool brother had more to do with it than you think."

"I don't know what that means."

The dark slashes of his brows hovered over cool, confident eyes as they narrowed. "It means you're fucking beautiful, and he probably told them he'd kick their asses if they ever asked you out." He shrugged. "That's what I would've done if you were my sister."

You're fucking beautiful.

Beautiful.

My tongue was heavy in my mouth, dry and wordless.

"Ask him. I bet you a drawing he tells you he warned a few guys off."

I laughed, more of a short, hysterical burst as the butterflies tripped over each other in my belly. "A drawing?"

"Yeah, if I'm wrong, I'll draw something for you, and if I'm right, I want a painting of yours."

"Why does it seem like we're always striking deals?"

He chuckled. "Maybe it's the only way I can get you to do what I want?"

"Or believe you?"

"Exactly." He splashed me, his smile broad, full lips stretched wide, reaching the soft creases around his eyes. He was golden skin, golden boy, and I was falling.

Our laughter quieted and I looked at the clock. "It's getting late."

The brightness of his smile lingered as he nodded. "We should go."

"Thank you for tonight, you can rest assured that if I fall into a body of water I will float and not drown."

"This is just lesson one, O'Connell."

"Really, you don't have to teach me."

He gave me a lopsided grin. "There you go again, not believing me."

I laughed and gave in. "When is lesson two?"

"Next week, same time?"

"We have that art history exam. We should study."

"We'll swim and then study after?"

Smiling, I laughed. "How did I get roped into helping you study?"

"I don't need help, but it's always better to study in pairs."

"Is that a fact?"

"It is." Kai pressed his lips together.

"You're probably right."

"I'm always right."

"Mm-hm."

I started toward the ladder, and once I was back on dry land, my fingers started to prune.

"You did good tonight," he said. "Meet me in the lobby, I'll walk you to Vigrus."

"Thanks."

It could have been my imagination, but I thought I felt the heat of his gaze following me until I was behind the locker room door.

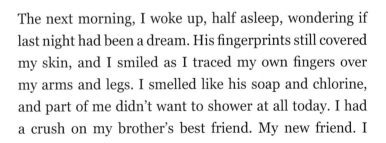

The next morning, I woke up, half asleep, wondering if last night had been a dream. His fingerprints still covered my skin, and I smiled as I traced my own fingers over my arms and legs. I smelled like his soap and chlorine, and part of me didn't want to shower at all today. I had a crush on my brother's best friend. My new friend. I wanted to see every drawing he'd ever created, float in a pool with him every night. I wanted everything I'd never dared to want before and my smile faded. Kai was the guy. The hottest guy at St. Peter's. Even Dev and Corbin talked about his sex life. He'd been the captain of their team. A legend in their eyes. I was the girl who had never kissed a boy.

You're fucking beautiful.

The husky sound of his voice thrummed in my ear, spiking my pulse, and each fingerprint he'd left behind lit like a flame. Maybe friends were all we'd ever be, but at least now I knew what it felt like to burn.

"Shower is open." Ari knocked twice, as usual.

I listened until her bedroom door shut before I stood and grabbed my towel from the back of my desk chair. The light on my phone blinked. A message from Daphne sat in my inbox.

Daphne: Hey. I'm sorry for yesterday. I love you, Pink.

Me: Are you home?

Daphne: For now. I'm taking your advice, about therapy.

Me: Yeah?

Daphne: Monday I'm checking into a treatment program. I want to be better.

A lump lodged itself inside my throat as I typed through a blur of tears.

Me: I want you to get better. I'm sorry I didn't help you.

Daphne: I wasn't ready.

Me: You are now?

Daphne: Yeah, Pink. I think I am.

Me: Can you call me?

Daphne: They'll take my phone when I check in, but I'll call you when I can. For now, it's probably best if I keep my calls for my family. Get my head straight.

Me: Love you, Daph.

She never responded, and I'd hurried through my shower, wondering if this treatment place would actually help her. Ari and Imogen were already gone by the time I was ready to go, and I walked by myself, with a head full of questions, to Beckett for breakfast. I was deep in thought, and when I sat down, I didn't realize Kai was at my table, chatting with Royal and Camden.

I expected him to stand, say he had somewhere to go, but instead he smiled and nodded his chin. "Hey."

A warm flush invaded my cheeks as he turned to continue his conversation with my brother. Camden stared at me.

"Good morning," I said to no one in particular, and Camden's eyes shifted from me to Kai and then back again. Wishing away the blush from my cheeks, I stood and asked, "Anyone want a coffee?"

Royal waved me off. "Already got one, Pink, thanks."

"Sure."

Kai stood, as well. "I'll come with you, I'm going to grab a cup before I head to the library."

I didn't miss the way Camden's perceptive gray eyes flared with curiosity. My brother was oblivious. "See you at practice tonight. Coach is going to kill us."

"He'll go easy, he wants us healthy for tomorrow." Kai raised his fist and Royal bumped it.

With another smile that made my heart skip, Kai followed me to the coffee counter. He kept his eyes forward; his hands shoved in his pockets and asked, "Did you get a text from Daphne?"

"I did. You?"

He exhaled and met my gaze. "Yeah. Looks like she's going to rehab."

"I'm glad." I fiddled with the strap on my bag.

"You think it will stick?"

"I do." I answered too quickly. "Well, I hope."

"Me, too."

We both stepped up to the counter and gave the girl our order. She gave Kai a suggestive grin, and he chewed the corner of his mouth. She was pretty, with dark hair and green eyes. I was envious of her womanly curves.

You're fucking beautiful.

A small smile popped across my lips and stayed there as she flirted with him. He thought I was beautiful. *Fucking beautiful.* That had to mean something. Or maybe that's what *guy* friends said to make their *girl* friends feel good. Kind of like how I'd told Daphne every morning she didn't look tired even when she had. I was so busy sorting through my thoughts I missed when he'd paid for both of our lattes. The girl gave me a dirty look when I thanked him.

"I can pay for my coffee."

"I can pay for it, too."

I huffed out an aggravated laugh. "You know what I mean."

"Actually, I don't. I haven't had my coffee yet, and my brain is literally functioning at thirty percent."

"Why don't you sit with us today?" I asked, taking a sip and burning my tongue in the process.

He turned to look at the table. Dev and Corbin had arrived and were in, what looked like, some kind of debate. Corbin scowled as Dev waved his hands.

"What are those idiots doing?"

My laugh bubbled up my chest. "I don't know, but I'm excited to find out."

He stared at me, his gaze tracing the line of my lips. I swallowed, wondering if he felt it. Felt the string attaching itself to each of our ribs, knotting and drawing us in with each twist. "I'm sorry it took so long for me... I mean... for us to be friends."

"Me, too," I said.

He smiled, and like it was second nature, he toyed with the end of my braid. "I can't go to the studio tonight. I need to sleep for tomorrow."

"That's probably a better plan than painting. We need a win."

"I need it."

"It's yours..." I whispered. "If you want it enough."

He let go of my braid, his eyes distant and fading as he asked, "What if I missed my chance? What if I'm not good enough anymore?"

"You're still their leader, Kai. Always."

His smile was small. "You'll be there, right? With Camden?"

"I might make him stand up and cheer with me."

"He'll love that." He glanced at the table. "I should probably head to the library. I've got a few things to work on before class. I'll see you on Saturday though."

I didn't want to watch him leave, watch as two girls sidled in on each side of him as he walked toward the doors. He was a leader, a magnet, drawing in everyone around him, and I was terrified I'd become collateral damage. The room fell into shades of green as I wished myself into the shoes of one of those girls. Girls he'd probably kissed once or twice, slept with, touched. Skin and hands and mouths. None of it belonging to me.

He pities you.

Little girl.

Little no one.

I shook my head, hating how fast I'd let my own insecurities, the witch inside my head, steal my smile.

Royal pushed his half-eaten bowl of oatmeal across the table as I sat down. "Finish this. Coffee is not breakfast."

"I'm not that hungry." But I spooned a bite of the maple and sugared oats into my mouth anyway.

Royal gave me a knowing smile. It stuck to my bones and made me feel a bit more comfortable in my own skin.

I finished the bowl, listening to Dev and Corbin argue about the relay team they would face on Saturday. It wasn't long before Royal gave them his opinion.

"Do you miss your quiet mornings alone in your room?" I asked Camden, half joking.

"Some days."

"You have a fridge? Get some milk and Cap'n Crunch. He'll never leave your bed."

Camden blushed. "Thanks for the tip."

"Anytime."

Camden nodded his head toward the coffee counter. "What was that?"

"What?"

"You and Kai?" Camden reached and tugged on my braid, mimicking Kai's familiar gesture.

I shrugged, failing at my own nonchalance, I avoided his eyes. "We're friends."

"Since when?"

"Since now, I guess. He's in my art history class."

"Who's in your art history class?" Royal asked.

I sighed. "Kai."

"They're friends," Camden said, a smirk burgeoning at the corner of his lips.

"Since when?" Royal asked, again, unnecessarily.

"He's in her art history class," Camden answered for me, enjoying himself more than I thought possible.

"Who's in her art history class?" Corbin asked and I groaned.

"Kai." Camden hid his smile behind his coffee cup, and I glared at him.

"We're friends. It's not a big deal."

Corbin laughed. "Kai doesn't do female friends, well, he does, but... yeah... you catch my drift."

Royal's iced blue eyes glared. "Corbin, I am not above drowning you today at practice."

Dev choked on his Fruity Pebbles.

"You guys are ridiculous. I'm friends with all of you. Kai, Dev, Corbin, Camden. But I'm wondering now why I bother."

"Pink." Corbin held his hand to his heart. "You push too hard."

My lips broke into an unwanted grin as I shook my head.

"Sorry." Camden gave me a repentant smile.

"I don't care if you're friends with Kai," Royal said, but I heard the way his voice betrayed him. I knew him as well as I knew myself.

"Why would it matter?"

"It wouldn't."

He wouldn't look me in the eye, and I was reminded about what Kai had said last night.

"Blue..." He lowered his coffee cup to the table. "When we were in high school... did you tell guys not to date me?"

His brows furrowed, and he picked at the white paper ring around his coffee cup. "Why would I do that?"

"That's not an answer."

"My friends knew you were off limits."

"Bro code... it's genetically programmed into us at birth," Corbin confirmed.

"Why would you do that? Wouldn't you want me with a guy you trusted?"

"I didn't trust my guy friends with you. I knew what they were like."

"That wasn't a choice for you to make." I could feel the bright orange flicker of anger at the corner of my eyes.

"Pink... most of those guys were d-bags. They were my friends, but there was no way in hell I'd ever let them near you, much less hurt you."

seven shades of you

"Maybe I wanted the chance to decide for myself." I shouldered my bag and pushed out of my chair.

"You're my sister," he said, his jaw set in a stubborn line.

The table was silent, not one of the guys, not even Camden, had taken a breath.

"That's my point. You're my brother, not my dad."

I didn't wait to hear his response, leaving my coffee behind I walked away. Pocketing my anger, I blew out a breath as the cold morning air hit my face and pulled out my phone. I typed out a message as I descended the stairs.

Me: I owe you a painting.

Me: I'm so mad at him.

Kai: Don't be mad. It's a guy thing. Bro code.

Me: Guys are stupid.

Kai: I agree.

I puffed out a watery laugh and wiped the tears from under my eyes.

My thumbs hovered over the screen. I wanted to tell him I missed him already, but that wasn't something you said to a friend, or to a boy with coffee-caramel eyes that made your bones melt. Instead, I tested the water, like last night, keeping my toes in the shallow end.

Me: I never said thank you, by the way. For saying I'm beautiful.

He didn't answer right away, and every second that passed, my heart sank another inch.

Kai: I didn't just say it, I meant it.

I brought my phone to my chest and squeezed it as I closed my eyes. The voices in my head muted as I painted their lips with crimson, sealing them shut. I opened my eyes. I didn't know how to reply without saying something over the top in my haze of red. Choosing to open the string of messages I had with Royal, I typed four words.

Me: Let me breathe, Blue.

Indigo

The entire Aquatic Center erupted as Kai's fingers touched the edge of the pool. He'd won the final race by three tenths of a second. Three. Tenths. It was infinitesimal, it was nothing more than a half of a breath, a lash falling from a fingertip, but in that small measure, the world became his. At least, the world that lived in this room. Every St. Peter's student, coach, and faculty member, including myself and Camden, were on our feet screaming like maniacs. Kai pulled himself out of the pool, his golden skin drenched with confidence as he stood and looked up at the bleachers, raising his right hand above his head, and curled into a fist.

Royal practically jumped him, and the rest of his team followed his lead, chanting, Cap! Cap! Cap! Kai was swallowed into the biggest group hug I'd ever seen.

"I was worried for a second," Camden whispered in my ear, clapping his hands.

USU had held their own in a few of the races, making the four-hundred medley the deciding race.

Three tenths of a second.

"Is it weird I want to cry right now?"

"Maybe?" Camden gave me a crooked smile, the same smile he reserved for Royal, and I poked him in the ribs with my elbow.

My throat felt tight as the guys slowly gave Kai room to breathe. His smile stretched over his face as he pulled his towel around his neck and shook hands with the guys from the other team.

"You have to work on that," Camden said.

Confused, I stared at him, and he nodded his chin toward the pool deck.

"It's written all over your face. You like him." he asked, more of a statement than a question, and my cheeks caught fire.

I bent down to grab my bag, avoiding his eyes. "Like I said at breakfast the other day, he's a friend, Camden."

"This is the same guy who ignored you last semester..." I gave him a dirty look. "Your words, not mine."

"He's also the guy who stood up—"

"I know." Camden exhaled and linked our hands. He squeezed our fingers gently. "He's a good guy."

"A good friend."

"Friend?" he asked.

"Yes, friend. You're as bad as Royal."

I tried to tug my hand from his but he held on tighter. "He's your brother. Isn't that what families do? Worry about each other?"

The guilt bubbled in my chest. I hadn't really spoken to Blue since breakfast yesterday. He hadn't responded to my last text, in a way, doing as I'd asked, giving me space to breathe.

"I was so alone in high school." The bleachers started to empty around us. I shook my head and swallowed, trying not to cry but for completely different reasons now. "Royal has always been bright and shiny, and I've always been on the dark side of his shadow. I know he wants to protect me, but at what point do I ever get to see the sun, Camden?"

Turning to leave, Camden's warm fingers wrapped softly around my elbow. "You deserve to be happy, too."

"Thank you."

"Just be careful. Kai is—"

"A friend. That's all."

Camden's smile was quiet as he nodded. "If you say so."

Did I wish it could be more? On every shade of yellow the stars provided. That didn't mean the universe was going to grant it. I'd lived long enough in the empty light of night to know the stars were liars. Bits of glittering gold spent on wishes long before mine. Dead light in a lost sky.

"I say so."

Camden left it alone as we made our way outside behind the crowd. It would be a few minutes before Royal and the guys finally made their way out of the locker room, maybe longer since they'd won and were most likely getting a congratulation speech from their coach.

The earlier rush I'd felt from the win had faded with the conversation I had with Camden. The silence between us was weird and bruised and I didn't like it.

"I'm sorry," he said as he zipped up his hoodie, the night air cold enough to fog with his breath. "I shouldn't have said anything, it's not my business."

I bumped my hip into his. "I'm basically your sister... I get it. But you don't need to worry about me, and neither does Royal. I'm an adult the last time I checked."

"Okay," he said, linking his arm through mine.

"Thank you." I kissed his cheek.

A few more minutes passed before Royal's team started to spill through the doors in waves. Sherman was one of the first to leave and gave Camden a scathing look as he passed us by. Camden dropped his hold on my arm and shoved his hands into his pockets.

"He's a jerk," I said.

Camden shrugged.

"Sherman is just one person."

"I know."

"Do you?" I asked.

"It's been a rough week. My dad wanted me to come home this weekend."

"He did?" I couldn't hide the surprise in my voice. Camden's relationship with his parents was beyond strained. He'd told me his dad had reached out a few times, but in my opinion, a parent's love was supposed to be unconditional, and what his mom had put Camden through was unforgivable.

"I said no. I'm not ready... to talk to my mom."

"That's your right."

Silver eyes found mine, and the defeat on his face almost crushed me. "You think I made the right choice, then? Not going?"

"If it would've hurt you to go? Then, yes. Yes, I do."

His lips parted into a small smile as I toyed with the sleeve of his hoodie.

"Hey, beautiful." Royal's voice cut through the night air as Camden's smile widened.

I turned toward the building as their lips met, I told myself it was to give them privacy, and not at all to look for a certain someone, but Kai wasn't there.

"Hey, Pink." My brother pulled the hood of my jacket until his arms wrapped around me from behind.

His hug was warm, and I hadn't realized how much I needed it until his familiar scent flooded my lungs. The lump in my throat was sharp. I wasn't used to going a whole day without talking to my brother, avoiding him this morning and this afternoon was childish. Maybe he was right. Maybe I was still that lonely little girl who needed his shadow to feel safe. I turned in his embrace, my cheek to his chest, he kissed the top of my head and whispered, "Breathe."

He held me like that, his arms around my ribs, and all the anger I'd had disappeared. When I pulled away, his smile was my smile again.

"Congratulations on the win."

He pulled his gym bag higher on his shoulder. "Barely, if it wasn't for Kai..."

"Where is he?" Camden asked, looking back at the front doors.

"He's heading back to Rockport tonight to visit his family after he's done talking to Coach." The private smile on my brother's lips made Camden blush. "Feel like playing your new recital piece for me tonight?"

"And I'm going to leave now."

I laughed as Royal tried to grab my wrist. "What? Hang on, let us walk you."

I waved at him over my shoulder. "Still breathing, Blue."

My dorm was quiet as I left the bathroom, cinching my towel tightly in my fist, I closed my bedroom door behind me. Ari was with Gus, and Imogen always spent the weekend with her boyfriend on Greek Row. After I threw on a pair of Royal's old Pioneer Lake High sweats and my dad's faded Joy Division t-shirt, I pulled my hair into a wet knot on the top of my head.

The room felt hollow with Daphne gone. Sterile white despite the blots of color she'd left in her wake. I hadn't packed up her things yet, and made a promise to myself that I would tomorrow. I should've gone to the studio tonight, but I was tired, and worried my fatigue was a sign my mood was changing. Sleep always helped, and I was getting ready to open my laptop and stream something to help me sleep, when my phone rang. My heart did a cartwheel as the number lit up my screen in bright blue light.

"Hello."

"Indie." He breathed my name like I was his saving grace.

Music and loud laughter filtered through the phone. "Kai?"

"Hey, I..." The background noise faded and I could hardly hear, but it sounded like he was talking to someone. "Sorry, it's fucking crazy here tonight."

"Where are you?" I asked.

"Stacks. Are you at the studio?"

"No, I'm in my room."

"Oh," he sighed and I could feel the weight of it through the phone.

"Are you okay?"

He didn't answer.

"Kai?"

"I don't know."

I looked at my face in the mirror, a blank canvas, no makeup, my shower pink cheeks, drowning in my hand-me-down pajamas. I wasn't Stacks appropriate, but I didn't have to get dressed up for the studio.

"Did you want to meet me at the studio?" I asked.

"It's late."

"Come over," I said on an impulse.

The air changed, or maybe it was just the rhythm of my heart speeding its way to an early death as he asked, "Are you sure?"

"Yeah... Yes. Come over. You sound—"

"I'll be there in a few."

"I'm in suite number four-oh-four."

"Four-oh-four."

"Kai, wait," I shouted and winced at the same time.

I thought I heard him chuckle. "Yeah?"

"Let me give you the code for the front doors, you'll need it to get in."

"I already know it," he said, and the line went dead.

I didn't want to think too long about how he already knew the code to an all-girls' dormitory. This was Kai Carter. Of course he knew.

I had ten minutes, not enough time to pull myself together, but enough time maybe to change into non-sleep attire and brush my teeth again. Scanning my room, I noticed one of my bras on the floor and decided to forego a wardrobe change, picking up my dirty laundry instead. Pins and needles invaded the tips of my toes and fingers by the time I finished brushing my teeth, and when I heard the knock on the door, I froze, bewildered and terrified.

"One sec," I called from the bathroom, quickly tapping my toothbrush on the sink's edge and wiping my mouth with a towel.

I can do this.

Didn't you look in the mirror?

The devil on my shoulder fought for the last word, but I took a breath and whispered, "You're fucking beautiful," before I opened the door with shaking fingers.

He was framed by the light of the hallway, his eyes hidden by the ball cap he wore. His black, long-sleeve shirt hugged every muscle on his arms and chest. Kai's jeans, worn and soft, hung low on his hips. His scent surrounded me, spicy and clean, and for a brief moment,

I was lost to the image. I almost missed it. The crack in his façade. The smile he forced to hide the strain in his jaw. The way his hands, usually casual at his sides or in his pockets, were balled into fists at his sides.

"Kai?"

"Can I come in?" he asked, pulling his cap even lower.

I stepped to the side, inviting him in, wishing I could see his eyes. Head down, he stormed into my living room as I shut the door.

"What happened?" I asked, worry taking root in my stomach when he finally looked at me.

His brown eyes were tinted with something I couldn't read. "I fucked up."

"Okay."

"It's not okay." He glanced over his shoulder toward the hallway. "Are your suitemates home?" he asked, keeping his voice low. I shook my head, and he let out a breath. "I was supposed to head back home tonight."

"I know, Royal told me."

"My dad bailed, he fucking bailed... said he had a last minute sale in Iowa, wanted to know if we could just talk over the phone." His laugh was derisive. "I should've known."

I took a few tentative steps toward him. "I'm sorry."

"I had a beer tonight." His brown eyes fell to the carpet.

"Okay."

"Why do you keep saying that?"

"I don't know what else to say. You had a fight with your dad, you had a beer. Are you drunk?"

"It was one beer, Indie."

"Then why are you upset?"

I was less than an arm's length from where he stood, and if I thought it would help, I'd close the distance and pull him into a hug, but this wasn't Royal, or Camden. I had no idea what Kai needed. He was a mystery, a ticking time bomb, and my finger hovered over the switch.

The knot in his throat bobbed, his hands relaxing at his sides, he said, "I don't want to be like him anymore... Drinking away my problems, pushing away everyone who gives a shit."

"You're not like him."

"I haven't had a drink all goddamn semester and then tonight..."

"You celebrated with your team because you earned your win... And now you're here, *not* pushing away the people who give a shit."

I bit the corner of my lip as the hard line of his mouth gave way to a soft, full smile. This smile was raw and broken, but perfect all the same. I'd never noticed the sun spot on his left cheek, and maybe this was the first real smile I'd ever received from him, as well. It defined his angles, his shadows, in ways I could never paint, in a color that didn't exist, revealing a dimple in his right cheek and a small freckle hidden near his hairline.

This was Kai Carter.

Nice to meet you.

"I'm here. With you. Probably shouldn't be."

"If you start spouting bro code I'll kick you out."

Kai's laugh filled the room, his violent purple giving itself over to a lighter shade of blue as he held up his hand. "No bro code, at least not tonight."

"Or ever."

"I make no promises." That elusive and genuine smile remained. "Thanks. For throwing me a rope tonight. I feel like an asshole, dragging you into my drama."

"I don't mind."

"It's late, I shouldn't have—"

"It's eleven-thirty on a Saturday. I'm just lame and had nowhere to go."

Kai's eyes danced slowly over my body, his lips breaking into a lopsided grin. "What the hell are you wearing?"

My cheeks flushed as I pulled at the hem of my t-shirt. "Pajamas."

"You were about to go to sleep... " His good humor dimmed. "Shit. I'm sorry."

"Kai."

He sucked in a ragged breath and avoided my eyes as he moved toward the door. "Thank you... for listening..." His jaw pulsed. "I feel like an idiot... shit... I'm gonna go before I—"

"Stay. You shouldn't be alone."

"I'm a big boy."

"Stay until you sober up."

"It was one beer."

"Stay."

He flipped his cap backward on his head, his eyes assessing me. "We could study?"

"Or... watch a movie. I found an old copy of *Surviving Picasso* at the library. That's kind of like studying."

His chuckle warmed my stomach. I didn't know what the hell I was doing, but I didn't want him to leave. My reasons weren't all selfish. I worried he'd leave, get into his head, and have more than one beer.

"A movie..." he mused. "That will give Royal and Camden enough time to—"

I put my hand over his mouth. "Shh. That's my brother. Girl code." His smile tickled my palm, sending a shiver down my arm.

He laughed as I dropped my hand. "To fall asleep... Get your mind out of the gutter, O'Connell."

Embarrassed, I changed the subject. "Come on. Follow me"

It was weird having a man in my room. Kai's body took up space, laid siege to the calm, and my heart responded. My stomach was heavy with butterflies as I watched him look around and absorb his surroundings. He gave Daphne's side of the room a cursory glance, his gaze shifting to the drawings I had tacked to the wall. I grabbed my laptop while he devoured the small collection of family photos I had hanging over my desk. Royal and my dad at his first meet. Mom, smiling over her shoulder, her hair speckled with blue paint. Dad holding me in his arms, his smile almost hidden by his beard, as I'd buried my eighteen-month-old face into his neck. Royal and I holding paint-stained hands in the studio, we were three at the time.

Kai laughed, pointing at the picture of Royal holding me over his shoulder this past Christmas, Camden blurred in the background. "This is my favorite. You look pissed."

I sat on my bed, and scooted toward the wall. Opening the laptop, I rested it on my legs. "My mom actually caught the shot right as he'd lifted me over his shoulder. I was more surprised than anything."

He stared at a picture of my dad working on one of his tattoo clients at Avenues, in a sleeveless shirt, his ink on full display. "He seems... intense."

"He is... I miss him." The scents of citrus and leather always made me homesick for him.

"It's cool he owns a tattoo shop."

"My Uncle Liam started it."

"You guys look... happy." He spoke as if lost in his own memories, pulling down a picture of me from last summer. Royal had taken it. In the shot, my hair was down, and the sun filtered through the window, obscuring my profile, illuminating my pale skin with an ethereal glow. I remembered looking at the picture and thinking I was weightless, a ghost with a paint brush in her hand. I'd had no idea he'd been in the studio that day until he'd shown me the picture. "I take it back," he said, his low, gravelly voice rattled my bones. "This is my favorite."

Another blush crept along my neck, filling my cheeks.

"The luck of good lighting."

Kai turned, his brown eyes fixed to the knot of hair on the top of my head. He swallowed and looked away, laying the picture on my desk.

"What's this movie about?" he asked, standing at the foot of the bed, his hands deep in his pockets.

"Picasso's love life."

He frowned. "That sounds like a shit idea for a movie."

I patted the mattress next to me. "It will help you understand him as an artist?"

My heart jumped as he sat down. "I doubt it."

"If it's terrible, I'll find something else."

"Oh, it's gonna be terrible," he promised with a smile, stretching his body until his back was against the wall next to me.

Kai's arm pressed against mine, the heat of his body stealing the breath from my lungs as I started the movie. We'd been almost naked together in the pool on Thursday, but here in this room, fully clothed, with buttered light, I noticed him. Everything was drawn out in intense, visible shades and lines. I couldn't stop staring at his capable hand where it rested inches from my pinky, or the curve of his chin, that sun spot on his cheek. The chocolate strands of his hair, peeking out from under his hat, all texture, and I wondered if it would feel soft or coarse sifting through my fingers. I memorized the thick strokes of his eyebrows, the small valley that carved his top lip, the dip of his nose. Kai kept his eyes on the screen, and I marveled at the hollow below his throat, that smooth patch of skin right below his Adam's apple. My fingers ached to touch him, to know his lines as well as my own.

He caught me as he turned to look at me, his lips drawing up at the corners, his eyes trailed over my burning face, my mouth.

His breath was sweet, with a hint of beer. "Are you bored already?"

I shook my head. "No."

Did he realize how easy it would be for him to kiss me if he leaned in one more inch? Coming out of my skin, I turned to watch the movie, and after a while, his body relaxed into mine. It could've been the even rhythm of his breathing, or the warm weight of having someone next to me, but for all of my effort, I couldn't keep my eyes open.

Kai

The light blue glow should have tipped me off that I wasn't in my room. I didn't usually fall asleep with my laptop on, preferring the darkness of a non-distracted submersion. It was overly warm as my eyes blinked open, a soft weight and the scent of lavender attempting to pull me back under. If anything, that signature scent should have jogged my sleep-addled brain, but it wasn't until I shifted to my side, my arm folding over her small waist, that her soft moan filled the room, reminding me exactly where the hell I was. Slender fingers fisted the fabric of my t-shirt, pulling me dangerously close as I breathed her in.

Indie close up, zoomed in, was too much to ignore. Freckles under her right eye. Her flawless palette of ivory. The barely there ridge on her nose. The way her hair seemed almost white at the root. Brows that fell sharp over her eyes. Scared to wake her, I lay there, frozen, in awe of the way the light from the laptop illuminated her golden lashes, wishing I could pull the hair from her bun, wishing I had the right to touch her.

I had no idea how late it was. My only clue the darkness outside her partially open blinds. The five a.m. alarm that I had set on my phone every day, no matter if there was practice or not, hadn't gone off, that was a good sign, but even so, as the question materialized, an empty anxiety filled my gut.

How long would I have here? Next to her? How long would I get to feel this content?

Fine hairs lined her face, and I didn't dare lift my hand to touch them, no matter how much I wanted to. I'd broken all of my rules, but inside this room, lying beside her, stealing time, I couldn't find the will to give a shit about right and wrong.

She'd answered her phone tonight.

Saved me.

I could have, should have, called Royal, or left the bar with Dev. Indie had been the only person I wanted to see, talk to. Her name the only contact I'd been able to muster up the courage to call. Rules be damned, I was happy about how this night had turned out. Even if this was all I'd ever have of her. A memory to remind me my life wasn't always disappointing. If not for her, I might've fallen for my own bullshit, gotten drunk, left my dad a shit-faced, angry, hateful message, and passed out on my cold mattress only to hate myself tomorrow. Watching the slow rise and fall of her chest, having no doubt this was the only place I should be.

"Kai," she mumbled my name, and I almost jumped until I realized her eyes were still closed.

Her lips parted, a breath hot against my lips, and my mouth watered. There's always that moment before you kiss a girl. Should I or shouldn't I? For me, the choice was always simple, I led with my dick. But I had this weird feeling twisting itself into tight knots inside my stomach. Like Indie had anchored herself there, reeling me in, and I had no way to stop myself from feeling it, from wanting her. I knew I shouldn't. Her innocence wasn't mine to take. But, she whispered my name again, and this time I was met with clear, bottomless blue eyes.

It could have been the way she held my stare, or the quiet way she pulled me closer when she noticed our bodies had aligned. Facing each other, side by side—my arm held her in place. Later, when I had more time to think about everything, this night, in coherent sentences, I'd remember the silent question in her eyes. Was this really happening? More than *should I or shouldn't I*. A sense of something *other* between us, this magnetic pulse in our veins. Indie's eyes dropped to my mouth as she tightened her grip on my shirt, telling me everything was now, not later, and my heart became this wild thing inside my ribs, begging, as she leaned in, her nose bumping mine, breaching our poorly built wall, and kissed me with soft, sleepy lips.

It felt right, too much and not enough, as she pressed her small frame against me, tugging the collar of my shirt, and maybe later, I would kick myself for not allowing Indie to ease herself in. But as her eager lips consumed mine, I rolled our bodies, pushing her deeper into the mattress, my lips moving rough and slow, kissing the soft curves of her mouth, coaxing, taking.

Take. Take. Take.

Until she opened for me. Tentative, and with wet lips, she explored my mouth. Her tongue darted, unsure over my bottom lip, causing a low, needful groan to rumble in my chest. Indie's hands instinctively pushed into my hair as our tongues slid together, the heat of her mouth drawing me in. I was hard and hungry and didn't stop to think.

Her scent polluted my better judgment, the easy give of her body beneath me, her fingernails on my scalp, the taste of her mouth, something I didn't care to categorize, all I wanted was more of it. Framing her hot cheeks in my hands, I kissed her top lip, bit her bottom, and smiled when she shivered. Smiling as her hands fell to my shoulders, I rested my forehead in the slope of her neck. Inhaling the powder scent of her skin, kissing the spot beneath her ear, neither one of us using the pause for air as an opportunity to stop, to raise a red flag. Indie touched her lips to my cheek, my jaw, and as I lifted my head, she bit softly at my chin, placing a tender kiss afterward. Like a masochist, I pressed my hips into hers, dying from the pain of it, half needing relief from the friction, half hoping she'd feel the ache, too. The pad of my thumb pulled a slow line over the seam of her lips, her chin—her cheek, as Indie watched me. The fascination in her eyes, giving her what she'd never experienced, and watching her feel it was something I could easily become addicted to.

Her smile broke across my lips as I kissed her again, this time with less hunger, more wonder than anything else. Her chin red from my stubble, she gazed up at me, flawless and pink. I took a slow breath, pulling her taste into my lungs, and dropped my face into her neck. Her lashes tickled my cheek as she turned toward me.

"We fell asleep," she whispered, the shy smile in her voice evident.

Chuckling, I said, "Please God, don't tell me I'm dreaming."

"You're not dreaming." Her fingertips trailed down the back of my neck, and I suppressed a shiver. "I'm sorry."

The vulnerability in those two words shook me.

I lifted my head, moving a strand of hair from her cheek, I said, "Don't be. I'm the one who should be apologizing." Confusion wrote itself across her brows. "I stole your first kiss."

"I kissed you." Her rosy lips broke into another small smile.

Resting on my elbow, I grinned. She seemed... proud.

I argued anyway. "I was overly persuasive."

She laughed, and my pulse came alive as her breasts brushed against me. "You didn't say anything."

"I didn't have to."

She raised her finger to the scar on my eyebrow, the scar I'd gotten while defending her brother.

"Maybe you are overly persuasive." Tracing the raised, ruined flesh, Indie whispered, "I'm glad it was you."

seven shades of you

Her fingertips lingered and I lowered them to my mouth, kissing her fingerprints, I asked, "What do you mean?"

"My first kiss, I'm glad it was you..." She lowered her hand to my chest. "Is that okay with you?"

I wanted them all. Every first she had, I wanted them to be mine.

She lowered her gaze, avoiding me as she said, "I don't want you to regret it. You know... in the light of day." I sat up and rested my head against her wall. She rolled onto her back and brought her hands to the flat plane of her stomach. "It's okay... if you say no... if you wished I hadn't—"

"I'm glad it was me." My voice was thick with nerves I'd never felt before. "I've been dying to kiss you, Indie, fucking dying to touch you..."

Her lips twitched and she pressed her teeth into the skin to stop them from trembling.

"And I don't know," I said. "I don't know what to think... what to do."

"Do you like me?" she asked.

I nodded.

"Do you want to kiss me again?"

The muscle in my jaw flexed as she stared at me. I wanted to tell her I wanted that and so much more with her, but I didn't want to scare her away completely.

"Yes."

Indie's face turned another shade of red, proving I had no fucking business lying next to her, kissing her, touching her. She shouldn't be with someone who'd had

226

a piece of half the female population at St. Peter's. And I was pretty damn sure her brother would feel the same, kick my ass for even tainting the precious skin of her lips. Indie should be with someone as pure as she was, someone worthy of her firsts. Even if the thought made me sick to my stomach, made me want to break this imaginary guy's neck. I couldn't hide from the truth. It's what she deserved, not some townie asshole who had something to prove.

"Then do it." She sat up, arranging her slim legs over mine. "Kiss me, Kai."

I could see her pulse as it fluttered beneath her skin, her pupils opening to a translucent black. I saw myself in her eyes and I liked it. I liked the image reflected. Tangible, whole. In her eyes, I was myself, no longer a fabrication. Honesty and desire. In her eyes, I was worthy, and maybe if I stared long enough, stayed within the crystal clear frame, I could become what she needed.

Taking her face in my hands, the heat of her skin scorched my palms. How much had it cost her to ask me? How much did she have to lose if I rejected her? Like I could ever say no in the first place. I leaned toward her as she closed her eyes. I kissed her lids first, feeling the silk touch of her lashes on my lips. I kissed the crease between her brows. I kissed her like I should have a few minutes ago. Worshiping her purity, her soft skin. I kissed the rise of her cheekbone as she tipped her head slightly, granting me free reign over the planes of her face. I brushed my thumbs along her jaw and stared at her mouth. Indie's lips opened as I kissed them, catching her quiet gasp on my tongue. I decided she tasted like a mixture of mint and sugar, and wondered if she'd had candy before I'd shown up at her door. She kissed me back, her hand wrapping into the collar of my shirt again with a violent tug.

I smiled, and she pulled away. "What?"

I tugged on her collar. "I think it's cute that you're aggressive."

Indie lowered her hand to my chest, and I hoped she couldn't feel how fast my heart raced. "I don't want to be cute, Kai."

"Cute is good."

"Cute is not sexy."

I trailed my knuckles across the new blush forming over her cheeks, following down to her chin and tipping her head so she'd look at me. So she'd believe it when I said, "You make cute sexy."

She pinched her lip between her teeth, shaking her head, she swallowed. "Kissing you makes everything in my head go silent." Indie took a breath, her eyes shimmered as she continued. "It's like a clean slate, a dry canvas. There's nothing but this singular shade of white, so colorless it's asking to be bathed in color... and it feels... I feel..." She blinked, her fingers curling into the cotton of my shirt. "Relief."

The weight of what she'd said lodged itself in my throat. I wanted to be her relief, because she sure as hell was mine.

"That was probably a weird thing to say."

I huffed out a laugh and kissed the corner of her mouth. "Only kind of weird, O' Connell." She moved to shove my chest, but I caught her wrists, pulling her next to me. "I like that you say whatever you want. You say what you mean, I wish I could do that."

"You can."

She smiled, waiting for me to expose some sort of truth about myself.

"All right." I stalled, trying to think past all the negative shit inside my head, when the perfect thing occurred to me.

"Last semester... I had this drawing of my mother I'd sold through Professor Hintz and was in the art building to pick up the money. I saw you there... before I knew you. You were in the hall, whispering to yourself... the most beautiful girl I'd ever seen. You took my fucking breath away. You didn't look at me, walked past me like I wasn't there..." I laughed at the memory. "I thought you were a ghost."

"Why didn't you ever say anything?" she asked, her face a mix of sad confusion.

"I saw you again. That morning at breakfast, and you were *his* sister... and out of principle, I decided to keep my distance." She started to pull away and I didn't blame her. I'd purposely shoved a wedge between us, purposely ignored her.

"You're such an idiot."

"It's how it is, Indie. Between guys. You don't mess with the sister."

"I'm not *the sister*. I'm a human being, with feelings, and it sucked wondering why you never made an effort to be a friend like the other guys, if maybe I was the reason you never stuck around." She lowered her chin. "And now I know."

"It wasn't you, Indie. It was my choice. I could've been like Dev and Corbin, but looking at you every day, being around you... I'd want more... I'd want to be the one who made you laugh, who got to tease and flirt with you, and I knew I couldn't. I knew I'd cross the line... Christ, I almost clocked Camden before I knew he was into Royal, because I thought he was into you."

A laugh bubbled over her lips. "You almost hit Camden?"

I licked my lips and smiled. "Yeah, told him to stay away from you."

She narrowed her eyes. "Like Royal told the guys on his team in high school to stay away from me?"

"Not the same thing."

"It's totally the same thing!" She tried to look pissed but the edge of her lips lifted, giving her away. "What changed?"

Nothing.

I still had no right to be here.

"You invited me over to watch a bad movie and seduced me."

Indie laughed so hard she snorted. "Is that what you plan to tell Royal?" My smile lost its strength and she noticed. "You're not going to tell him... are you?"

"He'd never allow it."

"He doesn't get to dictate my life."

I picked up her hand, running my thumb over the smooth skin of her palm. "Royal and me... everything is tangled up. His boyfriend lives with me. I'm his best friend. He knows me, how I was..." I made myself look straight into her eyes. "How I am... we're finally back to normal after all the shit from last semester... but this... us... he'd never forgive me, Indie."

"Then we don't say anything—"

"Indie—"

She shook her head, cutting me off, "Yet...we won't say anything yet. We can tell him we're working together in the studio, ease him in. Royal knows you, Kai. You're right about that. He knows how loyal you are. How hard you work. How much your friendship means to him. How much your family matters to you. How you almost threw away your future to protect *him*. You like me, and I like you, let's start there and see what happens."

"In secret?" I asked. "That's not fair to you."

"I'm tired of everyone telling me what I need, deciding what is and isn't good for me. Even my own brain, feeding me lies about who I am. I know what I can handle, what I want."

"What do you want?" I asked, taking a few inches of space and stealing one of her deep, rough breaths.

"This."

She kissed me as my morning alarm chimed in my pocket. Her hands in my hair, my palm on the back of her neck, our lips urgent, racing against time. Without breaking away from the kiss, I pulled my cell from my pocket, pressed the side button, silencing the annoying chirp, and threw it on the floor.

I could give her this. *This* I was good at.

Indigo

We'd fallen asleep again, his nose buried in my neck. The blunt pads of his fingertips peeked under the hem of my t-shirt, and as the morning light set the room in an orange flame, I smiled with swollen lips. Stinging from his kiss, from the coarse stubble along his jaw, I dragged my fingers across my chin. I turned on to my side, earning a low groan from the cute, sleepy boy next to me. Kai's large body took up most of the bed, but I wasn't complaining. I'd gladly spend every night trapped by the cage of his touch.

Every night.

I stared at his thick lashes, at the sun spot on his cheek, at the sleep lines created by my pillow, marking this morning as mine, and wondered if I'd get another night like this. Worried when his eyes opened, if the burn of the sun would remind him that I was untouchable. Off limits. And my *every night* would become *never again* and *thank you so much for the movie*, and his *I've been dying to touch you* would fade into *I should have never allowed this to happen*. The doubt set my palm on his chest, and I fell into the simple beat of his heart.

I'd kissed him. I'd kissed Kai and it was every shade of red. Red velvet. Burgundy. Cherry. Candy apple. Crimson. Cardinal. Fire engine. Pillar box. I wanted to keep kissing him, keep moving forward. Uncover unknown shades. Create our own. Keep touching until his heart raced again, until it kept pace with mine. Until the tips of his fingers, barely resting on my stomach, became the flat plane of his palm searching for more of my skin. Until the ache inside me pulsed. Until I asked him to relieve it.

You're empty.

Empty.

Empty.

Empty.

"Hey," he whispered, moving his fingers from my stomach to the small curve of my hip.

His voice closed the shutters on the voice in my head. Leaving the witch without a view.

"Hey." I rubbed my lips together as the pupils of his eyes stretched the coffee color of his irises to a thin circle.

Kai squeezed my hip. "You okay?" he asked.

"Yeah." I bit back my smile, trying to keep myself as casual as I'd been before we'd fallen asleep.

He rolled onto his back, taking his hands with him and yawned. "What time is it?"

The butterflies in my stomach rioted as I sat up, creating more distance from his heat. The room was cold and its temperature invaded my skin, stealing the remnants of his touch. I glanced at the clock on my desk.

"Nine."

He yawned again, sitting up on his elbows his lopsided smile appeared. He was a man at ease. "Nine," he repeated, his voice scratchy and gruff. "I should probably get going." My heart deflated. And maybe he saw it in my expression. As he played with the hem of my shirt, he said, "I didn't mean it like you're thinking."

"What am I thinking?"

Kai sat up completely, his hand on my thigh, he leaned toward me, "Come here." With my back against the wall, I draped my legs over his lap and he kissed my cheek. "I'm not bailing."

"Okay."

"I figured... don't you usually have breakfast with your brother?"

"Not always... it's Sunday. He's probably still in bed with Camden."

"Thanks for that visual, O'Connell."

I laughed. "I do what I can."

He cupped my face, his eyes searching mine, he asked, "Do you have plans today?"

"No."

"You do now."

Kai's mouth was warm, and his taste chased away the shadows as he kissed me.

He pulled away, his lips brushing against my chin as he spoke. "Let's go to that gallery in town."

"There's a gallery near here?"

"No, in Rockport."

"Rockport?"

"Yeah, there's this awesome hole-in-the-wall diner on the way."

"Is this a date?"

"It's art and greasy food." When I didn't say anything, he smirked. "Yes, Indie. I'm asking you on a date. You up for it?"

"Art and greasy food..." I hummed and tapped my finger on my lips. "Do I get to pick the playlist on the way?"

"You can play whatever the hell you want as long as I get to do this whenever I want." He pressed a kiss to my mouth, my jaw, and I shivered. "Let's go on a date," he whispered into what seemed to be his favorite spot, the crook of my neck.

"Okay."

When he lifted his head, his smile crinkled around his eyes. "I'll head to Garrison and shower. Meet you back here in like... an hour?"

"An hour works for me."

A date...

A comfortable quiet descended as we both looked at each other. His dark hair was disheveled, falling over his forehead and curling up a little over his ears. My smile took its time and so did his, starting at the edges with slow grace as we both realized this was happening. We were happening. I had a real date. The lump in my throat formed out of nowhere.

"What will you tell Royal?" he asked, pushing a fallen strand of hair behind my ear.

"I'm going to Rockport with a friend to check out a gallery." It wasn't a lie.

"Close enough..." He shifted and stood, bending to pick up his phone from the floor. "I don't like you lying to your brother. It will make everything worse if—"

"Indie," Ari yelled as the front door slammed.

"Jesus, Ari." I heard Imogen shout in a whisper. "If she was sleeping you probably gave her a heart attack."

"If she's even here." My bedroom door flew open. "See, she's probably with—"

To their credit, neither of them gasped.

Kai chuckled at their wide-eyed expressions as I quickly scooted to the edge of the bed and stood. He ignored them and I wished I could do the same. There was no way to explain why Kai Carter was in my room at nine in the morning without telling them the truth. And what if he spent more nights? That intangible *every night* I hoped for. How would I explain those away?

"I'll pick you up in an hour," he said.

I nodded, and he grabbed his ball cap from my desk, placing it on his head backward, he moved toward the door. Ari and Imogen stepped to the side. "Ladies," I could hear the smile in his voice. "Always a pleasure."

Ari waited until the front door clicked shut before she hit me with her first wave of questions. "Kai Carter was in your bedroom."

"I'm aware." I sank down onto my mattress.

"Why?" she asked.

"He came over last night to watch a movie for class, and we fell asleep."

Imogen laughed. "A movie for class?"

"Yes."

"Kai Carter came here to watch a movie for class?" Ari asked, her full lips pinching into an incredulous frown.

"That's what I just said."

"And he fell asleep?" Imogen asked, and I sighed.

"Yes, *we* fell asleep."

Ari took a few hesitant steps into the room, glancing at my rumpled sheets. Her eyes darted back to my face, assessing me. The longer she stared, the harder it was for me to stand still. I could feel the flush on my cheeks, and Imogen bit her lip.

"Indie…" I didn't like the placating tone of Ari's voice. "This is what he does, you know that, right?" she asked. "He's slept with—"

"I know." I hadn't meant to raise my voice. "I know what he was like."

"What he *is* like." Ari gave Imogen a knowing look and I bristled.

"He's not like that with me. We… we kissed, that's it."

"That's only because he's your brother's friend." Imogen spoke under her breath.

"She's right." Ari sat down next to me on the bed. "About him being Royal's friend." She glared at Imogen. "That's why he wouldn't play her like that."

"Like every girl on this campus?"

"Do you know him?" I asked, and Imogen didn't answer. "Do you?" I asked again, and she shook her head. "I didn't think so."

"Indie, I—"

"Kai is more than his reputation." I picked at the fabric of my sweats. "I like him, and it doesn't matter who he's... been with... right now... he's with me."

"He is?" Ari asked, and when I turned to face her, she smiled.

"I think so. He's taking me to breakfast and this gallery in Rockport."

Ari's tan cheeks flooded with a wide grin. "Shut up, like a date?"

"A real date."

"You have a date with Kai Carter!" Ari started to bounce on the mattress.

Imogen rolled her eyes, but a smile twitched at the corner of her mouth. "You can't wear overalls," she said.

"Why not?" I complained, and Ari giggled.

"Imogen has a point..." Ari stood and rummaged through my closet.

"What about that sweater you wore to that frat party we went to last semester?"

"Yes! Imogen, you are a genius." Ari giggled as she pulled the deep green sweater from my closet and tossed it at me.

"Pair that with skinny jeans." Imogen turned toward the door. "You can borrow my tan booties."

"I'm not wearing... booties."

"You're wearing them." She disappeared down the hall.

Ari grabbed a thin black scarf and handed it to me. "I mean, how did this happen... better yet, when did this happen?"

"It's a long story, and I only have an hour to get ready."

"I want an excerpt."

I exhaled and threw the scarf on the bed. "Grab my dark blue skinny jeans..." I pointed. "Right side of the closet." She did as I asked, and I debated on how much I should tell her, deciding that Kai's personal stuff with the therapist, and his family, didn't need to be a part of the story. "Kai likes to draw, apparently he's really good at it, too. He's sold a few pieces through Professor Hintz."

"No shit?" she asked as she threw the pair of jeans onto my bed.

"True story, he changed his major, and is trying for Hintz's TA spot. I'm helping with the painting portion of his portfolio."

"Helping how?"

"We work together in the studio, and he's in my art history class. We watched *Surviving Picasso* last night, well, before we fell asleep."

"And kissed." She smirked.

I touched my fingers to my lips and managed to control my smile. "I kissed him."

"He obviously likes you if he's taking you on a date. Kai Carter doesn't date."

"My feet are a size bigger than yours, if you buckle them as tight as you can, you'll be fine." Imogen placed her fancy shoes, the ones I never intended to wear, on the floor next to my bed.

"Thank you."

"Of course." She gave me a tired smile. "I'm sorry about what I said... You're my friend and—"

"I understand. And I'll be careful."

"He better be careful, if Royal doesn't beat his ass, Gus will."

"I'm not ready to tell Royal yet."

"He doesn't know?" Ari asked.

"No." I laid the sweater on the bed.

The tension from earlier rolled in like a gray fog. "It's my choice... for now. Promise me you won't say anything. To anyone... boyfriends included."

They were hesitant to answer but agreed after a few long, heavy seconds.

"Don't wear that black scarf. It's frumpy." Imogen ordered, but squeezed my hand before she left the room. "And have fun."

"I got to meet Gus for breakfast, but you should shower first." Ari offered, picking up the black scarf, she examined it again.

"Thanks."

She hung the long black piece of fabric on a hanger in my closet and turned to face me. With a serious look on her face she asked, "Wasn't it you who told Royal he shouldn't have to hide his feelings for Camden?"

Subtle.

"I'm not hiding. I'm delaying."

She tipped her head to my messy sheets. "This is hiding."

"I don't even know what *this* is yet."

Her smile was small. "You know... and so does he."

He won't want you.

Not worth the trouble.

240

I folded my trembling hands over my arms and across my chest after she left. Uncertainty made a home in my throat. Royal was the pair of lungs in my chest. The blood in my veins. The pulse in my wrist. I'd never kept anything from my brother, and what Ari said was true. When Royal and Camden had started dating in secret, I'd told him they shouldn't have to hide their relationship. *A beautiful thing can only stay in the shadows for so long before it starts to wilt.* But this was different. Royal had set up these rules for me, these limitations, without my permission. Maybe he wouldn't care, maybe he'd fist bump Kai and say *take good care of her. I know where you live...* or something equally ridiculous.

He was my mirror.

And I was his.

I studied my reflection in the framed glass hanging on the back of the door.

He'll know.

He'll see it.

I wanted to go on a date. I liked a boy, liked having his hands on my face, his eyes on my mouth, his kisses on my lips. I wanted to ignore the shadows as they gnashed their teeth, expecting payment for my secrets before I even had the chance to keep them for myself. I wanted to be a girl. Just a girl in a car, in a diner, in a gallery, holding *his* hand. A girl who didn't have to take meds every day. A girl with a brother who'd understand, for once, all I wanted was to be normal.

Chapter 21

Kai

Camden and Royal were asleep when I got to the dorm. But I wasn't as lucky as I left the bathroom, fully dressed with wet hair, ready to bolt.

"I thought you were in Rockport with your dad?" Royal asked.

I hated lying to him. I was a lot of things, but a liar wasn't one of them. I slipped on my smirk, choosing to focus on the way he and Camden were positioned on the couch. Both lying down, Camden situated between Royal's legs and resting his back against his boyfriend's chest.

"You guys seem... cozy." I casually slapped Royal's big toe. He was too tall for the blanket he had spread over both him and Camden, and his foot stuck out where it sat on the arm of the sofa.

He didn't smile. "What happened? I thought you guys were going to talk."

"I guess he had more important shit to do."

"Sounds like my parents," Camden muttered.

"He bailed?" Royal scowled, looking far more pissed off than he needed to be.

Especially since I'd spent the night with his sister, and a large portion of my morning making out with her like a freshman in high school. Now, I was about to lie through my teeth so I could take Indie out on a date, without his consent. I was definitely the worst friend on the planet. Most definitely going to hell. I didn't deserve his concern; I deserved to be punched in the junk.

"He had a work thing."

"On Sunday?"

Camden not so nonchalantly elbowed Royal in the ribs.

"Ow, what was that for?"

I laughed as I grabbed my keys from the coffee table. "I think your boyfriend is finally learning social cues."

"You were being nosy." Camden's smirk never ceased to catch me off guard.

"I wasn't being nosy."

Royal leaned down and kissed Camden on the neck. Trying to give them some privacy, and possibly leave without being questioned, I turned toward the door as Royal whispered something into Camden's ear.

"Come to breakfast with us?" Royal asked before I was able to make a clean getaway.

"Can't, I've got plans."

"Don't forget. Coach canceled weights tomorrow and wants us in the pool at the ass crack of dawn instead."

I had forgotten. "Shit, thanks."

He tapped his temple with his finger. "I've got your back."

Grinning, I flipped him off and waved at him one last time before I escaped. Proud I hadn't uttered one lie. Lying by omission could go fuck itself.

The sun was high in the sky, burning the dew off the quad, and thankfully it wasn't freezing inside my car as I slid in over the cracked vinyl seat. The heater hadn't worked since my senior year of high school. Most of the shit in this car didn't work. The wipers were fickle as hell, and there was more rust than blue paint on the hood. I wasn't embarrassed; this piece of shit was a tank and got me where I needed to go. I kept it clean and running, but as I pulled into the Vigrus parking lot, I assessed the passenger seat, trying to picture Indie sitting there, and my stomach turned.

What the hell was I doing? All my bone-deep insecurities manifested again. Wasn't I just stealing kisses and touches? Stealing time from a guy who had a real car and a real future with her. Someone who wasn't fighting the urge to drain a bottle of whiskey every night. Who actually had a plan and didn't derail his life on a whim. I should turn around, park my ass at Garrison, admit what happened to Royal, and get my ass properly kicked. I wouldn't fight back. But I'd texted Indie after I'd gotten out of the shower, told her I was leaving in five minutes. Not showing up would be a colossal asshole move. The idea of hurting Indie was a punch to the gut, more painful than any wrath Royal would rain down on me, much worse than my prideful thoughts about my stupid car.

Pulling my phone from my pocket, I texted her.

Me: Just pulled in, I'll be up in five.

Her response was immediate.

Indie: You don't need to come up.

Me: I should come up, it's the polite thing to do.

Indie: Too late, already on my way down.

I slipped my phone in my pocket and waited. Only a few students dotted the lawn this morning. Most of them looked hung over, or were dressed for a morning workout. I recognized one of the girls as she walked by the car and was glad she didn't notice me. Jesus, I really was a whore. I didn't have enough time to dwell on all the senseless shit I'd done the last two-and-a-half years. Indie emerged from the side door of the building with her lips between her teeth as she eyed the parking lot. Her knuckles were white as she clasped her bag, all her nerves surfacing in the way she kept her head down, her shoulders tight. She had no reason to be nervous, though. The sun illuminated her creamy skin, her pale blonde braid stood out against a bright green sweater, and Christ, her jeans fit her like a second skin. I gulped as her eyes found mine. Was she wearing heels? She took a step and tripped over her own feet. Her cheeks turned scarlet as she shook her head, a shy smile forming on her lips as I got out of the car.

"You okay?"

"I'm fine." She giggled and dropped her face into her hands as I approached. "Hopeless, perhaps. These shoes are a deathtrap." She toed them off and leaned down to pick them up. The light tan boots dangled from her fingertips as we walked toward my car. "A loan from Imogen. I only wore them to make her happy. I have Chucks in my bag."

A laugh burst past my lips. "You could have told her no."

"Imogen doesn't take no for an answer."

"Well, you look hot either way."

Goddammit, did I really just say that out loud?

"Hot?" She wrinkled her nose.

"I'm serious. I like this color on you." I pulled on her braid and chanced taking her hand in mine. I didn't recognize any of the lingering students.

She curled her fingers and exhaled. "Thanks."

I pointed to my bucket of rust. "Sorry about this, it's—"

"A car that runs." She smiled as I opened the door for her.

"On her good days."

All the uncertainty I'd had seemed unnecessary once I was in the car looking at her looking at me. She reached across the console and I met her half way. Her lips tasted like mint Chapstick, and, for maybe a half of a minute, I didn't care if Royal might walk by, or anyone who knew us, all I wanted was to kiss her, taste her, feel this new fullness building inside me, pushing out all the empty like it was never there in the first place.

Indie's lips seemed fuller somehow as she pulled away, and I choked back a groan as she licked them.

She eyed the ancient cassette player. "I don't suppose there's an outlet for my phone?"

I chuckled. "No, ma'am, but if you open the glove box, I have a Bluetooth speaker you can connect to. Just set it on the dash."

Indie put on her paint-covered shoes and worked on getting her playlist to connect as I pulled out onto the highway. It was a forty-or-so minute drive west to Rockport. The coastal town was small and affluent for most, the rest of us lived on the outskirts, scraping by on local jobs and drowning in debt. I planned on showing Indie the better parts of the place I grew up, she didn't ever need to see the rest.

The Bluetooth speaker came to life and she clapped. "It works."

"Most of the time. Won't the music app eat up your data, though?"

"That's okay. I always use the school's WiFi. I have plenty."

A girl with a sweet voice started singing about red balloons. "What is this?"

"My favorite eighties' song. Figured it went with the car."

I laughed, and she smiled, pleased with herself. "This is a '92 Impala."

She shrugged. "Close enough."

I wanted to kiss the smug smile off her face.

"It's a good car."

She ran her fingers over the gray surface of the dashboard. "I like it. I like old things."

"It was a hand-me-down from my dad. He fixed it up when he was still working as a mechanic." I didn't like the wistful sound of my voice, begging for a time that no longer existed.

"Does he still work on cars?"

"Nah, doesn't have the time, I guess. I wish he would though." I don't know why she made it easy to say the things I'd never say out loud to anyone. But when I looked at her, those big, honest, blue eyes asked for the truth. Asked for nothing less. Asked for me... "He was different then. Around more, loyal, loving even. His distance grew with every mile he put between me and my mom, selling shit parts at high prices across the country. Finding new reasons he shouldn't stay home... I used to think it was my mother who kept him away, but over the years, I wondered if it was me, too."

"I don't think it was you or your mom." I kept my eyes on the road as she spoke. "Some people fight their demons by planting roots. And some run away..."

The tone of her voice made my chest ache, and I fought to speak. "You believe that?"

"My dad planted roots, and my mom ran away. They were apart for nine years before they had me and Royal."

"And they're solid now?" I asked, taking my eyes off the road to look at her.

She smiled. "As a rock."

"I don't want to be like him... I don't want to run away from my family."

"You haven't."

No, I hadn't.

But I almost did.

The night with Daphne, the booze, the almost death by asphyxiation. I swallowed past the growing pain in my throat and said, "You're the one who should be a therapist, not Royal." Her laugh hung in the air making the dull interior of the car seem brighter. "Can I pay you in pancakes for our time today?"

"Ha-ha."

I reached for her, keeping one hand on the steering wheel, I laced our fingers together. Her skin was warm and soft, and I tried not to think about how good it felt to kiss her, to have her body molded under mine.

"Royal will be a great therapist," she said.

"You're good at it, though, listening. I'd rather talk to you than Brian any day."

"Then talk to me." Indie squeezed my hand and blushed.

"Can I ask you a question first?"

"Why am I scared to say yes?"

My shoulders shook as I laughed. "Don't be scared."

She blew out a breath. "What's the question?"

"Why don't you ever wear your hair down?"

She leaned back into the seat, visibly relaxing.

"It gets in the way when I paint." She stared out the side of her window. The trees whipped by, smearing the highway in green.

"But you're not painting today."

I had fantasies about her damn hair. Pulling my fingers through it, having it touch my bare chest, feeling it brush against my cheek as she kissed me, pinning me beneath her. Her answer wasn't what I expected and it cooled my heated thoughts.

"I guess I've always just tried to blend in." She whispered something I couldn't hear as she faced the window again.

"Indie." I squeezed her hand. Softly, I said, "Hey… look at me."

She turned, her eyes pale and empty.

"I get it…"

She nodded, color leaking back into her irises.

"What just happened?" I asked, grateful when she gave me a small smile.

"I spend all this energy trying to keep it all quiet, and I'm good at it. Sometimes I'm not."

"The stuff in your head?"

"Yeah. I can't always silence them."

"Did they say something?"

The grip she had on my hand lightened. "The usual stuff. I think every girl at some point struggles with insecurities, mine just happen to be more…vocal." Her laugh was half-hearted. "Can I pay *you* in pancakes?"

"I only take payment in the form of kisses."

"Done."

I let the car drift to a lower speed as the light ahead of us turned red. We rolled to a stop and I rubbed my thumb along the top of her hand.

"Take your hair down."

Indie pressed her lips together, quiet as she considered me, her cheeks flushing with color.

"Please."

She pulled her hand away from mine, and I thought I'd pushed her too far when she raised her fingers to the elastic in her hair and twisted it free. The light turned green but there was no one behind us as I extended my arm over the console, taking her wrist lightly between my thumb and finger, I lowered her hand to her lap. The pulse at the slope of her neck became visible as it quickened, the scent of lavender filling the car. I was drunk with it, with the feel of silk as I ran my fingers through her braid. The waves fell over her shoulder like gold. A river of gold in the palm of my hand. I wanted to smell it. Bury my face in it. Hold it in my fist and kiss her.

Indie's sweater dipped lower than anything she usually wore, her breasts rising and falling as I pulled the thick mass of waves around my fist. "You're gorgeous," I whispered, beside myself, pressing my foot on the brake, I gave in. She lifted her chin, her lips close enough I could almost taste them. "I have to kiss you... right now."

"Right now?"

"I can't help it. You're too fucking pretty."

She laughed and I caught it between my lips. This kiss was different from this morning. The lazy, early hours had dwindled away, leaving behind a brush fire of need. My fingers tangled in her hair, drawing her closer, she bit my bottom lip. Hungry, I pulled away, my jeans painfully tight along the zipper. I took a minute to catch my breath, letting her hair tumble from my grip. The light had turned red again affording us a few more minutes to stare, to come down from our high. It was too soon when she picked up the elastic that had fallen into her lap and put it in the pocket of her jeans. Indie shook out the waves, and I was jealous of her fingers as the signal turned green. Reluctant, I let go of the brake.

I didn't miss the smile forming on her lips as I stole a few glances in her direction. She was like a whole different person with her hair down. It was thicker than I thought it would be, longer, too. It spilled over her shoulders and covered her breasts, sitting just at her waist. She looked older, braver?

Indie held out her hand, and I liked the way her small palm, her delicate fingers, were consumed by mine.

"Thank you," she finally said.

Confused I asked, "For?"

"For making me feel beautiful."

Indigo

"You *are* beautiful," he said, slipping a piece of my hair behind my ear.

My hands lay empty in my lap and I stared at them as I blushed. "Thank you."

A cover of *Every Little Thing She Does Is Magic* played from the small Bluetooth speaker. "I actually know this song," he said.

"I love this version, it's sort of sleepy and blue."

I glanced across the console. Kai's smile was pulled into a dimple as he steered the car left into a rundown parking lot.

Cracked white vinyl siding that had yellowed over time seemed to hang heavy, fighting its own weight, as furry moss grew from underneath the eaves of the house in front of us. Tall firs lined the overgrown lot on either side; their arms reached out and brushed the rooftop in the light wind. *Darryl's* was etched onto a long wooden sign and it hung from the porch by a rusted chain, one side longer than the other, most likely broken and repaired without a proper measurement. If it wasn't for the two other vehicles parked in the lot, and the steam pouring from the chimney, I would have figured the place was closed.

"I promise, the food is phenomenal." Kai watched me with a grin.

"I love it."

He turned off the engine. "They have this ongoing contest... you have to either eat a dozen eggs with all the sides, hash browns, bacon..." Chuckling, he shook his head. "Or a pound of pancakes. It's totally unhealthy but I've always wanted to try it."

"What do you get if you win?"

He bit his lip and ran his hand through his hair. Even under the ivory-colored Henley he wore, I could see the flex of his bicep. "They take your picture and put it on the wall... forever. It's sort of a legendary thing."

The way he'd said forever made me giggle. His dark brown eyes were wide, like a little kid would look at his new toy car at Christmas.

"You should do it," I said.

He laughed. "Today?"

"Why not?"

God, were his eyes beaming?

"Because I want you to agree to another date, and if I eat that much food I'll be terrible company."

"Another date?" I asked, letting the butterflies in my stomach have free reign.

"I hope so." The warmth of his hand soaked through my jeans as he squeezed my thigh. "Stay put."

Kai opened his door and slammed it shut before I had a chance to ask him where he was going. He jogged around the front end of the car and opened my door. He held out his hand and laced his fingers through mine.

"Ready?" he asked, and I wanted to tell him I was ready for anything, as long as he was a part of the equation.

I grabbed my bag with a nod and let him lead the way inside.

The scent of cinnamon and bacon grease greeted us as a bell jingled over the front door. Wood paneling, wood floors. The small diner was covered in all-things wood. Old, sturdy wood booths with brown cloth cushions wrapped around the dining room, leaving a few four-top wooden tables in the center. The heat from the kitchen billowed through the room, the windows trickled sweat along their panes. Classic rock played from what looked like the world's last standing jukebox. I fell deeper in love with the place every second. I wondered if Darryl was the owner, or if the namesake was someone long gone, a legend in his own right. There was a seat yourself sign, cross stitched, the fabric frayed around the wooden frame, hanging from a lone cash register. The floors stuck to the soles of my shoes and Kai's grip on my hand tightened as he led me toward a booth near the back.

"This okay?" he asked.

"Perfect."

He let go of my hand, and, as I sank into the booth's deep seat cushion, I admired the wall. From left to right the entire space had been covered in pictures of smiling faces. Some of the snapshots had to date back at least twenty or so years. Grinning, I absorbed as many of the faces as I could, then glanced around the restaurant wondering if the few people scattered about might be one of the people on the wall.

"I used to come here with my mom every Sunday." Kai focused his eyes along the wall of fame. "She'd order a cup of coffee, no sugar. Lots of cream..." His lips twitched. "She'd goad me into ordering the pound of pancakes. And I ordered them every time. When I was little, I wondered why she only ordered coffee, but as I got older, I realized she knew the whole time I'd never finish the damn pancakes. She just knew that for me, the fun was in the ordering and in the possibilities."

"She shared them with you?"

Kai huffed out a laugh. "Yeah." He reached across the table and I covered his hand. "She did."

His knuckles were rough against the palm of my hand. Lost to the history of the moment, I hadn't noticed the waitress until she plunked down two plastic-covered menus.

"Kai Carter, well, well, well..." She clicked her tongue and smiled. The smile bled into the soft wrinkles of her cheeks, the red stain on her lips stuck to her front teeth. The badge pinned to her orange and yellow top had the name Genie spelled out with black marker. The name somehow fit with the mop of silver curls poking out from under her hair net. "How's your momma doing?"

Kai sat up, slipping his hand into his lap, he said, "Not great, if I'm being honest."

"I'm sorry, honey." She placed her fingers on his shoulder, her skin paper thin, the veins in her hands seemed fragile. "I'll have the girls say a prayer for her next Wednesday at church."

Kai's lips parted as if he was about to smile, but didn't have the strength. "Thanks, G, she'd love that."

The woman turned her attention to me. Her dull green eyes sparking with curiosity. "Who's your pretty friend?"

"G, this is Indie, we go to school together."

"Indie... Like *Indiana Jones*?"

"No, ma'am. Indigo, like the color blue," he corrected, and I felt my cheeks heat. I liked the way my full name sounded in his gruff voice. Almost desperate.

"Indigo," she whispered with a flourish of her hand. "A beautiful name for a beautiful girl."

"It's nice to meet you."

"And so polite. Please... tell me this is a date."

Kai's cheeks actually flushed. "It's a date."

She squeaked and looked over her shoulder toward the kitchen. For a minute, I thought she was going to tell the whole restaurant we were on a date, but she clapped her hands and asked, "You bringing her home to meet your momma?"

"It's our first date," he said.

"So?"

His laugh was patient. I might've liked watching him squirm a little under the pressure. "I'm taking her to that gallery in town."

"That art gallery is closed on Sundays."

He started to swear but caught himself. "It is?"

"Sure is. Everything is closed on Sundays 'cept us."

"That's okay." I playfully kicked his foot under the table. "You owe me another swim lesson. Remember?"

"That could work."

The flirty tone of his voice pulsed in my fingertips, itching to touch him, his skin, his lips wet with pool water, mine to kiss. The pulse spread through my body as I thought about his hands on me. On my back, my thighs, my stomach, this time without that precarious line. Was I ready for this? For him? My heart tripped as it sprinted.

You're just another girl.

He thinks I'm beautiful.

The noise in my head faded, and I caught the tail end of Genie and Kai's conversation.

"...well, Marvin is cooking today. I'll make sure he don't burn her eggs."

"I told Indie she had to get the pancakes."

She raised her brow. "You'd think after all these years this boy would get something different. Cheap date, making her split pancakes like you used to do with your momma."

Kai laughed, his shoulders relaxing into the seat cushion, he held up his hands. "I promise, she can have her own plate."

Genie grabbed the menus. "Two short stacks?"

He nodded and asked me, "Do you want coffee?"

"Yes, please."

"Two coffees, cream and sugar—"

"On the side. I know, I know." She winked at me and leaned down. Whispering, she said, "He's a good boy, don't let him fool you."

She tapped the menus on the tabletop and left for the kitchen, barking at one of the customers as he waited at the cash register. "Hold your horses, Saul, I only got two legs."

"She's crazy," Kai said, pulling a few packets of jelly from the small plastic holder against the wall.

I watched as he stacked them in order. Grape. Strawberry. Grape. And so on.

"All the best people are crazy."

His eyes met mine. "Indie... Shit. I didn't mean crazy. I—"

Laughing, I knocked his tower of preserves to the table. "Kai... I wasn't offended."

He picked up the jelly and started to build again. "I shouldn't have said that."

"Why? Because I'm crazy?" I asked, the humor in my voice wavering.

"You're not crazy." He took the last packet and tossed it gently across the table.

It bounced and landed against my roll of silverware. "I'm not crazy..." I tried to smile. "All the time."

He was quiet, and I raised my gaze from the table. I could see the questions brewing in his eyes.

"I wish I could hear them," he lowered his voice, "the voices in your head. I wish I could tell them to leave you alone."

seven shades of you

Pressing my lips together, I fought my growing smile. In the end, I lost the fight. I felt his regard as it warmed my face and neck. "You do... in a way."

His shoe pressed against mine under the table. "How?"

Nervous, I picked at my napkin and explained. "You make them harder to hear." I wet my lips, thinking of the least date-ending way to say what I wanted to say. "You make me feel seen... It's solitary being trapped inside my head all the time... I'm happy, less alone."

"Hey." His rough, warm voice scratched my ribs, made them separate. Made it easier to breathe as I made myself look at him. The smooth expanse of his throat moved as he swallowed. "With you... I don't have to be anyone but me. No fake bullshit, Indie. It's suffocating, every day, but not with you. I guess you make me feel seen, too."

I packaged up his words, wrapped them in red, and hid them for later. Later, when I was alone again, I'd open them up, let them break me open; let them become a permanent fixture. A wall to protect me from myself.

Genie picked that moment to bring our coffee. Kai thanked her as she piled a mountain of sugar packets in the center of the table.

"Be right back with your order."

Kai offered me the tiny metal carafe of creamer and I poured some into my cup. We sat in a comfortable silence until we took our first sips and smiled at each other when we both sighed.

"It's good," he said, setting his cup on the table.

"So much better than that place near campus."

He took another sip, and I watched as he toyed with the small legion of sugar squares. "I want to ask you something, but it's probably rude."

"Now you have to ask me," I teased, and his smile returned.

"Will you always be on medication?" He spoke with honest interest and not in a way that suggested he'd be bothered if my answer was yes.

"I will. My meds are good now, but they might change. Brain chemistry is a difficult thing to nail down. My dad told me he used to hate his meds because they made him feel like a zombie. He tried to wean himself off once, ended up in the hospital."

"No shit?"

"It was after he got back together with my mom. She made him happy, and he thought he didn't need them anymore. We'll always need them, though. And therapy."

He dragged the tip of his finger around the rim of his cup. "Have you ever been hospitalized?"

"No. I'm lucky to have my dad. We help each other. He swings more manic. Stays awake days at a time, trying to finish a painting or a project. He loses time, it can be scary, but it's not often. We see it coming, and we help him. He does the same for me, but I tend to have deep downs. Those are the days I wish for his mania."

"Are those days a frequent thing?"

I laughed at the serious, thick slash of his brows. "No. Don't worry, I promise it hardly happens. I stick to the plan better than my dad ever did. Medication and therapy."

"I'm not worried. It's just hard to picture *you*... down."

I made a show of frowning, and he laughed.

"That's a great visual, thank you."

I took a sip from my coffee. "Anytime."

Genie brought us the two biggest plates of pancakes I'd ever seen. Kai had to explain how short stack equated to three gigantic, almost inch-thick pancakes. I was one-hundred percent sure the people who'd eaten a pound of these brick-style hotcakes had found themselves in an early grave. We ate in our own sated bubble, and I found myself wishing Royal was here so I could watch him die a happy little food death alongside me. Thinking about Royal, and how I'd sort of lied to him this morning about going to Rockport with a friend, made it difficult to stomach another bite.

Dropping my fork onto the plate, I groaned. "No more."

Kai chuckled and wiped a drip of maple syrup from the corner of his mouth. "You tapping out already, O'Connell? And you said you liked carbs."

I pointed to the wall of pictures. "Those people like carbs. I'm just an amateur."

His head fell back as he laughed, and I wanted to kiss his Adam's apple. Like he could read my mind, his gaze settled—smoldered—over me as he asked, "Ready to get out of here?"

He rested his hand on my knee under the table. "Yeah."

The place was empty by the time we left, giving Genie more time to ask me questions as Kai paid our check.

How did we meet? What was my major? What kind of flowers would I want on my wedding day?

"All right, Genie. It was good to see you again." Kai wrapped his hand in mine, eagerly tugging me toward the door, away from her inquisition.

"It was good to see you." She waved at me as we left. "Don't be a stranger, Indigo."

As Kai opened the passenger side door for me, I asked, "I don't know... what do you like better? Lilies or tulips?"

"Ha ha." He kissed away my giggle with maple-covered lips. "Now get in the car."

Once Kai was settled in the driver seat, he backed out of the parking lot, and as he turned onto the highway, he said, "Roses. They're traditional."

My lips quirked into a small smile. "I like roses."

"What color? Let me guess... pink?" he asked, the dimple in his cheek deeper than I'd ever seen it.

"Pink... Always pink."

Kai

I should've known the gallery was closed on Sunday. Rockport was that kind of town. Small and out of the way. Not a place you'd ever want to visit on purpose. A place where Christian values only meant something one day a week. Those *values* measured by how much money you had in your bank account.

"I'm sorry about the gallery," I said, breaking the silence.

It had started to rain, the tires of the car whirred in protest. A fine mist evaporated from the asphalt. I'd driven this road over a hundred times, in the rain and snow, rushing to get back to campus. Today felt different. I wanted to take my time, ease off the gas. Stare at Indie a little longer than I should.

"It's okay. Another time."

The windows were up, but the air circulating from the vents shuffled a few strands of her hair around her face. With her hair down, she seemed older, less fragile as she gazed out the window. It had felt right, having her at the diner with me. Darryl's was my church. This morning, as I was getting ready, I'd tried to picture her, sitting in a booth where my mother had once sat. Eating my memories and making them her own. The real thing had been so much better. She fit. Belonged there. Reminding me how far I'd fallen. Drinking. Girls. Maybe I'd been trying to purge myself of all the good. My mother. My responsibility to her. To myself. It was so much easier to be angry than to accept everything. To blame my dad, blame the disease. Indie made me want to accept it. Accept that the past was gone and that the future was uncertain, but viable, if I only let it breathe.

My mother would die.

She'd disappear from our booth at Darryl's forever.

My father, who knows where he would be. I wanted to accept that I had no control over any of it. I wanted to be twenty-one, on a date with a hot, smart, interesting girl, and revel in the fact I might get to touch her for real this time. I wanted to know that I was living. That the rain beating like a drum on the windshield was the beat of my pulse.

Live. Live. Live.

It hit me, then, in the quickest of flashes. The night I'd almost died, maybe it had been subconsciously premeditated. My pulse had screamed then, too.

Sleep. Sleep. Sleep.

I wasn't tired anymore.

I was waking up.

The music she'd chosen for the ride back was bright and endless, and I was awake with it, with her. It felt fucking good. I felt good.

Reaching across the console, I held her hand and said, "Another time... I can work with that."

She blushed as I lifted her knuckles to my lips and kissed them.

"Do you think the pool will be empty?" she asked.

It would be pretty early by the time we got back, and I knew some of the guys, even if Coach hadn't made it mandatory, swam laps on their off days. If I wasn't with Indie today, I'd probably be in the water this very second. But it was the Sunday after a meet, and the guys would undoubtedly be hung over.

"I don't know, I don't think so," I said, disappointment settling itself between us.

She lowered her chin, her eyes on our clasped hands. "This is harder than I thought it would be."

What was hard? Being with me? Dating?

"I kind of screwed everything up, didn't I? I'm not the best planner in the spur of the moment."

She lifted her head. "No, that's not what I meant." Hesitating, she rubbed her lips together. "I'm not ready for our date to be over, but it feels like maybe it is."

"Let's play it by ear, see if anyone's there. If there is, we could go to the studio," I suggested, her smile resurfacing again.

Hiding was a lot harder than I thought it would be. If Royal wasn't her brother, none of this shit would matter. I'd show up at the pool and the guys would cat call and then leave us alone, if they didn't leave first.

"Okay."

Indie's thumb rested on top of mine. The high of the afternoon flooded my veins, my heart knocking hard against my ribs. The feeling never faded, lingering all the way back to campus, our fingers intertwined the whole way home. But as we pulled into the parking lot behind the Aquatic Center, I immediately recognized the silver pick-up truck parked near the back entrance.

"Shit. Coach is here."

Indie stared at the offending vehicle through her window, her fingers flexing in my hand.

"I'm sorry," I said.

"It's not your fault," she said, and the tone of her voice made me think she thought it was her fault.

"It's not yours either."

"If I was any other girl this wouldn't be an issue. We wouldn't have to sneak around."

"If you were any other girl we wouldn't be on a date."

The few freckles she had on her cheeks faded with her blush.

"I mean it, Indie, this makes me sound terrible. But if you were any other girl, I would've left your room this morning and probably never called you again."

Admitting this to her, out loud, in the dense space between us, where the words had no place to hide, where the mask I put on every day revealed itself, my heart rebelled. Yes. Indeed, I was the man-whore she'd most likely heard about. I was *that* guy. That idiot who used other people to make himself feel better. Feel anything at all. I tried last semester, when I'd dated one of my hookups longer than I should have. Karma had caught up to me, though; she'd cheated on me with Sherman.

I waited for regret to dull the open blue sky of her irises, but she squeezed my hand and said, "I know."

"You know?"

"I do..." She pressed the tips of her fingers against mine, measuring the size of our hands. "We might not have been friends last semester, but I have eyes, Kai. I see the way every girl on this campus looks at you. Aware and wanting. Some with hurt, and others, they can only hope to hurt."

Letting go of her hand, I lifted her chin. "What about you? How do you see me?"

Looking straight through me, she said, "It depends on the day. Sometimes I see you in violet. Violent and strong. Sometimes in gold, when you think no one is watching." She smiled, and the air in my chest ignited as she appraised me, each second that passed, she exposed, unearthed another nerve. Indie brought her fingers to her lips and lowered her lashes, heat flooding her face. "Lately, red."

"You see me in colors?"

"All seven shades of the spectrum." She wet her lips as my thumb dusted her cheek. "That's a weird thing to say, isn't it?"

I cupped her face in my palms, forgetting that we were in a parking lot where anyone could see us, shelving Royal and his overprotective bullshit and kissed her. Slowly, Indie's lips rediscovered mine. Sweet and gradual as my hands slid into her hair. The thick strands tangled in my fingers as she gripped my shoulders. The edge of her fingernails dug through my shirt, and I groaned into her mouth.

"Sorry," she whispered.

"Don't be. I liked it."

She laughed and rested her forehead against mine.

"Indie..." I inhaled her warm scent. "I like that you're not like every other girl on campus. You're not weird... you're honest. I'd rather spend my time with you, being real... than spend another night faking it with a stranger."

Tipping her head back, her eyes glittered as she smiled. "Then take me to the studio."

Heat from the kiln smothered the studio space as we walked in. Thankfully, though, there didn't seem to be anyone around. We didn't have to hide here, but I wanted to be alone with Indie as much as I could. Keeping her brother out of the loop gave us almost no options, and I was starting to feel like the studio was our safest bet.

"This was what I wanted to show you," she said, looking over her shoulder at me with a smile. "Dr. Greenbaum bought the wrong size last semester and said we could stretch our own canvas if we wanted."

"Dr. Greenbaum?"

Indie stopped in front of the large, chain-link storage gate in the back of the studio. She entered the combination on the padlock and it clicked open.

"He teaches a found materials class in the summer, but sits in for Professor Foss sometimes in advanced painting. He orders all the supplies, too, and..." She swung open the door. "He ordered two rolls of canvas in the wrong size. Said we could do what we wanted with them. No one has used them yet."

She linked our hands and pulled me into the large storage space.

"Yet?" I asked, smiling at her enthusiasm.

"Here... help me," she said, pointing at a seven-foot-tall roll of canvas leaning against the wall.

"Holy shit."

"Right?" Her face opened as her lips spread into something magnificent. She was in her element. "Each roll has one hundred yards. That's three-hundred feet of primed canvas just waiting to be used."

I chuckled. "That sounds dirty."

"That's something Corbin would say."

"Do I need to remind you, you're better friends with Corbin than I am?"

Barely able to suppress her smile, she said, "Come on, I can't carry this by myself."

"Carry it where?"

She nodded her head to the empty area near the kiln. "My parents used to do this with us when we were little. They'd roll out a huge piece of canvas and only let us use our fingers to paint."

Taking on as much of the weight as I could, I walked backward toward the spot she'd indicated, dropping the roll to the ground and asked. "We're going to finger paint?"

She shook her head, her lips tipping up at the right corner. "Have you ever heard of Yves Klein?"

"Yeah, didn't he create his own shade of blue?"

"Yes... I kind of love that you know that."

I kissed her forehead. "I'm smart when I want to be."

She exhaled, her eyes dissecting my words, her expression made me feel like I could be anything I wanted to be as long as she always looked at me like she was right now.

"*Anthropometries*," she said. "Klein used what he liked to call 'living brushes' to create art that seemed to move across the canvas. I found out about his work while I was researching the color blue."

"I kind of love that you researched the color blue."

"It's my dad's fault. He's obsessed with the color."

I played with a piece of her hair, tucking it behind her ear, understanding the word obsession better than I ever had before. She hadn't pulled it up yet. The golden waves fell well past her shoulders to the middle of her back. Gold wasn't right, though. Each strand seemed to have its own shade. Gold, straw, white, buttery blonde, and caramel. Indie had her own color. Just like Yves Klein's blue, she could trademark her own new shade of yellow.

I tapped the roll of canvas with my foot. "So what does this Klein guy have to do with finger painting?"

She laughed. "He had people cover their naked bodies in paint and –"

"Naked?" I swallowed, a little shocked and turned on.

A red hot stain reached the tips of her ears. "They used their bodies as the brush."

"Naked?"

"Yes." She stared at me.

I stared back.

My heart beating loud enough it echoed through this entire damn studio, I asked, "You want to paint naked?"

Indie's laugh was nervous as it giggled over her lips "No... No. I meant *they* were naked. I figured we could just have fun. Totally PG-13 fun. "

Was it wrong I felt disappointed and relieved? I could think of nothing better than being naked, covered in paint, Indie's hips in my hands, her hair dipped in blue, painting my chest as she straddled my waist. Blood pumped through my swollen veins as the image unfolded in front of me like the roll of canvas we were about to paint. But I'd said Indie wasn't just another stranger and I fucking meant it. I wouldn't use her. If I ever had the chance to be with her like that, it would mean more than getting off, than fulfilling some insecurity inside myself.

"Naked finger painting..." I teased. "Let's save that for date number three."

Laughing, she kneeled down and pushed the canvas, unrolling it over the floor. "If you make it to date three."

Her face was flushed as she looked at me from under her long lashes, her lips full from my kisses. There was no doubt I'd get a date three. But I played along.

"I'll be on my best behavior."

Turned out being on my best behavior proved more difficult than I'd imagined. Watching Indie focused, stripped out of her sweater, down to just a tank top and jeans, not giving a fuck that she'd ruined her clothes as she spread paint across the canvas with the bare palms of her hands, was sexier than anything I could have conjured up. She'd slipped a few times, laughing as she fell onto her living work of art, leaving behind little imprints of herself. Blue paint curved under her breasts—dripped down her arms—etched the perfect lines of her ass. She'd pulled her hair back before she'd started, but the pale wisps of blonde that had escaped were sticky with color.

She'd talked me out of my shirt and shoes, and I was busy leaving my footprints along the right side of the canvas, when I noticed her stealing glances at my bare chest.

"What? Do I have paint on my face?"

"No." She shook her head and stood.

Dollops of paint fell from her fingertips as she moved. Pressing the palm of her hand to my chest, she said, "I wanted to touch you."

Indie was shy, but brave in ways most girls weren't. Most girls played games. Wanting you to figure out what they were thinking. Indie said what she wanted. Asked for it, hell, even took it. It was unnerving and perfect.

"Yeah?" I asked, trying to sound casual.

I ended up sounding as raw as I felt.

"Dying to," she said, repeating what I'd admitted to her last night.

Could she feel how fast my heart beat under her palm?

She brushed her fingers over my chest, up to my neck, and framed my face. Lifting onto her toes, she let her lips slowly drag along mine. I didn't kiss her back, leaving my arms at my sides, wondering what she would do next. An involuntary moan sounded in my throat as she sucked on my bottom lip. I gripped her waist, unable to resist, and pulled her lip through my teeth. Her fingers were wet with paint as she trailed them over my jaw. She shivered as my right hand slipped under her tank top, resting along the silk line of her hip; I pulled her against me, knowing she'd feel how hard I was. How much I wanted her.

She broke our kiss with a breathless gasp, a quiet smile playing at the corners of her mouth, she said, "I might've gotten a little paint right here..." She wiped her thumb over my cheek.

"Worth it."

Indie took a step back, pulling the same lip I'd bitten between her teeth.

"I told you this would be fun."

I looked down at her handprint on my chest, and I had to agree she had a point. She smiled and handed me a fresh bucket of paint.

"This stuff is never coming off, you know. You'll have paint in your hair for weeks."

Looking over her shoulder, she said, "Worth it."

I told myself it was the challenge I'd heard in her voice as she repeated my words. Or perhaps, I had more selfish motivations. But as I watched her kneel down in front of me onto the canvas, I couldn't help myself.

"Hey, O'Connell..."

She lifted her head and her eyes widened as I dipped my hand into the same bucket of paint she'd given me.

Tilting it to the side, I scooped out as much paint as I could and threw it toward her, watching as it covered her shoulder and splashed onto the canvas, the color bursting out in stuttered images. She ducked and laughed, and to my surprise, fought back. Indie stood, grabbing the rag she'd used earlier, sodden with blue paint, and aimed for my face.

"You throw like a girl."

Her eyes narrowed. "You did not just say that."

"You're cute when you're mad."

She picked up her bucket, ready for war. "Ready to get messy?"

I grinned. "Hell yes."

Kai

Picking a flake of paint from underneath my nail, I smiled.

"I think that's the first genuine smile I've seen from you." Brian swiveled his chair back and forth. The pen in his hand a drum on his khaki-clad knee.

"Don't get used to it."

His eyes fell to my hand. "You've been painting?"

I sat up and leaned my elbows on my knees. Brian sat up in response. This was my favorite thing to do during our sessions. He always tried to make me feel as if we were on equal ground physically by either mirroring my posture or getting down on my level. I didn't know if that was a *him* thing or a therapy thing, but I noticed it all the same and purposely changed my position often to test my theory. I called it the posture game. Not very original, but it worked.

"I started my Teaching Assistant job last week," I explained. "I'm working mostly in the drawing classes.

But I've found a new respect for painting. I'm at the studio almost every night."

I didn't mention that the hot blonde I was dating was more incentive than the actual act of painting, but what he didn't know was none of his business.

"And you haven't had a drink?" he asked, leaning forward.

I sat back, waiting for him to mimic my movement, when he did, I gave him a truth. "I had a beer a few weeks ago, but I haven't had a drink since."

"And you mentioned your shoulder wasn't bothering you anymore?" He cleared his throat, picking invisible lint from another one of his boring sweaters.

I had some pain every now and then. But nothing like it had been at the beginning of the semester. Last week, Brian had mentioned that stress can manifest as pain, and it made sense. Since I'd changed my major, and started working with Professor Hintz, I felt more like myself. I stopped giving a shit about what or who my dad was doing. I couldn't stop him from being an asshole. But I could be there for my mom when he was. I could still be me, but with more breathing room. Indie taught me that. She lived every day with a negative voice in her head telling her to give up, but she fought it. She made me want to fight, too. Fight for myself.

"Did you ever talk to your dad like I told you to do?"

"No."

Brian zeroed in. "Why not?"

"I tried and he didn't want to talk."

"Try again."

I crossed my arms, and he leaned back, his arms open at his side, jacking up the posture game.

"Kai... he's the root."

"I know." I exhaled, but kept my arms crossed and my jaw clenched.

Brian eyed my crossed arms, read my closed-for-business attitude, and swiveled in his chair again. His laid-back approach would've been almost artful if I hadn't seen right through it. "This friend of yours. The girl who helped you with your portfolio. You've mentioned her a few times."

"Indie." Her name lifted the anger from my shoulders. The beat of my heart slowed, and I swear I could smell lavender. She'd completely infiltrated my head.

"Tell me about her." Tap, tap, tap, his pen bounced on his knee, his smile widening as he watched me relax.

"She's my best friend's sister. She's a cool chick."

"You like her?" I shrugged. "Your entire mood shifted just now when I mentioned her."

I nodded my head, debating on what to say, if I wanted to say anything at all, if I wanted his advice. "She's a cool chick."

His chuckle made my lips twitch, and I fought my own smile as he spoke. "You said that already."

"It's complicated."

"Relationships usually are."

I sighed, staring at him. His smile reached his eyes. He thought he'd won. Maybe he had.

"We're dating," I said.

"That doesn't sound too complicated."

It didn't. Not on the surface. I wonder what he would say if I told him we hid in the studio every night painting, making out like kids, or how we haven't been on another date since the day we went to Rockport because our options of where to go were limited because we're afraid her brother might freak if he found out. Royal knew I hung out at the studio almost every night. He knew Indie had been helping me with my portfolio for Professor Hintz, but he took my relationship with his sister at face value. To him I was like Dev or Corbin. A guy on the team who had befriended his sister. Nothing more. And if he did find out about us? I'd never know if he was pissed because we lied about it or because it was me she was with—the jock who'd told him he got laid almost three times a week when we first met. Camden, though, I never missed his curious stares, or his knowing smile. He was insightful as hell for a guy in his first-ever relationship.

It was complicated as fuck keeping my hands off her during breakfast, and on rare occasions, lunch. I usually had to leave. The urge to hold her hand, kiss her cheek, her mouth, bury my nose in her hair, which, thank God, she wore up because I didn't think I could resist if it was down, would start to wear on me. I wanted to pull her chair closer to mine every time Corbin told her a joke and made her laugh, or when Dev smiled at her. Most days I had to excuse myself and eat in the library. Royal didn't care or notice. It was my M.O. Indie noticed, and I hated watching her smile fade every time I left, hated that she couldn't get up and leave with me.

"Tell me what you're thinking." Brian's pen was paused midair above his knee. "You're tense again. What happened?"

The tension roped itself around the muscles of my shoulders. I had no one to talk to about this, and maybe telling Brian could help. But I had a feeling he'd tell me exactly what I didn't want to hear. Tell me what I knew was right, but wasn't ready to admit to anyone other than myself. Indie had said telling Royal wasn't an option yet. Everything was new, and spending time with her, just kissing, painting, falling asleep with my hand on the warm curve of her hip, I'd give up beer forever to keep everything the way it was. I wasn't ready to lose this fucking feeling in my chest. I wasn't ready to let her go.

"Like I said, she's my best friend's sister. His twin sister. The guy I almost got expelled for."

Brian's brows stitched together. "He doesn't approve of you guys dating?"

"He doesn't know."

Understanding dawned over his features. "That is complicated. Why not tell him?"

"He's protective of her. In his mind, when it comes to his friends, his teammates, she's off limits."

"Your actions in December protected him... his boyfriend. He knows you, knows you have his best interests at heart. You're his best friend."

"That's the problem. He knows me. He watched the carousel of girls leaving my dorm last semester and knows that I struggle with drinking. I'm not worthy of the ground that chick walks on."

"In his eyes or yours?"

I didn't answer.

"You're assuming a lot. You've made great strides in understanding your dependence on alcohol and how it relates to your triggers. I'm sure he's noticed. You can't change your sexual history, but if you're respectful of his sister, it shouldn't matter."

"I wanted to talk to him. But Indie thought it would be better to wait, see how everything between us plays out before dragging him into it. But now... we're together, and it feels too late. Even if he would've approved. We've been lying to him for a few weeks—well, lying by omission—and that's not going to go over well."

"You've put yourself in a difficult spot," he said, his tone more parental than necessary.

"You think?" I crossed my arms again, and the tension found its way to my jaw.

He ignored my visible irritation and pressed another button. "What happens if this all blows up? Do you think you're in a place you could handle that?"

"Are you referring to my drinking or my proclivity for violence?" Shifting to the edge of my seat, I squared my shoulders, my anger vibrating down my spine.

He didn't flinch. "Both. You know in AA they say you shouldn't date for the first year of your sobriety."

"I'm not an alcoholic."

"No, you're not. But you self-medicated for a long time. Alcohol. A *carousel of girls*. Do you think you're in a good head space to share your whole self with another person if you can't even tell her twin brother?"

I stood abruptly and the chair rattled against the wall. I spoke through my teeth. "I'll see you next Tuesday."

"Kai." He stood, too, and shoved his hands in his pockets. I wanted to tell him the leather patches that covered his elbows made him look pretentious. But that would be counterproductive. Wasn't I trying to prove that I was an adult capable of making good choices? "I only want to see you succeed. You've come so far in such a short amount of time. Take or leave what I've said, I only ask that you think about it."

With a curt nod of my chin, I turned and walked out the office door. This felt like a developing pattern with him. Push, pull. Push, pull. I didn't truly breathe again until I saw her standing by the elevator. Indie leaned against the wall, her ankles crossed with a book opened in her hand. She wore her oversized overalls, the ones made with more paint than denim. Her hair was up in a knot on the top of her head, a pen sticking through the golden waves, holding them in place. She looked sexy as hell. Confident. And as I approached, she lifted her nose from the book, her lips breaking open in a gorgeous smile.

"Last week you said your appointments were biweekly now." I wrapped my arms around her waist, falling into the heat of her body, I kissed her parted lips.

She tasted like toothpaste, smelled like lavender, like her. The weight on my shoulders, the knots tied in my neck, unfolded. Indie's book dropped to the ground with a muted thud. She curled her fingers in the collar of my hoodie, using it as leverage to pull herself up, closer, and I groaned when she licked my lips.

"No appointment. Came to see you." She spoke between kisses and hell if I wasn't crazy for this girl.

"Mmm." I hummed as her fingers ran through my hair.

"I missed you at breakfast," she whispered against my mouth.

"Didn't want to fight it today."

She pulled away and searched my face. I kept my expression neutral. I didn't want to talk about this. I didn't want to waste any time we had with topics that made her look at me with regret. "I'm going to tell him. I am."

I let out a long breath and attempted to smile. "I know."

She had to know the longer we waited, the worse it would be. And fuck you, Brian. I could handle myself if things didn't go well. I wasn't weak anymore. I would do the right thing, even if it meant, in the end, I didn't have either of them in my life. The thought alone almost made me sick.

Indie's hot hands warmed my neck. "Hey. It's going to be okay. He'll understand. I'll tell him over spring break. He can't wig out. My dad won't let him. Not if he sees how happy I am."

Worry surfaced in her eyes, the shadows hovered, and I wanted to change the mood, rewind the clock a few seconds where all I could see was her heart-stopping smile.

"How happy are you?" I asked, teasing her lips with my teeth.

She shivered. "Very."

The elevator doors opened with a ding and I stepped back, giving us an appropriate amount of distance. A skittish-looking kid with acne and Coke-bottle glasses breezed past us without a glance. The likelihood that we'd run into anyone we knew here was slim, but to be fair, I never thought I'd run into Indie when I had either.

I stuck my hand in-between the doors before they closed. "After you?"

She bent down and grabbed her book, stuffing it into her bag. "Thank you."

Once the door slid shut, I took the forty-second, private ride as a challenge and pushed her against the wall. She giggled as I kissed her neck, her jaw, and as all the blood in my body pumped below my belt, I pressed myself against her seeking friction. She tilted her hips with a breathless exhale as we rubbed against each other like tweens on a basement couch, like how we'd tortured ourselves over the last few weeks on her bed. I gripped her hips, holding her in place, and I didn't care if this piece-of-shit elevator still smelled like cat piss, or that I might actually come in my pants, I wanted. Wanted, Wanted, Wanted, and...

The light of the lobby slashed through the doors as they opened and we broke apart instantly. Her breasts rose and fell with each deep breath, her cheeks were flushed, her chin red from my three days' worth of stubble. Indie's eyes were almost black, her pupils stealing the color from her irises. I adjusted myself as casually as possible as she walked out of the elevator ahead of me. The pain throbbed throughout my entire body, and settled in my spine. My head didn't clear until we were outside and the clean, damp air stripped away her scent, her heat.

"Are you ready for the quiz?" she asked, keeping a foot between us as we walked, her smile reserved as she stared toward the building where we shared our art history class.

We sat next to each other now. But the classroom was another public arena with too many eyes. Another place where I couldn't hold her hand, lean too close, touch her at all. Spring break wasn't far off, and I wasn't sure if I could last that long. I wanted Indie to be mine and I wanted it to be known.

"I think so. Studying with you has been a big help."

She laughed, and I stared at the smooth line of her neck, the pain in my spine intensified.

"We study?" she teased.

"We study too much. Are you ever going to get back in the pool?"

"Let's go tonight?"

"With the meet on Friday, practice might run late. But everyone should be gone by eleven."

"Text me, and I'll meet you there."

"Not at eleven o'clock at night. I'll come get you."

"This again?" She rolled her eyes. "You realize I walked alone on campus all the time before we started dating."

"I try not to think about it."

Indie broke the unspoken rule and closed the distance between us. Her fingers errantly touching mine, she whispered, "I secretly like how overprotective you are."

Goosebumps marched up my arm as she pulled away.

"Good. Because I'm not going anywhere... anytime soon."

Indigo

"That's freaking fantastic," Royal said, ignoring my grunt as he squeezed the air out of me.

I squeaked and laughed, which made me feel dizzy as Camden squeezed me from the other side. Royal's bed creaked from the weight of all three of us.

"Blue, I can't breathe," I gasped again, and Camden was the first to let go, rolling onto his back.

Royal didn't let go and I buried my face in his chest. I'd been avoiding moments like this. Choosing to hide in my room after dinner until I could go to the studio. It wasn't easy lying to my brother; I figured he'd eventually see it in my eyes. Smell the lie on me as it festered like black mold on my skin. His scent washed away the acrid scent fogging up my head, and I was home again.

"I don't even care if you barf up those tacos you had for dinner tonight, I'm that proud."

He kissed the top of my head, letting me go. The heat of his body faded into the mattress as the lie sprouted from its roots with rotting gray buds. Camden laced his fingers through mine, and the hot pin pricks of tears in my eyes surfaced.

Proud.

How would Blue feel if he knew?

The thought burned in my stomach.

"Which painting are they featuring?" Camden asked, neither of them aware of my mental breakdown as I stared at the tiny constellation of holes in Royal's ceiling. Small dots, probably caused by thumbtacks, made a great distraction for eye contact.

"Three. I titled it *A Dissection of Inheritance*. I only finished the second one last week. The showcase will be the final week of school."

"This is big, Pink, don't they only feature juniors and seniors?" Royal took my other hand in his.

This had once been my safe space. Between Blue and Camden. But I'd built a barrier, and every time I hung out with Kai, the wall got higher. I could hardly see over it anymore.

"Professor Hintz is making an exception," I said.

"Isn't that who Kai works for now?" my brother asked, pushing himself up onto his elbow. "Don't get mad..." he started, picking at the pillowcase hem beneath him. "But I'm kind of jealous Kai gets to watch you paint now."

My laugh was nervous. "He doesn't watch me. He's doing his own thing like everyone else."

"You know what I mean... I miss it. When will I get to see them? The paintings?"

I wanted to tell him. I could tell him. Right now. Camden was here. He'd help me, wouldn't he? I was pretty sure he'd already figured everything out anyway. I didn't need to wait till spring break. My dad was a great buffer, but Camden...

An alarm sounded, stealing my courage and the opportunity as Royal groaned. "Ugh, practice."

He leaned over me and I shoved him in the ribs. He laughed as he kissed Camden.

"Get off," I mumbled into his shirt and pinched his waist.

"Ow. Shit, Pink, that hurt." He sat up, giving me back the air in my lungs.

"I hope it leaves a mark." I grinned as he lifted his shirt. Sure enough, there was a red welt on his skin.

"Look what you did," he said, his irritation all for show.

Camden squeezed my hand as he chuckled.

"Sure, you guys just lay there and laugh at me." Blue jumped off the bed and grabbed his gym bag.

"We'll only laugh until you leave, then we'll talk about what a baby you are," I said, scooting over to the other side of the bed.

Royal slung his bag over his shoulder and placed another kiss on Camden's lips. "I'll be home later than usual."

"I'll be here." Camden gave him a small smile that said *I love you* in the quiet, simplest of ways.

I watched my brother's face heat, watched as he rubbed the back of his neck, reluctant, wishing he didn't have to leave.

"Will you be here when I get back?" he asked, and I shook my head.

"I have work to do." It wasn't a total fabrication. I would, in fact, work on my painting until Kai showed up.

The proud smile he'd worn a few minutes ago reappeared. "Maybe I'll stop by after—"

"Don't..." I stammered as his smile fell. The voices in my head rejoiced.

Liar.

Liar.

Liar.

They laughed as the witch scraped her fingernails against my skull. The noise like grinding metal, I sucked in a breath, trying to hear myself think, and Royal noticed.

"It's okay, Pink. Don't worry about it. I get it." His lips formed a flat line as he watched me fight the static. After a second, he smiled again, his voice like alcohol in my guilty wound. "You want to wait till it's finished. Just like Dad."

I've never waited, not once, to show my brother something I was working on. His words spread a million more miles between us and all I wanted to do was cry. This distance was my fault. My lie.

Once he was gone, the silence in the room shifted as Camden turned to face me. "He'll understand."

I stared straight ahead as I sat up, pulling my knees to my chest, my eyes feeling overfilled and empty at the same time—the voices louder than they'd been in weeks. "I don't know what you're talking about."

Camden drew his knees to his chest, too, his head gently thumping against the wall as he sighed. "I think you do."

You know.

Slut.

You let him use you.

"Stop." The word came out of me with a forceful whisper. My fists at my temples, I heard Camden's intake of breath.

"I'm sorry," he said.

"I'll tell him." I turned and faced Camden, the wide set of his eyes, the pale color of his cheeks. I'd scared him.

He'd never seen me like this.

Never watched as the voices tried to pull me under.

They're not real.

They're not real.

I repeated the phrase over and over again in my head as I stared at him.

"Okay," he said, reaching for my hand.

Everything was so quiet. Like the cottoned white silence of being under water. Like the feel of Kai's lips on mine.

Everything is quiet

Everything is quiet.

"I'll tell him," I repeated. "When I'm ready."

He moved closer, until his shoulder touched mine.

Everything is quiet.

It was almost midnight by the time Kai showed up at the studio with wet hair, wearing basketball shorts and a hoodie. I'd wanted to call off our swim lesson, but his smile made me grateful I hadn't texted him. The guilt I'd struggled with earlier had found its way into the studio, and the painting I'd been working on had taken on a much darker shape.

"I feel like I should leave you to it?" he said as he stepped closer to the canvas. "There's so much black..."

The majority of the piece was covered in black paint, thick rivulets of rust cut through the negative space, breaking up the monochrome.

He looked at me, uncertainty breaking through his wonder. "It's kind of creepy."

If you could hear her you'd understand.

I wanted to tell him.

The witch inside my head licked her fingernails as I glared at my painting. A macabre representation of what it was like in my brain every time she spoke.

"I don't know if I'm going to keep this one," I admitted.

"Why not?" he asked, raising his hand like he wanted to touch it, but kept his fingers an inch away from the wet paint.

"Are you still up for swimming?" I asked, changing the subject, and he smiled.

"Yeah, ready if you are?" He leaned down and kissed my forehead. "Hi."

I folded my arms around his waist, letting the soft material of his hoodie press against my cheek. He smelled like fabric softener and chlorine.

"You all right?" he asked as I pulled away.

"Bad night," I said and removed the painting from the easel.

"Want to talk about it?"

I threw the canvas into the large trash can near the wall.

"I want to swim."

He looked over my shoulder at the painting sticking halfway out of the green plastic bin.

"Sounds good to me."

He let me brood on the way to the Aquatic Center. I was stuck in my head. I didn't even look at the few straggling students as they passed by on the lawn. I found my gravity, though, by the time we got to the front doors, when it was safe for him to hold my hand again. The heat of his palm centered me.

Inside the lobby, he tugged on my braid. "See you in a few."

I gave him my first smile of the night, his shoulders visibly relaxing as I nodded. Inside the locker room, I pulled myself together. I was the one who wanted to feel this out. To see where this thing with Kai would lead before we told my brother. Camden knew my brother in ways I never could. Maybe he was right, Blue would understand. I laughed because it was the first time I actually let myself realize that Camden had admitted to me that he knew about us. He knew and he wasn't going to say anything. Suddenly all the guilt I had seemed overdramatic. Camden knew and the world was still spinning. Everything was quiet, and Blue would understand. I reiterated this to myself a few times, as I unknotted my braid, letting the guilt cascade down my spine with the strands of my hair.

Lighter already, I opened the door that led to the pool. Kai sat on the edge, his feet and legs dangling in the water.

He laughed to himself.

"Something funny?" I asked as I sat down next to him.

He ran his fingers through his chocolate brown hair, almost black when it was wet. "I almost forgot how hot you looked in that suit." Warmth leaked into my cheeks, down to my neck. His gaze gave me confidence. "I barely survived last time."

I rolled my eyes. "I'm glad you lived."

His bare arm brushed mine as he turned to look at me. Almost nose to nose, he said, "Me, too."

Kai tilted his head slightly to the left as he closed the distance between us. His hand ran along the curve of my neck, his fingers tangled in my hair as I opened my mouth, letting his tongue slide past my lips.

After a few sweet seconds, he broke the kiss, resting his head against my brow. "You seem better now."

"I am," I whispered. "Today was one of those dark days I told you about." I kissed his cheek, his jaw, and risked the truth. "I don't want that to scare you away."

He framed my face. "I'm not going anywhere, remember?" A somber shadow covered his features. "Don't hate me..."

He lowered his hands to my waist. The shadow parting like storm clouds as he smiled and pulled us both into the water. Kai kept our heads above the surface, and I scrambled to find the floor of the pool with my feet. He laughed as I caught my bearings, and I splashed him in the face, his smug smile somehow both enraging and endearing.

"You suck." My pouting only made him smile wider.

"Come here," he said, grabbing my waist and pulling me toward him.

The skin on my legs, my arms, my exposed belly, puckered as the heat of his body permeated mine. We'd been skirting around each other for weeks, he'd sleep over, we'd make out, he'd put on the brakes, and we'd fall asleep. But skin to skin. Like this. His hands on fire, on my hips, his arousal resting against my stomach. He was tangible. Alive, like fire dancing over water. The ache between my legs uncontainable. Kai had been in my bed more nights than not, but this... nothing between us besides a thin layer of fabric, was more intimate than we'd ever been.

I could see the pulse in his neck; feel the hardness of his body as his fingertips trailed over my ribs. He kissed his favorite spot, the hollow between my throat and clavicle. He followed a path along my jaw to my ear. His breath warm and damp against my ear. "I want to make you feel good."

My heart was a wrecking ball, crashing fast and swift against each rib, against my sternum as the thumb of his right hand dipped below the waistline of my bikini. My pulse pounded in my fingertips as I rested my hands against his chest. Weak for him, my lips parted as he kissed me so slowly I wanted to drown in the softness of his mouth, in the sharp bite of his teeth as he scraped them along my upper lip. Raising my arms, I draped them around his neck, lifting my body, my legs winding tightly around his hips. Kai held me in place, a low moan sounded in his throat as I rocked against him.

He breathed my name, his fingers digging into the flesh of my backside, dragging my body down onto his. He shuddered, groaned into my mouth as his soft kisses became violent. Violet like the boy I'd watched from afar for so long. His colors were mine now, and I wanted to be what he needed. I reached between our bodies, reaching for him, wanting to feel all that desire in my hand, but he stopped me, grasped my wrist.

"Wait." He kissed me again, drawing my hand up and placing it on his shoulder.

Kai's mouth moved over mine, the rhythm of our kiss matched the rhythm of his hips, and I whimpered as he pushed against me in the perfect spot. Kai backed us into the wall of the pool and our teeth bumped together. He rubbed against the same spot, and I moaned as his fingertips bruised my hips. I welcomed the pain of it, of him. Something simmered under the surface of my skin, under the bone and blood, itching and screaming, I clenched my teeth as his mouth brushed over my jaw, my neck. His right hand skated across my stomach, and I trembled as he hesitated, his thumb teasing the elastic hem of my suit.

"Yes," I said, answering an unspoken question as his brown eyes, now black and hungry, held me tightly against the wall.

Kai's chest heaved with each breath, he was torn, drawn out in shades of red and orange. Painted in stark waves of want. I counted ten breaths before he rested his forehead on my shoulder and whispered, "Not like this."

A faucet of cold water turned itself on inside me. Everything was weighted and saturated as a lump formed inside my throat.

Not like this.

Not right now.

We should stop.

A collection of his three worded phrases had me wondering if he meant *not with you.*

Embarrassed and self-conscious, I gave him my own three words as he lifted his head. "I should go."

"Indie..."

I pressed my lips together, fighting the emotion building behind my eyes and extricated myself from his hold. He didn't say anything as we both lifted ourselves from the water. I couldn't look at him as we neared the locker room doors. Humiliation flooded my cheeks as he spoke, his tone unsure. "Meet me in the lobby?"

I nodded and watched as the door of the men's locker room closed.

He doesn't want you.

He sees you.
And he doesn't want it.

I felt it. Felt him against my stomach, against the pulse between my legs. He was hiding from it. From me. Maybe from the guilt he harbored, too. Kai wanted me and I wanted him, and I couldn't let this crappy day end this way. I was twisted up with need. This desire growing inside me was at full bloom, and I wanted to be brave, wanted to know what it was like to let the knots inside me unravel.

Not like this.

Not right now.

We should stop.

I didn't want to stop. I didn't want his chivalry. I wanted his hands, his mouth—his heart.

With a shaky breath, I took a step, my fingers trembling as I placed them against the men's door and pushed it open. I could hear the water as it rained down against the shower floor. The white noise of it loud enough to blot out my wild heart. The room was exactly like the women's facilities. Rows of lockers hid the showers and toilets in the back. I walked past a few rows and paused when I saw a locker open. A St. Peter's swim bag sat unzipped, Kai's basketball shorts and hoodie spilling from within.

Like this.

Right now.

Please don't stop.

I let my feet move me toward the showers, the steam hovered as I got closer, and as I rounded the last row of lockers I found him.

He didn't gasp or jump. He was frozen, arrested, framed in heat as he swore under his breath. "What are you doing?"

Skin, miles of defined, tan skin, uninterrupted muscle, sculpted and graphic. His naked body wasn't like any of the statues I'd learned about in art history. Everything about him was explicit. His chest was red from where the hot water had beat against him. Smooth and wet, I wanted to measure each muscle, follow them down to the indentations along either side of his hips, to the place where all that desire gathered, heavy and thick. I met his dark gaze as he stood there, unashamed, glorious, like a god among men, he commanded the space between us as if to say, I dare you to come closer.

"Indie," he cautioned, or maybe pleaded, as I took the last few steps.

The hot water coated my skin, too, as I stared up into his wet lashes. His jaw was fixed, his nostrils flared, and despite the heat billowing around us, he shivered as my fingertips trailed over his chest, down over the muscles in his abdomen, along the sharp grooves of his hips, until my thumb dusted through the line of dense, coarse hair and lingered.

"I want to make you feel good." I gave him back his words, made them my own, hoping he'd understand that like this, flesh to flesh, there was no place for his chivalry. "Show me how."

Kai lifted my chin with his left hand, his right circled my wrist as he leaned down and bit my bottom lip. His nails gently trailed up my arm, his hand falling from my face as he sipped from my lips, his tongue licking and tasting. He didn't try and stop me, didn't utter any words as his fingers snapped open the front clip of my top. There was a part of me that wanted to cover up, afraid he wouldn't like what he saw. The girl still standing outside the locker room door in a wake of insecurity. But he pulled his lips from mine, his eyes shining like onyx as his hands cupped my breasts. Kai swallowed, his throat working, his touch reverent. All the heat in my body pooled below my belly, between my legs, as he licked drops of water from my neck, his hand slipping under the fabric of my bottoms, and my breath caught in my throat.

His name stuttered from my lips as his fingers drifted lower, parting me open, relieving the pain, bathing me in blue and gold. Kai's hot mouth claimed mine, silencing my breath, taking it in his lungs, giving us a secret of our own as I fell apart under his touch.

"Show me," I said again, needy, wanting him to burn alongside me.

Kai's left hand laced with mine, never breaking our kiss, he guided our linked fingers over smooth, hard flesh. He made a desperate noise as he moved our hands in slow strokes, up and then down. He felt foreign and flawless, the heat of his body in the palm of my hand, he groaned, releasing my fingers, letting me take the lead. His kisses came faster, frantic, his touch more demanding as I learned the map of his body. He kissed me, drank me in until there was no color, only light, washes of white light, a crest of a wave, as I held on with one hand to the strength of his broad shoulder.

He told me to let go, to feel it.

Feeling.

Feeling consumed me.

It started with that one point of contact, his lips, his fingers, down to my toes. It was shocking and vivid. I was exposed for him, with him. My cheeks flamed as my body rattled from the inside out, as his body quaked, as his heat poured over my fist. Kai's head fell into the crook of my neck, his smile spreading over my skin, and as I caught my breath, his fingers trailed over my belly. His hands held my waist and he lifted his head. With full lips, he smiled so loose and real it hurt a little to look at.

My heart squeezed as he kissed a bead of water from the bow above my mouth, his hair sopping over his brow, he palmed my cheek, and I leaned into the touch. "I never wanted to push you."

"You didn't."

"Promise me you'll tell me if I ever go too far?"

"I promise to always tell you what I want."

"I like giving you what you want," he said.

Kai dragged his thumb over the seam of my mouth and I inhaled. My arms around his waist, I leaned up on the tips of my toes, kissing his chin, his mouth, and cupped his face between my hands. "You're all I want."

Chapter 26

Kai

"Feeling shy today, Carter?"

Royal laughed, swatting me in the hip with his towel. Staring at the shower stall, I hesitated, his laugh making everything that had happened here last night feel wrong. I could still taste her on my lips this morning when I'd snuck out of her dorm. Tasted her as my muscles had protested with each rep on the bench press. Tasted her even as her brother walked past me and turned on the same shower I'd shared with Indie the night before.

"Hurry up, I don't want to be late for breakfast," he said, shaking his head, a confused, but amused smile on his face.

I nodded, heading to another stall, and tried not to feel guilty about the vivid images running through my brain. Visions of her skin under the light of the locker room, pale like cream, or better, under the low light of her dorm room, warm and powdered. Images I could almost touch, her pink cheeks, her face as she came for the second time in one night. I liked watching her come, watching her cover her mouth as I tasted her, sprawled out on a tiny twin bed, opening herself up to me, for me, watching as she let go of everything was a fucking privilege. I couldn't even imagine what it would be like to have her completely, to be her first, to be inside her, to know all of her vulnerabilities, for her to know mine.

But now, showering not five feet from her brother, what I'd allowed to happen last night, I had to bite back the nausea, the feeling of disgust as it burned in my stomach. There was no coming back from this. I balanced two worlds. One with Indie, where everything had begun to click into place, where I could finally look at myself in the mirror and believe the smile reflected back. One with Royal, where everything was wrong, where the lies I'd told ruined and hurt, and the reflection I looked at everyday was intolerable. Each weight, getting heavier by the day. Would he kill me? Would I blame him if he did? I wondered, if given the chance to hear the beat of my pulse every time I looked at his sister, if Royal would understand.

She was my more.

I closed my eyes and let the cold water set into my skin. Let it numb my fingers, hoping it would quell the memory of her skin. The cool water rinsed my mouth of her taste, my head of her scent. I was empty. And later as I got dressed, I found, even with Royal next to me dressing, as well, all I wanted was to see her, to fill myself back up again, no matter the consequence.

"You seem tired," he said as we walked through the lobby doors.

The clouds hugged the tree tops, the smell of pine and dirt a welcome greeting.

"I didn't get much sleep last night," I admitted.

Royal shrugged his bag higher on his shoulder, his grin familiar and assuming. "Was it Laney again? She's been asking about you. She's in my human behavior class."

"It wasn't Laney."

"So it *was* a girl," he stared at me, a smart ass smirk on his face, awaiting confirmation.

Averting my eyes, I used the puddles pooled along the sidewalk from the earlier rain storm as a distraction.

"Nah, I had to study."

"Is *study* code for getting laid? Because you weren't at the dorm this morning when I woke up."

"Christ, Royal, are you my mom now?"

His smile faltered, and like a coward, I turned away.

"You used to tell me..." His sentence abruptly ended, and I forced myself to face him. If he figured it out, if he asked, I'd tell him. "Wait..." My heart furious in my chest, my palms clammy, I shivered as a bead of sweat trickled down my neck. "I think you might actually like this girl."

I scoffed, my laugh unbelievable to my own ears. "What girl? Royal, I was studying."

"You never bring chicks back to the dorm anymore. You're not partying. You've cleaned up your life..." Royal's eyes were wide, excited. He looked at me like he could see it all, like he knew... like everything wasn't about to fall apart. "You have a girlfriend."

I shoved his shoulder. "Calm down, O'Connell. You might shit yourself."

"I'm right." He clapped his hands. "You have a freaking girlfriend." I didn't answer. My tongue was swollen with so many things I couldn't say. After thirty seconds of waiting each other out, he was the first to speak. "You have a girlfriend and you didn't tell me?"

Pushing my fingers through my hair, I exhaled. "It's complicated."

"It can't be more complicated than when I admitted to having the hots for your *male* roommate."

"Honestly... I think it might be."

"Try me."

We stopped short in front of the stairs leading up to Beckett. How could I admit to everything without it setting off a bomb? The words were grenades, and no matter the way I told him, if I pulled the pin, there was no scenario where someone wouldn't get hurt. Where our friendship wouldn't be totally annihilated. I wished then, as he stared at me like a brother, like a friend who wanted me to confide in him, to trust him, that I would have. I should have trusted him, told Indie from the start of it all he needed to know.

But it was a little late for what could have been, and like the total asshole I was, I asked of him what I didn't deserve. "Trust me, I want to... but I... it's new, okay... and I've never felt like this about a chick, and I don't want to jinx it."

His lips broke into a slow smile as he pulled on the strap of my bag, tugging me back and forth. "Look at you, all tied up in knots over a chick. She's gotta be epic... Can't wait to meet her."

I wrestled his hand off the strap, my laugh more of a mask than genuine. "Fuck off, I am *not* tied up in knots."

I was free.

Because of her, I was free.

"Whatever you say, man."

Royal's smug grin only made me feel worse, but I kept my well-constructed façade in check as we ascended the stairs. I didn't allow myself a glance toward our usual table in the back as we entered the cafeteria. I wasn't sure I could keep my feelings from Royal if I saw her right now. If I saw the heart shape of her face, her lips, he'd read me like an open book. Hell, being in the same room with her was probably a bad idea. If I got a whiff of her lavender scent, all the memories from last night would flood my pulse. My mouth watered as I remembered what it was like to be between her legs.

Shit.

I needed to get the hell out of here.

"Everyone's here." He waved and nodded his head in a silent conversation with someone, probably Camden. "Come on," he said, like I didn't have a choice, like I didn't bail on breakfast more often than not.

Involuntarily, I turned and faced the table, meeting her bottomless blue eyes, and knew I wasn't going anywhere. She lowered her gaze, watching me under covert lashes, and despite all the secrets I tried to bottle up, hidden behind indifference, I smiled as color washed over her cheeks. She bit her lip and I was back in her room, my hands on her thighs, my mouth between her legs, her addictive moans lingering in the air. A flash of heat radiated down my neck and chest. I was hard for her as I walked across a room filled with over a hundred students, worse, with Royal a few steps ahead. Apparently I had a death wish.

"'Bout fricking time, I don't know what takes you two so long," Corbin grumbled around a bite of a breakfast burrito.

Royal smacked a kiss on Camden's cheek as he took his seat. His bag landing with a thump on the floor. "Thanks, Pink," he said, grabbing one of the three burritos from her tray.

She held my stare as I lowered my duffel to the floor next to Royal's and sat down across from her. Indie handed me a wrapped burrito. "I got one for you, too."

"Isn't she the best?" Corbin asked, and I knew better than to answer.

I gave her a quick thank you and dug into my breakfast, stealing glimpses of Indie while everyone yammered on about the spring formal. Part of me wanted to flee to the library. At least there I could have my dirty thoughts in the privacy of my favorite study room. Indie was just as quiet as me. Was she thinking about last night, too? Could she still taste me? Feel me? Was she burning? Her cheeks in a perpetual state of pink, she shredded her napkin into tiny pieces. I was transfixed by her elegant fingers. I imagined them covered in paint as she spread color over her canvas, saturated with water as she wrapped them around my...

"Indie, you love that movie." Royal's voice shut down my oversexed brain faster than a kick to the nuts.

"What movie?" I asked as casual as possible.

Fine golden hairs tickled the right side of her jaw where her braid hung over her shoulder. The phrase *Love is Love* stretched across her breasts against purple cotton. Her face was clean of all makeup. Under the natural blush, the faint freckles I loved on her cheeks popped. She looked at me, caught me staring, and pressed her lips together. It made me want to kiss her. Could she tell I was uncomfortable with need? Need for her. Need to be under the shower, in her bed, getting off on the feel of her skin.

"Sixteen Candles," she finally answered.

I wet my lips and looked at the table. "Never heard of it."

"Seriously?" she asked, drawing me into her smile. "We'll have to fix that."

"Even I've watched that bullshit." Corbin dunked his burrito in a cup of red salsa, then green before shoving it in his mouth.

I wasn't hard anymore.

"It's not bullshit." She was offended and adorable as hell.

"It's stupid chick bullshit." Corbin grinned, exposing the black pepper stuck between his two front teeth.

"You've just insulted her religion." Royal threw his napkin onto Corbin's plate and Dev laughed.

"I think it's cool," Camden said. "I've never been to a dance."

"Wait... How is any of this related to Spring Fling?" I asked.

"The theme..." Corbin held up his hands, spreading them out like he was opening up the scene. I could almost hear him say, '*Picture this...*' "Sixteen Candles."

"Sixteen Candles, for the dance's sixteenth anniversary," Dev added. "I'm totally wearing a baby blue suit."

"Ugh... the eighties." Corbin's scowl created comically deep, comma-shaped creases around his mouth.

Indie shoved him. "I love the eighties."

"She really does. It's our parents' fault."

Indie narrowed her eyes. "You love that movie, Blue. You cried when they kissed over the cake."

Corbin choked on his orange juice and everyone at the table laughed, even Camden.

"That was you!" Royal teased. "You're such a liar, Pink."

Indie's expression clouded. Royal and I both noticed, our eyes on her, waiting for the voices in her head to clear.

"Thanks, Pink." Oblivious, Corbin snickered as he balled up his empty wrapper. "You always give me the best ammunition."

The storm evaporated from her eyes as she high-fived Corbin. "Anytime."

"Holy shit... I just had the best idea." Corbin leaned into Indie's personal bubble. He was too close, and when he tugged on her braid, tension curled in my fist and jaw. "You should go to the dance with me... like a date."

"Hell no!" Royal and I said in unison.

"What? Why not?" Corbin's attempt at incredulity was pathetic.

His smirk was already stretching his lips before he even got the question out. Fucking button pusher.

"That's my sister, asshole."

"I'm not good enough for your sister?"

"No." Again, Royal and I spoke at the same time.

Royal's shoulders shook with laughter as he held up his fist. "See, Kai understands."

Indie's cheeks drained of color as I bumped my knuckles against her brothers'.

Camden reached across the table, squeezing her hand, he shot Royal a glare. "Last time I checked, it sucked having other people dictate who you could and couldn't date."

"Camden, my man, you're my favorite." Corbin held up his fist, but Camden left him hanging. "It's cool. I get it, bro. I don't like to touch people either."

Camden's brows furrowed. "You just tried to touch me."

Sometimes I forgot how socially awkward he was.

"I'll get him to fist bump me one of these days," Corbin whispered into Indie's ear, and she giggled. "So, what do you think? You want to go to formal with me, Pink?"

Indie wouldn't meet my gaze as she chewed her bottom lip. My knuckles, my teeth, my muscles, ached as my entire body tensed. Corbin got to have these precious minutes at her side. He got to whisper into her ear, ask her to the Spring Fling. It was irrational, but I hated him as I waited for her answer. Hated his confident smirk, his money, everything he had that I didn't, but mostly I hated that Royal hadn't tried to shut him down this time. He held his boyfriend's hand, whispering about something I couldn't hear as the madness of jealousy thickened my blood.

"I appreciate the invite, but I'm holding out... I'm waiting to see if my friend needs a date."

"Really?" Corbin actually seemed bummed out, and like the terrible person I was, I smiled.

I fucking smiled and didn't give a shit who saw me.

Indigo

He had the attention of the entire class. There were only fifteen students in this introduction to drawing class, but each one of them watched in awe as he sketched a quick human eye with a dry erase marker on the whiteboard. Kai's deep, rich timbre made the room feel whole, it breathed his words, and as I snuck in, I shut the door as quietly as possible. I didn't want to disrupt his flow. I'd watched him struggle with my medium all semester. Struggle with paint, with the brush in his hand. Not once had he shown me one of his drawings. Quick sketches here and there. Ideas he wanted to transfer onto canvas. And he was getting better every day, but watching him now, the detail he stretched out with a mere marker, he had me completely captivated.

His light laugh made my heart skip as he smudged his thumb under the eye. "This isn't the best example to demonstrate shading..." The classroom filled with quiet laughter. "But you see my point about line. You have to start small and build out..."

Professor Hintz stood from where he'd sat at one of the front tables. "That's our time today, have your shading assignments to Mr. Carter by the end of the day tomorrow." A student raised their hand. "No, Miss Cavanaugh, you cannot work on it over spring break. Deadline is Friday."

Kai wiped his hands on a small towel and set it on the front desk as the students filed out of the room. I sat in the back with my legs crossed, a smile on my face. He looked handsome in his navy button down and gray slacks that fit to his trim waist like they'd been made just for him.

Professor Hintz pointed to the whiteboard. "You're better than that."

Kai pushed his fingers through his hair, his grin changing his stark features into soft, warm lines. "I know."

I cleared my throat and both the professor and Kai turned their heads. Kai's smile spread into dimples.

"Isn't this class a little advanced for you?" Professor Hintz asked as he shuffled through a stack of drawings on his desk.

"A little."

"I'll give you twenty minutes, Mr. Carter. I need help grading these..." He held up the same stack he'd been ruffling through. The grimace on his face made Kai chuckle. "Can I even call them drawings?"

"They tried their best."

A grumble resonated in Hintz's throat. "Twenty minutes." As he walked by my table, he tapped me on the head with his stack of papers. "Always lovely to see you, Miss O'Connell."

Kai's dark eyes met mine as he walked toward the back of the class. "I don't think I could concentrate if you were in this class."

"No?" I asked and uncrossed my legs.

My heart accelerated as he leaned down, taking my chin between his thumb and forefinger, he whispered against my lips, "No." His breath was minty, like the peppermints I'd learned he kept in his gym bag. "I couldn't go the whole hour without doing this."

His eyes were black, his pupils snuffing out the chocolate color of his irises, and as hot lips pressed against mine, the grip he had on my chin relaxed. Kai slid his hand down to my neck, his mouth urgent as he kissed me.

"Hi." I nipped his lip as he pulled away.

"Hey."

I don't think I'd ever get used to his smile. This one, in particular. The one he reserved for me. Equal parts red and violet, his true colors.

"When will I ever get to see one of your drawings?"

He offered me his hand and I took it as I stood. "This week."

"You say that every week."

Kai let go of my hand, his energy nervous as he grabbed a black folder from his desk. He unhooked his bag and placed it inside. "I'm not like you, Indie. I have to work at my craft."

"I have to work on my craft, too."

"You're beyond talented."

I pointed to the whiteboard. "And so are you. You drew that in less than three minutes with a dry erase marker. I got goosebumps thinking what it would look like with a proper pencil."

He shouldered his bag and rounded the desk, closing off the space between us. He framed my face with his hands. "You got goosebumps?"

"I think the entire class got goosebumps."

"I think they're finally starting to listen to me." His thumbs trailed over my cheeks.

"I wish I would have gotten here sooner," I whispered. "I like watching you teach."

"Yeah?"

He lowered his chin, his nose dusting the tip of mine.

"Mm-hm."

Two sweet kisses and my legs were jelly.

"Did you skip your English class?" he asked, dragging the pad of his thumb over my lips.

"Nope. I turned in my paper early. I don't have to worry about Dr. Girri and her obsession with dangling participles until after spring break."

He let out a defeated groan. "Don't remind me."

"About Dr. Girri?"

He pulled back, linking his hand with mine, he led us through the classroom door into the empty hallway. "No, about spring break. I'm not going to see you for an entire week." I smiled, and he squeezed my hand. "I'm glad my suffering is amusing to you."

"Suffering…" I pressed my lips together to suppress my giggle. "I'll miss you, too."

"It's more than missing you." His serious tone took me off guard. "I can count on one hand how many times I've slept in my own bed this last month. You're going home, and I'll be here waiting for my home to return to me."

The air in my lungs stilled, like the gray surface of a lake, waiting to be broken. I waited for the witch in my head to appear. To tell me he was lying, using me, but there was nothing but perfect silence.

My feet planted to the floor and Kai turned to look at me, a confused look on his face.

"Did you mean that?" I asked.

He shoved his hand through his hair, making the strands shuffle and stick in messy but effortless waves. He rubbed the back of his neck, his posture almost vulnerable. His self-confidence only measured in the sure way he held my hand.

"Yeah." Kai's Adam's apple moved under the smooth line of his throat. "Indie, I think of nothing but you. All day, every day. And every time I look at your brother, I get sick because these feelings I have for you… I don't want to let them go."

Releasing his hand, I touched his chest, curled my fingers into his shirt and he wrapped his around my braid. "You won't have to."

He nodded his head slowly, as if absorbing the idea that we might be an actual possibility. Be something other than clandestine touches hidden behind my bedroom door, more than secrets heavy under our skin.

"I can't see a way, Indie. A way this won't hurt him."

I reached up to the tips of my toes and placed a kiss at the corner of his mouth, to his chin, and he relaxed into me, his chest falling with even breaths.

"Let me worry about Royal. I think telling him when we're home will be a good thing. It will give him time to process, and if he has a hard time, my parents will make him process."

Kai's warm grip settled on my waist. "I want it to be that easy."

A group of students rounded the corner and he let his arms drop to his sides.

"It will be." Reaching out, I claimed his hand. "I bet a part of him already senses it."

Kai looked down at our connection. "The twin thing."

We followed the group of students toward the exit, and even though I was bold enough to hold his hand here, in this little world of art and us, I reluctantly let go as I squinted into the mid-day sun.

"Royal and I are connected in so many ways. Most people don't understand it or they think it's creepy. You know he picked this school specifically? He knew they had an art program and he wanted us to be together. Most siblings are dying to get away from each other. Royal is stubborn, but he loves me. I waited to tell him because I had to be sure about us. I'm sure, Kai. If I'm happy, he'll be happy. It won't matter." He raised his brows, doubt etching creases into his tan skin.

"You saw how he reacted when Corbin asked you to the dance."

My smile stretched across my face. As much as I shouldn't, I'd liked seeing Kai flustered and jealous.

"That doesn't even count, Corbin wasn't serious, and besides, I told you, Royal pulled me aside that same day and said if I wanted to go with Corbin he'd deal with it. Who I show up with at the dance is irrelevant. He just wants me to be careful. The twin thing, remember, he knows more about me than most brothers do."

"We shouldn't have lied to him." Kai stared ahead, ignoring the two girls waving at him from the quad.

"Let me worry about Royal," I repeated, and he exhaled a long breath.

I wanted so much to reach over and take his hand in mine, soothe his stress with a quick kiss, in the open air. I didn't recognize anyone on the lawn, and for a second I wanted to risk it.

He swore under his breath, his jaw tense, as he slipped on the fakest smile I'd ever seen him wear. "Hey, Laney."

One of the girls who'd waved at him approached us. She wrapped her arms around his neck, giving a quick peck on his cheek. I'd never felt so small... so invisible.

He doesn't see you.

Doubt invaded the quiet hallways inside my head.

"I feel like I haven't seen you in forever," she whined, flipping her long, red locks over her right shoulder. She was tall with lean legs that had been poured into a pair of skinny jeans.

"I've been busy." Kai shoved his hands in his pockets.

"Who's your friend?" she asked, her eyes assessing me, the smile on her face just as fake as his.

"This is Indie, she's—"

"Royal's sister," I interrupted. "He swims with Kai."

"Oh, I know Royal," she practically crooned. "So hot, wish he was into girls."

I didn't miss the way she flashed her lashes at Kai. Was she trying to make him jealous? Had they slept together? Everything, all the rumors I'd heard about Kai, I'd stuffed them away inside a black box. Who he used to be shouldn't dictate who he'd become, but it was a hard pill to swallow when the rumors manifested in real life as a gorgeous, leggy redhead who'd just kissed your boyfriend in front of you.

"You guys look so much alike, you're twins, right?"

"True story."

Look at her.

Look how beautiful.

I blinked, pushing the voices back into a closet and smiled. She was beautiful. And maybe Kai had a past with her. But she didn't have him now. Her lips parted in a smile I recognized. Bitter. Resentful.

She eyed my overalls. Her nose wrinkling, she said, "Love your outfit. Very low maintenance."

Kai's brows furrowed, his dark eyes hard as he stared at her. "You should see her paint, she's amazing." The strict line of his jaw gentled as he dropped his gaze to mine. A teasing smile curling at the corners of his mouth, he said, "Talented and hot, I bet your brother had to kick some serious ass in high school."

Laney's giggle fell flat. "Such a flirt, Kai." She reached her hand to touch his arm, and in a silent denial, he stepped back. The smile on her face trembled as she fought to keep it in place. "There's a party at Stacks tomorrow, you should come."

"Got plans."

Someone called her name from the lawn. "Gotta go," she said, her confidence pooled around her feet. "See you around."

She didn't offer me a goodbye as she walked away. Since I was thirteen, I'd grown used to the way pretty girls treated me. Like I'd done something to offend them. For the longest time I let the voices in my head, my uncertainty—the witch—tell me they were right. It wasn't until Laney had spoken in her sweetest voice, openly mocking me, that I realized that maybe I'd been viewed as a threat to their precious egos all along.

"Wow. She's pleasant."

Kai chuckled, bumping me in the ribs with his elbow. "She usually is. She was being a jealous, mean girl."

"She shouldn't be, she's beautiful."

"She tries too hard."

"Harder than paint-covered overalls?"

He lightly pinched the bottom of my braid. "I like these fucking overalls, okay?"

I nodded, holding my bag to my chest, my cheeks heated. "Okay."

We fell into a slow stride, stretching out our time together before we made it to Beckett and parted ways. I'd eat lunch with Royal and Camden, and he'd help Professor Hintz grade assignments.

"You have plans tomorrow?" I asked, attempting to hide my disappointment.

I wanted to spend the night with him before I left the next day for Salt Lake. The butterflies in my stomach took flight, fluttering inside my hollow stomach as I thought about what I wanted to do. I was ready, ready to be with him in every way possible. I wanted to give him that final piece of myself to hold on to until I came back.

"With you." He rubbed the back of his neck and pushed his left hand into his pocket. "I have something for you."

"Oh."

Blush crowned the tops of his cheekbones. "Don't get too excited... or I'll chicken out."

I dramatically swept my fingers over my lips like I was zipping them shut. "Not a word of excitement will be uttered."

He tugged on the strap of my bag as we stopped in front of the cafeteria. "You know, right? That girls like Laney are assholes because they wish they were as beautiful... as good as you."

I could hear my pulse in my ears as tears pricked at the corners of my eyes. I spoke past the knot in my throat. "I'm kind of starting to figure that out."

Because of you.

Because you see me.

Kai scanned the front steps of Beckett and took a step closer. "I want to touch you right now."

I let go of the strap of my bag, let my hand dangle at my side as I turned enough that my fingers would brush his. I heard his breath hitch at the contact.

"You can touch me all you want tonight," I whispered.

His thumb, daring, trailed over the top of my hand. "Looking forward to it."

Chapter 28

Kai

"Coach has lost his mind." Royal sank down onto the bench, sliding his palm over his head, he removed his swim cap.

Out of breath, I nodded. "Get used to it."

One of our teammates, Max, sauntered past our lockers with a towel around his neck. "You guys are looking a little green."

He tried to hide it, but it was obvious he was winded. After a few seconds, he curled over and sucked in a huge breath. "Christ, I can't..." Max struggled through his laughter. "The man is a sadist."

"I love it." Dev clipped Max on the shoulder and he almost fell over.

"Show off," Royal muttered.

"Ass licker." Corbin snickered as he leaned against his locker, his cheeks red.

Dev snorted, but when he sat down, he winced.

"Quads?" I asked, and he sighed.

Rubbing the sore muscles, Dev nodded. "Killer practice tonight."

We were all dying. The entire team spent. Coach always worked us the hardest before a long break. His philosophy was that our parents would make us soft with home-cooked meals, and to make up for it, he'd drill us on our last practice until everyone on the team wanted to puke.

"I never thought I'd say this..." Max wiped his palms down his face. "But after this bullshit, I hate swimming."

"It's the worst." Corbin groaned as he opened his locker.

My shoulders hurt, my abs were on fire, and as much as it sucked, it was pretty awesome, too. "You fools love it."

"Amen," Dev said and our palms slapped loudly with a high-five.

"Stacks?" Corbin asked as he slipped off his suit.

"Can't." Max unzipped his duffel. "I'm gonna shower and hit the road. I have a long-ass drive ahead of me."

"Same, but I'm not leaving until the morning. And honestly, all I want to do is pass out." Royal chuckled as he stood.

"I've got plans," I said.

"With who?" Dev stared at me.

"No one, you nosy bastard. I have a project to finish for my painting class," I lied.

"Boring." Corbin rolled his eyes. "You in, Dev? And don't even say you have to sleep, your flight leaves after mine tomorrow."

"Alright, alright, I'm in."

"Sweet." Corbin pointed at me, then Royal. "You guys can suck it."

"Be careful, he might take that as an invitation." Sherman, the asshole, snickered as he passed on his way to the shower.

"Sherman, you can totally suck it, too." Corbin fluttered his lashes, and I held my fist to my mouth to cover up my laugh.

Royal's shoulders shook, his own suppressed laughter coming to the surface as the vein on Sherman's forehead pulsed, and he flicked us off.

"Be careful," I said. "That looks an awful lot like an invitation."

"Not if he was the last guy on Earth," Royal said under his breath.

"What if I was the last guy on Earth?" Corbin puffed out his chest and stuck out his bare ass.

Royal's eyes went wide, his face morphing with disgust, and as we all fell apart with laughter, Sherman scowled and walked away.

"Pretty tempting, Corbin." Royal shook his head and grabbed his towel. "But *only* if you were the last guy on Earth."

Corbin held a fist to his chest. "Honored, dude."

"You guys are fucking weird." Shutting my locker, I grinned.

"You love us, don't lie." Royal clapped his hand on my shoulder.

I did love these guys. I'd lost my official spot as captain, but they still looked at me like a leader. We were there for each other, and except for the handful of idiots who'd chosen their bigotry over their teammates, we were family.

Family.

I stared at Royal, my brother, and it finally snapped. This line, this tight wire. I was in love with his sister. I was in love with Indie. My mouth went dry as the conversation continued around me.

Royal's brows dipped, his blue eyes looking deeper, seeing me. He leaned in. "Everything okay?"

"I..." My skin was cold, but sweat beaded on my forehead. The truth was right there, in the thin air, but I couldn't grasp it. It slipped through my fingers as my heart raced. "Yeah, man. Just tired."

"I know what you mean," he said as we headed to the showers. "I'm hoping Camden and Indie will share the drive with me tomorrow."

"I'm sure they will."

"Don't keep her up late, okay?"

I almost tripped. "What?"

Royal tilted his head to the side, and I wondered what my face looked like. If he could see the fear, all the things I was too afraid to say out loud.

"You said you had a painting to work on."

"Yes, in the studio. I have a painting to work on in the studio."

"The studio." He nodded slowly, his smile growing as he stared at me like I was an idiot. "Where my sister and you practically live now... Indie's working on something tonight, too, or we would've headed to Salt Lake after practice." Royal turned on the water and the stall filled with steam. "Just tell her not to work too late. I need fresh eyes for the drive."

Rubbing my neck, I avoided his eyes and turned the knob on the opposite stall. The sound of the water hitting the marbled tile, I hoped, would cover up the lie in my voice. "Sure, if she's still there I'll tell her."

"Thanks."

I let the hot water spill over my face and into my ears. Closing my eyes, I listened to the noise in my head, all the lies, and hoped, when he finally knew everything, I would still get to call him my brother.

"Do I want to know?" I asked as Indie frantically cleaned off the small coffee table in the living room of her suite.

Her face was beet red, her eyes darting over the wood surface. "Ari thinks she's funny."

I picked up one of the many foil packets and grinned. "I think she's pretty funny."

Indie collapsed onto the couch. Her hands covering her face. "I'm so embarrassed. Imogen went away with her boyfriend to Mexico for break and Ari thought this would be a funny gift."

I sat next to her, dragging her legs over my lap. "They're just condoms, O'Connell."

She peeked at me through her fingers and I laughed. "There is no such thing as 'just condoms'."

"When Camden and Royal started..." I cleared my throat and threw the condom I'd picked up onto the

327

coffee table. "Uh... dating, I stuffed Camden's bedside drawer with condoms and lube as a joke."

"Ew." She lowered her hands as I rubbed her calves. "I could have gone to my grave never knowing that."

"It was awesome."

"Poor Camden, he probably blushed for days."

"Days."

My fingers found their way under the hem of her baggy overalls. Her leg was smooth to the touch, her skin hot. Like always, I wanted more, and as I kneaded the muscle of her calf, I inched my way to the top of her knee.

"That feels good." Indie rested her head on the arm of the sofa. "I feel like I stood all day."

"Did you finish it?"

"No. I started the second piece over. It didn't match the first one like I wanted." She closed her eyes as I dragged the tips of my fingers over her knee, down the side of her leg. "I don't want to disappoint Hintz."

"You won't."

"Don't be so sure."

"When it comes to you, I'm sure about everything."

She opened her eyes, and I focused on the thin silver halo that surrounded the blue of her iris. I hadn't captured it like I'd wanted, and the drawing hidden in my bag suddenly seemed amateurish. Maybe I wasn't sure about all things pertaining to Indie. My stomach flipped as I thought about her seeing it.

"Can I borrow some of that confidence?" she asked.

"Only if I can borrow some of your talent." I reluctantly pulled my hand away from her leg and squeezed her foot. "Sit up, I have something for you."

Lifting Indie's legs, I stood from the couch. I couldn't meet her eyes as I rummaged through my bag and pulled out my black sketchbook. I flipped through a few of the pages and grimaced. Nothing here was worthy enough to show her, not even this. My thumb traced the curve of her lip on the page, and I took a deep breath.

I started to talk as I turned to face her. "I worked on this forever."

Her hands were outstretched, expectant. I wanted to chicken out, show her the drawing I did of Mt. Hood. But her bottom lip was pinned between her teeth, her cheeks flushed, hopeful, and of course I'd never deny her what she wanted.

I sat down next to her and laid the sketchbook in her waiting hands. "I wish I was better. At so many things."

She didn't speak as she opened it. As she turned the pages with reverence, pausing to absorb the pictures, the lines. Mt. Hood. The lake near campus. Beckett House on a slow, lazy Sunday morning. Royal and Camden on the couch. Each drawing more personal as she moved through the book. My mom in bed, on the porch. The field by my house. I stared down at the pages, nervous and unsure. What did she see when she looked at the world through my lens? Was it good enough? Indie lingered on a sketch of my mother. It was unfinished. My mom had fallen asleep before I'd been able to get the lines right. A drop of wetness landed on Indie's hand and she sniffled, wiping it away on her knee.

Indie's lashes were damp, her eyes shimmering as she touched the curve of my mother's smile. My work had affected her. It felt wrong to feel good about your girlfriend crying. But I did.

"She's beautiful." Whispering through another sniffle, she said, "This is my favorite."

I swallowed through the ache in my throat. "You haven't gotten to the end yet."

She lifted her eyes. "Kai, I—"

"Keep going." I rubbed my sweaty palms on my jeans.

She flipped past a few more half-finished sketches, and her breath hitched as she came to the last page. Indie's fingers shook, causing the page to tremble. Everything in this sketchbook had been drawn with a plain pencil. Everything, except for this. For her. I'd drawn her face a thousand times. A. Thousand. Times. It wasn't until I'd added color did it truly start to take form. Take shape. Coming alive on the paper, like she was there looking back at me.

With wet cheeks and awe in her eyes, she looked at me now. Her lips had swollen with tears as she brushed them away with her fingers. I was vulnerable, open for the slaughter, on this couch, with her.

"Is this how you really see me?" she asked, each breath cut short and hard as she tried to hold back her emotion.

I glanced down at my drawing. Golden hair filled the white page in waves, crowning the top of her head. Certain pieces wrapped around sprigs of lavender, and if you looked close enough, you'd see it in her azure eyes like sea glass, lined with silver, the hidden word, whisper, repeated in a spiral toward the center of her pupil. I'd created this so everything, every one of her features were elevated and bright. Her lips slightly open, more red than pink. Her cheeks more rose than peach.

"Yes... and no." I wiped the moisture from under her eyes with my thumb. "It's nowhere near as good as the real thing."

"I love it."

She gripped my shirt, craning her neck until she was kissing me. Salty lips claimed mine, and I devoured her taste until she pulled away to admire the drawing again with a smile.

Indie pressed another kiss to my chin. "I would have never painted myself in such bold colors. I would have picked something more muted, subdued. My dad has this thing he always says. It's like his I love you. He tells us that we belong to color. And I didn't realize that I never believed him... I mean... not that he loves me, I know he loves me." She gave me a watery smile, and I curled my fingers through hers. "But, Kai..." Her voice cracked, and she pressed her lips together, shaking her head as she stared down at her likeness. "I believe him now. I believe you."

I lifted the drawing from her lap and placed it on the table. Cupping her face, I kissed her once, and again, and again. My pulse raging with each taste of her lips, I fell into the soft warmth of her mouth. Her fingers pushed into my hair as I gripped her waist, dragging her closer until she straddled my lap. All of my sensible thought went out the window. The worn denim of her overalls, familiar under my palms, gave way as she shrugged off the straps.

The fabric pooled around her hips, and I wanted to strip off her tank top, touch her skin, her breasts—memorize the pink of her nipples as I kissed them. As I whispered the words I love you into her flesh.

Five.

Four.

"I love this," I breathed, lips to neck. "And this." Lips to lips.

Three.

I was on the mark, my arms over my head. The water in front of me, tempting me to break through it. I wanted her to believe it. To believe me. I wanted to trust this exposed nerve, this ache. I wanted to have the courage to say what I fucking felt.

Two.

"And this," I whispered as I trailed my thumb across her jaw.

One.

"I'm in love with you, Indie."

Indigo

Tears welled along my lashes. I didn't want to cry. I didn't want to be the girl who was shocked by those five words. *I'm in love with you.* And the longer I stared into his eyes, I realized he meant it. His drawing was proof enough, and maybe I'd had a fleeting thought that it was too good to be true, maybe the voice in my head had tried to ruin this moment. But I wouldn't let her out, not now. Not with him looking at me like this. Like I was truly as beautiful as the girl he'd drawn inside his sketchbook.

His thumb rested on my lip as a tear escaped down my cheek. It trickled under his touch and pooled against his skin.

"Please... don't cry," he whispered as he wiped away the tear. "It's okay... if you don't love me, it's okay. Indie—"

"I love you," I blurted, and Kai's lips broke into a wide grin. "I do, I love you." I wiped at my eyes. "I love you." I kissed his smile.

"Yeah?" he asked, kissing me back.

With my arms around his neck, I pushed him deeper into the couch, tasting his lips, slowly, until his eyes closed. "Yes."

I'd fallen for Kai. I'd fallen for him the day he'd stood up for my brother. His sacrifice painted in blue across my heart.

He held my face. "This feeling, Indie. I wish I could explain it better."

"I already know... You showed me."

"The drawing?"

"All of it. That's more than a sketchbook, Kai. It's a part of you, a part of your heart. You let me open it. I got to see the world through your eyes, see the things you loved so much you had to draw them, had to remember them forever. You had to give them a second life, one only you could capture. In your eyes I saw myself as something more... and more is all I ever wanted."

"I want to give you that," he said, his eyes sparking with a dark flame I'd felt down to the bone. I ached for it. "You deserve it."

I rested my hand on the slope of his neck, his heartbeat pounded under my palm. "And so do you."

He swallowed, fidgeting with the thin strap of my tank top. "I believe you," Kai repeated what I'd said earlier in a rough whisper.

I placed my lips against his, kept them still, waiting. My tongue stole a taste. My mouth parted in a small smile, and I nipped his bottom lip, teasing. An attempt to draw him out first. Kai's nose brushed mine as his grip on my waist tightened. I gasped when he stood, lifting me. His hands skated to my backside, holding me, my thighs squeezing against his hips as he walked us to my room.

"Ari and Imogen are gone for break?" he asked, his breath hot against my skin.

"Yes."

"Good."

He gave into the standoff, his mouth crashing into mine. This kiss commanded my body. Demanded that I give in. And I did. Kai lowered me to the mattress, his lips leaving me raw as he stood at the foot of the bed. Reaching behind his neck, he pulled his shirt over his head. His chest a golden canvas. Stone, carved into ridges and valleys. Shadows that dipped on either side of his hips, promising power and strength, and though I feared it, I craved it, too. I wanted to know what he was capable of, if given free reign over my body, if I'd survive him.

Leaning over me with hooded eyes, he pulled my overalls all the way off, letting them fall to the floor.

"Is this okay?" he asked.

He always asked. And I always said, "Yes."

Every night we could, we'd explored each other, touching with our fingers and mouths, somehow finding the will to stop before it went too far. We'd find ourselves in the pitch black night, under covers, with subdued voices, but we never dove in, never took that last inevitable step. I wasn't holding on to my innocence, I'd already gifted it to him, in every way possible but one, and as Kai pulled down my underwear with his thumbs, I knew tonight I wanted it all. My fingers knotted in his hair as he kissed

seven shades of you

my thigh. The soft strands sifted through my fingers, in contrast to the stubble on his chin, and the way it burned the sensitive skin between my legs. White and Red.

"Kai..."

The pain of expectation settled itself inside me. Coiling low, the pulse ached as I lifted my hips, inviting him to soothe it, to take me there, but he stopped. Raising his eyes to mine, he kissed me below my belly button, placing wet kisses along the line of my hip. He lifted my tank top, and I helped him by removing it, along with my bra. His palm fit perfectly against my breast, the rough tips of his fingers lingered over the curves, until his mouth was on mine again, and my hands worked open the button of his jeans.

Kai's lips never left mine as he pushed his pants down, leaving on his underwear. The cotton material felt foreign as it brushed against me. I wanted skin on skin. My fingers swept below his elastic waistband, and he groaned as I took him in my hand. The biceps in his arms stretched, defined as he held his weight over me. Kai's teeth dragged over my chin, my jaw, and all that power, that strength I needed, started to build as I pushed my hand up and down. Letting go, I tugged on his underwear and he took them off, kicking them to floor. Kai was bare and hard, pressed against my inner thigh, I shuddered. His kiss was messy, needy, and I shifted my hips, trying to show him what I wanted. He went still, resting his forehead against my shoulder, he caught his breath.

"Keep going."

Doubt clouded his expression as he asked, "Keep going?"

I gripped his waist, lifting my lips to his with a deep kiss.

"Yes..." He rolled his hips, and I moaned at the friction. "Keep going."

Not enough.

You're not enough.

Kai kissed me, his fingertips ghosting over my stomach, around the curve of my breast, and back down over my ribs. Like the drawing, he saw the whispered words in my eyes and whispered words of his own against my lips as his fingers slid between my legs.

Perfect.

Beautiful.

Love you.

Want you.

And when I was close, when the twisted knot of desire threatened to break, he rolled to the side of the bed, reaching for his jeans. The cool air made me shiver as he rolled back toward me with one of the condoms in his hand. I tried not to blush, tried to maintain the heat of the moment, but he saw through it.

"We can stop, we don't have to do this."

His fingers untied the muscle in my thigh, and the pulse he'd created inside me came to life all over again.

"I know, and I don't want to stop."

"Okay."

His gruff tone woke the butterflies in my stomach as he tore open the packet.

Kai kissed the slope of my neck, his teeth on my skin, the lobe of my ear, and whispered, "Take down your hair."

I did as he asked, feeling every bit of his violet as he watched. The hungry color consumed me. The pain of it started in my chest, working down my limbs, dripping to the tips of my fingers, pulsating between my legs. Kai's hands framed my face as his lips slid along mine. His fingers slipping into my hair as he gently pushed my knees open with his. I breathed in the scent of his skin, tasted the salt on his lips, and imagined, as his tongue swept into my mouth, the rhythm of our hearts aligning. He reached down between us, the pressure overwhelming as he gradually guided his way inside me.

I stopped breathing, and Kai placed his hand between my breasts, skimmed his nose along my cheek, and reminded me with a softly whispered, "Breathe, Indie."

My name, strained on his lips, he was splitting apart as much as I was, and I found my breath as he pushed deeper. Kai held my gaze, his body firm and solid above me, taking me, holding me.

"Okay?" he asked, and I nodded.

I waited for pain, but all I could feel was this perfect intrusion. I took a chance, raising my hips, and he swore under his breath. His eyes fluttering shut as his brows pinched together. His features almost tortured. I wanted to give him relief, wanted his eyes to open, and when they finally did, he kissed me hard and slow. Long, drawn-out kisses matched the way he moved his body, like the way he cut through the pool, shaping and forming himself into the current. Pulling our connection to its limit, he glanced down between our bodies, a bead of sweat dripped down his neck, and as he pushed inside me again, I tasted it on my tongue. Tasted him.

There were no more voices trying to cut me down, no sickness bleeding through my veins, just the steady feel of his hands, the intimate color of our eyes, and the sound of our bodies. The muscles in Kai's back were strung between broad, tight shoulders. I ran my fingers along his spine, grasping for skin as I felt the bottom drop, as his pace chased my climax to its peak.

"Indie," he said my name as my legs trembled around his hips.

His fingers fisted the hair at the nape of my neck as he pinned my bottom lip between his teeth. The sting of his bite muted by the low groan in his chest. He dropped his forehead, surrendering to the feeling, and even though I'd started to feel a pin point of soreness between my legs, I kept his rhythm, held his face, kissed him until he collapsed into me. Sweaty and hot.

His skin puckered as I drew a line down his back with the tip of my finger. Rolling himself onto his elbow, he kissed my forehead and I closed my eyes. Kai's lips pressed against my lashes, my cheek—my mouth. We kissed each other with swollen, full lips, without technique, with tongues that still wanted more. We kissed to find our breath, to find each other after the fall.

He rested his hand on the plane of my stomach, his fingers painting shapes on my skin as he spoke. "Did I hurt you at all?" He cringed, his big brown eyes searching mine.

"No, you didn't hurt me." I smiled, pushing my fingers through his damp hair. "I feel different, is that dumb?"

"It's not dumb." Kai sat up, grazing his knuckles over my cheek, he stared at me. "It's not the same, but you were my first... in a way. I've never been with anyone I cared about. Never had sex like that."

"Sex like what?"

"Good sex, Indie. Sex that matters. You felt..." Kai's jaw clenched. "I never wanted to stop. Ready for dumb?" he asked. "I was afraid to let you go. I panicked for minute. I've never been a part of someone like that. It was disorienting." The smile on my face formed of its own accord and he chuckled. "You liked that, huh?"

"A little bit, yeah." I leaned over and kissed him. "I might've loved it."

"I love you." He took my hand and I laced my fingers through his.

"I don't have to meet Royal until seven."

"Want me to stay?"

"I always want you to stay."

He grinned. "Mind if I shower?"

"Want some company?"

"Never have to ask, Indie. Never ever have to ask."

Kai

It was only a week. Seven days. Saturday to Saturday. But having Indie like this, with her legs around my waist, her damp skin, skin that tasted like sex and salt, pressed against me, her breath in the crook of my neck as I pressed my chest to hers, giving into her softness as I came, I didn't think I'd last one day without her. My fingers trailed up her back to the nape of her neck as she kissed me with messy lips. Her hair thick through my fingers as she rode my hips, the six o'clock alarm on my phone long forgotten as she shuddered against me.

We were both a mess again, the shower we'd taken last night useless, and as we caught our breath, the scent of us filling our lungs, she whispered, "I wish I didn't have to go."

Strands of her hair stuck to her red cheeks, pushing them behind her ears, I said, "I'm going to miss the hell out of you."

Her smile spread slowly. "I hope so."

Indie's phone chirped, warning us our time was coming to an end.

"That's probably Blue." Indie's smile faded as she turned to look at the clock on her desk. "He'll be here in fifteen minutes."

She made an attempt to untangle herself, but I held her in place. I kissed her neck, her lips, licked them open until she was kissing me back. Almost hard again, I groaned and pulled away. "Fuck." I grunted, burying my nose in her hair as she pulled me into a hug.

"I'll text him, tell him I woke up late."

I lifted her at the waist, a tight shiver escaping as I broke away from her body. Laying her back on the mattress, I hovered over her. "He'll show up anyway."

"He will."

Placing a kiss on her forehead, I sat up and swung my legs over the side of the bed. Resting my elbow on my knees, I stared at her naked body. Her skin was flawless, not one tan line or blemish beyond the paint under her nails and the goosebumps prickling over her stomach. Fucking perfect.

"Seven days," I said out loud, and she sat up and stood.

I told myself not to stare, but I indulged in one last look as she slipped on a tank top. I handed her the underwear stuffed under her pillow, and she blushed. After I watched her get dressed, I figured I should probably do the same, ignoring the hard-on that would torture me for the next week, I cleaned up and put on my boxer briefs and jeans.

She picked up her phone and expelled a relieved breath as I pulled my t-shirt over my head. "He's running late."

Indie started to braid her hair, but I stopped her, pulling her into an embrace, I said, "Leave it down."

"Okay." Draping her arms around my waist, her blue eyes serious, she asked, "Are you worried about talking to your dad?"

I shrugged, not wanting to waste my last few minutes with her talking about my family bullshit. "We'll work everything out." I grinned. "Brian will be very pleased."

Indie didn't smile. "Don't do that. Not with me..."

"Do what?"

"I want a real answer, Kai. You don't have to fake it with me. You can always tell me the truth. About anything."

I stepped away and took her hand in mine. "I should've spoken to him sooner... it'll be tense. We can't fix everything in one week, but we'll get through it."

"And if it doesn't go well... promise you'll call me if you need to talk, if you need anything."

"He told my mom he wanted a divorce over Thanksgiving break, then comes crawling back not even a month later after banging some other chick. It's not *going to go well*. I'm angry, Indie. But I won't do anything stupid this time." I lowered my eyes to hers, held on to the clear crystal color. "I've got too much to lose."

Her phone chirped again, and I exhaled a weighted breath. I wanted to stay, put her bags in the trunk of Royal's car, hold the door open as she got in, and lean down and kiss her before she left. I wanted one goddamn normal moment, where everything wasn't tainted with a lie. I wanted five more minutes.

"I better go."

She held onto my hand, her grip tight. "I love you, Kai."

Lifting her chin, I kissed her one last time, lingering longer than I should have, I whispered, "Love you, too."

I'd been staring at my father's car, parked in the driveway, for the last ten minutes. The morning sun glinted off the red paint, and I found myself welcoming the glare. It made it easier to ignore the overgrown grass, the missing shingles. The patches of dandelions were out of control, crawling across the lawn and pouring over the edges of the sidewalk. Guilt warred with irritation as I finally stepped out of my car and onto the cracked concrete driveway. The house looked like shit, partly my fault, partly his. Last year I'd made sure I was home as much as possible to maintain the yard, made sure to come home whenever I had time between meets and work and classes. I used to pick up all the slack, and then some, left behind while my dad travelled for work. I'd learned as a child, in his absence, I had to be the man of the house, had to fill his shoes, keep my mother's world as pristine as possible. It didn't matter if I was thirteen or twenty-one, the holes my father left behind had to be repaired. As I ascended the stairs to the front door, navigating past the tall weeds, a sinking feeling filled my gut. I'd left her to fend for herself.

The front room was dark, the curtains pulled shut—the smell of stale sweat hung in the air. "Mom?"

She coughed, and I followed the sound to her bedroom. The door was open, and she smiled as I walked in. "Hey, sweetheart."

She'd lost a considerable amount of weight. Her cheeks hollower than they had been in January. Was her hair thinner? I looked around the room, her wheelchair was tucked away by the closet door. Her tray of medications sat on the dresser top, everything seemed to be in its usual place, except the television was muted, and her clothes for the day were still spread on the foot of her bed. And despite the sunlight spilling over her blanket, her skin, she looked cold. Tired and wrung out.

"Where's Dad?" I asked and kissed the top of her head.

Her cough was wet, her face pinched in pain as she pressed the button on the side rail to raise the head of the bed.

"He's in the shower."

"Have you been sick?"

"I'll live." Her smile didn't reach her eyes. "I'm glad you're home. How was the drive?"

I sat on the side of her bed and held my hand to her forehead. "Mom..." She sighed at the alarm in my voice. "You have a fever."

"It's nothing."

"Mom..." I stood, checking over everything again. "Has the home health nurse been here?"

"Kai."

I rummaged through the meds on her dresser looking for Tylenol.

"Kai," she almost shouted and I stopped.

"It's just a fever."

My head fell forward as I braced myself against the edge of the dresser. Shame hung from my shoulders, the burden of it too significant to bear. I'd put her through so much this winter. I should have come home, should have...

"I'm fine, sweetheart."

I turned to face her, tears stinging the corners of my eyes. "It's never just a fever."

"Maybe not." The smile on her face was thin, as thin as the skin on her sharp cheekbones. "But I feel okay. And you're home, and that makes me happy."

I grabbed the bottle of Tylenol off the dresser and opened it, spilling two pills into my palm.

"I missed you," I said as I sat back down on the side of the bed. "I'm sorry... I should have been here, I could've—"

"You were taking care of you... like I told you to do. Don't feel guilty for letting yourself have a life. For finally doing something you want. I can't wait to see the painting you've been telling me about. Did you bring pictures?"

Her smile trembled, weak, but genuine, a smile I didn't deserve.

"I feel like him. I feel like I abandoned you." I squeezed the pills in my fist as I grit my teeth.

"You hardly abandoned me." She laughed, the hoarse sound of it unfamiliar. "You call me, you check in, that's all you should have done, baby. You're a young man, and it was about time you started living like one."

"Take these," I said, grabbing her water from the bedside table.

She stared at me. "I don't need another nurse, Kai. I need a son."

"Take these, please. You have a fever."

"I'll get some applesauce." My father's voice startled me.

He stood in the doorway, his dark hair wet, in a pair of jeans and long-sleeve shirt. A premonition. Every time I looked at my father, I got a glimpse of my future. A future I never wanted. A man I never wanted to be.

"Applesauce?"

His brown eyes met mine. "She has a hard time swallowing lately. If you came home once in a while, you'd know that."

"Fuck you."

I stood abruptly, already halfway across the room, ready for a fight, ready to shatter him, shatter the mirror that haunted me.

"Kai," my mother cried out, her voice cracking, and I caved.

My dad's stoic jaw relaxed, his eyes sad and apologetic as he took a step toward me. "Let's not do this... she's sick."

I took a step back. "When has that *ever* stopped you?"

Everything was broken.

Nothing felt the same.

Anger had taken root and its hold on me was deeper than I'd thought possible.

I felt thirsty for the first time in weeks. Last year, I would have stormed out of here, driven to the nearest bar, and drank until everything was blank and quiet and numb. Until I no longer cared about what or who was right.

I love you, Kai. Indie's voice whispered inside my head. My bones hurt. My head ached. I was exhausted. And all I wanted to do was get inside my car and drive back to campus. But she wasn't there. And regardless of where I lay my head tonight, my anger, the shit I didn't want to face, would all still be there when I woke up.

"I need you to listen to me." My dad glared at me, and for the first time I noticed the dark circles under his eyes. Weariness wrinkled around the corners of his mouth. "If you pull the same shit you did this winter, I swear to fucking God, I'll—"

"Kyle..." My mom coughed, her face splitting with pain. "Stop..."

"Mom?"

Her shoulders shook as she gasped for a breath, the heavy, wet crackle of her lungs suddenly silenced.

"Mom!"

My dad pushed past me and scooped his hand under my mother's neck. She sputtered as he cradled her head, tilting it back, her eyes went vacant. I was paralyzed, and when he looked at me, his face white and frightened, every ounce of anger I had in my heart was replaced with terror as he yelled, "Call nine-one-one."

Indigo

M*e: Half-way home.*
Me: In the middle of nowhere, listening to Royal and Camden argue about the merits of pop music.

Me: Also... side note... Camden's apparently terrified of bees.

Me: Being forced to listen to these weird instrumentals from Camden's cultures in music class...

Me: Send. Help.

Me: Just drove over the Utah state line.

Me: We've been home for an hour and mom is crying... again.

Me: Missing you.

I dropped my phone onto my lap and watched as the sun smeared the horizon in burnt tones of purple and pink. The empty feeling inside my chest had spread to my stomach, and I'd started to regret not eating more at dinner. Mom and Dad were able to fend off the entire

O'Connell clan for one night so that they could have us all to themselves. I was sad at first, missing my uncles and their families, but after I'd been unable to reach Kai all day, something dark had begun to spread its wings inside me. My dad had been the only one who noticed my mood at dinner, but I was able to smile through my lie. And it wasn't even much of a lie, I was tired from the drive.

It wasn't like Kai to ignore my texts. At first, I thought maybe his phone was dead, or he was busy with his mom. But as the day progressed without any contact, my anxiety made it more difficult to discount every little thing my brain could conjure. Rockport wasn't that far from campus, but he'd had little-to-no sleep, and what if... I couldn't think about that scenario for too long. The vacant feeling it left behind was unbearable, tight, and hollow. He was fine. Probably busy.

The previous night, everything we'd shared, what we'd done together, it all started to filter through. The voices I'd been able to successfully lock away all day, here, miles away from Kai, where the familiar scents of home could make me believe it had all been a dream, where my father's macabre paintings stared down at me, here in my family's studio, those voices had begun to take root again. They knew me best inside these walls, knew my fears, my heart, and poisoned me with tiny seeds of doubt.

He got what he wanted.
This is what he does.
Look what you let him do.
I'm in love with you, Indie.

He loves me.

Filthy.

Loves me.

Loves me.

"He loves me."

I shook my head and stood in front of the blank canvas, leaving my unanswered texts on the floor. I was about to start working when my phone came to life. I couldn't help the way my heart leapt from the bottom of my stomach, it had been hiding there all day, and it crawled back between my ribs, furious, as I leaned down and grabbed my phone.

The number was unfamiliar.

"H-hello," I stuttered as I fumbled the phone in my hand.

"Pink!"

"Daphne?"

"Back from the dead," she said, her laugh rich and deep.

"Oh my God, Daphne... You sound..."

"Different. Sober. It's crazy, right?"

If I didn't know her better, I would've missed the slight, insecure shiver in her tone.

I leaned against the wall, my smile wide as I huffed out a laugh. "You sound so good. I miss you."

"Miss you, too, Pink." Her speech was muffled as if her whispered words were hidden inside the palm of her hand, covering the phone, keeping her secret safe.

"Are you still—"

"In rehab? Yeah. But I'm at this residential facility in New Hampshire now. I'll probably be here another six months."

The smile on my face faded. "Six months."

"It's good, Pink. I need to be here."

Hearing her admit it showed more of her improvement than the warm quality of her voice had.

"Listen, I'm calling because... well... I'm calling because I'm supposed to apologize to those I've hurt while using, and I wanted to call you so many times... but I wasn't sure what I wanted to say."

"Daphne... you didn't... you never hurt me."

She exhaled, the exhaustion reached through the phone, and my eyes burned for her.

"I was a shitty friend. Selfish. I lied to you, made you worry. I might not have done anything concrete, but when I was using... I pushed people, pushed everything good away. Did shit I should've never done. Scary shit... I'm sorry, Indie... for real... I never wanted you to know how weak I was..."

The silence stretched and I heard her sniffle. "I wish I could hug you."

"I wish you could hug me, too." Another sigh. "I'm good though, okay. I wanted you to know I'm good. My parents have gone through this, addiction is kind of a virus in my family, crazy contagious, but I'm working through it."

"Will you come back to St. Peter's?"

"No. I don't think it's a good idea. I need a place where I can have a fresh start, be my authentic self without fear of remembering who I used to be."

I understood her on some base level. I feared every day who I could become without proper medications, without the love of my family. "Fresh starts are always a good idea."

Her laugh was wet. "Shit, I'm monopolizing the conversation. My therapist told me I need to work on that... How are you? How's your sexy swimmer brother, is he still with—"

"With Camden, yeah."

"Man, I was hoping he was hooking up with Kai by now, at least that would make me feel a little better."

I laughed, confused. "What do you mean?"

"I figured Kai was in the closet."

My dad walked into the studio, and I held my finger to my mouth and he smiled, stepping quietly to his canvas.

"How would Royal and Kai being together make you feel better?"

My dad chuckled, and I held the phone away from my ear and shushed him.

"...the night we hooked up."

We hooked up.

My smile shattered.

"Wait, who did you hook up with?"

"Kai."

His name hung inside that distant static between here and there.

"So stupid. Never. Ever. Have sex with the campus man-whore and expect him to care afterward. I knew better." She giggled, the sound of it made me nauseous.

"When?" I whispered, swallowing back the metal taste in my mouth.

He got what he wanted.
This is what he does.

"I fucked up over winter break, I was so wasted, so was he. You know how these things go." No, I didn't. I didn't know anything. "I kept my ego intact after he completely blew me off, hoping he was into your brother." She groaned. "Ugh, all the mistakes I made when I was using... I should probably call him and apologize, too."

Tears spilled over my lashes and I wiped them away. I had no right to cry.

Winter was before me. Before us.

Blew me off.

Didn't call.

Won't call.

Got what he wanted.

The witch was alive and well, feeding on the sticky memories inside my head. The red thoughts, fresh and new, she devoured them all.

"I should go," I found myself saying before I could stop the words.

"Oh... okay."

"Thank you for calling." The robotic sound of my voice alerted my father, and his keen blue eyes held mine.

"Hey, Pink?" she whispered.

I stared at my dad, the tears falling heavy on my cheeks, he stepped toward me.

"Yeah?"

"Thank you for being there for me... when I didn't deserve you."

Her candid tone pulled me from my downward spiral.

"I'm glad you're getting help," I managed to say and meant it. "Take care of yourself, Daphne."

"I will. I promise."

I probably should have said more. Told her to *hang in there, get well soon, you've got this*, but all I could muster was a simple. "Good-bye." And ended the call.

My dad didn't hesitate, wrapping me in his big, warm arms. My face burrowed into his chest, his citrus scent filling my lungs as I fractured. He held me together, my shoulders shaking as I cried. I had no right to be upset, had no right to care who Kai had slept with, but this somehow felt like a betrayal anyway.

Dad's heavy palm rested on the back of my head, his deep voice rumbled as he spoke. "Talk to me, baby girl."

His long beard tickled my neck as he squeezed me close. I didn't want to let go, but I knew my father, and if I didn't start talking soon, my anxiety would become his, and I couldn't let him bear that burden for me, knowing how much he already held of his own. Pulling away, he wiped the tears from my cheeks with his thumbs. His inked arms, muscled, even now with his beard more salt than pepper, he was my home, and I found it easier to breathe, having him this close.

"Dad..." My voice cracked.

I had no idea where to start. My dad was my safe space. I'd never hidden anything from him, but if I told him this, told him how stupid I was, how naïve, he'd look at me differently. I could handle my voices, my doubt, but I wasn't sure I could handle his disappointment.

You're filthy.
Disgusting.

He lifted my chin, his face serious as stone, but open in a way that only I could understand. His clear eyes held secrets, like me, and the doubt I harbored, he could read it like it was written on my skin. "Don't give them your silence, don't let them win... talk to me."

I did. I told him everything. I told him how I'd watched Kai from afar for so long. How I'd fallen for him so irrevocably. How I wanted to have something of my own, and how I was afraid if I'd told Royal my feelings he wouldn't have understood. I admitted to myself, and to my dad, though irrational I'd worried that he wouldn't let me have Kai, this one thing that we both shared, for myself. I told him how I gave myself to this boy, this boy who had the world on his shoulders, who'd loved my brother enough to risk his future, who took care of his mom, who'd said he loved me, who'd slept with my friend and never told me. I told my dad everything through swollen, tear-drunk eyes. We sat on the floor, my head on his knee as I cried, as I purged the witch from my system and spoke aloud every hateful word she'd infected me with.

"Maybe he was afraid to tell you about Daphne. It's no excuse, but sometimes we do stupid shit to hold onto the people we love."

"He didn't have to tell me about Daphne. I know that... but I wish he had. I wish he would've trusted me enough to know I wouldn't have cared."

"As much as you trusted Royal not to care?" he asked, the sadness in his voice unmistakable. I sat up, meeting my dad's cool blue gaze. "Love is a twisted thing. It hurts as much as it heals. It's painful to watch you go through this…" The rough skin around his eyes crinkled. "But it's important that you do. You can't love someone with your whole heart if it started with a lie. Dishonesty is a shadow, Pink. It's a shadow you can't smudge away with your thumb, and even in the night, when everything is dark, it will follow you. It infiltrates every good thing. I might know from experience." He smiled, and I leaned my head onto his shoulder.

"You and Mom?" I asked, and he nodded.

"It took us nine years to find each other again after we let the lies of our life destroy us. Don't let that happen to you." He cleared his throat, stifling the emotion I could see building in his eyes.

I started to cry all over again. Breathless, my heart ached. I didn't want Daphne's admission to ruin what had happened last night. I didn't want her words to hold any truth. I was more than a hookup. More than a one-night-stand. I was… *more*.

"Kai hasn't called or texted?"

I shook my head, and the strain of my silent answer could be seen in the straight line of my father's shoulders.

"That boy better be dead in a ditch somewhere…"

"Dad." I gasped, my fingers shaking at the thought.

"If he doesn't call you… I'll drive down there and kill him myself."

"Not before I do." Royal's angry declaration filled the studio like a flame, gobbling up the oxygen in the room.

"Blue…"

357

His eyes were rimmed with red, his cheeks pale and wet.

"How long?" he asked from where he stood in the open doorway.

"Son," Dad cautioned, but Royal glared at me anyway.

"How long?" he demanded, his hands balled into fists at his sides.

"Royal... please listen." My tears had begun to fall in earnest. I stood on shaky legs, my father right behind me. "I love him."

Royal's entire posture buckled. His shoulders sank, his face white and sad, he stared at me. "Kai?"

Royal held a quiet vigil under the frame of the door as I told him how I'd fallen in love with his best friend. I told him about our late-night studio sessions, and how they'd turned into something Kai and I had never expected. How his friend had become my friend, and how I wanted to make sure that what had developed between Kai and me was real before we risked telling him. I told him Kai was the only boy to ever see me, to ever want me, and with heavy, wet lashes, I told him that Kai had fallen for me, too. How Kai had purposely kept his distance last semester out of loyalty for Royal. I told him Kai would never hurt me, even though the voice inside my head laughed and reminded me that he already had.

"You could have told me, Pink." I made a step toward my twin and he took a step back. "I told you the minute I thought I was attracted to Camden. Do you know how scary that was for me? You... you lied to me... We tell each other things. We trust each other. Or, at least... I thought we did."

"That's not fair. You said it yourself, Blue, you'd told all your friends to stay away from me... that you didn't want them hooking up with me. What was I supposed to do?" I was yelling now, my anger bursting like orange stars.

"Exactly. *Hooking up*. Indie, it's what he does! Kai doesn't give a shit, he doesn't deserve..." His sentence lost steam toward the end and his eyes widened. Royal mumbled to himself about it being complicated and something else... about being tied in knots? I couldn't hear, but it was as if he stumbled on a memory only he could see. He raked his fingers through his hair, and he stared at me, his anger wilting at the edges.

"Royal..." My dad rested his hand on my brother's shoulder. A look I couldn't decipher passed between father and son.

"You haven't heard from him..." Royal asked, his jaw tight. "Since this morning?"

My brother turned, walking toward me and I shook my head, watching as his fury morphed into a steely shade of silver. Royal pulled me into a hug, freeing the sob stuck behind the dam inside my chest, soaking his shirt, and whispered, "He better fucking call."

Kai

The house was quiet and dark as I shut the front door behind me. Heavy legs led me to the couch where I collapsed. When I closed my eyes, I tried to draw some sort of picture behind them. Anything but the image of my mother in that hospital bed with tubes coming out of her arms, her throat, anything but the horror show— like a coward—I'd left behind. I mashed my eyelids shut, let the burn shore up against my lashes, and let the rage clog my throat. I screamed until it hurt, until all I could see were the spots behind my eyes. Exhausted, I allowed myself to break. The weight in my arms anchored me to the couch, to this pitch blackness behind my eyes, to the fight. I wouldn't open the fridge and drink myself asleep. I'd sit here and roar. Scream until I was raw with noise, until the quiet rhythm of my mother's ventilator no longer haunted me.

Disoriented, I woke up, what I assumed was several hours later. The room was filled with rays of gray light. The front window curtains were parted only a few inches, allowing the morning sun to spill across the floor. I felt hungover, and I hadn't had one drop of alcohol as an excuse. It hurt to swallow, like I'd downed an entire gallon of whiskey, and binge smoked a carton of cigarettes. My neck pinched as I sat up, shooting a sharp pain down my shoulder. A crack in my lip split as I yawned, the bitter taste in my mouth made me nauseous. The sick feeling brought a rush of memories to the surface from yesterday. Startled and desperate for the time, I reached into my pocket for my phone, remembering as I grasped inside the empty pocket, I'd left it in my mother's room when I'd called nine-one-one. I hadn't spoken to Indie since I'd left her dorm yesterday morning. I wanted to hear her voice. One good thing to remind me that not everything in my life had come apart at the seams.

I stood too quickly, dizziness from lack of food—I couldn't even remember when I'd eaten last—hit me like a sucker punch. I closed my eyes to gather myself, my head aching as I found my center.

My mother's room was a mess. I tried, and failed, to hide from the details scattered on her bed, on the floor. The paper backing from the paramedics' AED pads seemed so innocent, like tiny white flakes, pieces of discarded paper, no big deal, strewn randomly on the floor. The comforter half wet with her urine and vomit, the room smelled worse than the hospital. My heart started to sprint as I took notice of all the little things. The Tylenol bottle, tipped and opened on the dresser, the pills sprinkled over the wood. This room was a still-life representation of chaos.

I grabbed my phone, and pressed the power button knowing I wouldn't be that lucky. I was right. It was dead.

I didn't look at the details as I left the room behind. I didn't want to remember any of it. I was grateful I knew CPR. That the paramedics had been able to stabilize her. That the pneumonia was treatable. I needed to get back to the hospital. See if she was breathing on her own. I didn't want that tomb of a bedroom to be the last place my mother had smiled.

There was always a charger in the kitchen and, after I plugged my phone into the jack, I opened the cabinet to grab a glass. The tap water had an almost metallic flavor, but it soothed the dry cracks inside my throat, so I didn't complain. The liquid hit my empty stomach like a brick and the nausea returned full force. I was searching for my mom's stash of Saltines when I heard the front door open. Glancing at my phone, I noted the red bar. Two percent. I could charge it at the hospital, I argued, but my head spun with hunger. If I was going to make it through this day, if I wanted to be there for her when she woke up, I needed to deal with my dad, stay put, and pull my shit together.

"Kai?" my dad called out my name, and I dropped my head, bracing my hands on the counter.

"In here," I shouted, wishing I hadn't.

The pulse in my head pounded like a drum, and I winced.

"Hey." His voice was as rough as mine.

His brown hair was greasy, flopping over his forehead as he ran his fingers through it. Dark circles created deep crescents under his eyes.

"She's breathing on her own."

"Really?" My heart jumped, and I noticed he had a small smile on his lips.

"Took her off the vent at five a.m. She was fighting it." He plopped down onto the barstool on the other side of the counter from where I stood. My dad's face fell into his hands. Hands I'd once thought were strong, but now seemed old and weathered. His entire body shook as he started to cry. I wanted to feel sorry for him, but I didn't have the strength. "She's strong," he sputtered into his palms and lifted his chin.

"I know."

He wiped at his eyes with the heels of his palms. "She asked for you. I told her I sent you home for sleep." Skeptical, he appraised me. "Did you sleep at all?"

"A few hours." I couldn't meet his eyes.

"Are you sober?"

My spine straightened. "Yes, I'm fucking sober."

"Don't act like I'm crazy for asking."

"Are you serious right now?" I shoved back from the counter, practically ripping the charger cord from the wall.

"Where are you going?" he asked as I shoved my phone into my pocket.

Clenching the black cord in my fist, I said, "To see Mom."

"Kai," he yelled before I could make it to the living room.

I paused, my back stiff, and asked, "What?"

"She worried herself sick about you after break... I worried, too."

I laughed without humor and faced him. "You've never worried about me, about us."

He grit his teeth, his head shaking back and forth. "You don't get it. You can't understand what it's like for me."

"For you?" I spat. "Please, by all fucking means, tell me how hard any of this is for you." I could feel the anger turning into tears at the corners of my eyes. I wanted to blame the lack of sleep, lack of food, for my sudden inability to hold everything in, but there was only so much one person could take.

He took a step forward, shoving his hands through his hair. "I worked my ass off to make sure she never had to be in a nursing home. I made sure you had a roof over your head, food in your stomach. You think your swimming lessons were free? Kai, I provided. I did what I fucking had to do. You're not the only one who's made sacrifices."

"How much did you have to sacrifice when you cheated on Mom?" I hated that my jaw was wet, that my voice had broken.

"Everything," he whispered. His jaw, I noticed, was wet, too. "I lost you."

"You were never here." I took a step backward toward the door.

As much as I hated the hospital, this, being here in this house, was worse. I'd give anything to rewind the last twenty-four hours. I'd never leave Indie's bed.

"I wasn't. And as much as you don't want to hear it, that was a sacrifice, too. I lost time. I lost you. I was alone. You guys at least had each other. I needed someone, too."

"You're right. I don't want to hear it." I turned to leave, but he called my name again.

"The doctor said she's too sick for home health, that we need to think about—"

"No, absolutely not, I'm not sending her to a nursing home."

"What are you going to do? Quit school? Ruin your future to sit here and play nurse all day? She wouldn't want that. She *doesn't* want that for you."

"I can't do this." I swung the front door open, and it wobbled on its hinges as it hit the wall.

I wanted to get in my car and drive straight to Salt Lake City. Forget it all. The thought made me feel selfish, made me feel like him. I didn't run. I didn't get the privilege of being "alone."

"She's dying, Kai." His words found their mark and I stopped, hesitating on the front porch, my chest quaked. "She wants you to be happy, you've given enough. Let her be happy, Kai."

"She agreed to a nursing home?" I asked.

"We've been talking about Hospice for a while, she wants to be comfortable. She's tired of being in so much pain." Any resistance I'd had poured down my cheeks, and my father's hand gripped my shoulder. "The doctor suggested Orchard House."

Orchard House was one of the nicest nursing facilities in the county. But it wasn't home. Images from her room assaulted me. The smell of stale urine, day-old vomit, stung my nose. I turned and faced the house I'd grown up in, the man who'd had no hand in raising me, utterly isolated, and weary. I thought, I wouldn't want to die here either.

"If it's what she wants..." I cleared my throat.

"It's what she wants."

I shrugged his hand off my shoulder. "If you need me I'll be at the hospital."

I should've gone in ten minutes ago, instead I sat, staring at all the missed messages and calls. One in particular had me wishing I'd never turned on my phone in the first place.

Indie: Blue knows, and it's a mess. God, I hope you're okay. Please call me.

Royal knew.

I didn't have time, room in my head, for another mess and had avoided the voicemail icon sitting in the top left corner of my screen for longer than I should have. With a long sigh, I opened my voicemail app. There were two messages. One from Indie and one from Royal. I figured I'd throw myself in the crossfire and listen to

Royal's first. Nothing he could say would be worse than your father telling you your mother was dying.

The message started and for three whole seconds he said nothing. When he finally spoke, his voice was eerily calm, like he'd taken those three seconds to buckle himself down.

"I don't know what to say to you, except that my sister is a wreck right now." He took another three seconds. This time when he spoke the threat in his voice was loud and clear. "Pink told me everything... and I'm trying really hard not to flip out, and maybe I should, someone needs to." His voice muffled as he whispered away from the phone, probably to Camden. "Why haven't you called her? I swear to God... this is why I never wanted her to hook up with one of my friends. You can get any chick on campus. Why her? Why Pink? Was it the challenge?" I wanted to tell him to fuck off, to yell into the phone. No, you goddamn idiot, I love her, but he exhaled and the defeat in his tone was the last bullet I could take before bleeding out. "She loves you, and I'd never take that from her, but she's not like us, man. She's not built like us. She breaks and it's big... and it's for good. It's for forever. So if you can't..." I heard him take four, even breaths. "If you're not ready for big, then you should stay the hell away from my sister."

I opened the car door and threw up on the pavement, coughed until my throat caught fire, spitting the remaining acid from my lips, I wiped my mouth with my sleeve. I was in love with her, but I didn't know how much of myself I had left to give. My mother was dying, and a part of me would be here, in Rockport, until she did. I didn't have a forever bone in my body. I was a twenty-one-year-old with too many masks, too many wounds. I couldn't ask her to wade through all of my bullshit, settling for the leftover scraps I'd give her. Royal was right, she wasn't built like us. She was built better. Deserved *more.*

My head hurt, my temples swollen and stretched as I raised the phone to my ear. It rang twice before she answered with a sleepy, "Hello."

Despite the pain in my stomach, and the way my heart rioted against it, I smiled. "Hey."

She instantly started to cry, and my smile vanished. "You're okay... I was so scared."

Guilt speared through me. "My phone died. Indie... I'm sorry. Please... please don't cry. I should've called. My mom's in the hospital and—"

"Oh my God, Kai, is she okay?"

It was my turn to lose control. My turn to let go, to let her see how weakly I was built. I broke down and told her what had happened, catching my breath as I cried. I was a five-year-old boy, with skinned knees, sobbing through the pain as it spread over my skin, as I told her that my mom was dying. That she'd almost choked to death on the fluid in her lungs. That I was helpless. That I was alone.

"I could drive there. Royal would drive me."

"No."

"You're not alone. Kai, I'm right here. Let me—"

"It's okay. You're not driving all the way back here to coddle me, Indie. I can deal with this. It's what I do." I hadn't meant it to sound as harsh as it had.

"I know you can handle it, Kai." She spoke softly, her voice like a cool cloth on my hot head. "I want to be there for you."

"My life... she has always been my life. Some things... I have to do alone."

She didn't say anything for what felt like several minutes.

"And your dad? Is he—"

"He's here."

Exhaling, I pinched the bridge of my nose. I wanted to tell her I missed her. That I wished she was sitting next to me. I wanted to hold her hand as I walked into the hospital. I wished she could have met my mom before I had to tuck her away in some sterile home for the nearly deceased.

"This feels different... like you're more than a few hundred miles away. Why does it feel like I've already lost you?" she asked, and I could hear the tears on her lips.

Hesitating, I swallowed the acrid taste in my mouth and told her the only thing I could. The truth. "I need some time."

"Time?"

"Royal called."

"He did?"

"Yeah, he left me a message. I don't want to be the wedge between you two."

"You're not." She raised her voice. "He's okay with it."

"Indie..."

"He's getting there. We were both worried when you didn't call. I was scared you'd gotten in an accident."

And he was scared I'd fucked you and ran. I didn't say that, though, but that's how little he thought of me. And rightly so. It's what I'd taught him to believe. It's who I'd used to be.

A beep sounded in my ear, my dad was on the other line. I lifted my gaze to the hospital doors. "My dad's trying to get a hold of me. I should go inside, see how my mom is."

It was a cop out, but I needed to hang up before I couldn't. Before I decided I didn't give a fuck about the truth, and let myself be selfish.

"Will you let me know how she is?"

"I'll call when I can."

"Kai..." She steadied her voice. "I love you."

"I love you, too."

Indie was all I wanted, but I'd learned at an early age from my dad's clichéd line, '*You can want it all you like, doesn't mean you'll ever get to have it.*'

Indigo

"Listen to me..." Dad lifted my chin, his smile hidden beneath his beard, crinkled around the edges of his eyes. "You know what to do. He asked for time, his mother is sick. Give him time. And if the time turns into goodbye... he's not the last boy you'll ever love."

I couldn't cry. Colorless, I didn't have anything left to spill.

"Did Liam tell you that when Mom left?" I asked without malice, with honest curiosity. I wondered if I would end up like dad. If I would end up alone for years, until something or someone finally found their way back to me.

He chuckled and pulled me into a hug. His breath was hot in my hair as he spoke. "You don't want to know what Liam said when Mom left." Dad leaned back, his hands on my shoulders. "Mom came back... we found each other again. But that's rare, honey. You're young and so is he..."

"I get it." I gave him half of a smile. "Time. I can do that."

Weak.

You're already breaking.

He used you.

Avoiding my dad's perceptive stare, I turned toward the car where my mother was hugging Camden for the fifth time.

"Let's go, Pink." Royal rested his arm on the frame of the car door, his lips stretched into a grin as he watched our dad drag Camden into a hug.

"Miss you already," Mom said, as usual. She kissed my forehead, handing me the pink dress we bought for the Spring Fling. "It'll all work out," she said, always so positive and sure, she squeezed me a little harder than usual.

"I hope so."

"If it doesn't... you know we're here waiting for you." She wrapped her arms around me again, this time the smile I produced felt real.

"Mom, the dress..."

"Screw the dress. I miss you already."

I laughed into her shoulder. "You already said that."

She pushed a piece of my hair behind my ears. I hadn't pulled it back yet, hoping to send Kai a picture, letting him know I was on my way home. Home to him.

Royal eventually put his foot down, and Mom gave us all one last hug before we hit the road. The ride home was quieter than I expected. Camden was lost in his notebook, scribbling music notes across his lined paper, and I wondered if Royal had turned up the radio, hoping he wouldn't have to talk to me. The week at our parents wasn't strained, exactly, but there was something off between Blue and me. We avoided eye contact during dinner time, and when our extended family came over for a night of board games, he purposely pit himself against me, something he'd never done before in our entire life. We were always a team.

I tried to ignore his silence and reread the meager texts I had from Kai, looking for something to hold onto inside his words.

Kai: Mom is looking a lot better. No more fever.

Kai: Sorry, I've been moving some of my mom's things to Orchard House.

Two texts.

His mom was dying.

He used you.

His mom was sick.

Stupid girl.

I pressed the camera app, raised the phone, and snapped a quick picture. No one noticed, and when I looked at the screen, I smiled. It was a decent picture. The wind from Royal's cracked window had shuffled my hair. My blue eyes were bright behind pale golden strands. I pressed send before I could overthink it.

Me: On my way home.

I didn't expect a reply, so I was surprised when my phone vibrated in my hand.

Kai: You look happy.

Me: I'm happy I'll be seeing you soon.

Kai: I won't be there. Have to get my mom settled.

Me: What about classes?

Kai: I sent out an email to my professors and Coach. I got approval to miss a week.

Kai: My dad is traveling, surprise, surprise. I want to make sure she's okay. New place and everything.

Another week. Another million miles between us.

Selfish.

He doesn't want you.

The witch was regaining her rule. Every day the voices had gotten worse. My dad told me I had to see Dr. Sand as soon as I got back, but there was this small piece of me, this tiny, self-indulgent spark that said, let her win. Let her make it better. I knew that was the monster inside me, the one my father warned me about. He'd always painted his away. His monster, the specter, showed up in a lot of his work. I'd never met mine, and I hoped I never would. Dr. Sand wasn't an option, it was a necessity.

Me: Is she still in the hospital?

Kai: No. We moved her today. This place is nice.

Me: Nice is good.

Twenty minutes passed without a reply, but I refused to put my phone in my pocket. I held on to it like a talisman, closed my eyes, and refused to let the witch whisper me into my dreams.

"Indie..."

My eyes slowly opened. The smell of gasoline filled my lungs as I yawned.

374

"We stopped for gas." Camden stared at me from the front seat. "Do you want me to run in and grab you anything?"

I shook my head, sitting up and stretching my arms. "I'm okay, thanks."

I debated on using the restroom, but decided against it when I realized we were at the place we'd stopped at on our way home last time. The toilet stalls had no doors. I could wait for the next stop.

"Good, that place freaks me out. I told Royal not to stop, but he didn't think we'd make it to the next city."

I laughed and stared out the window at my brother.

"He's never been this angry at me before," I whispered.

"He's not angry." I turned and faced Camden. "He's hurt."

I folded and unfolded my hands in my lap. "That's worse."

"Maybe. Give him time."

I huffed out a laugh. "I'm giving everyone time, it seems." Camden gave me a confused look. "Kai needs time, too."

"Royal said Hospice is involved now... I don't know... Maybe it's a good thing that he's getting some help. Maybe he'll have more time to just... be."

"I have a feeling he doesn't know who he is if he's not helping her." I picked up my phone from the floor where it had fallen, I assumed, while I slept.

"That's something he'll have to figure out on his own."

"Why?" I asked, hating how petulant I sounded. "Why can't I be there to help him?"

"You can be... Royal was there for me... when I was ready."

"Kai isn't ready."

It wasn't a question, but Camden answered it anyway. "Maybe not, but you can be there when he is." His smile was soft.

"And what if he's never ready?"

"Then he's missed out... it's his loss. Not yours." Camden's silver-green eyes glimmered as he reached over the console and squeezed my knee.

"What'd I miss?" Royal asked as he slid into the driver's seat.

"Nothing, we were debating whether or not it was worth it to use those bathrooms again." Camden gave him a pointed look, and a slow smile spread over my brother's cheeks.

"And?" Royal glanced over his shoulder.

"Hell, no. I still haven't gotten over the last time," I said, and Royal laughed.

I wanted to bottle the sound of it. It was the first real laugh I'd gotten from him since he'd found out about Kai.

The car started and Royal looked at me through his rearview mirror. "If you really need to go, Pink. I'll go in with you. Stand guard at the door."

If he and I weren't two hearts, two sets of souls weaved together through DNA, history, and something only we understood, it would have seemed like such a small offer. But as his eyes held mine through the mirror,

I saw his olive branch for what it was. He would always be there. He was my big brother, my protector.

"Awe, thanks, Blue. I always wanted a potty guard."

Camden didn't crack a smile. "That was a terrible joke."

Royal, on the other hand, snickered like a school boy. "So terrible."

"Whatever, Blue. You love me and my bad dad jokes."

Our eyes met again in the mirror, and his smile widened. "Yeah... I guess I do."

He didn't turn up the music this time, and I took that as another good sign. I listened to him and Camden talk about Royal's new tattoo. A string of musical notes from the song Camden had played at his winter concert last semester were now permanently placed along Royal's left collar bone. The conversation felt lighter as the trees blew by, and the closer we got to campus, the harder it was for me to ignore the phone in my hand. Kai still hadn't texted. It wasn't until we were about fifty miles from campus that my phone finally vibrated.

Kai: How do I do this?

My fingers trembled as they skated across the screen.

Me: Do what?

Kai: Leave her here.

I typed out a response and then deleted it. Six times. I had no idea what to tell him. Nothing I could say would make it easier for him to leave his mother behind in a foreign place. I pressed the call button and the phone rang four times before he answered.

"I wish I was there," I whispered, and he said nothing. "I know that wouldn't make any of this better, but at least you wouldn't be alone."

I kept my eyes on my lap and pretended like I wasn't in the car with two other people. "I wish you'd let me be there for you, Kai."

I could hear him breathing, slow and even, and in the silence, his sadness bled through, blue and thick.

"I don't know how," he said, his words ripped and raw. "Your brother's right, Indie, you need someone who's capable of so much more than I am right now."

"Your love is enough." I closed my eyes, pressed my lips together to stop them from shaking.

"Indie... I can't—"

"Don't do this." I wiped at my cheeks. "Don't push me away."

I heard another voice in the background and he answered some unknown question. "That sounds good, tell her I'll be right there."

"Kai?"

"Indie, I have to go." He exhaled and the pain of it split me open.

Done with you.
Throwing you away
Used you.

"You deserve more than this," he whispered, before ending the call.

I could feel Royal and Camden's eyes on me. The pressure pushed down on my shoulders as I held in the sob trapped inside my chest. *You deserve more than this.*

Angry tears threatened to leak down my cheeks, but I blew out a breath and composed myself.

"Everything okay?" Royal asked, and I could hear the tension in his voice.

I nodded, finding my own voice, taking a steady breath, I said, "Yeah, his mom is in the new place now. He got permission to miss a week of school to make sure everything is in place."

Royal's posture relaxed. "That's good news."

"Yeah... the best." I stared out the window and ignored Camden's knowing stare. "Can you turn up the music, Blue? I love this song."

You deserve more than this.

The car filled with guitars, but the synth beat wasn't enough to drown out the voices.

He's a liar.

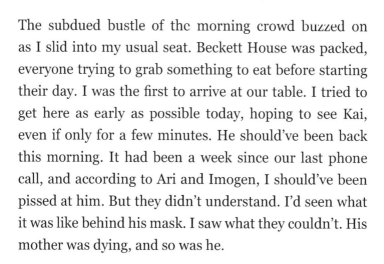

The subdued bustle of the morning crowd buzzed on as I slid into my usual seat. Beckett House was packed, everyone trying to grab something to eat before starting their day. I was the first to arrive at our table. I tried to get here as early as possible today, hoping to see Kai, even if only for a few minutes. He should've been back this morning. It had been a week since our last phone call, and according to Ari and Imogen, I should've been pissed at him. But they didn't understand. I'd seen what it was like behind his mask. I saw what they couldn't. His mother was dying, and so was he.

379

Royal and Camden walked through the front doors, and I sat up taller. My brother met my gaze from across the room, his smile falling as he shook his head. I stared at the door. Kai wasn't there.

"Hey, Pink." Corbin pulled out the chair next to me. "You okay? You look a little pale."

My heart raced as it deflated, begging, but I was left with an empty feeling as I slipped on the best smile I could. "Not feeling so great."

Corbin opened his protein drink. "Seems to be going around. Sherman puked at weights today." He snickered. "Best thing I've seen all year."

"What are you talking about?" Dev asked, setting his full tray on the table.

"Sherman yarfing because he's a pus—"

"Hey, my sister is at the table." Royal sat down and Camden followed.

Royal nodded his chin at my tray. "Aren't you going to eat?"

I pushed my unopen box of *Cheerios* toward him. "Not hungry."

He and Camden shared a look, and I purposefully changed the subject. "How was the gym besides Sherman and his abdominal fireworks?"

"It feels weird without Kai, man." Corbin picked at the grapes on my tray. "Have you heard from him?" he asked my brother. "How's his mom?"

Royal avoided my eyes as he said, "He actually called me this morning. His mom is good, he'll be back tomorrow."

"You spoke to him?" I sat up, my heart raging again. "What did he say? Is everything okay?"

My brother clenched his jaw. "Yeah, Pink. Everything is okay... *with his mom.*" He spoke, placing an emphasis on "with his mom."

"Oh." I glanced around the table and found everyone staring at me. "Glad to hear it."

"Same," Dev said. "We need him if we're going to beat Western Idaho again next week."

I picked at the edge of my tray, ignoring the way Royal watched me. He was always watching me lately. I'd promised him I'd speak to Dr. Sand and I had. I had another appointment tomorrow, the thought made me think of Kai. Would he be there, too? All I did was think about Kai. *You deserve more than this.* His last words ate at me every day. And every day the witch in my head told me he was a liar. I was starting to believe her. I didn't know what I deserved anymore.

"No way." My brother's voice broke through my mental digression.

"Why is everyone looking at me?" I asked with a nervous laugh.

Royal frowned. "Ignore these idiots, please."

"I think she was ignoring us already." Corbin threw a grape at Royal and Camden chuckled. "Do you—"

"Come on, did you forget what I said the last time?" My brother glared at Corbin, a silent threat in his eyes.

Corbin flicked him off and turned his attention to me. "Do you or do you not have a date for Spring Fling?"

He had no idea how much it cost me to answer.

"No."

"Go with us." Corbin's smirk was directed at my brother, and Royal groaned.

I narrowed my eyes. "Us?"

"Me and Corbin," Dev clarified.

"Like a double date." Corbin's lips reached to his ears.

"No." Royal answered for me and I grabbed my box of cereal.

Opening it, I said, "Sure."

Camden smiled and Corbin pumped his fist in the air.

"You sure you can handle us?" Dev asked.

His dark skin made the blue of his eyes sparkle as he waggled his brows.

The first genuine laugh I'd had in over a week bubbled past my lips, and I noticed Royal's face light up at the sound. "I think I can handle you two just fine."

Camden leaned across the table. "Do you know what you're getting yourself into?"

"Not really, and it feels... good."

"I will break both of your necks if—"

"Simmer down, O'Connell. We'll have her home by midnight."

"Eleven," Royal countered.

"One," I argued, and Royal's smile, once again, mirrored mine.

He hesitated, reading me like only he could, and gently brushed his foot against mine under the table. "Twelve-thirty, on one condition."

Corbin grumbled.

"You have fun, Pink."

Kai

He tapped his pen on the sole of his shoe as I stared at the letter B on his name badge. Five, maybe ten minutes had passed without a single word spoken, and I started to doubt the benefit of coming here today. I risked running into Indie, but my mom had asked that I continue my therapy, and I agreed that maybe it could help. It wasn't a secret that I was struggling. The last few days had proved harder than I thought. Alone, with my father away, I'd wanted to finish off the six-pack he'd left in the fridge. I'd almost stopped at the liquor store on my way back to campus. I didn't even want the alcohol, didn't want the numbness I knew it would offer me, but for some reason, I couldn't shake the thought of having it, of just holding the option in my hand.

"Kai." Brian finally broke the silence. "Let's start small, okay." He held up his hands in surrender. "You're here… that's good."

"I'm here." Leaning back in my chair, I closed my eyes. "I'm not, though."

"Can you explain that?"

I sighed and opened my eyes. "I'm here. I'm there. I'm fucking worried."

"Orchard House is a great facility."

"Facility." The word in itself made me angry.

"Let's try something." He leaned forward, resting his elbows on his knees. "What if it was the other way around? Let's say you injured yourself. You were paralyzed from the waist down."

"It doesn't work like that."

He smiled. "Humor me."

I knew where he was going with this, but I waved my hand for him to continue.

"So you're paralyzed, and your mom has spent the majority of the last ten years taking care of you. Over those ten years, you watch as she slowly starts to disappear. She smiles less. She's lost weight. Maybe she's quick to anger. Maybe she's more tired than usual. You start to notice she's not doing the things she used to. She's stop caring about the hobbies she has, slipping up at work, barely making it day to day because she's consumed with stress. She's balancing everything on her shoulders and refuses help when it's offered. You're watching this person you love die, and you swore you were going to be the one to die first."

I sucked in a breath and rubbed my fingers over my eyes. I hadn't realized I'd started to cry until I couldn't breathe.

"What would you want her to do, Kai? Live or die?"

"Live," I stuttered the word.

"Live," he whispered.

"I feel like, by living, I've abandoned her."

"That's how you see it. And that's what you have to work on. You aren't abandoning her. You're giving her a last hope. Do you think she wants to part from you knowing that her death could be the reason you fail?"

"No." I wiped my face with my shirt sleeve.

Brian leaned back and the chair creaked as he stared at me. "From what I can tell, you've been grieving the death of your mother for years... maybe it's time to celebrate her life before it's too late."

"How?"

"Just like you said earlier... by living."

Living.

The concept should be easy. But the weight of my phone in my pocket was hard to ignore. When would it ring? Would she be gone already? Would I have time to get there before she passed? The spring sun was warm, not a cloud in the sky, but still, everything seemed surreal. Like the painting we'd learned about in art history. Bright but sad. I'd skipped all of my classes again today, hiding in the library, working on assignments and emailing my professors, letting them know I wasn't there, but still working.

I scanned the lawn, looking for her, for Indie. I'd been lucky this morning and hadn't seen her at the

Behavior Health Center. I wasn't ready to see her yet. I knew myself well enough to know if I saw her; the chances of me caving were pretty high. I reached into my pocket and pulled out my phone. Staring at the picture she sent me, I smiled. She looked happy and that's all I wanted for her. My life was like a field riddled with landmines, one wrong step and I'd take everyone down with me.

Slipping my phone back into my pocket, I headed toward the Aquatic Center. The large wood and glass building stood like a beacon against the green of the fir trees. This was my place of forgetting. Maybe the place where I could understand what it meant to live, and as I opened the doors, the sweet, humid scent filled my nostrils. I had a rare moment of peace. Nodding to the girl at the front desk, she blushed as I smiled and made my way to the locker rooms. It was loud and perfect, the voices of my teammates echoed off the marble floor and metal lockers as the door shut behind me.

Corbin was the first to notice me, and of course, nothing that kid did could be chill. "Carter's back." His smile was wide, but there was something sad underneath it, or maybe I'd imagined it.

The locker room quieted down, everyone's eyes were on me, and as I passed my teammates, I was welcomed back with strong hands. A clap on my shoulder or a fist to bump. Even coach watched me with warm eyes as I passed his office.

I raised my hand in greeting. "Hey, Coach."

"Hey, kid, good to see you."

I offered him a smile, and as I turned toward my locker, I was greeted with a familiar pair of cool blue eyes.

"Hey," I said, holding onto the door of my locker, I exhaled a long breath.

The locker room started to buzz with chatter as Royal unzipped his bag. "When did you get back?" he asked.

"This morning." I lifted my shirt over my head and stuffed it in my locker.

"How's your mom?"

I winced, the question a constant reminder that I'd left her behind.

"The same."

His hand rested on my shoulder and I lowered my head.

"I'm sorry... I—"

Turning to face him, I said, "I'm the one who should be apologizing, Royal."

He gripped my shoulder once and let go. "You should have talked to me. But I understand." He nodded his chin at Sherman and I realized he was staring at us. His contempt was written in the stiff stretch of his shoulders. "Sometimes hiding is necessary. But I'm your best friend. I'm the last person you ever have to hide from."

I could have told him I wanted to tell him from day one, that it was Indie's idea to wait, but it wouldn't change anything. We both lied to him.

"I should have told you."

He punched me in the chest, and I chuckled. "A week ago I probably would have punched you a lot harder. But, I've had time to think about everything."

"I deserve worse," I said, pulling my swimming trunks from my bag.

Royal locked his eyes with mine. "Do you love her?"

The muscle in my jaw pulsed as I nodded.

"Then I know you'll do the right thing."

I didn't know what his definition of right was. Stay? Walk away? I'd already made my choice.

"And..." he glanced over my shoulder, leaning in, he whispered, "Camden told me I needed to get over myself... We owed you one."

He reached into his locker, using the opportunity to avoid eye contact, I asked, "How is she?"

"Indie?" he asked, pulling up his swim trunks. "I think she misses you. But she won't talk about anything with me."

Sitting next to her in class was going to be painful. The scent of her skin, the heat of her body. Knowing what it was like to touch her, have her... my chest hurt just thinking about it. Maybe I could ask my art history professor if there was an online course option.

"Get this..." Royal laughed. "Corbin and Dev are both taking her to the Spring Fling."

My mouth went dry. "No shit?"

"Maybe I was too quick to forgive you. See what you started... asshole. By next semester there will a freaking line outside her dorm door."

I fisted my swim cap in my hand, my molars aching as I crushed them together.

"Ready?" he asked, seemingly unaware of my shifted mood.

No.

I wasn't ready for any of this.

389

"Yeah," I managed to say.

But as he handed me a towel, a knowing smirk formed on his lips, and I started to think he wasn't as oblivious as I thought.

Indigo

Brown.

It was the color of his eyes.

I threw my arm out with as much power as I could. Assaulting the canvas with thick splotches of coffee-colored paint.

I dipped my brush in the next bucket.

Black.

Like his pupils when he took from me the last thing I could give and never gave it back.

I didn't throw the paint this time. Smearing my brush in high arches, I cut through the river of brown. It was dark and uncomfortable to look at. It was how I felt on the inside. He hadn't shown up for class, and if Royal hadn't told me he was at practice the other night, I wouldn't have ever known he was even on campus.

Erased and fleeting.

There was no place for violet or red here. Only this... a muddied interpretation of what he'd left behind. It was dramatic and immature, and I was capable of better, but this was what I did. I plastered myself onto tightly stretched squares—rectangles of white—and hoped I'd find myself again somewhere in the chaos.

Wiping my hands on my overalls, I picked up a clean brush and dipped it in blue. *Azure Waters,* to be specific. I grabbed a stool and started at the top, directly in the center, and dragged the color down, slicing it open, and like my father, I let my monster free. My specter was formed like a wave, it ate at my confidence like a riptide through a weak shoreline. I was the sand tumbling in the *azure waters*. It was soundless in the depths of my mind, where time didn't exist, and I was free to indulge in my insecurities. This was my place of remembering. Who I was. What I wanted. And those voices... how they knew me so well.

> **Poor girl.**
> **Stupid.**
> **Worthless.**

I didn't stop painting. I kept adding layer after layer until I found my tears again. I needed to break. I hadn't really let myself fall apart since the night I'd cried in my father's lap. I'd held myself together, pulled the shutters on all the intrusive whisperings. Dr. Sand had told me to cry, to paint, to let myself feel the loss of Kai. The loss of trust. In order to heal, I had to face my demons.

Kai loved me. Wounded me.

> **Discarded you. Used you.**

I picked up the brush in the brown paint and slapped the canvas with another flood.

"People break up, Indie. Things you cannot control will happen. You will get hurt. You will be happy. Just remember the tools you have, the support system you've built."

Dr. Sand's words, like an alarm, shook me back to the present. Pulled me from all of my disordered thoughts and I kneeled down in front of my painting. Brown paint pooled on the ground as I stared up at the canvas.

A quiet laugh broke past my lips and I wiped my cheek in the crook of my elbow. "What a mess."

I'd never truly lost time like my father had, and maybe tonight I hadn't either, but as I stood, took a step back, I didn't recognize the piece in front of me. A long, shaky breath expelled from my lungs and I felt... better.

Kai's silence hadn't pulled me under.

The hardest part of all of this was the guilt. What if his mother hadn't gotten sick, would we be together? The thought made me angry at myself. I didn't blame her. Kai had decided what he could and couldn't handle. I waited for my brain to laugh at me, to tell me Kai never loved me at all, or something just as cruel, but all I could hear was the soft piano playing from my phone. I picked up my cell and turned off my playlist, it was late, and I needed to head back to my dorm.

I'd missed a message from Royal.

Blue: Camden is staying at my place tonight. Call me if you need me to walk you home from the studio.

As I started to type my reply, the studio door opened.

Tall and striking. His shoulders were broad and strong, his chocolate hair fell over his forehead. He looked the same, as if time had reversed back to that first night in the studio. I didn't think the time apart would have changed him, but I'd thought, perhaps the image I had of him, where he smiled at me, his eyes alive, his mouth soft, as our bodies had become one, was simply a figment of my imagination. Kai avoided me as his tired eyes roamed over the large painting behind me.

"Is this for the showcase?" he asked, and the sound of his voice, gruff and worn, gave me goosebumps.

"I think it might be."

Kai lowered his gaze and met my eyes. A shiver pricked along my limbs. "I don't know why I came here." For me, I wanted to say but didn't. "That's not true." He shook his head, the rise and fall of his chest matched mine, faster with each second. He took a few steps, leaving less than two feet between us. His scent stole my breath. "I owe you an apology."

What we shared was worth much more than just an apology.

I waved my hand, unable to form words, the burn in my eyes unbearable, I swallowed down the surge of emotion. "No."

"Indie..."

I grit my teeth, shaking my head, my whisper was wet. "I don't want an apology, Kai."

I want you.

"I didn't mean for this to happen..." He pushed his fingers through his hair, his dark eyes messy like the painting behind me. "I'm sorry I hurt you. I'm sorry I don't know what the fuck is going on in my head. I'm sorry I can't be what you need right now."

I'm sorry you fell in love with me.

I'm sorry I wasn't enough.

These things... stayed on the tip of my tongue, and when he reached for me, I turned my cheek, avoiding his touch. "I understand."

He exhaled, his hand falling to his side. I stared at the tips of his fingers, questioning myself if I'd made the right choice. If I'd let him touch me, it could've sparked something inside of him. If the feel of my skin would've brought the color back and maybe he'd see all we needed was each other.

But, the silence was a monochromatic slate of gray.

Kai was close enough I could see the shadows, the weight of a thousand worlds inside his eyes, and my guilt resurfaced. This was bigger than my hurt feelings. My heart was broken, but his was spent.

"I understand," I repeated, but this time I meant it. "You have to be there for your mom. You're stronger than you think... I don't know what I'd do if..."

If I lost my dad or my mom, it would feel like the world had ended. Looking at him, I could see the small changes I hadn't seen at first. The golden tan of his skin was dusky. The dark circles under his eyes were deep. The muscles in his arms seemed leaner. He was fading away right before my eyes. Without thinking about the repercussions, I eliminated the distance between us, wrapping my arms around his waist, my cheek pressed into his chest. Kai didn't move as I absorbed his scent, his heat, and after a few seconds, his arms draped around my back, pulling me even closer.

He rested his chin on the top of my head, his deep voice vibrating down to the marrow in my bones as he said, "I missed this."

I held back my tears, held in the *I love you so much* I wanted desperately to say, because he didn't need my guilt trips. Kai squeezed his arms around me, trying to hold us both together. He needed this. Not me. And I'd take what I could get, even if I knew nothing would change.

"I'm here, Kai. For you… no matter what."

He pulled away, scrubbing his palm down his face, and swore under his breath. "I can't ask that of you…" He took three steps backward. "I shouldn't have come here." Pushing through the studio doors, he said, "Don't wait for me, Indie."

I couldn't follow him. If this was what he wanted, if I ever wanted to find a way to move on, I had to let him go.

"Girl, you look fabulous." Ari smiled as she released the final strand of my hair from the hot iron. Golden waves fell over my shoulders, framing my rose-stained cheeks. "How come you never wear your hair down?" she asked, covering the locks with a light mist of hairspray.

"It's messy when I paint." I stared at myself in the mirror. "Kai liked it when I wore my hair down."

She gently slapped my bare shoulder. "Didn't I just say you're not allowed to think about him tonight?" Ari ran her fingers through my hair, separating the waves, giving them a more natural appearance. "You're going to the dance, and you're going to have fun. And I'm telling you right now, Dev is fine as hell, and if you get a kiss at the end of the night, I want details."

I pinned the corner of my mouth between my teeth, suppressing my smile. "Corbin and Dev are just my friends."

She hummed. "Sure, and I'm the Virgin Mary."

"Ari, come on. They're doing Royal a favor, taking his sister, who was dateless, to the dance of the year."

"Is it weird they don't know about you and Kai, or is that just me?"

My smile faltered. "I thought we weren't saying his name." I stood, smoothing my hands down the silk fabric of my dress. "Besides. There's no me and Kai, remember."

"I think if he could see you in this dress he'd come crawling back." Ari's lips broke into a wide smile. "Corbin and Dev are going to fight over you, and I can't wait to watch who wins."

"You're a little crazy, you know that, right?"

"It's why Gus likes me, I keep shit interesting." Ari pointed to the foot of her bed. "Imogen left her rose-gold open toes by the bed for you."

"I can't believe she's not going," I said, slipping my right foot into the delicate heel.

Ari tugged on the bodice of her green dress, revealing more cleavage. "She'll be there taking pictures for the paper."

"It's not the same," I said and turned to look at myself in the full-length mirror.

I didn't recognize the girl in the reflection. In her pink silk slip dress, the fabric barely dusting the floor, she seemed taller... sexy. Her skin was flawless, her lips parted and full, the color of a rose petal. Her blue eyes were deep and cobalt against the light color of her dress. She was paint free and confident. She was exquisite.

Ari stood next to me and whispered, "He has no idea what he gave up."

"Don't make me cry."

"If you cry, I'm not redoing your makeup."

Laughing, I nodded. "Good point."

A loud knock on the door made me jump and both Ari and I laughed.

"Put this on and I'll get the door." She handed me a tube of gloss.

I did as she ordered, placing the gloss in a small clutch I'd gotten to go with the dress. Royal's laughter echoed through the suite, and my cheeks flushed with nerves as I took one last look in the mirror.

Fake.

Ridiculous.

I didn't close my eyes, instead I held my gaze and whispered, "Tonight is for you."

"Holy shit, Pink." Royal's smile stretched into dimples as I turned to face him. He stared at my bare shoulders. "You're bringing one of those sweater things, you know what I'm talking about, something to cover—"

"A shawl?" Ari laughed. "Hell no, this girl does not need a cover-up."

"Says you," Royal grumbled under his breath, and his boyfriend's lips twitched.

"You look gorgeous." Camden kissed my cheek.

"Thank you." I flexed my fingers at my sides. "You both look very handsome. I like the matching ties."

Camden and Royal were both wearing dark gray tailored suits. Their silvery green ties reflected differently in each of their eyes, creating their own shades of blue and green.

Royal took Camden's hand and said, "I might need you to hold me back if Corbin and Dev piss me off."

Camden looked at my brother, affection in his eyes, and chuckled. "You're on your own."

"I love you, too." Royal leaned in and kissed him on the mouth. "Should we go?" he asked, his face and neck flush with color.

"I'm ready." I hugged Ari. "I'll see you there."

"Try to live a little," she whispered before she let me go.

Royal took my right hand as Camden took my left, I looked at my brother and said, "Don't let me fall."

"We won't."

Kai

"Turn it down, Kai. I'm tired."

I muted the television and stood, grabbing the water pitcher by the side of my mom's bed. "I'll refill this. Be right back."

I made my way down the hall and smiled at the two nurses behind the desk. Lifting the pitcher so they could see it. "Seven-hundred milliliters."

"Thanks, Kai." Nikki, one of the nurses said, "Don't fill it all the way, she's close to her limit."

"Will do."

My mother's ins and outs were closely regulated here. Orchard House so far had proven to be a pretty decent place. The staff was good to her, the nurses seemed like they actually liked their patients. Although my mom was obviously depressed, she said she liked it here, too.

I filled the pitcher to the three-hundred-and-fifty mark, no ice, and replaced the lid. Nikki eyed the pitcher as I passed and gave me a small smile. I nodded my chin, keeping my attention on the floral wallpaper as I walked down the hall to room one-seventy-two. A small painting of an apple tree hung above the number placard on her door.

Mom was on her side, eyes closed as I walked in. I poured water into a cup with a straw, and before I had a chance to sit back down, she asked, "Why are you here?"

"Where else would I be, Mom?" I sighed, shaking my head I pulled the chair closer to her bed and sat down.

"School. Practice. It's Friday right? Don't you have a meet this weekend?"

"It was this week and we lost." I leaned back, pinching the bridge of my nose.

"Do you have a headache?"

"Always."

"Go home, Kai."

"Stop it, Mom."

She gripped the hem of her pillowcase in her fragile-looking hands. "No... you stop this right now. I don't want you here."

"Mom, come on..."

She was agitated, her arm trembling, and I almost called the nurse, but a few tears trickled down her cheeks. "It hurts too much."

"I'll call the nurse, I think you can have morphine..."

"Not the pain, watching you... it hurts to watch you."

I sank back into the chair, deflated. "I'm sorry."

She squeezed her eyes shut. "I want you to go home, Kai."

"I can't... I don't want to leave you," I argued, but she opened her eyes at the crack in my voice.

"I know." She patted the side of her bed, and I leaned closer, resting my hand on the mattress. Her hands were cold and thin as they covered mine. "But I need it. I need you to go so I can feel better."

"You don't want me here?" I hated my childish tone. I was supposed to be here for her, not the other way around.

"I really don't, baby." She smiled. "I love you too much too keep you here, and watching you mope around, it's like the Grim Reaper sharpening his scythe."

"Tell me how you really feel." I gave her a lopsided smile.

"You never do that anymore."

"What?"

"Smile." I lifted one of my hands and tucked a piece of her hair behind her ear. "I miss your smiles."

"I smile, Mom. You're just always sleeping."

Even her laugh sounded tired. "They give me the good drugs, here... It's Friday night... shouldn't you be out with that girl you were telling me about?"

"We're not together anymore."

"Is that why you stopped smiling?"

I gave her a watery smile. "I think it might be one of the reasons, yeah."

"Kai, my life has been small. Small town. Small experiences. But I was lucky, because God gave me a huge gift when he gave me you... and I need you to listen to me... really listen, Kai. I need you to go—"

"Mom."

"Listen." She raised her voice and her face paled. "I'm not telling you to stay away, but I'm telling you to live your own life. There is nothing small about you, Kai Carter. You have always lived big, and I don't want to be the reason you stop. Don't stop for me... I've gotten everything I've ever wanted... in you. And watching you like this... it's worse than death."

I didn't think it was possible for a grown man to cry as hard as I was in that moment. With drenched cheeks, I sucked in a deep, harsh breath, sucked the air through my nose, my mouth, like I was a toddler.

"Can you do that for me... can you promise me you won't stop."

My entire body nodded. "Yeah, Mom, I promise."

Her pillowcase was wet, her tears soaking into the fabric, she asked, "Get a tissue for me?"

"Of course." I stood faster than I intended and was dizzy on my feet. Grabbing a few tissues from her night stand, I handed them to her.

"Do you have a picture of her?" she asked, dabbing at her nose.

"Of who?"

"The girl who made you smile."

I pulled my phone from my pocket, and opened up the picture Indie had sent me on her way home from Utah.

"Her name's Indie," I said, holding the screen so my mom could see it.

Mom's smile was next level as she stared at the picture. "Kai... she's so pretty."

I looked at my phone, rubbing the back of my neck, a smile stretched across my lips. "This picture doesn't do her justice."

"Why aren't you together anymore?"

"I screwed up."

"Can you fix it?" she asked, the hope in her eyes lit a fire inside my chest.

Could I fix it?

"I want to," and as I said it, my heart took on an urgent rhythm.

"Call her right now." Mom looked at me like I was stupid, and I laughed.

"It's not that easy, Mom."

"It's always that easy."

"She's at the Spring Fling."

"The what?"

"A dance at school."

"What time does it start?"

"It started an hour ago."

For the first time in two weeks, my mother's eyes were clear, no hint of shadow, or pain as she stared up at me and said, "Then you still have plenty of time."

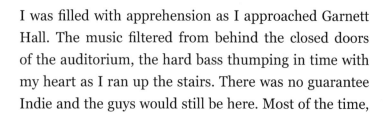

I was filled with apprehension as I approached Garnett Hall. The music filtered from behind the closed doors of the auditorium, the hard bass thumping in time with my heart as I ran up the stairs. There was no guarantee Indie and the guys would still be here. Most of the time, people made an appearance at these types of things before leaving to go party somewhere without the faculty and staff as chaperones. Spring Fling was sort of huge, though. St. Peter's was older than dirt, and sixteen years ago, the Board of Directors had decided to throw a charity gala to help raise funds for the school's defunct athletic department. This was more than a dance, and I was banking on that fact, hoping everyone was still here sipping nine-dollar glasses of punch.

I'd made it back from Rockport in a record thirty minutes, without getting pulled over, and didn't bother to stop by my dorm to throw on some slacks and a tie. I would most likely stand out like a sore thumb and make a fool out of myself once inside, but after what my mom had said tonight, I didn't want to let her down. It made sense, what she'd said. It was why I'd changed my major in the first place. I'd fallen back into my pattern of pushing away everything in my life because I'd felt guilty I *had* a life. It wasn't selfish to live. I promised her I wasn't going to stop trying. I would do this for her, for me. And maybe like Brian had said, when my mom did pass away, because yes, she was going to die, at least she'd go knowing I was taken care of, that I was happy.

Even the girls selling tickets were dressed up, and I didn't miss the way they gawked at me, like I was out of my mind, as I handed them the eighty dollars required to attend.

"You know it's a formal... right?" Her vapid, hazel eyes scanned my jeans and Stacks t-shirt.

"Shit, really? I didn't know." I grinned, and she narrowed her eyes before I walked toward the auditorium.

Dim lights lit the wood floor in a warm glow. Everything was doused in pastels. The tables were covered with starched white cloth, bouquets of multicolored tulips sat in crystal vases in the center. Eighties' music blared from the overhead speakers, the dance floor at the center of the room pulsed, illuminated, and alive. Ignoring the curious eyes, I walked deeper into the room. The place was packed with dark suits and overly bright dresses, and as I scanned the surrounding tables, I came up empty. I recognized some of the faces, a few of the guys from the football team snickered as I walked by.

"Couldn't afford a suit, Carter?" Some asshole from my high school elbowed his buddy, and I shrugged with a forced smile.

The crowd dispersed a bit, opening up my field of vision, and I spotted Royal and Camden, hand in hand, whispering to each other next to one of the food tables. Bracing myself, I walked to where they were standing, taking even breaths as I went.

"What are you doing here?" Royal darted his eyes to the dance floor and then back at me.

I followed his gaze and wished I hadn't. Indie's smile was radiant as she laughed. Dev twirled her in time with the music, and the overhead lights lit her hair like a halo. The pink, silky-looking fabric of her dress clung to all of her curves, slight and perfect. The tiny straps on her shoulders exposed all of her creamy skin, soft and...

"Kai, man. What the hell?" Royal punched me in the shoulder. "If she sees you, you'll ruin her whole night. Don't make me hate you."

"Nice to see you, too." I smiled at Camden. "You look good."

"I know," he said and straightened his tie.

"I'm serious, get the hell out of here. Don't do this to her." Royal's lips were set in a firm line.

"I'm here for her." I pushed my shoulders back, found my height, my back bone.

"You can't push in and out of her life whenever you want. I told you. She's not built like that."

"I messed up... and I can't expect you to trust me, but please believe it when I say, I'm in love with your sister, Royal, and I'm here to make it right."

He relaxed, his eyes drifting to the dance floor, he said, "If you hurt her again, we're done, and that's after I kick your ass."

I chuckled. "Seems reasonable."

He nodded his chin toward his sister as the lights dimmed. Indie's smile was nervous as Dev took her hand and pulled her into his chest. A slow rendition of "99 Red Balloons" started to play, and my stomach dropped as she draped her arm around his neck. Maybe I was too late. Maybe there was nothing left to fix.

"You better break that up before I do." Royal's lips lifted slightly, but his guarded expression held. "Fix it, Kai."

I stepped onto the dance floor, bumping into a few couples as I hesitated. Dev whispered something in Indie's ear. Her cheeks turned pink, and my hands started to shake. I was fighting against rage and fear as I moved closer. Dev noticed me first, his lips breaking into a smile, and then just as quickly, his smile fell as he gauged my mood.

"Indie..."

She heard my voice, her arm falling from around Dev's neck, her eyes glittered under the low light. Up close she was even more beautiful. The little makeup she had on highlighted her cheek bones, but didn't hide her perfect imperfections. Her freckles still dotted her cheeks. She smelled like lavender, and if Dev wasn't standing right here, I'd reach out and touch her, see if her skin was as soft as I remembered, as soft as it looked.

"Dev, I'm gonna finish this dance... if that's okay with you?"

Dev's eyes darted between me and Indie. Confused. "Sure, I should find Corbin anyway."

Indie pointed to the other side of the room. Corbin had his tongue down the throat of a petite brunette.

Dev laughed and shoved his hands in his pockets. "Guess I'll be hanging with your brother, come grab me when you're done."

I kept my eyes on Indie as he walked away. She kept her eyes on the ground. The music continued, its melodic rhythm pulling us together. I brushed my knuckles against hers and she shuddered.

"Will you dance with me?"

She laced our fingers together, a silent agreement. I lifted her arm until it rested on my shoulder. The tips of my fingers trailed over her skin, stealing her heat. She wet her lips as she gazed up at me. We didn't say anything. Her arms around my neck, my hands on her hips as we moved to the music. Indie pressed the length of her body along mine, and I submitted to the vulnerability, to her. She could tell me to leave, tell me there was no way I could repair the damage I had done, and I'd walk away, with the feel of silk on my fingertips, and her scent in my lungs, knowing I'd try again the next day. And the day after that.

I lowered my chin and placed my lips to her forehead, whispering against her skin, I perched myself on the tip of her knife. "I don't want to stop."

Her breathing accelerated, her eyes shimmering, she asked, "Stop?"

"Living... " I held her face in my hands, watched as her lips trembled. "I almost lost my mom... and it scared the shit out of me... but I know now, all these years, I've been watching my mom die and I was following right behind her. I don't want to stop, Indie. Living... loving you. I fell in love with you, and it was the first time in forever that I can remember feeling actual happiness in my life."

"What if after everything... I'm not enough?"

"Indie... you're enough." I kissed the smooth spot between her brows. "You. Are. Enough." I said each word slowly, kissing the tears on her cheeks. "You are so much more," I whispered against her cheek, my hand on her neck, my thumb feeling the heavy thud of her pulse. "I know I messed up... and even though I don't deserve—"

"You do, though" she whispered. "You deserve happiness, Kai. You deserve the love you give."

I rested my forehead against hers. There were no lights. No sound as the color of the room swam around us.

"I believe you," I whispered the familiar words, our words, against her mouth, and she smiled.

Indie curled her fingers into the collar of my t-shirt, pulling away any remaining distance. And it didn't matter that Corbin, somewhere behind us, hollered and whistled over the music. Tentative kisses gave way to parted lips. Peppermint and salt. Parted lips became two weeks' worth of goodbyes, and as my fingers tangled in her hair, I wondered if she could taste my regret. I wanted her to taste my truth, all seven shades of it. That I was indeed, built just like her, with a tongue that could taste the red on her lips, the torrent of orange on her skin, see the yellow in her pulse, the vibrant green hidden inside the blue of her irises, heard her name, Indigo, every time I closed my eyes at night.

I'd found the forever in my bones as she broke away from our kiss, and I felt the violet color of her touch as she traced the curve of my lip with the tip of her thumb. As if she'd tasted every last one of my thoughts, she whispered, "I believe you, too."

Indigo

Large crowds usually made me nervous. Navigating in a tiny space, even worse. I tended to hide against a wall, or disappear in a corner. Today was no different. The small art gallery on campus was overflowing with students, faculty, and even a few art aficionados from Portland. The Junior and Senior Showcase was a collection of handpicked talents, and the fact that my three paintings were hung on the wall next to some of the most amazing work I'd seen, beyond my parents, was overwhelming. Today I couldn't hide. Today I had to stand in my little black dress, Imogen's idea, with my hair down, like a golden beacon, and I had to stand alone.

My parents couldn't afford the drive down, and Royal and Kai had a swim meet. Camden would be here soon, though. His class ended at five, and as I wiped my clammy palms down the soft fabric of my dress, I gave shy smiles to the curious attendees as they passed. They mumbled

411

their opinions as if I wasn't right there, standing with my heart on the wall.

"Interesting use of color."

"So dark."

"Did you see what she did with the blue... it's hard to look at."

"I love it, it makes me uncomfortable."

I love it, too, I wanted to say, but I was struggling to keep my voices in check. At times not knowing which was real. Was it the witch whispering her disapproval, or were the words really coming from the people around me. Large crowds were noisy, distracting, making it easier for my anxiety to reach chest-tightening proportions.

"What was your inspiration?" a young man with a warm smile asked as he stopped in front of my exhibit.

I didn't dare look into his eyes, nervous and unsure of myself, I turned and faced my paintings.

"Honestly," I said, "each piece has its own inspiration." I pointed to the first one. "This one started as an experiment." The man's light laugh gave me confidence. "But then it became something more. I wanted to create something that fought the norm of shape and line."

"You succeeded." Facing him again, his eyes devoured the canvas. He had on a black, button-down shirt, tucked into jeans and an expensive-looking watch. I couldn't gauge his age. He seemed older, but could easily be around Kai's age, as well. "This one." He stepped closer, looking up at the center painting. "It's angry."

The middle piece was the most personal, but I didn't tell him that. The dark blue slash down the center unveiled that sleeping monster inside me, and I hoped, by giving it life on the canvas, it would stay there, live and breathe outside of me.

Feigning indifference and keeping it light, I said, "I painted it during a break-up."

"Then you're single?"

If I was better at social situations, I could have maybe harmlessly flirted to be polite, but I was already chewing the corner of my lip with nerves, uncomfortable with the attention, and stumbled over the truth. "I have a friend... a boy..." I stuttered on a laugh. "I have a boyfriend." My cheeks were hot as he stared at me with a smile that made me think he didn't care if I had a boyfriend or not, like I'd just given him a challenge.

"He's not here..."

"Sorry I'm late." Camden, a bit out of breath, swept in, taking my hand in his, he kissed my cheek."

Relief washed over me as the man's smile evaporated. "The boyfriend?" he asked.

Camden was about to interject, but I clasped his hand and said, louder than necessary, "Yup. He's my boyfriend. I mean, yes, this... this is my boyfriend, Camden."

I gave Camden a wide look, praying he would understand, and that his lack of social prowess, for once, would not hinder him. The confusion on his face faded as he nodded his head. He kept a tight grip on my fingers, not taking the stranger's offered hand to shake and said, "I'm the boyfriend."

The man let his arm fall to his side, not giving Camden another glance, he asked me, "Are these for sale?"

"No," I said too quickly and the corner of his lips fell into a flat line. "I've never sold anything before," I admitted.

I didn't think I could. Especially not the middle one... but in keeping it, I'd have a constant reminder of what I almost loss, off that thing inside me, ready and waiting.

"That's too bad," he started, but I cut him off.

"How much?" I asked, and I heard Camden clear his throat.

The man slipped his hands into his pockets. Ignoring my question, he admired the last painting. "Why red?"

The last painting was a monochrome of red. Red for love. For the way Kai made me feel when he touched me, kissed me, told me I was beautiful and perfect and his.

I shrugged, keeping my secrets, and lied, "It's my favorite color."

He pulled out his wallet and handed me what looked like a stack of one-hundred-dollar bills. "Nine hundred... I think three a piece is reasonable."

I stared at the cash in my hand. "Nine-hundred dollars?"

He laughed again, incredulous. "Yes."

"Do you really want to sell them, Pink?" Camden whispered, and I met his worried gaze. "Maybe think about it, talk to your dad?"

The money was heavy in my hand, everything I'd worked for these past two semesters was worth more than nine hundred. Everything Kai and I had been through bled across those canvases. I folded the bills and handed them back.

"Thank you, it's a generous offer, but they're not for sale."

Disappointed, his smile was forced. "I understand." He leaned in, reading the white sign with my name on it. "I'll keep an eye out for more of your work in the future. You're very talented, Miss O'Connell."

I thanked him again, my heart beating a thousand miles an hour as he walked away.

"I didn't want your paintings hanging in his house." Camden let go of my hand, and I smiled at his irritated scowl.

"Why?"

"He seemed... slimy?"

Bumping my hip into his, I said, "At some point I'm going to have sell my work, and I don't think I can afford to care if the buyer is slimy or not."

"Not today, though." Camden's lips parted into a grin.

"Not today."

He pulled his phone from his pocket, his face lighting up as he swiped his thumb over the screen.

"Did Royal win?" I asked, but he didn't answer.

He didn't even look at me. Raising his eyes to the center of the room, his smile came alive. I followed his gaze, the butterflies in my stomach fluttered awake. Royal and Corbin and Dev were weaving through the crowd. I kept looking, waiting to see where Kai was, waiting for him to immerge, but by the time they made it to where I was standing, I realized, with a gnawing, sinking feeling, he wasn't with them.

"What are you guys doing here?" I asked my brother as he folded me into a hug.

Royal made it, and my friends... warmth bloomed in my chest as the sting of emotion pricked at the corners of my eyes, but I was proud I didn't ruin my mascara.

"I might've lied, our meet was this morning in Rockport. We wanted to surprise you." Royal stepped back, giving his teammates a turn to hug me, too.

"This shit is fancy, Pink." Corbin glanced around the room. "We should have worn our suits." He gave Dev a dirty look.

"What? How was I supposed to know this thing would be formal? She's always covered in paint. You can't get more casual than overalls, man." Dev looked down at his jeans and button-up with a frown.

"You could have shown up in your swimming trunks and I wouldn't have cared. You guys came... Thank you."

Corbin draped his arm over my shoulder, pulling me toward him, he said, "Aw, Pink, we wouldn't miss this. You're our best cheerleader."

"What about Camden?" I asked and they laughed.

"He's alright, I guess." Dev smirked, and I loved the blush that bloomed on Camden's cheeks.

Corbin and Dev scanned the room, commenting more on the women than the art, when I leaned in and whispered into Blue's ear, "Where's Kai?"

"His dad was at the meet today."

"He was?" Allowing hope to fill my tone, I asked, "How did it go, I mean, did they—"

"Talk? Yeah... Kai went to Orchard House with him, and said he'd try his best to get here before it ends."

Kai and his father had been attempting to work through their differences after his mother was admitted to Orchard House. The facility offered grief counseling and they had gone to a few sessions together. Kai had been hesitant at first, but when his dad made an actual effort to get him to go, Kai gave in, hoping that his dad would really be there for him and his mother this time. Even though the path they treaded was rocky, at least they had chosen to walk it. Together.

My phone was in my purse in the back room of the gallery, and I was internally kicking myself for not keeping my phone with me. I wanted to text him. Tell him not to rush. To stay with his family because it was way more important for him to build his bridges than to come here and stand with me in front of paintings he'd seen already, every night in their evolution.

"Text him and tell him not to worry about it, if he makes it great, if not, that's fine, too," I said and Royal pulled out his phone.

The guys made their rounds, and the crowd dwindled a bit. My feet were killing me from standing in one place, and even though Professor Hintz had said we could mingle, I was fine staying in my own little bubble. Another twenty minutes passed, and I itched to get outside, to take a breath of air that wasn't saturated with overly expensive men's cologne. Pulling my hair over one shoulder, I offered Royal a small smile from across the room, and sighed. He pulled his phone out of his pocket for the fifth time since he'd been here and steered himself toward me through the sea of people.

"Want to take a break? Step outside for a bit, Pink." His twin intuition must have alerted him, and like he usually could, he'd read my mind.

"I think I will."

"Come on."

Camden was talking with one of the professors and waved at us as we headed toward the front door.

"Let me rescue Camden, meet you outside?"

"Sure."

He gave me a kiss on the cheek. "See you in a minute."

The tips of my toes ached, the small, strappy heels I had on were too high, and I wished for my Converse as I made my way through the room, smiling as I went despite the pain. People smiled back, parting for me as I moved, nodding with recognition, though none of them were familiar. I was caught up, in my head, thinking about if this was what my life would be like if I continued to pursue being an artist. Parties and galas and exhibitions. Heels and dresses. Would I get to be me? Would I get to be comfortable in my own culture? I was wrapped up in all the questions, and as I opened the front door, I didn't see him at first.

The setting sun warmed my arms, the wet breeze rich with pine, filled my lungs. I'd closed my eyes, cleansing myself of the room, and when I opened them again, he was there.

It was straight out of a movie, Kai leaning against his car, dressed in dark jeans and a long-sleeved, hunter green Henley. His chocolate hair needed to be cut, but I loved the way it hung over his forehead. His jaw was shadowed with a day's worth of stubble and I knew exactly how it would feel against my lips, rough and perfect. He had a bouquet of pink roses in his hands, his dark coffee eyes captured me as the gallery door closed. Kai's smile reeled me in.

My hair caught in the breeze, and the long tendrils drifted, tickling my shoulders as his strong hand claimed my waist. "You look beautiful," he said, handing me a half-dozen roses wrapped in a pink bow at the stem.

"I didn't think you were coming." I reached up to kiss his lips.

Just as I hoped, his chin was raw against my skin, his lips soft and the contrast made me dizzy with heat as his tongue tasted mine.

Kai smiled against my mouth. "Are you surprised?"

"Yes," I whispered, unable to keep my lips off of his.

"I thought about bringing a cake for us to kiss over, but figured I'd save that for your birthday."

I laughed, shoving him in the chest. "I knew you liked the movie."

He pulled his bottom lip through his teeth, suppressing his smile. "You didn't really give me a choice." Kai shrugged as I smelled my flowers. "I liked *The Breakfast Club* better."

"I think I can be okay with that." I threaded our fingers together, placing another light kiss to his lips. "I'm glad you're here."

"Sorry I'm late."

"Don't be, I'm glad you got to spend time with your family."

I didn't miss the way the light darkened in his eyes. "It's touch and go."

"He showed up today, though." I gently squeezed his hand, and he exhaled.

"He did." Kai gave me a crooked smile, and my stomach flipped. "I don't want to talk about him. I want to talk about my hot, artist girlfriend who almost sold her paintings tonight for nine-hundred dollars."

I narrowed my eyes, biting back my smile. "I swear I have no privacy anymore between you and Camden and Royal…"

He chuckled. "Royal still doesn't know about our swim lessons."

"I get one whole thing to myself," I teased.

"You get to have me all to yourself." His arm wrapped around my waist, pulling me closer, running his fingers through my hair with his other hand. Kai's smile radiant as he leaned down and kissed me with hungry lips.

Breathless, I whispered, "All seven shades of you."

Three Years Later

It was the first Christmas I could remember that it hadn't snowed. The sky was cloudless and endless as I stared through the large studio windows. My father next to me, and in our silence we spoke to each other, knowing the other's quiet movements, we breathed.

"Do you think it will snow tomorrow?" I asked, my eyes lingering on that infinite blue.

"I hope not." Dad smiled despite his anxious tone. "I don't know why the hell your brother thought it would be a good idea to get married the day after Christmas."

"You know why," I said and turned to face the studio door. "Camden has the hardest time during the holidays. This is Royal's way of making it about them, and not about the parents who chose to abandon their son."

"I always had hope his father…"

"I think we all hoped."

"He'll always have us."

I could hear my family laughing in the other room, my cousins, Ava and Quinn, arguing over who had the better football team, St. Peter's or Washington Heights. Camden was probably hiding on the couch, grateful he'd graduated before the other half of the O'Connell clan had infiltrated St. Peter's College. Our family was loud and touchy, and as much as he liked to pretend he was annoyed at times with our overzealous love for one another, he was always there for it. Like me, quiet, in the background, with a smile that whispered, 'I love you, too.'

We were family.

All of us.

And now Kai and I...

I exhaled a long breath and my dad noticed.

"What's on your mind?" he asked, and my throat closed on the words I was afraid to say.

"Indie..." Kai called out as he walked into the studio. "I think your Uncle Kieran is about to pop a blood vessel."

My dad laughed. "Kieran?"

"Yeah, Ava just told him she's dating the Silver Wolves' quarterback." Kai laughed as he snuck his arms around my waist, pulling my back to his chest, his hands resting over my belly.

He pressed a kiss to the top of my head and the heat of his hand, protective over my stomach, made the burn in my eyes real, made the words I needed to say that more present.

You'll fail.

"I won't," I whispered and hoped no one noticed.

I wasn't that fortunate. Dad rubbed his beard through his palm, his perceptive gaze holding mine as he said, "Talk to me."

Kai pulled me a little closer. "Declan…"

"Dad."

Kai and I both tried to speak at the same time and my dad chuckled.

"Sorry, baby." Kai leaned down, whispered in my ear. "Go ahead."

Dad waited me out, waited as I found my courage, holding my hands over the top of Kai's, I said, "I know it's not ideal… but Kai got a great review this semester from the head of the Art Department and they're giving him a full-time job."

"Adjunct professor while I work on my masters," Kai added.

"And it will be hard, I know… with my senior year and everything, but I think we've figured out all the kinks," I said.

"They offer married housing." Kai spoke, and I could hear the nervous edge in his voice.

"Married?" Dad asked, a little too calmly.

"I'm pregnant," I blurted and felt Kai's intake of breath.

We both waited for my dad to say something, anything. He was sifting through his own voices. Worry. Anger. Surprise. Trying to figure out which uncertainties were valid, and which were the fabrications of his own brain.

He ran his hand through his hair, his eyes, iced and sharp, focused on Kai.

"Dad?"

"I was going to ask her..." Kai's voice was thick, and I wished I could see his face. "To marry me before we found out. It's not about the baby."

"The baby." My dad's eyes fell to my stomach.

"My mom told me I'd be crazy not to marry this girl the day she met her. And a part of me wishes I would have asked her before my mother..." Kai's voice cracked. He waited a few seconds before he spoke again, his tone sure and brave, and my lips broke into a wet smile as he said, "I love your daughter, and I'll love this baby. And if I learned anything at all from my mom before she died, it was that you never know how long you have. Years, months, and I hadn't started living until I met Indie, and I don't want to stop."

Kai loosened his hold around my waist, his hand lacing through mine, I looked up at his handsome face. Beautiful in his stark truth, bold as if he dared my father to doubt him.

"Are you scared?" Dad asked me, and I squeezed Kai's hand for strength.

"No... and yes. I know Kai will take care of us."

"What about..." The knot in my dad's throat bobbed as he pointed to his temple. "Are you scared the baby will be like us?"

"No," I answered honestly. "If he's lucky, he'll have you to teach him."

"Him?" My dad's lips twitched with a smile.

"We found out the gender before we left for break," Kai said, the pride in his posture unmistakable.

"So you have it all figured out, then?" he asked.

"For now." Kai let go of my hand and stepped toward my father. "I'll take care of them."

My dad rested his hand on Kai's shoulder, pulling him into a hug he whispered, "I never doubted it."

The emotion bubbled over, not that I was ever good at holding it at bay anyway, but the pregnancy hormones made it that much harder. Tears streamed down my face as my dad pulled me into the hug.

"When are you going to tell your mom?" he asked, releasing his hold on us.

"After the wedding, tomorrow," I said. "We don't want to steal Royal's thunder."

"And the rest of the family?" he asked.

"We're thinking maybe a need-to-know basis for now."

"Especially, Liam," Kai said, and my dad laughed.

"We're telling Kai's dad when we get back to campus." Needing his warmth, I wound my arm around Kai's.

"Pink..." Royal yelled from the living room.

"And Royal?"

"He already knows."

The creases around my father's eyes deepened as he grinned. "Of course he does."

"Pink." Royal huffed out a breath. "Hurry up, Camden is about to play our reception piece for tomorrow."

Blue took in our expression and it didn't take him long to figure out what we were just discussing. His smile fell into a lopsided grin. "Great news, right?" he asked and my dad nodded. "Mom's waiting for you in the living room."

Dad walked toward the door, stopping, he asked, "Did you pick out a name yet?"

"We want to name him Sky."

Another shade of blue. Another extension of you.

"Sky... I like it," he said, giving me a private smile before he left through the studio door.

"Told you he'd be cool, Pink."

"Fine, you were right," I conceded and Royal's eyes widened.

"I'd like the record noted."

"It's been time stamped." Kai smirked. "Now let's go listen to Camden's moody bullshit."

THE END

A Letter to the Reader

Writing about depression, mental illness, is something I hold as a major responsibility. Suffering with anxiety and depression myself, I always want to bring a reality to the page, but in a way that offers hope. You are not alone. And on your worst days, and on the darkest, there is someone waiting for you to reach out. Sometimes you won't want to, sometimes you'll want to quit, but I want you to know I hope you don't. I hope you know, no matter how big, or how small, there is a light at the end of the tunnel. Easier said than done, I know, but I want you to pick up that phone, make that appointment, go to dinner with that friend, even if it's a millimeter wide, it's a ray of hope.

If you are struggling with depression, anxiety, or affected by anything mentioned in this book, I ask you to reach out.

National Suicide Prevention Lifeline
www.suicidepreventionlifeline.org/

Call 1-800-273-8255
Available 24 hours everyday

NAMI CRISIS
https://www.nami.org/Find-Support/Living-with-a-
Mental-Health-Condition/What-to-Do-In-a-Crisis

Acknowledgements

It's crazy to think I've typed "The End" on another book, another story, another part of my heart. I hope you enjoyed this book, this story. As always, my biggest thanks goes to you, the reader, for spending your time in a world I created.

Thank you to my beta team, my editing team Elaine and Kathleen. Timelines and commas and typos, oh my. You keep me sane.

Thank you to Becca, and all your gorgeous support, work and art that helps me maintain a brand and a name people can recognize.

Thank you to all my friends! Book world and beyond. Thank you for waiting on me, on my deadlines, and making my introverted ass get out of the house from time to time.

Thank you to John Hughes for teaching me what romance is all about.

Thank you AJ's Crew, every single one of you rock my world. Thank you for encouraging me no matter how long I take, to stay true to who I am as a writer, and not allowing me to bend to the market. You guys keep me in my lane, and I am grateful for that.

Thank you to all of my author friends for helping me, networking, advice, and late-night therapy sessions.

Thank you to the blogger sphere for always helping me get the word out!

Thank you to my family, to my kids, my hubby, and my work family too. Your continuing support makes all of this possible.

Thank you to the voices, though you keep me up at night, because of you, I am free.

As always, if you are in my life, you know you are loved.

Much love and side hugs, Amanda~

Available on *Spotify*.
https://open.spotify.com/user/12150951606/
playlist/5FwGWC43QOfCar5MW
qGWo1?si=z9tbD6ucTlaisnOBbtnxQQ

About The Author

Amanda lives in Utah with her family where she moonlights as a nurse on the weekends. If she's not busy with her three munchkins, you'll find her buried in a book or behind the keyboard where she explores the human experience through the written word. She's obsessed with all things Austen, hockey, and Oreos, and loves to connect with readers!

Stay up to date by signing up for her newsletter
http://bit.ly/NewsLetterAMJBooks

Connect with her online

https://www.facebook.com/AMJOHNSONBOOKS/

Instagram @am_johnson_author
www.instagram.com/am_johnson_author

Other Books by
A.M. Johnson

Forever Still Series:

Still Life

Still Water

Still Surviving

Avenues Ink Series:

Possession

Kingdom

Poet

Twin Hearts Series:

Let There Be Light

Seven Shades of You

The Rulebook Collection

Breakaway

Stand Alone Novels:

Scared Hart

Erotica:

Beneath the Vine

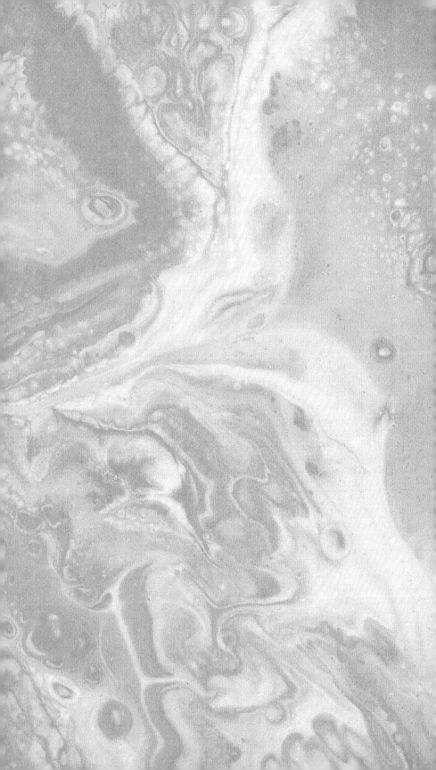

Made in United States
Orlando, FL
01 April 2022

16384647R00267